Until Aber Falls Into the Sea

Frances Myers & Zi Weate

Front cover illustration: Christopher P. John

ISBN: 0 86243 743 1

Published and printed in Wales by
Y Lolfa Cyf., Talybont, Ceredigion SY24 5AP
e-mail ylolfa@ylolfa.com
website www.ylolfa.com
tel (01970) 832 304
fax 832 782

1

Before and Sly

THIS IS LOIS'S STORY. It starts on the evening when Lois had no idea what was about to happen to her, and her friend Luke had his heart broken for the first time.

Lois, a first-year student at Aberystwyth University, was undergoing those life-changing experiences familiar to everyone who has ever been to University. Lois had never harboured dreams about University; she had fashioned her life on her sister's, except that she had chosen to go to a College of Further Education rather than stay on at school, influenced in her decision by her boyfriend of the time, Sid. Initially, she intended to study geography but, at the last moment, chose Biology. Her choice was limited to five Universities, because she was not studying Chemistry at A-level; Aberystwyth was one. Having visited the place in the spring, she knew that she would be happy there. The sun had shone; the Principal's garden was golden with daffodils.

To be at the seaside was a novelty, somewhere to satisfy the little girl inside her. Once she had been awarded an A grade in O-level Chemistry to sit along side her A-levels, her place was secured. Apart from an uncle, she was the first of the family to attend a university. When her geography teacher first suggested it, she had hesitated, wondering whether her mother, who was about to retire from her cleaning job, would be able to afford it. Lois supposed that, like her older sister, Veronica, she would get a job and contribute something towards housekeeping. Veronica had left school after she had spent two years failing her A-levels, more because of laziness than stupidity.

The girls were so different in appearance that it was difficult to believe that they were sisters. Veronica, known to the family as Ronnie, was small, blonde, and very petite. Lois was tall, had jet-black hair and an olive skin. Lois's mother was forty-four when Lois was born, the younger child of her second marriage. Lois was aged five when her father died, and her mother had to bring up her family on her own. Lack of money was always a huge issue for them all, but it entitled Lois to receive a full grant from the Local Education Authority and, with extra income from a part-time job, she thought that she should manage very nicely.

Her friend David, unofficially adopted into Lois's family circle after a row with his father, had offered to pay her fees from the money he was currently earning as a male model, which earnings supplemented wages he received from working part-time in an up-market clothes shop in Chester. His father, to whom David would not speak, also subsidized him.

Lois had been at university for a month, two weeks of which had been the worst of her life. She pined for Chester, and the friends who shared her tastes in music, dancing and partying. Life in Aber was proving disappointing. 'Quiet Life' by Japan had recently been play-listed on Radio One, and she had thought how apt it would be for her. She had discovered no one in Aberystwyth who shared her tastes. No one else had leapt the A-level barrier to get to Uni. For two weeks, Lois had attended lectures and practical sessions, and each time she entered the lecture-room, someone exclaimed, 'What has she got on today?'

Everyone she had met liked heavy rock or disco tunes to make you weep. They dressed in jeans and sweatshirts and were boring. Lois loved clothes and make-up, and dressed outlandishly. While she recognised that appearances were unimportant, music and dancing were vital, and she couldn't imagine dancing to Echo and the Bunnymen with any fellow student.

Towards the end of a depressing day, she sat at the window, watching the sea and trying not to dwell too hard on the fact that the Freshers were doing the Birdie Song at the Prom party. Finally, in desperation, she accepted an invitation to go to the Students' Union with some of the girl's from Alex (her hall). Alexandra Hall was a beautiful Victorian building, nestling under Constitution Hill, at the end of an elegant Victorian promenade.

A visit to the Student's Union entailed a pub-crawl beforehand. Everyone wore their best jeans and sweat shirts; Lois squeezed into her tightest black dress, which had once belonged to her mother. Lois had altered it, so that it was skin-tight, with a slit in the back, which allowed her to move her legs enough for dancing purposes. Her hair was a sleek curtain of blue-blackness. Her exotic appearance astonished the other students in Aberystwyth, in 1981. Walking up steep Penglais Hill in the tight dress and high-heeled, stiletto shoes was difficult, and her acquaintances strode on ahead, walking easily in their desert boots and Kickers. Her shoes came from a jumble sale. Someone with feet the same size as hers had finally decided to part with their 'fifties stilettos, and Lois had come away with ten pairs, in assorted colours, purchased for twenty pence a pair.

Lois arrived at the Students' Union half an hour after the others, surprised to find that the place where she had eaten lunch for two weeks was now a dance floor, and 'I Travel' by Simple Minds was playing. No one was dancing, but she launched herself into the room and danced. Japan, The Bunnymen, U2, Scritti Politti, Joy Division, New Order, The Psychedelic Furs, Depeche Mode all followed. Eventually, other people arrived and danced, and a glimmer of hope rose up in Lois's mind. After about two hours, she went to fetch a drink, and sat down at a table near the edge of the room, to survey the revellers. Almost immediately, a boy with red hair and a fluffy red jumper sat down beside her and asked,

'What's wrong with The Clash, then?'

Lois said there was nothing wrong with The Clash; she hadn't recognised the start of the record, and she had needed a drink.

'Where did you learn to dance like that to 'New Life' by the Depeche Mode?'

'Have you seen the video?' He had. 'Well, when I saw it for the first time, I thought, 'Dislocation Hips', David Gahan, moves like that, so I taught myself to do it. I spent hours practising it. I think I do it quite well.'

Lois had made her first Aber friend, Luke. They danced some more. On the way home, Luke told her that he was reading Economics, was mad about the Clash and loved collecting records. He also told her about his friends: Malc (Japan freak, reading Geography), and Fenn (punk freak – he missed out in the seventies and was making up for lost time, reading American Studies).

Lois said that her friend, David, had recorded all her records onto tape, as she had no turntable, but had not labelled any of the tracks, so she had the 'Quiet Life' album, but didn't know what the tracks were called. Luke promised to bring Malc round to meet her in Alex, and said they would sort out her tracks for her.

Next morning, Luke, Fenn and Malc arrived, and looked after her thereafter. Luke was already madly in love with her; Malc wanted to befriend her because she was the trendiest student in her year, and he collected friends; Fenn thought he might be in with a shout because he was a blonde bombshell.

The group began to lunch together; the three friends took Lois to some Hall nights on the Pier, where the D.J., Lord John, would play Simple Minds and New Order, if they nagged him enough, and to the Students' Union on Friday and Saturday, where their third year friend, Mitchell, knew what was what.

On Saturday, they made her tea. Luke was a good cook; Malc thought that he was but could hardly boil an egg. She stayed the night with them, sleeping in Luke's room, while he slept on the floor in the other room. They made her a boiled egg for breakfast, which is how she knew Malc couldn't boil an egg. They read the papers and had a walk up Pen Dinas, to the Memorial built to commemorate the Battle of Waterloo. When David came to stay, they were equally nice to him, even if they were in awe of him, his good looks and his cool car, a red Triumph Stag.

David had driven from Chester, taken Lois out to dinner, and they had stayed up late, catching up on things. They were quietly eating lunch next day, when the Plyn boys started lobbing food at him. Plynlimon was the boys' hall, but they ate their meals with the girls, in the large dining room in Alex. David was incensed; it took all Lois's powers of persuasion to prevent him from taking on the whole lot of them. Lois's newly found friends offered to put them up for the night. When he left, they gave vent to their curiosity, and asked why David and Lois were just friends. Lois explained that David was great as a friend, but, as far as girls were concerned, he was completely untrustworthy.

She met David through Sid, her first boyfriend. He was in the Sixth Form at her school, when she was in the fourth form. He was eighteen, she was fourteen, already attractive and looking older. Sid had first noticed her when David was away from school, recovering from a skiing accident. David and Sid were the bad boys of the Sixth Form, practically joined at the hip, always up to no good, sleeping around and partying and, inevitably, for the time, going to see obscure punk bands. Sid was bored without David, and spent a lot of time gazing out of the window; otherwise, he might never have fallen under her spell. Once he had noticed her, it became something of an obsession with him, to have someone like her on his arm. He was competitive, essential if you hung around with David. He enquired about her, and finally discovered that she was Veronica's sister, and her name was Lois. He began to greet her by name, which confused her. Eventually, he asked her to go to a Sixth Form party. She declined, knowing that her sister would hate her for it if she went. Instead, they played tennis after school, and soon had a very grown up relationship. They avoided all Sixth Form socialising and, once David recovered, the three of them became inseparable.

David was an Adonis; he was six feet two, had blonde hair, blue eyes, a clear skin and the most wonderful presence. Girls found him captivating, and boys were envious. Unlike Sid and David, Lois was a swot, and collected a string of A grade O-levels, A-levels and S-levels. Sid and David began to work for their fathers while Lois was in her last year at school, which is one of the many reasons why family relationships were so bad in both families. After only a few weeks, Sid's father died from a heart attack, leaving Sid and his family devastated and obliged to move house. Sid, the eldest child, found a more responsible side to his character, and as David's circle of friends grew wider, the boys saw less of each other. David remained very close to Lois.

Eventually, Sid had casual sex with another girl, someone that he had known at college. Lois would never have been any the wiser, except that Sid felt obliged to write to the girl, to say that he never wanted to see her again, as he was overcome with remorse. Lois found the letter on his desk, and was shocked and dismayed. She wanted to break off with him, but he pleaded that his father's death had made him behave out of character, and that the shock of them finishing would distress his mother and family. Finally, Lois succumbed to his pleas and excuses, but decided that she would finish with him when she went to University.

Her only confidantes were her sister and David. David went to see Sid, punched him very hard, and never spoke to him again. Since that time, she and David had grown closer but there was no romance between them. David continued to treat girls with little respect. One of his phrases was, 'What that girl needs is a dammed good fucking.'

On the third Saturday of their acquaintance, Lois, Luke and Malc planned to enjoy an evening of theatre and go to the Union afterwards. The third year Drama students were putting on an evening of Directors' Projects, and the 30 tickets would go to the first arrivals at Theatr y Castell, the Castle Theatre. Luke drove down the promenade in his Mini, and allowed Malc to turn the car round, while he went to fetch Lois from her seafront room in Balmoral. Lois was lucky to have a single room in those days, when most first years had to share. The room, in fact, had a spare bed for David, when he came to stay.

Luke thought how stunning she looked, in a very short tartan dress, a second-hand one, red tights and red, calf-length boots. Her hair glistened, and her make-up perfectly highlighted her smooth skin and high cheekbones. Her large brown eyes and jet-black hair made her look like a porcelain doll.

She was to stay with the boys in their rooms on Trefechan Road. When they found Malc, Luke remembered that he had forgotten to bring his Union card, and Malc told him drop them off at the Castle Theatre and drive home to get it. He said that he wanted to waste no dancing time after the evening of Drama. Luke, by leaving now, would lose his chance to sit next to Lois in the theatre, but Malc insisted that Luke go. Lois felt sorry for Luke and, as he drove away, she smiled and waved, and melted his heart yet again.

They bought tickets and programmes for the three of them. The first performance was to begin at seven o'clock. The theatre was prohibited from selling alcohol, but included with the £1.00 entrance fee was a dreadful glass of wine for anyone not discerning enough to be tempted, and, as we are talking students here, everyone except Lois took one.

Lois and Malc found seats in the foyer and waited. Malc was

delighted that he had sent Luke to fetch his card, and now proceeded describe the Directors' Projects. A tall, blonde girl and a raven-haired punk came into the foyer.

Malc whispered, nodding towards the dark girl, 'That's Finlay's girlfriend, Lynne, and her best mate, Rhiannon, a townie. Finlay is one of our star performers.'

He stood up to greet them, and the two girls came over and kissed him.

'Well, hello, Malc,' Lynne said. 'Glad to see you're support-ing our Drama Department. Because Finlay's directing, I've had to come every night so far, but at least you get a glass of wine.'

Finlay's girlfriend was very classy, in a dark, punky sort of way, thought Lois, who felt a little neglected. Lynne wore a black velvet dress, nicely cut, which was skin-tight to the thighs and then flowed out into handkerchief points. She had a black jacket around her shoulders, and a very small, black, leather handbag, expensive-looking, tucked under her arm. Rhiannon was graceful, tall and slim, and had near waist-length, wavy, blonde hair. She wore a well-tailored, dark, man's suit and a bow tie. She looked nervous and jittery and kept smiling shyly at Lois and everyone who passed.

The foyer had begun to fill up, and although the performance was not due to start for another half an hour, once the available tickets had gone, people began to drift away. Luke had not yet reappeared. Lois studied her programme, aware that Malc and Lynne were ignoring her. Malc must have become aware of her discomfort because he suddenly cut off Lynne in mid-sentence and said, 'Oh, I haven't introduced you to my fresher friend, Lois.'

He always used this term 'my', even though Luke had made friends with her first. They exchanged a few polite words, then, Lynne turned back to Malc and spoke about people Lois did not know, until she spotted some people she wanted to be with, and hauled her friend away.

'See you later. Are you coming to the do afterwards?' Lynne

called over her shoulder.

'No, we're going to the Union. See you around.'

'Rhiannon doesn't say a lot,' Lois said.

'Neither do you,' Malc said.

'I don't know what to say to people like that, so confident that they make me feel inadequate,' Lois answered truthfully.

'Don't worry, you'll soon settle down, and you've got the three of us to look after you. That's Dickie Bedford over there. He's the Head of Drama and everyone has to lick his arse to get on. He gives me the creeps.'

'Here's Luke.' Lois stood to wave to him.

Malc disappeared into the cloakroom. Luke sat down next to Lois. 'I think Malc's just seen Lucy, his ex-girlfriend, or maybe Sly, his other trendy fresher friend,' Luke said.

Malc approached with a student in tow. 'Lois, meet my other fresher friend, Sly.'

Lois stood up to meet a young man, who was slightly taller than she; he had short brown hair, was dressed in a baggy suit, and had amazing green eyes, which gave her the uncomfortable feeling that he could read her mind.

Sly said, 'Hi, Lois, nice to meet you. I've heard a lot about you.' He had a lovely Welsh accent.

She managed to say the old line, 'Only the good things, I hope'

'Only good things,' he answered, with a smile that sent her into a fluster. He looked moody, but when he smiled, his whole face lit up and she found him captivating. Somewhere in the theatre, a bell rang.

'We'd better go in.' Malc broke the spell.

'And it's the bell to galvanise me into action, too. I'd better go and do some work, to justify my presence here. Excuse me. I'll see you in the interval, okay?' Sly hurried off and the three of them, Malc leading, sauntered into the main hall.

'Is Sly in the production?' Lois asked. Malc said yes, and gave her a résumé of the piece they were about to see. Lois sat between Malc and Luke. The play was short and soon over, the applause died down and the lights went up. Malc was in raptures over the performance given by Lucy, his ex, and Lois joined him in praise. Luke said very little, but he had noticed Lucy wave to Malc at the end, and he thought it would be a good idea to invite her to the Union. The audience had to leave the auditorium for scene changes, and the wine was passed around again as they stood in the foyer, this time unable to find chairs, so Lois and Luke stood near the door while Malc went off in search of Lucy.

'If he's so crazy over Lucy, why did they finish?'

'Oh, don't ask me,' Luke replied. 'They went together for about a term and a half in the first year, then Malc finished with her. It had something to do with Fenn. Lucy got off with him one night, and Malc found out, ages after it had happened, and had a fit.'

'A bit nasty of Fenn, to do that to a friend.' Lois was surprised.

'Well, they weren't such good friends then, but they got closer later, and when Malc eventually found out, he preferred to finish with Lucy and keep Fenn as a mate.'

'Better to have forgotten all about it, surely?'

'Not Malc. He believes in fidelity and loyalty.'

They gossiped on like this for a while, and then Sly was back.

'So, Luke, are you all right?'

'Yep. How's it going?'

'There's not much to do, really. Dickie is bullying everyone, so I thought I'd escape. You going to the Union later?'

'Yes; do you want a lift?'

'Yes please. I've forgotten my card, but Malc said he'd sign me in.'

Luke and Lois exchanged glances and laughed.

'Have I said something funny?' Sly asked, puzzled.

'No, it's just that Malc sent Luke home to collect his card,'

Lois told him.

Sly laughed, too. 'Malc's in a funny mood tonight. I've never seen him chase after women before.'

'Let's hope he gets her.' Lois raised her wine glass and felt a lot better.

'Did you like the play, Lois?' Sly asked.

'Lucy's coming to the Union,' Malc said, flopping down and interrupting their conversation. 'She's changing now and she'll meet us at the next interval. She's pissed off at Dickie for being such a prat over the productions, so she'll come out with me instead of going to the party.'

Malc seemed pleased with himself, and Lois and Luke smiled at each other, relieved to see him so relaxed and happy.

'I bet you don't think much of the next bit,' Sly said. 'It's a long song, really boring, but after that there's a brill project called Doomsday. See you in the next interval.'

Sly was right about the next project. Lois lost concentration after a few minutes, and thought about the Union and the music, longing to dance. Suddenly, she spotted Sly, standing on the far side of the hall, staring at her. She rapidly looked away but, after a few seconds, her eyes drew back to him. He saw her looking, but he neither smiled nor waved, just continued to stare. She felt herself blush, highly embarrassed. It occurred to her that he could be looking at someone else, so she glanced over again and smiled. He smiled back. She tried to concentrate on the songsters. Malc nudged her and whispered, 'Can't you take your eyes off him?'

'Who? Do you mean Giles?' Malc just smiled.

* * *

Lucy joined them at the next interval, and Lois took to her straight away. Sly didn't appear this time, to Lois's relief, because she didn't know how to react to him. She wasn't used to people staring at her so intensely with no reason, 'unless he fancies you,' a little voice inside her head cried. Nonsense, she thought. I've only just met him, but she knew that she was attracted to him and was unsure how to act.

The final production was a feminist play about a suppressed housewife, a comedy that involved much shouting and throwing props around. When the wife finally murdered her overbearing husband, blood squirted everywhere, much of it landed on Lois's legs, splashing her stockings with red. Only Malc and Lois noticed this. Malc guffawed and Lois, infected by his mirth, was crying with laughter by the end of the play. Their laughter brought them together a little, and she was distracted from thinking about Sly, until they met him again in the foyer.

Malc proved to be a natural leader. They bundled into the car, Malc driving, Luke in the front, and Lucy, Sly and Lois squashed into the back, Lois in the middle. Although she and Lucy were small, Sly squashed up close to her. It was like electricity, when they touched. She was sure that she was imagining it, and kept on telling herself so as they drove up to the Union, but whenever she shifted a little, the pressure of his thigh against hers was constant. She wasn't sure if she liked this guy's attitude. If he liked her, surely he could come up with something more subtle than staring blatantly at her and pressing his leg against hers.

Malc and Luke were speculating on who would be at the Union, where Saturdays brought the same faces every week. The music didn't suit 95% of the student population, who were well catered for elsewhere. Lois supposed Sly must have similar tastes in music to Malc and Luke.

Luke went to talk to Mitchell, the D. J., while Malc bought the first round of drinks. The four of them sat in a corner and waited for the place to fill up. It was not quite closing time in town, it took fifteen minutes or so to walk up the 1:4 hill to the Union, and then it would fill up.

Malc chatted to Lucy; Sly and Lois sat in silence, until Sly asked her where she came from. The ice broken, they began to talk about themselves and their families.

The two girls went off to the cloakroom, after a while, to freshen their make-up.

'You like music, don't you? Have you seen Sly dance yet?' Lucy was powdering her nose. 'He's brilliant, really fantastic. I can't describe the way he dances, but it's great to watch. Malc says the same about you.'

As they walked back to the disco, Lois decided to test Sly's talents. 'Echo Beach' started as the girls reached their table. The place had filled up by now but there was plenty of room on the dance-floor. Lois loved this record and loved to dance to it. Her heart leapt a little, as it always did, when she got up to have the first dance of the evening. Sly moved beautifully; they had a similar style, and, instead of dancing alone, as she usually did, she was at ease with him as her partner. Lois waved to Luke as he bopped around the floor. Mitchell played their favourites. They were dancing to record after record: the Bunnymen, Level 42, Heaven 17, The Cure, Orange Juice, Bauhaus, the B52's, Haircut 100, DAF, the list was endless. As one record finished, Lois thought of another she wanted to dance to, and it was played.

At a quarter to one, they sat down and Sly went to fetch more drinks. Malc moved over to Lois and asked, 'Getting on okay, are we? He fancies you like mad.'

'Malc!'

'All right, make up your own mind. Never let it be said I interfere with other people's love lives'

'How are you doing?' Lois asked, to divert Malc's interest from her and Sly.

He made it clear that things were no better between him and Lucy.

Lois shrugged and asked, 'Where's Luke?'

'Sulking somewhere.'

'Why?' What's the matter?'

'Oh, nothing. He's okay, but I think he'd rather be on his own at the moment.'

When Sly returned with the drinks, he had bought an extra bottle of wine. She looked at it quizzically.

'I thought that you might like to prolong the party and dance some more, after this, at my place. I'm really in the mood, now I've met my dancing partner. Just us, though. There's not enough room for everyone'

She found herself enthusiastically agreeing to the invitation. Sly forced the bottle of wine into his jacket pocket, more dance records came on, and they were back on the floor. At one-thirty, Mitchell put on a slow record, and the place cleared instantly. Luke threw the car keys at Malc and said he could drive. When Luke asked, 'Ready, Lois?' she told him she was going back for a coffee with Sly.

'Suit yourself,' Luke snapped, and walked away.

Malc said to Sly, 'Make sure Lois gets back to Alex safely.'

'Don't worry, Malc; I'll take good care of her'.

They exchanged 'Good nights' and Lucy and Malc set off after Luke. As Sly and Lois left the building, Luke's Mini went hurtling past, and Lois caught a glimpse of Luke's face, set firm and tight.

They walked downhill, passing the Physics and the Botany and Zoology buildings, skirting the edge of the sports hall and the running track, passing through the Botany gardens and into the car park outside Pantycelyn. The night was clear and mild; stars twinkled above them. On the west coast, the sea is warmer than the land in the winter, and autumn lingers almost into December. The Campus was beautifully landscaped, every path bordered by bushes and creepers, and, with one week of October left, the night air was scented, and the dew made the earth smell as does after rain on a summer evening.

Sly offered Lois his arm. She often walked home arm-in-arm with Malc, or Luke, or David. It was just friendliness. Was it friendliness, too, to be invited back for more wine? Her conscience pricked. 'There's magic in the air. Can you feel it? I've really enjoyed tonight. I hoped that it would not end,' she said sweetly.

Sly sighed. 'It hasn't yet, Lois, and the magic is within you; it never has to end, never.' He squeezed her arm as they negotiated the steep steps alongside the Botany building.

'This is my territory, the Science Departments. They look good, don't they?'

'You enjoy your subjects, don't you? You seem proud of everything, even the Department buildings.'

'I love Biology. It explains everything,' she exclaimed.

'Surely, not everything?' He laughed. Lois began to explain her feelings at being in the university, her enthusiasm and her hopes.

'I wish I could feel the same way. I never wanted to do the Drama, or the Classical Studies, just Art, and that will always come from me. I don't feel I need all the lectures and all the studying, I just wanted three years to be an artist, but they have to stick all the irrelevant work on, too. It will be another two years before I choose what I want to do.'

'It's worth it, though, isn't it? It's the same on my course. I have to struggle with Organic Chemistry this year and do Botany for two years, before I choose my Honours year subjects, but it might all help in the long run.'

They spoke about their subjects and about the recent theatre evening, until Sly said, 'Well, here we are. My room is at the back. It used to be a storeroom, or something.' Sly indicated a small extension at the back of the hall, one storey high, with a large oak door. 'Iolo is the only neighbour, and he's so smashed out of his skull, he never worries me. It's mushroom season, you see.'

'I'm a Biologist. I go on fungal forays.'

'What on earth is a fungal foray?' Sly asked.

'Don't ask. I'll tell you some other time.'

Sly fumbled for his key and opened the door. There was a smell of polish, reminiscent of Alex, but stronger here. 'The bathroom's right opposite my room.' The corridor lighting was dim. Sly unlocked the door and ushered Lois in. 'It used to be a double, I think, but they made it single, especially for me.'

'Did they?'

'I haven't a clue, but I'm the only fresher in this hall to have a single room.'

'Oh, you've got a three-quarter bed. Mine is tiny. Well, all the beds I have seen in Alex are. What did you have to do to get this?'

'Reckon they notice a star when they see one. I'll go and get some glasses and a corkscrew. I won't be a minute.'

Lois took off her jacket and hung it over the chair at Sly's desk. She looked around her and saw the customary kettle, mugs, tea and coffee, the books, tapes and tape deck, but it was unlike a typical student room; it was more like her own. On the walls were small postcards, a few of Sly's sketches, a couple of posters, one of them a Bunnymen one. The desk was neat and, for a male, the room was very tidy.

She brushed her hair, touched up her make-up, and sat down on one of the floor cushions, her back against the wardrobe. On hat-pegs above the bed were a trilby, a black baseball cap and a beret. A real baseball jacket hung behind the door.

Sly came back in and announced, 'Success! I've found glasses and a corkscrew. I had to wake Dafydd up, to get them.'

'Did he mind?'

'No, he only wanted to know who the other glass was for. I told him Malc. I think he's a bit worried about me.' They both laughed. 'Choose a tape to play, Lois, and we'll drink glass of wine, to toast good music.' She selected 'Crocodiles' by the Bunnymen, and 'The Correct Use of Soap Magazine'. It was past two o'clock in the morning, and wine usually made her sleepy, but Sly's stimulating companionship kept her wide-awake. They laughed and talked about University, the other students and their mutual friends.

'What do you think of Fenn?'

'I don't know him as well as Luke and Malc. He's okay, I suppose.'

'Does he fancy you?'

'I think he fancies anything in a skirt, doesn't he?'

'Luke does. I mean, he's infatuated with you.'

'What makes you say that? I think he sees me as a special friend. He's never made any, well… you know… he's never said anything.'

'He wasn't very pleased that we were together tonight.'

'Oh, don't, Sly, please. I feel a bit guilty about it. Malc was in such a strange mood tonight, that Luke was confused. He's so sensitive, and I suppose he thought that he and I would be together and have a good bop around. I don't think he fancies me, honestly'

'I wouldn't blame him if he did.'

She smiled, far more relaxed now. The wine and the music helped, but she knew that, eventually, she would have to make a move. She toyed with the response she would make if Sly invited her to stay the night. Instead, he asked her to name her favourite tracks for dancing.

At three-thirty, she said, 'I really ought to be going now, and let you get some sleep.'

He was sitting cross-legged on the corner of the bed, and came to sit beside her on the floor. 'Lois, I know that this is going to sound crazy, but I feel crazy. I think I love you. I think I've known that since I first set eyes on you tonight, but I didn't believe it completely until now. I love you.'

'You can't love someone so fast; it isn't possible. You have to know them properly, to be able to trust them,' she said, quite shocked.

'It is possible; it happens all the time; it's happened to us.'

He was so earnest that she almost believed him. She had never believed in love at first sight, but she did have very strong feelings for him, and she was confused, speechless. He kissed her. She felt strong desire, but she couldn't let herself do this, could she? Her body said something very different from her mind. The kissing decided it, so she simply committed herself to him, united in desire, in fascination, and without thought.

'When I got up this morning, I didn't think that the day would end like this, that I could meet someone like you, who would mean so much to me.' Sly said.

'Neither did I. I felt I was going a bit mad when I first saw you; I thought everyone could tell that I'd been captivated.' Lois actually blushed.

'I'm, so glad that you felt that way, too. I could hardly speak to you, let alone take my eyes off you. You've put a spell on me. I really want to make love to you; it's intense, so authentic, I can nearly touch it. Listen, I know how strange that sounds, I know all about the lies boys and girls tell each other all the time; how they will say anything: I love you, it'll be all right, and, I'm on the pill. It's not funny, Lois. We are talking real life, and people just don't know how to be honest. They will say anything for sex. I don't mean everyone, but I think about these things. I like philosophy; I like to think. I've thought about this situation millions of times, and I can honestly promise you I am telling you the truth. I'm not drunk; I've only had a few glasses of wine. Are you drunk?'

'No. I'm not stone cold sober, either. I have never been drunk. I can't afford it. I'm poor.' Lois was deadly serious.

'Good, then. That's a good start. Most of these things happen when people are drunk. Alcohol lowers people's inhibitions and then they want sex. Please listen to me while I try to explain to you what is happening here. I think we are both clever people and, if we take a risk on life tonight, we might just discover something about ourselves that we will have forever to cherish. I love you and I would like to make love to you. Please, can I?'

Lois nodded and he bent to kiss her. Sly made love to her with tenderness, and worked hard to give her pleasure. This wasn't student sex; it was different. They had discovered something: they were sexually compatible, and it's not Chemistry, it's Biology.

Afterwards, Sly exclaimed, 'Christ, I feel wonderful, really wonderful!' Then, almost immediately, he struck his forehead. 'Oh, no! I've just done something I always promised myself I would never do. Lois, are you on the pill?'

'Yes, I am?' Lois said.

'Oh, my God, to go from ecstasy to complete failure, back to ecstasy again, in a few seconds. That's not nice. I just got carried away.' He sank back on top of her. 'So, you weren't a virgin?'

Concerned and puzzled, she answered, 'No, Sly, I wasn't.'

'Have you had many lovers?'

'None like you.'

'But many? You seem to know exactly what you want.'

'Just one, actually.'

'Where's he now?'

'I have no idea and I don't want to know. He broke my heart, and it was the most intense pain of my life. Please don't talk about this. You are taking me from ecstasy to failure. Please, don't make me think about it.' She was becoming agitated.

'I'm sorry.' Seeing her reluctance to talk about it, he said, 'We won't talk about it now, but I am fascinated and entranced. I want to know everything about you. I am as hungry for knowledge about you as I am for your body.'

They spoke endearments and affirmed their love for one another, as new lovers must. A little later, after more love-making, Lois asked, 'What would Malc say if he could see us now?'

'I don't suppose he'd understand. I mean, it looks a bit tacky. We only met each other tonight and, here we are, screwing the living daylights out of each other. I don't care what anyone thinks,

I know that what we did was real and oh…. just wonderful, and, Lois,' he looked gravely at her, 'it will go on being real and wonderful,' he gave her a glass of wine, and added, 'for the rest of our fucking lives, Lois. I've met the girl I'm going to marry.'

She smiled and responded, 'To the rest of our fucking lives.'

He came to lie next to her and looked at her again, one finger caressing her body. She could feel the electricity in his touch, as though there ought to be a visible spark. She watched, fascinated, mesmerised. They made love again. Later, high on love, Lois said, 'I have to go to the loo. Where is it?'

He handed her his dressing gown and asked, 'Would you like a shower?'

'No, I'm never going to wash again. I like the smell of you on me, the smell of sex and spunk.'

'I'll be here, to top it up every so often.' He smiled wickedly. He showed her across the hall and put the latch on the door. When she came out of the bathroom, she met Iolo, who introduced himself.

'You and Sly make good lovers, from all I can hear,' he said.

'Sorry to disturb you.' She blushed

'Oh it's not disturbing me; it's making me horny.'

She hurried back into Sly's room, where he was ready to make love all over again. 'I've just met your next door neighbour,' she said, with a coy grin.

'Was he smashed?'

'I certainly hope so,' she said as she shed the gown and crossed over to the bed. They had finished their wine and struggled under the covers to sleep, and it was five-thirty in the morning. Lois lay on her side, Sly curled up behind her, his knees in the crook of her knees, his body pressed close to hers.

Sly woke and went to the bathroom. When he came back, she was still asleep. Outside, the birds twittered, but the hall was quiet. She moved sleepily on to her back, he gently lowered himself beside her and, very gently and lovingly, aroused her yet again. Their sleepy love pattern would be repeated in the days to come, but on this first morning, she could think of nothing lovelier than dreaming of his body and his love, and waking to find that, while she had dreamt, her dream had become reality.

2

During Sly

AT TWO-THIRTY the next afternoon, they were sleeping heavily when the sound of loud voices stirred Sly. He sat up and rubbed his face. Finding Lois next to him came as no surprise. He had dreamt of her all night. Lois woke, surprised to find herself in Sly's room. Outside, Welsh voices were shouting, 'Come on, Davies, you lazy cunt. Stop slobbing around in your pit. You've missed lunch and you're about to miss tea. Come on out, you toad, and make us some coffee'

Lois looked worried, but Sly said, 'It's two of my so-called friends, Dafydd and Melfyn. Don't worry, they'll go away.'

Someone kicked at the door. 'Davies, let us in. We know you are in there.'

'Fuck off, Dafydd. I'm asleep,' Sly shouted back. Lois laughed and pulled the sheet around her, just in case. This wasn't how she'd imagined Sly's friends to be. Too late, Sly realised that they'd never taken the latch off the lock, and two young men suddenly leapt into the room, as surprised as Lois was that the door had been left open.

'Oh, sorry, Sly. Didn't realise you had company.'

'Well, you never asked, did you? Now, if you still want some tea, you can make some. If not, piss off.' Sly said all this with a wide grin.

'Aren't you going to introduce us?' the other guy asked.

'Okay, okay. Dafydd and Melfyn, meet Lois. She's a girl. You both look like you've never seen one before,' he said, still smiling.

'Hello, Lois,' they chorused.

'Hello, Dafydd and Melfyn,' she replied, as evenly as she could to the two men, staring at her lying naked in bed with one of their friends. They looked more embarrassed than she did.

'Well, nice to have met you. We'll go and ask Iolo if he could find us some coffee.'

'I'll put the kettle on,' a muffled voice replied from the other side of the wall. 'I'm awake now, thanks to you two pricks.'

'You can lock the door behind you,' Sly shouted after them. 'Sorry, Lois,' he said with a grin. 'Anyway, it's about time I made you breakfast.'

He leaned over and kissed her good afternoon, only to find that food was the last thing on his mind. Realising that there was an audience next door, he flicked the switch on the tape deck and covered the sounds of their lovemaking with music.

Passion spent, Sly got up to make toast and tea. Lois crept out to the loo and washed her face. Every bone in her body ached, her back and pelvis especially. When Sly returned, she stretched and groaned.

'You've almost killed me. I feel like I've been fucked for a fortnight. Every bone in my body aches, and I've strained muscles in my back I never knew I had.'

'Well, you know what they say about aching muscles. It's lack of use that does it. We'll soon get you into practice. I feel bloody fantastic. I want to tell everyone I know all about you. I feel drunk with happiness.'

'I think we can leave that to Dafydd,' Lois said.

'Yes, and we'll have to tell Malc soon, because Dafydd's bound to say something. He's like an old woman, just because he never gets anywhere with girls.'

'Oh well, I suppose everyone will have to know eventually, won't they?'

'As I intend to spend every night and day with you, they'll soon catch on, whatever we say. Do you want a shower? Why don't we have one together and wash ourselves clean?'

'Marvellous but, first, I want some tea. I'm really dehydrated.'

'By the time we're ready to leave, it will almost be time to go to Malc's.'

★ ★ ★

Eventually, showered and refreshed, they left the hall and, hand-in-hand, walked to Alex. The sun shone, the tide was in, the sea was calm, and there were many students on the promenade. Sly wore black jeans, a Bunnymen T-shirt, baseball pumps and his Bunnymen raincoat. Lois thought he looked even more gorgeous in daylight. She, with her face scrubbed, looked like a twelve-year-old as she danced alongside him. As they came to the main entrance, two girls came out; Sly introduced them as Gina and Ali, and there was a bit of banter before they left.

'Are you all right? You went a bit quiet,' he said, pulling her close to him again.

'Yeah, I'm fine. Just couldn't think of anything to say.'

'Gina and Ali are doing some of my course. They are Drama and Art. They're good fun. They are in Alex, as well. They don't like it much.'

'I've seen them around, but I don't know them.'

She opened the door to her room and Sly stepped inside. He was struck by the extraordinariness of it. A huge window overlooked the sea. The room was of a similar size to his, but Lois had transformed it from an ordinary student's room into a small shrine to her heroine. Over the bed was an imitation fur rug; white fur rugs were scattered on the floor; posters and prints of Marilyn Monroe decorated the walls; fans and feathers were attached to every possible anchor. The top of the wardrobe held fancy boxes and hatboxes. The dressing table was covered in bottles of perfume, and her cosmetics were neatly organised in a large plastic toolbox. The desk held books and photographs of family and friends.

Sly had many questions to ask but, for now, he just looked. The bookcase held numerous tiny boxes, a complete Art Deco tea set, and boxes of biscuits and cakes; on the window ledge were more books and a tray with glasses and drink. A decanter was full of sherry. The whole room had a 1920s feel about it, but it was as modern as she was.

'Lois, this room is so you; you've done wonders with it. I love it.'

He sat down in the chair at the window and pulled her onto his lap.

'This room is my little corner of Aber that I carry with me all the time. I'm at home here.'

He felt at home here, too. He set her on her feet and stood up. He had noticed her tape collection, which hung from the ceiling in a long strip, each cassette having its own pocket.

Lois said she must change, and he continued to move around, prying into the things that everybody wants to pry into: drawers and cupboards.

'So many shoes for one person.'

'They are a passion of mine,' she answered. She selected a red and grey dress with three-quarter-length sleeves and a small collar. The top was plain, but the skirt was pleated round and looked very 1920s. Before she had put it on, they made love in the sunlight that streamed into the room. Afterwards, he asked her for a cigarette.

'You smoke?'

'Only when I'm blissfully happy,' he replied.

She handed him a black Sobrani from a silver box, lit it for him and handed him an ashtray.

'My Lois, my lovely Lois, so much style.'

Then, the bell for tea rang, which meant it was six o'clock. She dressed quickly. Sly lay naked on the floor, watching her apply make-up and select jewellery. 'I'm ready, Sly,' she whispered. She looked like a dream. He stirred himself and dressed, aware of how scruffy he looked in comparison. She kissed him and asked, 'Will you carry the wine?'

'We'll be late, and you know what Malc will say.' Sly teased.

They chatted as they walked to Annedd Deg, about Monroe mostly. She was a real idol to Lois, who could describe her every film, her life, and who felt a real compassion for the film star. They rang the bell.

Luke and Malc lived with six others, sharing one kitchen and one bathroom. Each had separate rooms. Malc, Luke and Fenn had the top floor. This weekend, nearly all except Luke and Malc were away, so they decided to have a dinner party, to celebrate the peace in the kitchen. Malc answered the door.

'Here's the wine, sweetest. Where's Luke?' Lois asked.

'He's in the kitchen, clucking over the stroganoff. Would you like a glass of sherry?'

'Sherry, great, let's go,' Lois said with a smile, following Malc into the kitchen. 'Hi, Luke, that smells wonderful.'

Luke turned round, smiling. 'Oh, Sly, did you two arrive together, eh?' His face fell visibly.

'Yes.'

Lois asked, 'What can I do?'

'Nothing. Everything's under control, thanks.' Luke turned quickly back to the stove.

'Would you like a sherry, Luke?' Malc asked.

'Take one up for me. I'll just bring this to a boil and be up, okay?'

Malc led Sly out of the kitchen.

'Are you okay, Luke?' Lois asked.

He seemed edgy. 'Yes, I'm, fine. I'll be up in a minute.'

She hovered, feeling uncomfortable, then decided to leave well alone and went to join the others.

The table was laid in Fenn's room. Malc and Sly were selecting some tapes.'What's wrong with Luke, Malc?'

'I don't know exactly. He's been drinking a lot this afternoon, but he seemed okay to me; a bit quiet, perhaps. Maybe, he's missing Fenn. We came round to Alex after lunch, but....'

Luke came into the room and finished the sentence. 'You weren't there. Natasha said she thought you were away for the weekend.'

'Well, I'm not. I'm here.' She smiled, trying to ease the conversation away from this. She felt awful. Like Sly had said, it could look a bit tacky to outsiders. 'I just wasn't there after lunch.' She shrugged and sipped her sherry.

Sly tried to draw Luke into a discussion about music. 'Malc always wants Japan to eat by. The Art of Parties. What's your choice, Luke, before we get outvoted?'

Luke answered sourly, 'Japan's fine for me, Sly. Anything.'

★ ★ ★

The food was excellent, the wine wonderful. Malc, Lois and Sly kept the conversation going, light and breezy, but Luke said very little. He insisted on serving all the courses and clearing them all away again, and once it was over, before Malc had even suggested coffee, he leapt up from the table and said he'd do the washing up. He collected the plates while the others sat in silence.

When he'd gone, Malc said, 'I'm really sorry, you two. This is worse than I'd expected. I'll make some coffee, and go and talk to him. I should have done so before.'

'No, Malc, I'll go. I'll help him with the washing up. We won't be long.' Lois took the remaining dirty cutlery down to the kitchen with her.

'Luke's crazy about her, Sly,' Malc said. 'He won't take this well. You'd better be good to her, or there will be trouble.'

'I will be good to her. I couldn't be anything but good to her. I'm in love with her. Yes, that fast,' he added, seeing Malc smile.

Downstairs, Luke was doing things slowly, to defer having to go back upstairs. He knew he was being childish, but he loved Lois, and last night, what happened between her and Sly shouldn't have happened. He wished that he'd never gone to Alex today, and found out about it.

Lois came down to the kitchen and picked up a teacloth. 'I've come to help you. We can't have the chef washing up alone. It was a superb meal, Luke.'

'I like cooking alone and I like finishing the job alone, too.' Luke spoke quietly.

'Well, you can't have it all your own way. We'll do this together, okay?' Lois tried to keep her voice light. She started to wipe the few bits of cutlery Luke had left. Upstairs, Malc put on Bauhaus, which came echoing down the stairwell. She sang along to it and tried to figure out what to say. Before she could think of anything, Luke said softly, 'You're going out with Sly, then?'

Was she going out with him? He'd talked of the future; of seeing her night and day, so she guessed they were going out. 'I suppose I am, yes,' she replied evenly.

'Did you stay with him last night, Lois?' She met his gaze and saw the pain in his eyes. Again, the question was so direct that it surprised her. She wondered how much she could tell Luke. 'Did you stay with him in Panty, have sex with him?' Luke's voice was hard.

She answered with a sigh, 'Yes, Luke, I did. It was unavoidable.'

'I never expected you to behave like that, meet someone and leap into bed with him. It's not like you. I know it isn't. What are you thinking of? You hardly know him.'

'Luke, it's not like that, it's different,' she said sharply.

'It always is, isn't it, different?' His voice was pure bitterness.

'Luke, why does it bother you so much what I do?' she asked, puzzled.

'He's spoilt it all. We were friends until Malc introduced you and now, suddenly, I'm forgotten. Love at first sight, eh, Lois? You knew, Sly knew, I knew and Malc knew. Oh, he must be laughing at me now. He bloody masterminded the whole fucking thing. You and Sly! What a fucking marvellous couple!'

'Luke, please be reasonable,' she almost shouted.

His brown eyes pleading, he said, 'We were friends, Lois.'

'We still are; nothing's changed.' Lois touched his arm and he looked down at her hand with a bewildered expression on his face. Lois tried to explain her feelings for Sly, while Luke froze inside.

'Please, Luke, we can still be friends,' she said gently.

I'm sorry. Of course, we can still be friends. I'm just being stupid, I guess. I'm tired, that's all. I'm sorry.'

Malc came into the kitchen and said that coffee was ready upstairs.

Lois and Malc went to Fenn's room, and Luke stayed in the kitchen, but appeared shortly afterwards, carrying a bottle of brandy.

As they left, Luke kissed Lois on the cheek and whispered, 'Have a good time, friend.'

She smiled at him and hoped that, tomorrow, everything would be as normal.

★ ★ ★

Once at the Union, Malc raced ahead to get the first round in.

'Hang on a minute,' Sly said, holding Lois by the arm, 'I want to talk to you. What's up with Luke?'

'He's upset about you and me, but we talked it over; he'll be fine. We are good friends, you know,' she explained.

'I heard him shouting. He didn't hurt you, did he?'

At first, Lois thought he meant hurt her feelings, then she realised that he thought Luke might have hit her. 'God, no, Sly, of course not. He was simply upset that things happened so quickly between you and me, I suppose. He didn't expect it.'

'Does he hate me?' Sly asked.

'No. His problem is more to do with his men friends. Whatever it is, it will blow over, so, forget it, okay? Don't you think we'd better go and keep Malc away from Dafydd, before the whole Union finds out what a scarlet woman I am?' They laughed together.

Aber was still dry on Sundays, and the Union, with its special licence, was packed. They came up behind Dafydd, Malc and Melfyn, and caught the end of a conversation. Iolo, Sly's neighbour in hall, had evidently been enjoying himself by spreading gossip, and he swiftly changed the subject now. They spent a nice evening with the boys, as Sly called them. Afterwards, Lois walked down to Sly's hall with the others and Malc drove off in Luke's car. It was cold, the sky was clear and filled with stars.

'"Two things fill my mind with ever increasing wonder and awe,

the starry heavens above me and the moral law within me,"' Sly quoted, and smiled, capturing the moment. 'It's all Kant to you,' he joked. 'You got any lectures tomorrow?'

'Yes, at nine, eleven and twelve, and a practical all afternoon.'

'You are joking?'

'No. I'm a Scientist, not a part-time Arts student, Sly. Thursdays, I have two lectures and the afternoon off, and Wednesday afternoon, of course, but David usually comes down then.

'Who's David?'

'He's a really old friend of mine; we were at college together. His Mum is staying with friends in Machynlleth. He comes to visit her on his day off and usually drives over to meet me on

Wednesday.'

Sly asked, 'Does he come every Wednesday?'

'He can't come for the next couple of weeks because he is away on business.'

'Good, otherwise, I may feel inclined to punch him on the nose. Maybe, in two weeks I'll be satiated with you enough to let you out of my sight for a couple of hours to see an old friend. Oh, why does life have to go on? I want you all to myself, no lectures and practicals to complicate it,' he moaned.

'Well, I have to go, darling; it's too difficult to catch up if I don't.'

They argued until Lois agreed to skip the first lecture, Organic Chemistry, for which concession Sly showed his pleasure by sharing it with her in their favourite way.

3

During Sly

THE FIRST COLLEGE DAY after they had met went by in a dream for Lois. When she woke, Sly was gently stroking her back and her hair; they made love in the peace and security of his room, before she had to leave for her two morning lectures.

Lois took lecture notes, but her mind was elsewhere. A fellow student lent her his notes from the first lecture, which she had missed. Her Zoology practical, which she usually enjoyed, seemed endless, and time weighed heavily. She tried to imagine what Sly would be doing. He had a lecture at two, a Drama class at three. At break, she went to the Union for coffee, and found Fenn and Malc there. Malc hurried off to a lecture, so she sat with Fenn and asked about his weekend.

'My weekend? What about yours? Malc's been telling me. I am shocked.' He tried to look sternly at her.

'Oh, Fenn, really, I mean, you're at it all the time,' Lois cried in horror.

'Not to the extent you are, according to Dafydd. It's shockingly poor behaviour. Can't you let the poor boy sleep, for fuck's sake?' Fenn laughed at the outraged look on Lois's face. 'So, it's all Sly now, and I'm blown out, am I?' he teased her.

'Well, Fenn, I decided that, if I couldn't have you all to myself, I'd have to take my heart elsewhere and make do,' Lois joked.

'Well, you certainly didn't hang around, Lois.'

Talk turned to Luke and Fenn said he thought that Luke would soon cheer up. It was a difficult subject for him, knowing the cause of Luke's distress, so he changed tack. 'Are you going to the Alternative disco on Wednesday? It's an Alternative to the Alex. It's a Pier party, at the Football Club? Do you want some tickets?' he asked.

'Yeah, why not? A good bop will set us all to rights. Give me two, Fenn.'

'Bringing Mr Davies along?'

'I might do.'

'Good. I'd like to meet the poor chap. I've heard a lot about him. I'll meet you at the White Horse at nine, we'll have a pub-crawl and then go, okay?

When she got back to Alex after her practical, she went straight into dinner. On the way back to her room, she picked up her post and found a letter from David, posted in Rome. "The women are all virgins here," he wrote, "so, I'm rectifying that." Lois smiled to herself. When she got up to her room, it was six-thirty; Sly was due at seven. A student called Gina arrived with some lecture notes for Sly, and Lois offered her a cup of tea. Gina looked surprised, but accepted. She was an outgoing girl and chatted easily until Sly arrived,

'Hi, Gina, what are you doing here?'

'Saving your arse, sweetheart, by lending you the notes. Let me have them back pronto, please? See you, Lois, Sly.' Gina swept out of the room.

Lois was glad to be alone with Sly. They settled to work, Sly on the floor, reading, and making notes; Lois at the desk, finishing sketches, completing the practical write-ups and writing notes on what she had drawn. It was nearly ten when she finished. Sly had hardly said a word to disturb her, but as she looked round for him, she found he had been watching her.

'You work too hard,' he said, putting his book down and coming to massage her back. 'I've been sitting there, bored, for ages.' He kissed her neck.

They spoke and joked about their respective subjects, and Sly stretched his stiff limbs. 'Is this your David?' he asked, pointing at one of her photographs. She nodded. 'Good looking fucker, isn't he? I hate him on sight.' Sly sounded sincere.

Lois turned to look at him in surprise. 'David's just my friend; he's really sweet; he'd do anything for me. He helped me get over Sid.'

'Oh, yes, the bastard that took your virginity. Is he here?' He examined the pictures.

'No. I wouldn't keep any of him on show, would I?' Lois said cautiously.

'No matter, I hate him, too,' Sly replied. His tone of voice alarmed her, but it quickly slipped her mind.

* * *

Studying together became the highlight of their days. Lois worked extremely hard and had a good influence on Sly. The amount of work given to her now by her tutors was considerably less than she had had in College, reading for her A-Levels. Here, she had to press her tutor, Dr. Wooton, for essay titles, and even then, he only set her five in the first term. Working hard during the week gave them free time at weekends, and they usually put aside Wednesdays for parties and Thursdays for each other.

Lois concentrated far better with Sly in the room. His presence allowed her to channel her energies to work, in order to finish quickly, so that they could make their wonderful love. Sly sketched her as she worked, or from imagination, and by the end of the first term, he had a complete portfolio entitled 'Images of Lois', containing pencil drawings, water colours, charcoals, oils and chalk.

The Alternative party was where Sly introduced Malc to Frankie. They met at the White Horse at the preordained time.

Luke came with Malc and Fenn and seemed in high spirits. Lois sat watching the others, completely at ease with the world. She wore a tight, black dress, high cut and ruched, to show off her figure. She had her hair in a high ponytail, and looked lovely. Sly wore his dark grey suit, a shirt and tie, and carried his trilby and a dark overcoat.

From the White Horse, they went to upper lounge bar at the Bell Vue, overlooking the sea. Students generally preferred the dark atmosphere of the cellar bar. At ten o'clock, as they were about to leave, a girl came in and looked around. Seeing Sly, she came over. 'Hi, Sly, have you seen Julia and Julia?'

'No, sorry, Frankie. They haven't been in here.' Sly said.

'I've lost them. We were on our way to the Football Club, I got talking to Giles, and now I'm not sure where they are.' Anxiously, Frankie looked around again.

'They probably went ahead, thinking you would follow with Giles.'

'Giles had to go to the Pier.'

'Well, come along with us; we're off in a minute, anyway,' Sly said, introducing everybody. Frankie joined them. She smoked incessantly as she talked, mostly to Malc, about her name, about her friends, and about the Carp boys. Carpenter Hall was another seafront hall, occupied by boys only, mostly animals, according to Frankie. Only Fenn seemed unaffected by this girl. Normally, anything relatively attractive in the room, and Fenn would give them the charm as soon as possible. However, he sat chatting quietly to Luke.

At the Football Club, Frankie's arrival heralded catcalls and whistles from the Carp lads, who, contrary Malc's prediction, were there, after all. Frankie waved madly to them, and then clung on to Malc for the rest of the evening. Fenn chatted to the D.J., Lewie. The first record to which Lois danced was DAF, 'Der Mussolini,' with Fenn. It was rapidly becoming their song. Sly didn't want to dance; he wanted to watch her. It was, in the end, a great evening for all of them. Malc showed all the signs of being interested in Frankie, and when Lois and Sly were walking home, they discussed it.

'Maybe Malc's met the girl of his dreams,' Sly said.

'Well, she certainly seems lovely enough to keep anyone from dreaming. She's good fun,' Lois agreed.

'She's sad, I think,' Sly said thoughtfully.

What makes you say that?' Lois asked, surprised.

'Well, she's good fun because she's taking speed; she's always smashed.'

'You're joking.' Lois had never known anyone who took drugs.

'I wish I were, honestly. She hates Aber and the course. She's almost gone home dozens of times.' Sly explained

'Jeez, I'd never have guessed. Perhaps, what she needs is a steady man to settle her.'

'And you think Malc is a steady man?' Sly asked.

'I was not thinking of Malc, actually. There's Fenn,' Lois said.

'Fenn? He hardly noticed her.'

'Exactly. It's completely out of character for Fenn not to notice someone as attractive as Frankie. I think he couldn't fathom her, and that's why he didn't make a play for her. He wasn't sure of her response.'

'Women's logic! Fenn ignores her, so he fancies her, and she makes a play for Malc, so she fancies Fenn. Honestly!' Sly laughed. 'Actually, Malc isn't her type. She's crazy about this guy called Freddie, in Carp, but he's got a girlfriend called Joy. She's a friend of Malc and Luke's. Do you know her?'

'Vaguely, she's really pretty, long dark hair?'

'Yes, that's her. Well, Frankie has tried everything to get off with Freddie, and I think he's weakening. Didn't you notice a lack of Julia and Julia, you know, Frankie's friends, at the party?'

Talk about other students soon lost its appeal, and then they got distracted by kissing in the moonlight, with Cardigan Bay as a backdrop.

★ ★ ★

Lois had two lectures on Thursday morning, and Sly had a tutorial in the afternoon. They missed them all. Instead, they told each other about their families, and Sly asked how Lois's mother had reacted to her sister Veronica's early marriage. Lois said she had accepted it very well.

'I'd marry you now, but you're too flighty for marriage, aren't you?' Sly pulled her close to him. 'I'm going to have to make you take me more seriously before you will be ready to accept my proposal, won't I?'

Lois wasn't sure whether he was joking, or not. He sounded deadly serious. She asked him about his family. He became very pensive, staring out to sea. 'Well, it's just me and my da. Manx, sort of Welsh for mother, died five years ago in February. She had breast cancer; it was horrible. I guess that I'm lucky, because I have got some memories of her. You can't remember your father, can you?' He looked at her hard. Not surprisingly, the conversation troubled him; he became very quiet and they looked out to sea, lost in thought. Sly's arm was around Lois's shoulder, holding her close.

Towards dusk, they wandered back from South Beach and decided to call on Malc and Luke. Luke was alone and he greeted them warmly. Lois asked how Malc had fared with Frankie.

'Well, that's a story and half,' Luke said. 'He walked her back up to Penbryn....'

'Penbryn?' Lois asked surprised.

'Yes, Frankie's a Radel girl.' Luke explained, as he put the kettle on to make tea.

'Really? She doesn't look much like a Radel girl.'

'Honestly! How long have you been here and already you've started to categorise people.

'Okay, okay' Lois laughed, pulling a face at him. 'Go on with your story.'

'Well, first, she threw up; then, she told him she was madly in love with Joy's boyfriend, Freddie; then she threw up again and passed out.'

'Had she been drinking?' Sly asked.

'No, but Malc says she speeds a lot, and too much of that and even a little drink doesn't help the situation.' Luke said, pouring out tea.

'Oh dear, so Malc's not a happy man, then?' Lois asked.

'Well, he's taking her to the Union on Saturday, so you never know what'll become of them. Are you two coming to the Union?'

In the end, they agreed to go to a Fringe theatre production on Saturday.

* * *

That Sunday, they woke late and dressed quickly, so they wouldn't miss the Panty Sunday lunch of roast lamb. They sat with Dafydd and Melfyn and, as they were drinking coffee, Luke and Malc came in. Malc was having Welsh lessons in the hall every Sunday afternoon, and Luke had come for the ride. They took Luke back to Sly's room, to wait for Malc, and he told them about the Union.

'I wanted to ask: do you two want to come to a film stars' party on Wednesday?' Luke said. 'You have to dress up as your favourite film star. I'm going as Charlie Chaplin and Fenn's going as Adam Ant. Are you coming?'

'Okay,' Sly said, 'Give us the tickets. Where is it?'

'The Pier. It's a private party, and it's free if you have an invite. There's this girl Catherine, someone that Fenn knows; it's her twenty-first, and her father is paying for everything, even booze.'

'Oh, poor thing! Does he have any idea what he's let himself in for?' Sly asked.

'I should think not, actually.' Luke smiled.

'It'll be great fun. Guess who I'll go as?' Lois asked.

'I really can't imagine, Lois,' Sly smiled at her.

'Okay, what about you? How about Humphrey Bogart? He would be easy to do. All you need is a white dinner suit.'

'As it happens, I have one.' Sly said, opening the wardrobe and pulling it out. 'It was my Godfather's. I thought it looked pretty special, so I wouldn't let him throw it away. I had it, instead.'

Lois had a dress similar to the famous white one worn by Marilyn Monroe in 'The Seven-Year Itch'. She had the voice and make-up off to a tee. All she needed was a wig. There were no costume-hire firms in Aber, and the one chemist that sold wigs only had a long blonde one. Armed with this and a photo of Marilyn, she looked for a hairdresser who could cut and set her wig to look like Marilyn's hair. The first two hairdressers shook their heads. On the afternoon of the party, she had almost decided to have her hair cut and bleached, and then she remembered seeing a smart, red and white hairdressers' salon on North Parade. Here, she met Huw, a gay hairdresser. On this first occasion, he made her laugh and cut and set her wig for her. He explained how to put the wig on over her hair, and refused to accept payment for the work. He also caught her as a customer by saying that she needed her hair trimmed.

Lois, with her wig prepared, felt excited about the party. She rushed to get tea at Alex, and wondered when David would be back from Italy. She hadn't seen him for two weeks, and felt rather guilty because she'd given him hardly any thought. She wondered how he'd react to Sly, and decided that, however much she wanted them to, they probably wouldn't get on. They were too different, but none of this affected her mood.

Sly was due at five o'clock. That afternoon, he had a technical meeting for the end of term production and, although he said he wasn't bothered, she knew he would be pleased if he got some of his ideas accepted. The play was Sean O'Casey's 'The Plough and the Stars'.

After dinner, she spent a long time over her toilette, slowly transforming herself into her heroine. Lois knocked on Natasha's door, to see her reaction, and found that Natasha was with another girl, whom Lois vaguely recognised from the dance at the Football Club.

'Lois, that's amazing. I had to think who the hell it was. You look just like your pictures,' Natasha exclaimed. 'Doesn't she, Gerry?'

Lois explained about the fancy-dress party, and twirled round, to give them the full effect. The noise brought other girls along, to have a glimpse at the transformation. Lois's spirits were soaring, and she invited Natasha and Gerry to have a glass of sherry with her. She put on a Marilyn tape and lit a Sobrani cigarette. Just then, her Bogart arrived. Sly, in a white tuxedo, had a cigarette in the corner of his mouth, and carried his heavy overcoat and trilby.

'Of all the gin joints in all the world, why do you have to walk into mine?' he said, walking into the room with a swagger. 'Oh, hello, everyone. Lois, you look brilliant, just like her.' His face was incredulous.

'It's a shame Bogart and Monroe never starred together.' Gerry commented dryly.

At eight-thirty, they set off. It was a calm night, so they got to the Pier without too much damage to the costumes. It was full when they arrived and, after a quick peep in the mirror, they made their way through the crowd, to find Charlie Chaplin, Groucho Marx, Adam Ant and Twiggy congregated in a corner.

'Lois, my God, that's brilliant. You're just her image.'

Lois was delighted that her costume had come off so well, and Sly felt immensely proud of her. The party was a huge success. Lois and Sly never met their hostess, who spent most of the evening phoning her father, to get the limit on the bar extended. All the drinks were free, so everyone had a good time. The music consisted of theme tunes to classic films. Sly and Lois danced to 'Diamonds are a Girl's Best Friend', with Charlie Chaplin, Adam Ant and Groucho Marx tempting Monroe with kisses, but not getting very far.

The other costumes were good, too. Clint Eastwood figured heavily; Lynne had come as Bette Davis (an uncanny likeness); Gina and Ali as Laurel and Hardy; someone else was Jaws; and there was a couple dressed as the Lone Ranger and Silver. The party mood heightened at about midnight, when they all sang Happy Birthday to their anonymous hostess, and her boyfriend, Toby, jumped out of her birthday cake. There were many drunken toasts to her benevolent father.

At one o'clock, as people were beginning to leave, Lois became aware of a rumpus at the back of the hall, and saw Joy (dressed as Bo Peep) throw a glass of beer at a very worse for drink James Bond (Freddie). Her first reaction was to find Sly, who had been at the bar, getting drinks. Joy stormed out, James Bond followed her, and Sly and Lois went to find the others, knowing that this had something to do with Frankie. Malc was holding Frankie's wrists, while she struggled to get free.

'Let me go, Malc. Just leave me alone.' Lois watched in horror, Frankie was screaming at Malc, tears rolling down her face. 'I just want to go.'

'No, you'll follow Freddie. Just let him alone. You've caused enough trouble tonight.'

Frankie's face was distorted with rage. 'I just want to go. Can't you see, I don't want Freddie, and I don't want you. I want Fenn.'

Malc looked as though he had been slapped in the face. He dropped her wrists immediately, and she ran sobbing to Fenn, who put his arms around her and shrugged at Malc, who watched in silent anger.

'Take me home, Fenn. Please, take me home.'

Lois picked up Frankie's jacket and draped it over her shoulders. Frankie was sobbing hysterically. Lois looked questioningly at Fenn, who shook his head. The music had started up again and people were drifting away from a scene they had not understood. Malc turned back to the table and swiped his glass onto the floor. Sly went over to him.

'Oh, that's fucking marvellous, that is. I was trying to help the crazy bitch, and all she wants is fucking Fenn.' He was white with rage and clenching his teeth. 'Well, I hope they'll be fucking happy together.' He sat down heavily and sighed.

Sly and Lois were very concerned about Malc, who seemed most annoyed at Fenn. Sly gave Malc the key to his room in Panty, so Malc could avoid having to return to Annedd Deg. He promised to call round and see them the next day.

Luke walked with him to the door and then came back.

'What happened, Luke?' Lois asked.

Luke told them what he had seen. Freddie was very drunk and, when he walked past Frankie and Malc, Frankie grabbed him and started kissing him. That's when Joy threw her drink at him and stormed off.

'What about Fenn?'

'He had no part in it. Frankie's smashed out of her brain. I don't think she knows what she's doing. She spent the day with Malc, and I think he thought....' he sighed. 'Well, you know, what he thought.'

'Shit. What a mess,' Sly said.

Luke decided to go home at this point, wondering why it was always he who was caught in the middle. All pleasure had gone out of the evening. When they got back to Alex, Lois was glad to unpin her hair and become Lois again, and find Sly was back to being Sly.

4

During Sly: Disputes and David

ON THURSDAY, SLY WENT to the Department at lunchtime, to find out whether he had been included in the technical crew for 'The Plough and the Stars'. Lois had a pile of biochemistry notes to study, so they made the most of the few hours they had. The fallout from the night before was considerable. After Sly had left, Lois was visited by just about everyone who had been involved. First was Malc, on his way back to Annedd Deg. He'd spent the night outside Frankie's door in Penbryn, determined to know exactly what he was dealing with and just how far she and Fenn had betrayed him. He felt exhausted and no wonder. He had taken Frankie's switch of allegiance very hard; his bitter experience with Lucy had just been repeated, this time with Frankie. Lois listened to his outpouring of grief.

'What's Sly up to that he isn't here on a Thursday?' Malc asked suddenly, as he was about to leave.

'That's more like you, Malc. He wants to help with the technical stuff for 'The Plough and the Stars', the end of term production, and he finds out today if he's in, or not.'

'Thanks, Lois, for the tea and for listening,' he said, reluctantly closing the door behind him.

After Malc had gone, Lois thought how much life would change if Fenn and Malc did have a huge row over Frankie; and what about poor Luke? Malc had called her the diplomat; well, she'd better employ all her diplomatic powers to cope with this crisis. Frankie turned up almost immediately. She was on her way to Alex and had popped into the Prom shop to get some fags, when she saw Malc walk past the window, and so she sat on the seaward side of the shelter on the prom, waiting for him to leave, so that she could come and see Lois. She told Lois that Fenn had been very sweet with her and that he hadn't taken advantage of the situation. They had spent the night together, but that was all. He wanted her to stop taking drugs and drinking before he was willing to commit himself. This seemed to have given Frankie an incentive to sort herself out. She told Lois how unhappy she had been in Aberystwyth. She said she didn't usually act like this, she was just desperate for something nice to happen amidst all the gloom and despondency. Lois, who understood nothing of drug dependency, advised her to try to stay straight for a while and allow her feelings for Fenn to settle. She also told her that she would have to try to explain herself to Malc, but Frankie thought that was too much to ask of her at present.

Eventually, Frankie left, and Lois opened the window. The sky was overcast, the tide was in, and waves splashed onto the prom. How the moods change, she thought.

At last, Sly came back.

'Hello sweetheart.' She hugged him to her. 'How did you do?' she asked, knowing from his face exactly what he'd say.

'I've been included; involved with set design, which is mega because there's this bloke, a third year Art student, who I really like; he's brilliant and he's in overall charge. I'll learn loads. His name is Mickie, he's a Scouser, he's ace.'

'Oh, you almost look pleased'

'I know I said I didn't care, but now I'm in, it's wonderful.' He kissed her gently. 'It will mean loads of extra work; meetings from nine in the morning until all hours, but I don't have to go to all of them, so there will be plenty of time for us, too.'

'Good. Maybe, I'll be able to make some nine o'clock lectures and understand some Biochemistry.'

There was another knock at the door. It was Fenn. 'Hi, I was just passing and thought I'd drop in.'

Lois knew what was on Fenn's mind, too. He wanted to know if they had seen Malc. 'Come in, Fenn. Like some tea?'

'No, can't stop. I'm cooking tonight, so I'd best be quick. I just wondered if you'd seen Malc, either of you, because he didn't come home last night.'

'He stayed at my place' Sly replied curtly.

Sly's taking Malc's side, Lois thought, not surprised. Fenn seemed in need of some support and approval, but he was unlikely to get it from Sly. Fenn wished that Lois were on her own, for she seemed to understand his position. He found it hard to speak openly with Sly there. Lois could tell that Sly was cross with Fenn, too, but she knew that was because he was so loyal to Malc. She saw it from all sides.

They didn't discuss it much after Fenn left; they turned up the music and made love, leaving the world outside to cope on its own for an hour or two. After tea, Luke arrived, and Sly, who wanted to finish some work, suggested that Luke take Lois out for a drink and a chat.

A week later, Malc and Fenn were being polite but distant to each other, Fenn and Frankie were spending a good deal of time together, Frankie apparently keeping off the speed and drinking more sensibly. Malc had thrown himself into his work, in an attempt to avoid the new lovebirds.

* * *

The worst storm of the winter came about half way through November. It had been brewing for sometime. The prom was off limits, and students and staff had to use the back entrances to all of the seafront buildings. On the Friday, after her Bio-chemistry practical, the friends congregated in Lois's room and watched the storm. She and Sly sat in one chair; Lois perched on his lap. Nick and Gerry were also with them. None of them had ever witnessed such a violent storm. Waves were crashing right over the prom; spray reached the third floor window; waves hit the roof of Alex. Everything seemed white, even though it was dark. The sea was seething, the wind howled, tossing Lois's curtains in a storm dance. Suddenly, they saw a small object flying towards them, and flinched instinctively, adrenaline surging. It was a small pebble, approaching with power enough to break the main windowpane. Water beat into the room, and they ran to the far side, their clothes drenched.

Gerry was laughing. The gale was inside the room now. Lois flew round, trying to save her notes. Sly went to find someone to help them. They couldn't stay here. He returned with one of the maintenance staff, who was obviously used to such disasters. Lois made him a cup of tea while he battled to fix a board over the broken pane.

'It's this Victorian glass, you see; it's far too thin to withstand storm damage; it goes all the bloody time.'

He eventually fitted the patch, and promised to replace the glass, once the wind had died down. The storm raged over the weekend. The building seemed to fall into a rhythm as the waves crashed against it. Outside, there was a constant chink, chink, chink, of ropes battering the flagpoles. It was difficult to sleep.

★   ★   ★

David came back from Italy, and arrived in Aber on the following Wednesday. Lois was in bed with Sly, when David knocked on her door. She left Sly in bed, grabbed her bathrobe, and went to unlock the door. Before she could stop him, David was in the room, holding a carrier bag in one hand, an orchid in the other.

'For you, my favourite girl in the whole world,' he said, bending to kiss Lois. Then, he caught sight of Sly, still in bed, staring savagely back at him.

'David, you're impossible; you ought to have said you were coming,' Lois said, but she was thrilled to see him.

'Wednesday afternoon is my time, remember?' David didn't take his eyes off Sly.

'Well, you ought to have more manners, barging in like this.'

'I can see I was interrupting something. Who is your lover, lover?' David said casually

'David, this is Sly.' She sat on the bed, took Sly's hand and smiled up at David.

'Hello, Sly,' David said wryly. 'Sorry to interrupt things. I'm David, Lois's best and dearest friend. How do you do?' A smile played around his lips.

Filled with loathing, Sly stared back at David. Nothing Lois had said about him had prepared Sly for this creature. He stood tall and proud, he was ridiculously handsome, with clean-cut features. He exuded confidence, power, and supremacy. Even Sly couldn't help being impressed. David's clothes were good quality, but David wore them so casually that it was clear that he expected only the best. It was also clear that David did not approve of Sly. If David was this handsome, Sly wondered what Sid was like. Lois had said that there had been a tussle between them over her. If Sid had won the girl, he must be something special. Jealousy racked Sly's mind.

'Listen, darling, I can see you are busy, so I'll pop round to Luke's. I've got a little present from Italy for the boys. I'll be in the Cabin in an hour. See you there. Oh, by the way, this is for you. I hope you like it. I'll put it here and you can open it later, when you're not so occupied. Bye Bye, you gorgeous thing.' He put a carrier bag on the bed and blew her a kiss.

Once he had left, she turned and kissed Sly. 'You're cross. Don't be. That's just David.'

'Just David? he growled. 'Why didn't you warn me that he looked like a Greek god? I don't know how he had the cheek to walk in here and make me feel uncomfortable. I practically live here'

She tried to placate him but he was implacable.

'He obviously thinks you're his.'

'Oh, don't be stupid. David is a really good friend. I've known him for years, it's not like that at all; in fact, he's not like that at all, either. He's really sweet underneath that brashness. It's just a display he puts on, a front.'

'Well, he makes a damned good job of it,' Sly said, and continued to grumble at her.

'Oh, Sly, please don't be mad. I love you, remember?'

Sly stopped suddenly, realising that she was right. It wasn't her fault. He softened.

'I'm sorry Lois. He made me mad. It's not you, I'm sorry.'

'Look, you don't have to meet him again today. I'll go and find him; he'll leave about six, to get back.'

Sly wanted to know how he knew Luke, so she explained about David staying with the boys when he spent a night in Aber. She reminded him that she'd already said he came to see her on Wednesdays. Sly was further placated. She opened her present and tried on the trouser suit that David had bought for her. Even Sly had to admit it suited her perfectly. Then, he wanted her to take it off again and get into bed.

Later, Lois arrived at the Cabin, where David was chatting up two girls. Lois recognised them as second year drama students. He left them as she walked in. 'You're late.' He kissed her, just touching her face with his lips.

'I was admiring my present. It's lovely, David.'

'Nearly every girl on the trip thought I'd got it for her. You should have seen their faces when I told them it was for my best friend.'

'I should be cross with you. You didn't make much of an effort to welcome Sly into my life.'

'You never warned me, and it was a bit of a shock, to find you practically in bed with a man. Luke tells me it's pretty serious.'

'It is, David. I'm crazy about him.'

'God knows why.' He was very dismissive.

'Hey, David, listen, this is very important. Sly is perfect for me, and he's crazy about me. It was love at first sight.' Lois patiently explained to David about Sly and her, and, even though he listened and told her he was delighted for her, she knew he was sceptical. David promised he would try to befriend Sly, and then he started to tell her why he had come down unexpectedly.

'I probably won't see you until Christmas. I'm moving to London. I've been offered a job with an agency.'

Lois was delighted for him. Apparently, he had made good in his career. When David had to leave, he gave Lois a lift back to Alex in his Stag. As he kissed her goodbye, he said, 'Make sure that boy looks after you okay, or I'll fucking kill him.'

'I will, my love, I promise. Take care. See you at Christmas. I'll be home on the Monday before Christmas.'

'That late?' He was disappointed; he was looking forward to her undivided attention.

'Yes, I'm staying on here, to use the library while it's quiet. '

'You take it all too fucking seriously, Lois,' he said, climbing behind the Stag's steering wheel and gunning the engine.

She stood waving until his taillights were lost to sight.

Sly also watched David's departure from Alex and, after seeing the car, he felt second rate compared with David, who had money, looks and the lasting friendship with Lois. Luckily, there were no rehearsals that evening, so she had time to soothe him. He was desperate to know about Sid. He asked to see pictures of him. She found a few, mostly taken at parties, or with David, larking around in a park. There was one of Sid and Lois, arms around each other, at a fairground. Sid was tall and blond, taller even than David. He was good looking but without David's beauty. Sly wondered what had made Lois choose him. She explained what Sid had done and how David's reaction was the start of their special relationship.

Gradually, she won Sly round, and David was forgotten. Later that evening, they went to another football party. Malc and Luke sported the shirts David had brought them back from Italy. They both adored David and couldn't understand Sly's hostility. Gerry, who now often joined Lois when she went out with the boys, found David intriguing. Fenn and Frankie were at the party, wrapped in each other's company, oblivious to anything else. Lois was pleased for them both.

★ ★ ★

Later, alone again, with gentle love and all consuming passion, Sly held Lois close and tried to wash away the bitterness he felt after the way in which Luke and Malc had praised David to the hilt. Watching her face as he made love to her, he knew he had succeeded, and he knew that David could do nothing to weaken this bond between them.

5

During Sly: the End of Term

ALL LECTURES AND PRACTICAL sessions for First Year students were cancelled in the last two weeks of term because of the Christmas Exams, which had to be taken in all subjects. Students didn't have to pass them in order to continue, but those who failed were re-assessed and more closely supervised. However, the June exams had to be passed, and Lois understood that revision of the first term's work would consolidate her position for those exams. She drew up a revision schedule and stuck to it rigidly.

Sly was increasingly involved with the play, which opened on the Saturday before the exam week and played until the end of term, the following Thursday. His drama exams were waived, but he had to sit Classical Studies and Art History. The older students told them how easy the exams were, but they ignored this, studied hard and did not go out during the preceding week.

Everyone from Pantycelyn intended to go to the play and to the party afterwards. They each paid £10 to buy the ingredients for an enormous punch. Lois bought the ingredients, and Dafydd and she mixed it in the large plastic bins Iolo used for his home brew. It was a brandy and champagne base, its potency masked with fruit juices and mixers.

While they waited for Malc and Luke to pick them up, Gerry arrived, wearing a blue dress. She usually wore trousers but, with a little effort, she looked very pretty. Lois was excited about the evening, the play and the party. Malc and Luke, dressed in suits and bow ties, had also made an effort, for Sly's sake. Luke looked gaunt. He had recently lost a great deal of weight, and Malc said he was not eating enough to keep a sparrow alive. He looked tired and his cheeks were hollow, but he sparkled this evening, and everyone was at ease.

Dickie Bedford was in the bar when they entered. He bought a drink for everyone. Lois thought he seemed a bit drunk, having only met him once or twice, and then briefly, but he chatted to her as though she were one of his students.

Once settled in the theatre, she watched avidly. Finlay Morrison was particularly good, as was Elin, another up and coming star. The play ended and the cast and crew appeared on the stage. Sly's smile lit the theatre. When the lights in the auditorium went off, Lois led the others to the bar, to wait for Sly. Eventually, he appeared.

'Bedford's in floods of tears, "One of my best, my darlings. You were all perfect," Well, at least, he's satisfied. He's pissed out of his brain. Although, thinking it over, I don't know about satisfied. Maybe, Giles can see to that for him.' Sly laughed.

'Talking about getting pissed, what about this punch, Sly?'

As they approached Panty, they heard the party before they could see it. In fact, it was a series of small parties, taking place in various rooms. Everyone was having an end of term spree; the hall committee had banished dissenters. Iolo's room was full of people, including Dafydd, Melfyn and a group of giggling Welsh women. Even Huw, the hairdresser, was there. Dafydd greeted them with,

'Hurry up and open your room, Sly. I want my ten quid's worth of booze. This man here cut my hair today. Great, isn't it?'

'Dafydd, you look like you've had ten quid's worth of booze already,' Sly replied, but he opened the door and they all piled in. They threw open the window and put the tape deck on full blast, trying to drown out the heavy rock music coming from upstairs.

They all found plastic cups and started on the punch. They cleared the room and started to dance, in there, in the corridor, and in the bathroom opposite. Everyone was very high-spirited.

At midnight, they started a conga, and took it right through Panty, into every room. Various people joined in. They found couples in secluded rooms, junkies in others (they lost Iolo to that), and party poopers who were in the TV lounge, trying to escape the noise.

After an hour, they were back in Sly's room, having picked up about a hundred people, who were now out in the car park, trampling the gardens and wrecking the cars unlucky enough to be out there. Iolo came back and took Gerry, Sly and Lois to the stairwell, where Dafydd was sitting on the stairs with a girl.

'He's chatting her up in Welsh, man. It's got to be heard to be believed.'

They crouched underneath the stairs and listened. Sly translated Dafydd's clumsy Welsh. After a short time, the girl became bored with it.

'I am too pissed for this,' she complained.

Dafydd launched himself at the girl, who stepped to one side. Dafydd toppled down the stairs and lay there groaning.

'Well, don't just stand there. Help me up.'

* * *

The party seemed likely to last all night. Malc had found a pretty student called Ilris and was talking to her. Luke was still bopping around with Gerry, Huw and Iolo. Suddenly, Dafydd threw up in the corridor. Lois and Sly took him outside, to sober him up a little, then mopped up the mess. Eventually, they settled him in the bathroom, with his head resting on the toilet edge, his back supported by a pillow. He fell asleep, or unconscious, they couldn't tell which. They returned to Sly's room.

Gerry and Iolo were lying on the bed, snogging; Malc and Ilris, Huw and Luke were asleep on various cushions around the room. At three o'clock in the morning, they decided to go back to Alex. It took them nearly an hour to make the journey that usually took twenty minutes. Lois felt really out of control; she didn't like it because she had drunk very little. She sat down on every bench, or wall, they came to. Back in Alex, she swayed around the room, fixed two more drinks and drank both of them. Sly was quite merry, but he had never seen anyone such a happy drinker as Lois. She stood in the bay window, swaying but not quite falling over, a huge smile on her face.

Next morning, Sly woke when Lois sat bolt upright and hit him in the stomach.

'Lois, what the hell's the matter?'

'Oh,' she said, shaking herself awake, 'it was just a dream, a nightmare. A monster was chasing me. It was really weird, weird colours and shapes, moving really weirdly. I can still see it now, if I close my eyes. It was really strange.'

Sly sat up, squinting in the bright light. It was well past midday. He had felt and heard nothing since they had crashed out that morning.

Lois looked ashamed. 'I think I had too much to drink last night' she said, snuggling against him. 'I feel awful.'

'Never mind, love; you enjoyed it.'

'Did I? I can't remember.'

He began to kiss her, whispering that he'd soon give her something to be ashamed of

By three o'clock, they had showered and felt more human. They climbed the hill back to Panty. As they entered by the oak door, they heard groaning from Dafydd, who was still in the bathroom. During the night, his pillow had slipped, and his head had fallen. It was now wedged under the U bend. Suppressing laughter, they helped to free him.

'Oh, my fucking head, and, ouch, my neck!' Dafydd gingerly turned his head from side to side, trying to ease the pain. 'Have I spent the night here?'

'Seems like it, boyo. Come on, we'll make you a cup of tea.'

At the thought of tea, Dafydd went a bit green again, but he came with them, all the same.

In the room, everyone slept on; Gerry and Iolo on the bed, Malc and Ilris lying on floor cushions, and Luke and Huw simply stretched out on the floor. Sly opened the door and surveyed the scene. He picked his way over the bodies and turned his tape deck off. Then, he switched over to Radio One. It woke the sleepers.

'Oh, for fuck's sake, Sly,' Malc snapped from the floor. Sly turned off the radio. Everyone stirred, sobering up and squinting.

'Morning, Lois,' Gerry ventured from the bed.

'Well, hello, chaps. A good night had by all, then?' Lois asked brightly. She felt fine now, but sympathised with them. 'How about some tea and toast?'

Everyone was dehydrated, but soon looked better, after sharing toast and tea, except Dafydd, who still looked green. He had hardly supped his tea and refused any toast.

'Come on, Dafydd.' Iolo said. 'Buck up. You'll soon feel better. Hair of the dog, that's what you need. There's still some punch left.'

Huw looked at Dafydd and said gently, 'Better out than in, Dafydd. Just think of fried eggs.'

Dafydd leapt up and ran to the bathroom. Everyone roared with laughter. Eventually, Dafydd came back, looking pink again, and had tea and toast.

'What the hell was in that punch, Lois?' Gerry asked.

'Just brandy and champagne. It shouldn't have been all that lethal.' Lois was puzzled. She'd calculated the mixture carefully, to ensure that it would be sensible to drink it.

'It wasn't lethal, until I put the tea in it,' Iolo said.

'What tea?' Lois asked.

'Mushroom tea, especially brewed for special occasions,' Iolo said.

'You spiced our punch with mushroom tea?' Lois asked.

'What sort of mushrooms?' Luke asked, puzzled.

'Magic ones,' Dafydd said.

Last night, they had all been tripping, and they hadn't known. Lois laughed until she cried. Luckily for Iolo, no one was angry; even Malc thought it was a scream. About five, everyone left, except Gerry, who stayed and helped tidy up.

'I wonder why the punch didn't affect you, Sly,' Lois said.

'I know when I've had enough,' he teased them.

'Wimp,' Gerry muttered.

* * *

Lois had three exams at the end of term, on Monday, Tuesday and Wednesday, and Sly had one on Thursday. On Thursday, Lois packed a suitcase for herself and one for Sly. Luke took the suitcases to Annedd Deg, where Lois and Sly were to spend the post-term week and pre-term fortnight because Panty and Alex closed on the Friday. Lois felt guilty about going home for just ten days, but she promised her mother that she would make more visits home in the spring term.

Once Sly had met her family, Lois knew that he would love them, and they would be free to go home at any time. Neither she nor Sly had to empty their rooms, so they had no need to pack up everything to store over the break. On their last evening, she bathed, put on a fitted black dress, and packed her cosmetics into an overnight bag, ready for the morning. Sly had arranged to meet her for dinner at nine thirty, in the Belle Vue, after the final performance.

Their table was in an alcove overlooking the sea, a truly romantic setting. It was the first time Sly had taken a girl out for dinner, and if ever a bloke had been with a beautiful girl, then he was with the most wonderful of them all. She looked radiant tonight; the hard work of the term over, she glowed now. She wore her hair in a French pleat. She could have been a film star. Her make-up was subtle, but stunningly effective, emphasising her big brown eyes and perfect skin. He still hadn't got used to people staring at Lois, and at him, when they saw him with her. Every time he walked into a room with her, he felt immense pride.

The meal was delicious, brought to them by unobtrusive waiters, who left them talking about their plans for the holidays, the term that had almost gone, about each other and their hopes for next term. Through the windows, the waves were also moving unobtrusively, making very little sound. Sly knew then, and probably never knew so clearly, the promise of Lois, the sheer beauty of her, binding him to her forever.

They had finished their meal before they noticed that it had started to snow. Gentle flakes drifted down, sticking to the windows, disappearing into the sea, or covering the dry pavements. By the time they left the hotel, the pavements were white. Arm-in-arm, they walked back to Alex and, from the window, watched the lights along the prom turn the snow pink.

'Perfect,' Sly whispered, as he undressed Lois for bed. 'I feel perfect with you, my Lois.'

* * *

When they woke next day, impatient for the students to go down and leave Aber to them, the world lay under a white blanket. The two morning trains were cancelled, and coaches postponed until the roads had been cleared. Gerry was waiting for her parents to arrive from Shrewsbury, and hardly anyone had managed to leave Aber by eleven. When they arrived at Annedd Deg, Fenn had only just left, to catch the midday train, (a student special), Luke and Malc, who were driving back together, were still waiting for the all clear from the AA. Sly was highly impatient for them to go and leave him and Lois alone.

After lunch, Sly phoned the AA, who reported that the main roads were clear and advised them to travel now, before more snow came. Finally, they left, Malc waving madly to them from the car's back window.

Once alone, they settled down to the pattern that was to dominate the next week. When Sly complained that he hated the idea of separation from her, Lois comforted him, reminding him that it wouldn't be for long.

On the day of departure, they would leave in the afternoon and travel together by train to Shrewsbury, where Sly would catch his connection to Ross-on-Wye, and Lois, her train to Chester. By Friday, the day after Boxing Day, they would be reunited at Lois's home, and travel to London, and be back in Aber a week before term started.

Sly reverted to David, and insisted on hearing more about him. Lois did her best to fill the gaps in his knowledge. Sly seemed more relaxed about David afterwards.

On Sunday night, they tried to cheer each other up, but Lois found herself sobbing uncontrollably in Sly's arms. She wanted to run away with him. She felt like a five-year-old again, begging not to go to school, knowing deep down that she must.

Next day, their mood was glum. The train hurtled along the single track; it was dusty, and unbearably hot, and slow enough to cut down to an agonising five minutes the twenty minutes timetabled for Sly's connection at Shrewsbury. They huddled together, drowsy from lack of sleep, yet determined not to doze for one minute of the three-hour journey. Sly's train was already waiting as they drew into the station. As he boarded, he had an overwhelming desire to jump off again, to stay with Lois, but the whistle went and the train drew slowly away. Lois waved tearfully until the train disappeared into the distance. She had half an hour to wait for her connection

On the train to Hereford, Sly stared out of the window, numb with misery. Exhausted, he slept, forehead pressed against the window, his right hand clenched, nails digging into his skin.

Lois woke when the refreshment trolley arrived. She had a coffee. After only twenty minutes sleep, she felt better. She started to think about home, and about Sly and his home, somewhere she knew little about. She had a mental picture of his house, and she fitted into it the faces she had seen in photographs. She remembered some of the events he had described for her. He would phone her tomorrow, as he had promised, and she could telephone him on Christmas day, at eleven, when his father would be at chapel.

6

During Sly: Festivities

DAVID WAS WAITING for her on the platform; and he drove her home, and when she arrived, Lois decided that retirement suited her mother, who was delighted to see her. Ronnie arrived later, just to say a quick 'hello'. Lois took her bags to her old room, at the top of the house, and found it exactly as she remembered it. She was bursting to talk about Sly, and the others allowed her to dominate the conversation with anecdotes of her life at University.

David and Ronnie went to wash up after the midday meal.

'Whoever he is, my love, he's doing wonders for your looks,' her mother said, cupping Lois's face in her hands. Lois asked nervously whether Sly and she could sleep together, when he came to stay.

'Would it make you happy? Are you sure he's the one?'

'Yes, Mum, I've never been more sure over anything. He's the one, you'll see.'

'All right, then, but remember, this is my house. All I ask is that you are discreet and respect the rest of the family.'

David was driving Ronnie home, when Sly rang Lois, and said that he had arrived safely and that he loved her. He was in a pub with his cousin, Morgan, when he called, having warned her that his father would not be pleased if he telephoned her every night, or if she called him unexpectedly, so she hadn't anticipated his call. He rang off and left Lois positively glowing.

Christmas came and went much as it had done in other years.

It was strange to have David at home and not Ronnie. Lois and David went into Chester, to meet old friends at the overcrowded Malt and Hops pub, where the landlord was only letting people in when others left. Someone recognised them and opened a window for them to climb through.

Louise and Carol, two old college friends, arrived and sat with them. Most people moved on to the clubs after midnight. The Grot was their old haunt, which, this evening, was ticket only. The foursome decided, instead, to go back to the flat of David's friend Tim, for coffee, before returning home.

Back at the house, they went upstairs to their bedrooms, and David stopped outside his door. 'Where's my Christmas kiss, then, Lois?' he asked, reviving memories that filled Lois with embarrassment and regret.

'Like last year, David?' she asked.

'Yeah, just like last year,' he confirmed eagerly.

'Sorry, sweetheart, that was before Sly.' She kissed his cheek lightly. 'Happy Christmas, David. Good Night.'

Left standing on the landing, David thought to himself, God, I hope you'll never feel pain like this, Lois.

* * *

Christmas morning felt strange without Ronnie there. David brought Lois tea in bed at midday and reminded her that her presents were waiting for her downstairs. She had gifts from her mother, David and Ronnie, and two packages from Sly. She opened Sly's presents last and with trepidation. In flat packets were two framed postcards of Monroe, photographs that Lois had never seen before. There was also a small box, containing a beautiful jet and opal ring. The card attached said, "This was my Godmother's ring. Wear it and, please God, love me for at least as long as she did. That will be a good start. I love you forever. Sly."

Sly's Godmother had died at the beginning of the year and Lois knew Sly had been very close to her. She slipped the ring onto the middle finger of her left hand and watched the colours in the opal change and the jet sparkle. Her mother and David opened Lois's gifts and thanked her.

She 'phoned Sly later, when he told her that his father had bought him a new Pentax camera for Christmas, which pleased him very much. Sly had loved the three prints, purchased from an exhibition on the Arts Centre of work by a final year student called Mickie Marshal, which Lois had given him. When she replaced the telephone, she started to count the hours before their next meeting, assuming from what he had said, that all was well with him.

In Monmouth, things were, in fact, going badly for Sly and his family. At first, he had ignored the cold reception that mention of Lois evoked. When he unwrapped the camera, he felt that he could forgive his parent anything. When he opened Lois's present and showed it to his father, the indifference was there. His father asked him to come to chapel, but Sly had declined with, 'No thanks, Da. Lois is phoning me at eleven.'

'What sort of person phones at eleven and prevents you from going to Chapel?'

'Someone who knows that I don't want to go to chapel. I'd rather talk to her.' He had taken the call upstairs, in his father's bedroom.

* * *

Sly could hardly wait until Friday, and when he reminded his father that he needed a lift to Hereford, to catch the train, his parent again disparaged Lois.

'Sylvester,' he said reproachfully, 'are you sure that you want to be wasting your time on this English girl? We always used to spend New Year as a family.'

'I have just done Christmas for your sake, now it's my time with Lois. I love her and I have missed her madly, and you're trying to pretend that she doesn't exist! It's ludicrous. She's real, she's my girlfriend and you just wish her away!'

'Sylvester!' His father faced him. For a moment, Sly thought his father was about to hit him.

'Well, for Christ's sake, Da, you won't even try to accept Lois. Ignoring her existence won't make her go away. She's here, and I'm going to go to be with her, whether you like it or not. Accept Lois, or, well, you'll see less and less of me.' Sly turned hopelessly and ran to his room. He lay on his back, listening to a tape. Eventually, his father came in.

'All this arguing is upsetting me. I'm getting angry and I don't like it,' he said, sitting down on the side of Sly's bed.

'So am I,' Sly said sulkily.

'Tell me about this girl, then. Is it serious?' his father asked gently.

'Very. I would like to marry her someday.' His father was very thoughtful, but he didn't respond, so Sly added, 'I've really missed her. It's been horrible for me. Oh, Da, what do you want me to do? I love Lois,' he cried desperately.

His father glanced round the room, looking for inspiration. His eyes settled on a photo of Lois that Sly had left out earlier.

'She's beautiful, not just in looks either. The girl loves me. She calls me her perfect boy. What's wrong with me loving her, Da?'

'Well, how about bringing Lois home to meet me, next term? I would like that. Then, maybe, I will begin to understand?'

★ ★ ★

Sly's train was due to arrive at three, and David, who had been out on the tiles all night, eventually drove up to the house at two-thirty, by which time Lois was really worried about him. He was grey with tiredness and, after a cup of tea, he went straight to bed.

Sly, impatient to see Lois, was afraid of missing a connection and arriving late. As the train approached Chester, it stopped for what seemed like hours. He had left his seat and was standing at the door with his luggage, growing angry, until, with a jerk, the train travelled the last hundred yards to the station. As he left the carriage, he saw Lois approaching, a wide smile brightening her face and sending a surge of excitement through him. They embraced eagerly.

'Oh, Lois, I've missed you. I can't believe you are here.'

'Is it really you, Sly? It seems so long ago since I held you. I love you so much, it hurts.'

'Where's David?' he asked, as they walked home together.

'He's in bed, recovering from last night. He looked rough when he got home, and it serves him right.' Lois replied.

When he saw 102 Houle Road, Sly felt excited about meeting the Bartlett family. I've bought your mother a tray of alpine plants; you did say she'd just built a rockery didn't you?' he said, as they came up to the front door.

'I didn't know you knew about alpines and rockeries,' she teased.

'Well, you're not the only one who knows about Botany.' They laughed.

'Mum, we're home,' Lois called and her mother came to greet them.

'This is Sly. Sly, meet my mother.'

She held out her hand to him, greeted him warmly and offered him tea. Lois took Sly into the sitting room and introduced the cats. He took one on his lap and stretched out his legs to the fire. A Christmas tree stood on a low table next to the TV. It felt very warm and welcoming in this house.

'Mother's chocolate shortcake is scrumptious. Try some,' Lois urged, when her mother set down a loaded tea tray beside them.

David, in his dressing gown, joined them a few minutes later. He looked tired. 'Hello, Sly. How're you doing?'

After watching the way David behaved, exactly like a member of the family, Sly began to revise his opinion of him. The two men found themselves talking amicably, until David said he was going to get showered and dressed, ready to help prepare the next meal.

Lois took Sly upstairs to her bedroom, which was the same now as when she had been living at home. Sly gazed about him and said, 'It's like a little girl's room, sort of unspoilt.'

'I've never wanted to change it. Everything has so many memories.'

While David and Lois's mother cooked, Lois and Sly discussed Christmas and played records upstairs. In the evening, they ate, drank wine, talked and watched some TV. Lois was thankful that David tried to include Sly in everything. He made no comment on the fact that she and Sly were to sleep together in her room.

The next day, they went into Chester; Lois showed Sly all the haunts that had dominated her life until she went off to Aberystwyth. On Sunday, they tidied up last year's leaves and found a spot in the rockery for the little alpines Sly had brought for Lois's mother. Sly watched Lois and David gardening together, and it helped him to believe that David was a family member, not a rival. On Monday, Veronica came over with her Bryan. Sly had learnt a lot about Lois, by watching her interact with other people. Sly grew fond of Mrs Bartlett, Lois's mother, and was not upset when she asked, Do you get on with your father, Sly?'

'No, not really. He can be a bit oppressive and he always thinks badly of whatever I do,' he said nonchalantly.

* * *

Luke came over on the Tuesday, to take Sly and Lois to a New Year's party at which Malc would also be present. They spent the night together in Luke's room, which was painted black, and seemed most depressing. However, Lois and Sly turned out the light and forgot the décor, as they snuggled up together and made love for the first time that year.

★ ★ ★

All too soon, it was time to get back to Wales. Lois and Sly had planned to travel by train on the Monday, but David, who wanted to see his mother, persuaded Mrs Bartlett to come along for the ride down to Aberystwyth. Snow had fallen again, covering the mountains and filling the valleys. It was a magical journey through the white countryside. Lois took her mother on a tour of Aber, and although most of the campus was closed, Mrs Bartlett said she got the feeling of the place. She had brought a hamper of food for them, but when David insisted on buying everyone a meal at the Belle Vue, they decided to save it until the next day. They fell quietly back into their old routine.

7

During Sly: Mickie

AFTER FURTHER SNOWFALL, the college delayed by a week the start of term. Aber was completely cut off from the outside world. Sly and Lois telephoned the news to their friends, although it had been all the national bulletins.

On Friday, they spent the afternoon on the promenade, making a snowman and having snowball fights. Suddenly spotting someone he knew, Sly pulled Lois out of sight behind a large yellow litterbin, and carefully made a pile of snowballs. He peered over the top of the bin and took aim. Lois peeped out and saw the snowball narrowly miss a small, blond lad, who looked all round him. Sly threw another snowball and hit the fellow on the side of the head.

Lois heard him shout. Sly peered over the top once more and was spotted. Sly ducked back as a snowball hit the shelter behind them.

'Come out and fight, you shit. I've got you covered.'

'A truce, Mickie?'

'Okay, Sly.'

When Sly stood up, a snowball hit him in the face. Wiping his eyes, he chased the other warrior and rugby-tackled him, bringing him crashing down in a pile of snow. When Lois caught up with him, both were covered in snow and were laughing.

'Lois, meet Mickie.'

'Hello,' she said, smiling at the young man.

'Hello, Lois. How are you? I owe you a favour; you bought

some of my prints from the exhibition.'

'Oh, you're Mickie Marshall! Hello.'

'What are you two doing back here, then?' Mickie fell into step with them.

'We've been back since last weekend, studying, Mickie, keen Freshers that we are,' Sly said with a smile.

'Sly, you're the laziest twat in the first year,' Mickie said. 'I know why you're here, you rascal.' Mickie winked at Lois and she felt herself blush.

He told them that Pauline, his girlfriend, was here, but very few other people had made it back yet. Mickie, in his typically Scouse way, explained that Pauline and he were having problems in their relationship. 'She's off her wick, and I'm at the end of my tether with her. I really think she's gone nuts, like.'

Mickie's Liverpudlian accent fascinated Lois, and he looked like a typical Scouser, too, in his donkey jacket. 'Hey, listen, are you two out tonight?' he asked.

'Yeah, shall we meet you at the Belle Vue at nine thirty?'

'Sure, Sly. I'll walk with you to the end of the prom; anything to avoid Pauline. I'll try and get her to come out, too, if she hasn't been committed by then.'

The Old College and the Victorian promenade had never looked more attractive.

'Isn't it beautiful? I love it here,' Lois said, gazing along its row of tall, elegant houses, curving along the line of the beach.

'Do you know how it all started?' Sly asked.

Mickie was interested; he knew something about Aber's history, but Sly was Welsh and, maybe, he knew even more. Sly began to relate the story of the University and its origins. He spoke fluently and with deeply held conviction.

'In Victorian times, there were only three universities that accepted the children of Welsh families: Oxford, Cambridge and Durham. There was no chance for students from Wales to use the

Welsh language, or to keep up tradition. A small group of influential people, all Non-conformists, one of whom was my great, great, great, great uncle, Sir Edward Anwyl, raised the money to build a wholly Welsh university. The unique feature of this venture was that it was entirely financed by public subscription, with money coming in from right across Wales, from Welsh people who wanted to send their children to a Welsh university.

'It fitted in nicely with the arrival of the railway and the completion of the promenade. The builder of what was the Castle Hotel, in anticipation of the railway boom, went bankrupt, and the hotel became what we now call Old College. Alexandra Hall followed very soon after. My da says that the Victorians were greedy; they built the hall too close to the prom. By squeezing it in under Constitution Hill, all of its foundations are under the promenade and they are slowly crumbling away. The whole promenade will go, one day, and Aber will fall into the sea.'

'I can't imagine Aber without its prom. It doesn't seem possible that one day, in hundreds of years' time, this will be very different, and we'll all be dead.' Lois was suddenly very sad.

'It's a long time off; don't worry about it. You've got a lovely, long life ahead of you; live for the day,' Mickie said. Mickie kicked the bar at the end of the promenade, and said he must go and see that Pauline was okay. He said, 'tara,' and hurried off towards the Pier.

'So that's Mickie Marshall, is it?'

Sly described his girlfriend, Pauline, as a stunning looking girl. Lois said, 'I think she sold me the prints. She was ever so snotty about it; hardly said a word to me. I nearly didn't buy them, except I really wanted them.'

'She's okay with me,' Sly said. 'She introduced me to Mickie. He's a brilliant artist. I bet he gets a first.'

★   ★   ★

When they arrived at the Belle Vue bar, Mickie and Pauline were at a table, Mickie seated and Pauline on her feet. Sly waved to them and went to the bar to get some drinks. Lois could hear Mickie's angry words. 'You leave now and, I'm telling you, you won't see me again, so sit down and relax. They're ordinary people, Pauline, all right? Stop this fucking nonsense; sit down?' he commanded.

Sly took Lois and the drinks over to Mickie's table and introduced the girls. Pauline smiled briefly at Lois, then, the sulky look returned. All her conversation during the evening was monosyllabic. Sly and Mickie enjoyed teasing each other about music, art and everything. Mickie began to include Lois by commenting on her dress sense and saying it showed creativity.

'I haven't got a creative bone in my body.' Lois replied

'You have. Look at the way you dress and dance. That is creative, of course, it is.' Sly joined in. 'Look at all those microscope drawings you do. That's Art.'

Lois changed the subject by asking about Mickie, who told her that he had started university life as a zoologist, too, and had transferred to Art and History of Art after one year.

'I liked the Zoology side. Oh, I've got lots of notes and stuff, if you'd like to borrow them, Lois.'

'Oh, thanks, Mickie. It would be a help,' Lois replied.'

Pauline muttered something under her breath and Sly looked curiously at her. 'You okay there, Pauline? You're not saying much.'

'There's not much to say, is there, except goodnight? I'm going home. I don't have to sit and listen to this mutual appreciation society.' She took her coat off the chair and walked out of the bar, pushing her way through the tables.

'Oh, hell! What have I done this time? I was only having a laugh.' Mickie sank back in his seat. 'Honest to God, I can't understand her, I really can't.' He lit a cigarette and drew heavily on it. 'She's pissing me off; I tell you that much.'

'Aren't you going after her, Mickie?' Lois asked, puzzled by Pauline's behaviour.

'What's the point, Lois; she's off her head at something, and I have to guess what. We'll row all night.' He took another couple of drags. 'Sorry, you two.' He thought about it. 'Maybe, I'd better go and make sure she gets home. Honestly!' He shook his head and took his coat. Sly said that they had intended to ask him and Pauline round for dinner the next evening. Mickie said he would come, and if Pauline cheered up, he would bring her as well, but he didn't hold out much hope.

When he'd gone, they went to the Pier and, then, back to Trechefan Road.

The next afternoon, they went to bed after lunch, tired still after the night before. Mickie rang the doorbell and roused them. He wanted to unburden himself about Pauline.

'Hi, Sly. Just got out of bed?'

'Yes, thanks, Mickie; some prat rang the doorbell.'

Sly, guessing the reason for this visit, led Mickie into the sitting room and asked what was eating Pauline.

'Oh, she's crazy. I tell you, it's finished. I can't put up with any more.'

'Put up with what?' Sly was interested.

'Listen, Sly, you're a mate, aren't you?'

'Of course I am, Mickie. Tell me all about it.'

'You're the last person in the world I should tell, but I hope you'll understand.' Sly wondered what Mickie was about to say next. 'You see, mate, Pauline's got it into her head that I fancy other girls.' He paused. 'Well, another girl; Lois, to be precise.'

Sly felt the hairs on the back of his neck stand on end. He suddenly felt cold. 'What do you expect me to do about it?' His voice was hard.

'Sly, just listen to me, okay?' Mickie knew he was on dangerous ground. His voice was low, all the joking gone.

Sly still couldn't understand why Mickie was telling him this. 'Okay, go on, then.' Sly was very suspicious.

'Tell me, Sly, how did you feel, when you first saw Lois?'

Sly remembered exactly how it had been, but all he said was, 'I fell in love with her on sight.'

'Yes, well there is something really special about her, not that I fell in love with her like you did. Pauline was with me in the Union, arguing about who to invite to a dinner party, and she said I couldn't take my eyes off Lois, that I was being cheap and blatant, staring at some girl. Christ, Sly, every bloke in the place did a double take at her. She's magnificent. I didn't know anyone she was with, I couldn't speak to her, I just sat there, gob-smacked. In Pauline's eyes, I suppose I did fancy her. I mean, it looked that way, but I don't know if I do. She fascinates me. It's the way she dresses, her movements, her face. She's so sensual. She turns me on every time I see her. I think I'm obsessed.'

No flicker of reaction crossed Sly's face; he just listened.

'Anyway,' Mickie continued, 'I didn't see her for a while. I told Pauline that she reminded me of someone I knew ages ago. It worked, until I discovered that you were going out with her. I envied you so much. I saw Malc, who told me about you and Lois. I saw you in the Old College library one evening, collecting references while Lois was reading and writing. I was on the gallery. I tried to sketch her, but every time I tried, I failed to do her justice. Pauline was looking for some notes amongst my stuff, just before Christmas, and she came across a huge pile of sketches I'd done of Lois. She was furious. I tried to explain that, if I could get it right, they'd make a first class series, but she was convinced that I'd drop her for Lois, at any minute. I wouldn't have, Sly. I'm not like that. I really like Pauline. Lois was just, well, something I was trying to capture. This sensuality; what many blokes must feel for her, I wanted to be the one to capture it. My Mona Lisa, if you like.

'Anyway, the next day, Lois bought those prints from Pauline, who just went mental. She thought something was going on. I was really pissed off not to have been there, because it could have been the perfect opportunity for me to have asked Lois to model for me. I reckon, if I couldn't get it in sketches, or in paint, I could work it out on film.' Mickie stopped, looked at Sly and wondered if he'd done the right thing.

Sly flicked the ash from his cigarette. 'Do you want me to ask her for you, Mickie?' His eyes were narrow and spiteful.

Mickie pleaded, 'Look mate, please, I'm trying to be honest. I know I could do some good work with her, but I know how you must feel.'

Sly laughed bitterly and turned his head away. 'You know how I must feel? You're joking. You sit there, telling me how sexy my girlfriend is, how she turns you on, and you know how I must feel! ' He spat the words out and struggled to find more. 'She's my girlfriend, Mickie; more than that, she's my girl, my one! I love her, for fuck's sake.'

'I know, Sly, and she's crazy about you, too. I can see that. I'm not conning myself. You're a lucky guy. I'm telling you this because you're my mate and you know how I feel. You feel it too.'

'You're not having her, Mickie.' Sly's voice was thick with emotion.

'For a model, that's all I want her for. God, I can't explain myself.' Mickie sighed, exasperated. He tried again. 'I do think she's the most beautiful person I have ever set eyes on; yes, I do see something in her face, something sensuous and sexy. I can't help how I react to her, but I wouldn't try to take her. I'm not that stupid. I just want to try to capture the essence of her.'

'No way, Mickie,' Sly said firmly. 'You can never capture that.'

Mickie looked crestfallen and agreed. 'Maybe you're right. Perhaps I ought to forget it.' He lit another cigarette.

Sly tried to understand. 'Look, Mickie, get to know her a bit and then ask her. Maybe, she'd like to model for you, but if she does, I'm coming along too, and if she doesn't, that's it, you leave her alone.'

'Christ, thanks, Sly. You do understand, don't you?'

Sly could forgive Mickie his honesty. He was unlike David, Luke or some of the others.

Lying beside her in bed afterwards, Sly felt uneasy. He had no cause to doubt Lois, who had never looked at anyone else when she was with him, but he realised how vulnerable they were. If they ever finished, he felt that he would die. He woke her gently, and whispered, 'Stay with me forever, Lois.'

'Of course, my love,' she answered, not knowing how much he had needed that gentle reassurance.

Next day, they tried, disastrously, to prepare a Chinese meal, which meant that Sly had to race to the Chinese Restaurant to buy something at the last minute. He left the door unlocked. Mickie arrived before Sly's return, and walked in without knocking.

'Have you got some, sweetheart?' Lois called from the kitchen.

'That depends on what you want,' Mickie said.

'Ah! Mickie. It's you. Isn't Pauline with you?'

'She's not with me. It's over; finished. I couldn't be happier, honestly.' He sat down wearily.

'Oh Mickie, I'm sorry.' Lois found it difficult to know what to say next, and an awkward silence developed. Sly returned as Mickie was cracking open the first bottle of wine.

'All right, Sly, join the party. Lois and I have just made passionate love over the kitchen table, but you can join in later,' he joked.

'Watch it, you scally!' Sly laughed at Mickie.

'Here you are, Lois. Let's have a toast to being snowed in, or to the world being snowed out, depending on which way you look at it!' Mickie was on a high.

* * *

The meal was delicious and lightened Mickie's mood. Afterwards, when Sly made a pot of coffee, they went upstairs to listen to music and relax. Mickie asked them if they'd like some dope. He explained how it accentuates your mood, and because they were both in good moods, they tried it. They watched Mickie roll a joint.

'This should be fun, if you two have never had it before. My brother gave it me for Christmas. We smoked a joint of it on Christmas morning, and I can tell you, it's strong stuff. God! Did that turkey taste good! Even the Queen's Speech was psychedelic.' Mickie lit the joint, inhaled deeply, and passed it to Sly.

They sat around and smoked until three in the morning, when Lois made up the bed in Malc's room for Mickie, and went to fetch him a glass of water. She found him already undressed and in bed, when she came back with the glass. He thanked her for a lovely meal.

'Remind me to ask you something tomorrow.'

'Can't you ask me now?' she enquired.

'No, but I'll ask you now if I can kiss you.'

Without waiting for an answer, he kissed her long and hard, not deeply or passionately. She stood and let it happen but made no overt response. When he finally pulled away, Sly was standing at the door, watching them.

'All right, mate? I'm just kissing your girl.' Mickie said, intensely embarrassed.

'I can see that, Mickie. No offence taken. Come on, Lois.'

Mickie studied Sly's face. It was set hard. Lois blinked heavily; the dope was really getting to her now. She moved to the door and said good night to Mickie. Sly slammed the door shut. Mickie couldn't imagine why he had behaved like that. He hoped Sly wouldn't blame Lois, who was so doped up that she would have agreed to almost anything.

The sight of Lois and Mickie kissing had jolted Sly completely. He had only gone to wish his friend goodnight. Now he felt bitterness and anger. 'Did you like kissing Mickie, Lois?' he asked her.

She sat down heavily on the side of the bed, feeling slow and dopey. Every time she blinked her eyes, she felt heavy.

'Did you like kissing Mickie, Lois?' he repeated.

She tried to focus on him, understand what he was saying. 'Did I kiss him?' she asked, not really knowing.

Sly's voice was soft now. 'Yes, you kissed him and I watched. Did you want him to kiss you like this?' He kissed her savagely. She said nothing.

'Did you want him do this, Lois?' He kissed her neck and shoulders, concentrating on a spot just below her ear, an area she could never resist.

Her breath deepened and she murmured, 'Oh, Sly.'

Caressing her shoulder and neck, he moved his hands to the back of her dress. 'Did you want him to do this?' He started to unbutton the dress slowly. He had watched Lois dress that evening and he knew that she was naked underneath her dress. He realised suddenly how close Mickie had come to Lois's flesh. He tried to remember whether, during the kiss, their bodies had touched. He couldn't remember. When all the buttons were undone, he knew Lois was aroused and so was he. He stood up and stripped slowly.

'Did you want him to do this, Lois, did you?' His voice was tight with anger now. She looked vacantly at him, unmoving, wordless. Her breathing was shallow. He pulled at her dress; it came off, but material tore somewhere.

'Did you want him to do this, Lois?' he asked, his teeth clenched. He pulled her down onto the bed, her legs hanging over the edge. Roughly, he pulled her legs apart and entered her, pushing his way deep inside her. She tried to protest. He knew she disliked being in this position; she liked their bodies to touch. He started moving inside her.

He continued to taunt her while he raped her, his anger, fired into lust by the dope, making him behave cruelly As the physical act peaked for Sly, Lois found the strength to raise her back from the bed. She pulled herself up, to bring his body close to hers, kissing his face, his lips. Rage gone, Sly found his own climax had overtaken the anger.

'I was trying to hurt you. I was going to hit you.' Sly's voice was muffled as he held her close.

'But you didn't. It's okay. It's alright, darling. I love you.'

She soothed him. When he looked at her face, he wept with shame.

'You didn't hurt me, Sly,' she said softly. 'It's the dope; Mickie said it accelerates moods; it made you go a bit mad, that's all. I shouldn't have let him kiss me. I'm sorry. I didn't know I was doing it.'

It took time for both of them to calm down and fall asleep. Next door, Mickie breathed a sigh of relief at the silence. Dope had sometimes made him feel sadistic, and he hadn't enjoyed the experience. It is very hard, to do things under the influence of drugs and then live with yourself when you wake in the morning. He felt he ought to drop the idea of using Lois as a model. He had already done Sly too much damage, and he was supposed to be a mate, he reminded himself. What an appalling way to treat a mate! He also felt guilty and ashamed. Eventually, they all slept; it was five in the morning.

★   ★   ★

Lois was the first awake. She went to the bathroom, drank two glasses of water, cleaned her teeth and rinsed her mouth with mouthwash. It was almost eleven o'clock but she felt refreshed after sleeping for only six hours. Outside, the sky was clear and the sunshine bright, promising another cold, crisp day. She lit the gas fire and began to put the room in order before Sly woke. She needed to forget the awful things that had happened in the depths of the night just passed.

Sly opened his eyes. A feeling of shame overwhelmed him; it took a couple of minutes to realise why. He saw Lois, standing with her torn dress in her hand, her face pale and pensive. He had to make things right between them, and there was no time like the present, unshaven and rumpled as he was.

Mickie also awake, was relieved to know that the lovers had patched up their differences. It was safe for him to show his face. Sly entered his room.

'Hi, Mickie, did you sleep alright?'

'Yeah, fine, lulled by angels.'

Sly said was going to buy newspapers, and told Mickie that Lois would make him tea and toast. Sly looked completely normal. Mickie wondered if he would say anything at all about the kiss, or try to ignore it. He went next door and found Lois wearing a silky dressing gown, her hair pulled up from her face and neck. Standing in front of the window, against the sunlight, he could see the outline of her body through the flimsy material. They drank tea and chatted. Gradually, her face took on a glow of its own. Her skin was clean and smooth, her eyes wide and clear. He had never seen her looking so lovely. Mickie was uneasy. He had to confront what had happened last night.

'I'm sorry about last night, Lois. It was a stupid thing to do. Sly had every right to be angry, but at me, not you. I'm supposed to be his friend. It was stupid of me. I'm sorry.'

'It's all right now. Sly understands. We've made it all right. That stuff we smoked has a weird effect on people. I don't think we'll try it again in a hurry.'

'No, maybe you should leave the drugs to those who think they can handle it, like me,' he joked.

The tension had gone; he had said what he had to say. Sly returned with the papers and they sat around companionably for a while, flicking through them. Then, unexpectedly, Sly asked, 'Have you told Lois about this modelling business, Mickie?'

Mickie was astonished. He hadn't expected Sly to broach the subject. 'No, I haven't got round to it yet.'

Lois was against the whole idea, when it was explained to her, until Sly said, 'I'm in favour, love. It would be fun for you and I'll come along, too. I need some sketches of you, to finish the series I'm working on. No pressure, mind; do it if you want to.'

Lois thought it over. 'Okay,' she said, 'but don't blame me if I'm awful.

As lunchtime approached, Mickie knew he'd have to go, but he wanted to speak to Sly on his own first. 'I'd better be off, I suppose. Will you see me out, Sly?' He picked up his bag and his jacket, and said farewell to Lois. 'I'll let you know when I've got the studio; it'll probably be Tuesday, okay?'

As they walked downstairs, Mickie thought about what to say. At the front door, he put a hand on Sly's shoulder and said, 'Sly, I'm sorry about last night, I really am. I fucked it up, didn't I?'

'It's okay, Mickie. That stuff made us all act weird.

'Don't feel bad about Lois, Sly. It was my fault.' He wanted to say more, but without admitting what he had overheard through the bedroom wall, that was not possible, and he concluded by saying, 'I feel like a shit, Sly, for betraying your trust after such a lovely evening, the food and everything, and then you persuade her to model. I owe you one, all right, mate?'

'Sure, mate. Just forget it now. Lois and I will forget it, so you may as well. There's no point in feeling guilty about it.'

Mickie hugged Sly, grateful for those words. Forgiveness was more than he deserved. As he walked away, he promised himself that, once the photo session was over, he'd forget Lois.

Mickie booked the studio for Tuesday and spent Monday preparing the backdrops. The session started, as Lois had feared, very badly. They did test shots all morning. Mickie made no jokes, and seemed to concentrate on the camera, while she held her poses interminably. Sly sat silently at the back of the studio. Lois had expected Mickie to be sympathetic to work with, instead, he seemed almost as ill at ease as she did. He barked instructions at her, and chain-smoked cigarettes.

'Relax, Lois, for fuck's sake,' Mickie shouted.

She resisted the urge to tell him to piss of, or to weep, and tried to think of nice things. During lunch, for which Mickie paid, he insisted that she drink wine. He refilled Lois's glass as soon as it was empty. When she went to the toilet, Sly asked, 'Are you trying to get Lois drunk?'

'No, just more relaxed.'

'Well, try to be nice to her. She doesn't respond to hostility. Do you want me to help? I could talk to her while you do the shots.'

'It's my session, Sly,' Mickie said possessively.'

'That is precisely why you should let me help. I know her; she does respond to me. I've made some sketches of her this morning, but in all of them she looks tense and unhappy. She can look fantastic when she is happy.'

Mickie studied the sketches Sly had made and selected a few of the type he wanted to reproduce this afternoon. Sly gave Lois the sketches to look through, and she remembered when he had made them. She forgot the camera and let her mind wander. From time to time, a memory would bring a radiant smile to her face. Mickie snatched the opportunity to take the pictures he wanted, while Sly talked to Lois as if they had been alone. It was hugely successful for all three of them.

'Okay, mate, I'll be in the Boar's Head. See you later. Lock up, would you,' Mickie said, carefully packing away his gear and unplugging the studio lights. He felt good about his work and was impatient to develop the films. Sly and Lois, too, felt that it had not been a wasted day.

8

During Sly: Zero Day

MICKIE TOOK A SELECTION of prints of his photographs to show Sly, who admired them and asked if he could have copies. 'These are yours. Mine are back at the department.'

'Can I have all these?' Sly was thrilled.

'Sure, you're in most of them. I reckon you deserve them. You saved the session for me.'

Sly admired the results that Mickie had achieved. He would be hard pressed to take photos this good, and Mickie was not even very interested in photography. 'Have you shown anyone else?'

'Only you and my friend Peter. There's enough there to make a portfolio for my MA, so it's all perfect.' Mickie looked ecstatically happy.

'You're going to forget Lois now, Mickie?'

'No, I'll never be able to forget her, but she's out of my system, now I've got her captured.'

'What are you going to call the series?'

'Well, Peter thinks "Lois", but I want to call it, and please don't take offence, Sly, but "Obsession".' Sly raised his eyebrows. 'Lois will never see it, and it won't go to exhibition unless someone sponsors it.

Sly reminded him that all who gained a first class art degree at Aber were awarded with an exhibition.

'Well, I'll call it "Obsessions" in the portfolio, and if it goes to exhibition, it'll be called "Lois", okay?'

Lois saw the photos and felt quite proud to have been the model.

* * *

The students filtered back to university once the snow began to melt. Sly had done well in the exams; Lois had come top in all her subjects. As the term wore on, Sly lost heart, and began to resent time spent away from Lois, so that his work suffered. One day, Sly was told to see his tutor, Amy John, who asked him the reason for this. He couldn't tell her about the feeling of loss, now term had started; how he hated College and all that went along with it, because it was stealing Lois way from him. He promised to pull himself up, and get on with work. He showed her the portfolio he had put together. She said it was good, but not good enough for him to rest on his laurels. She added that he was expected to attend lectures, write the essays and present himself for the practical Drama classes. She dismissed him, having given him a fair warning.

Sly tried to settle down, and began to catch up, but he still missed those lectures that coincided with Lois's free time. He was dissatisfied when she refused to do the same for him. Lois's courses were going well; Biochemistry was the worst subject, and Nick helped a lot, and she spent time with him and Max, discussing the work. Sly grew to know Nick quite well. Nick had a part in the play 'Bent', an amateur production; Sly coached him and listened to his lines, helping him make the most of his words. Eventually, Nick brought his friend Gwyn along, too, as he was playing opposite him. Sly became interested in Drama again, and things settled down.

Frankie, about to leave for good, came to pick up her belongings. She left a note for Sly and Lois, saying that she wanted to keep in touch. Lois was sorry they had missed seeing her.

Malc and Luke decided to have a party early in February; a

belated joint celebration of their twenty-first birthdays, which had fallen during the long summer vacation. They booked the Union for a Saturday, hired caterers and invited everyone. David agreed to come down for that same weekend. The night before, a party was to be held at Nick's country cottage.

Lois and Sly were in Alex, when Lois had a haemorrhage during their love-making. She was embarrassed. 'Don't worry; it's just a breakthrough bleed; it happens sometimes.'

Sly wondered if she could be pregnant. Lois dismissed the idea and Sly bowed to her superior Biological knowledge. The idea of fathering a child by Lois seemed pleasing to Sly. Lois said she was fine, and they accepted Nick's invitation to his party. They would bunk off College on the following day, so they could all have a good night.

Nick and Luke drove them out to the country cottage. Lois and Sly went in Nick's car and the others went with Luke. They took sleeping bags, wine and torches. There were four bedrooms at the cottage, but little bedding, and the toilet was outside, at the back. The nearest neighbour was over a mile away, and the darkness was almost complete, when they approached the cottage. It was a clear night and the sky seemed crowded with stars.

Gwyn welcomed them. 'You're here at last, then. Better late than never, so they tell me.'

The cottage smelt of burning logs and smoke. All the rooms downstairs had open fires and were nicely, if sparsely, furnished. Gwyn's girlfriend, Bronwyn, was with him. They supplied strawberry wine and sloe gin (all homemade), and baked potatoes with salad, and huge quiches, along with lots of nibbles. Gwyn was something of an odd character, known to sail through exams with little application to study, and sometimes to behave eccentrically, but he was the life and soul of the party on this occasion. Lois found her attention wandering. Gwyn put on a Fall record and threw himself and Bronwyn around the room a bit, then he played the Anti Nowhere League. 'This is my favourite,' he drawled, in an exaggerated Welsh accent.

Lois found Sly and they talked quietly together. The evening was uneventful. They drank a lot, had delicious food, and enjoyed the entertainment Gwyn inadvertently put on. They played a couple of childish games, then, Sly asked where he and Lois were sleeping.

'This is my room, you can have it. Just remember, though, there's another room through here, and you can only get to it by coming through this one,' Nick warned, having shown Sly where to sleep.

Sly got undressed and into bed, thinking that he had enjoyed the evening, in a funny sort of way. When she came into bed beside him, he took Lois in his arms.

Downstairs, there was a bottle of sloe gin for the others to finish. They played a drinking game. Bronwyn went to bed during the first game, and left the five of them alone. Nick wished he'd put Sly and Lois in the back room, where they wouldn't be disturbed if anyone else wanted to go to bed. He played the game cannily. He had already been sick once that evening and didn't want to repeat it. Luke came off worst and had to drink four fingers. After pouring out the gin and gulping it down, nausea overcame him. He stood up quickly.

'I have to be sick,' he said.

The others let him go, laughing at his stupidity for drinking it in the first place. Gwyn took the opportunity to slip off to Bronwyn. The others left the game and shared the dregs of the bottle. Outside, Luke was sick the moment the fresh air hit him. He didn't mind; it meant less calories and he had eaten rather a lot. It had been a lovely evening; he loved all evenings that he could spend with Lois. He sat outside for a while, breathing deeply. He felt tired and wanted to go to bed. As he went into the hall, he heard the others laughing. He thought it best not to disturb them, so he crept up the stairs that he supposed led to the bedrooms. As he started up, he heard noises, creaking springs. He realised that the stairs led directly into the bedroom.

Looking back, he knew what was going on, but at the time, he was so drunk that he continued to the top of the stairs and surveyed the scene. Lois was on top of Sly, moving herself to stimulate him. As they came to a climax, Lois caught sight of Luke, standing at the top of the stairs, like a ghostly figure. She stared at Luke, horrified that he could watch her as she came. The feeling of shock seemed to last for ages; she was powerless to do anything. As Sly's climax subsided, he, too, caught sight of Luke. No one said a word.

Luke looked pale and horrified at what he had seen. He turned, ran back down the stairs and out of the door. He had to go home. He fumbled for his keys, dropping money and the torch from his pocket as he made his way through the darkness to the car, stumbling many times and falling twice. He banged his knee and hurt his shoulder. He had to get away from there, from the awfulness of what he had seen. He climbed behind the wheel, his face streaming with tears. He backed down the lane and away. The vision of Sly's hands manipulating Lois's tiny hips for his own pleasure wouldn't leave his mind. 'The dirty bastard,' he shouted to the silent countryside.

'How long had he been there?' Sly demanded, pulling himself up from the bed and fumbling for his cigarettes.

'I don't know. I saw him just as we were coming.' Lois began to hyperventilate.

'He stood and watched us?'

'Yes, Sly. I couldn't do anything. It was too late, I'd lost control,' she gasped. In her memory was the image of Luke, staring at her.

'Christ, well, that fine, isn't it? He gets his kicks watching us screw. God, it's horrible.' Sly was outraged. The ecstasy he had felt a moment before had gone. He couldn't believe that Luke had stood and watched him and Lois during their most intimate moments. No one else would have come upstairs or, if anyone had, would have been acutely embarrassed, and would have slipped away. Luke had come right to the top of the stairs and watched.

'I'm going to kill that bastard.' Sly said fiercely. 'Shit, how he could do it?'

'He's drunk, Sly. For Christ's sake, leave it.'

At this moment, they heard the screech of car wheels as Luke backed his car down the lane. Lois ran to the window.

'He's taken the car. God, he's so drunk, he'll kill himself.' She grabbed her clothes and began to pull them on. Sly grabbed her arms.

'What do you think you're doing, Lois?' He was furious.

'I'm going to find Luke. Sly, please, he's upset, he's gone home. Heaven knows what'll happen.' She struggled against his grip.

'Leave it, Lois. It's his problem. Leave it.'

'No, Sly, I can't, please.'

She was panicking about Luke. He was an old friend and he was in danger. She resisted Sly's grip. 'Please, Sly, he's my friend.'

'He's a pervert; he stood and watched us screwing.'

Lois broke lose and ran downstairs. Sly dressed hurriedly and followed her down into the lounge.

'Where's Luke?' she asked.

'I don't know. He went outside to be sick.' Malc answered. 'Has something happened?

'He came upstairs and he saw me and Sly in bed.' She added, 'We were making love and he stood and watched. Oh, Malc, I think he's taken the car and gone home.'

'Shit.' Malc grabbed a torch and went outside to look.

'Hold on. I'll come with you.' Nick had no idea what had made Malc act so promptly, but he wanted to help.

Lois sank down next to Gerry and burst into tears. Gerry tried to comfort her.

Malc and Nick saw that Luke had taken the car and gone. 'Shit,' Malc said. 'Why did he have to go snooping around?'

'What's going on, Malc?' Nick enquired uneasily.

Malc took a deep breath. 'Basically, Luke's mad about Lois; he always has been, he's really screwed up, practically anorexic about her and, I suppose, seeing her with Sly threw him off the rails. God, Nick, he's pissed as a fart. He shouldn't drive.'

'I could drive you back,' Nick offered.

'You're in no state to drive either. Look at you.'

Nick had to admit this was true. He couldn't even steer himself straight.

'Are you sure that we're not overreacting, Malc?'

'I'm sure we're not. Luke's been teetering on the edge of something like this for ages, since Lois first started seeing Sly. She knew initially, but I've kept a lot from them since. Luke shares his thoughts with me and I try to keep him steady, but it's become a losing battle.'

They walked back to the cottage in silence. As they came in the door, Lois looked up gravely. Malc confirmed that Luke had taken his car and gone. Lois was beside herself. There had to be something they could do but Malc was adamant that they should wait until the morning. He tried to comfort Lois. Sly said not a word.

Nick said, 'I'll set the alarm for seven. I'll be sober by then. You'll feel better in the morning, Lois. It's amazing how much better things look in the daylight.

Sly said sulkily, 'I'm not getting up at seven to find Luke. It's stupid. He'll be fine.'

Malc glared at him. 'Look, Sly, you don't have to get up. Come later, with Gerry. Me and Lois will sort it out.'

'Why does Lois have to go?' Sly asked angrily.

'I want to go. He's my friend.'

'I'm your boyfriend, and you're just going to leave me here, while you go running off, looking for your friend. Lois, for fuck's sake, he's in the wrong. Let him sort it out.' He was shouting; he hadn't meant to.

'It's not a matter of being in the wrong. Luke's in trouble and he's our friend. I have to help him. I'm really worried about what he might do. He's upset.'

'I'm upset. He's ruined my evening, creeping around, spying on us. He stood there and watched us. He didn't have to it. I didn't make him. I didn't say, "Hey, Luke, want to come and watch, while I screw Lois?" I've done nothing wrong, but everyone's so worried about Luke. They've forgotten what actually happened.' Sly was really angry now, his foot tapped impatiently against the wall behind him.

'Grow up, Sly. Lois is right, anything might have happened; just let us work it out,' Malc snapped. Sly stared angrily at him.

'Oh, shit! I'm going to bed. Come on, Lois,' he ordered.

'I'll be up in a moment.'

Indignant, Sly went upstairs. He couldn't believe this attitude. He had every right to fuck Lois; she had always wanted him to, and now Luke was making a mockery of it all. He felt angry and bitter. When Lois climbed into bed beside him, he turned away from her and, when she touched him, he shrugged her off crossly.

* * *

Lois was already dressed when Malc came upstairs. 'Ready?' he whispered, aware of Sly's sleeping form.

'I'll be down in a second.' She went over to Sly and shook him awake. 'I'm going now, Sly. I'll see you later.'

He tried to protest, but Lois was determined. Undecided about whether to leap up and go after them, or to forget it, he lay still, hurt by Lois's reaction. He fell asleep again, without resolving why he felt so bitter and cruel.

They drove in silence, half-expecting to see Luke's car smashed up at the side of the road. There was no sign of it, until they arrived at the house and found it parked outside. Malc opened the door; the house was silent. Most of the boys were still sleeping; it was about quarter to eight. Fenn came downstairs and gave them a friendly greeting.

'Where's Luke?' Lois asked, convinced that something was wrong. She rushed upstairs to Luke's room. The door was locked; she tried the handle then banged the door with her fist, shouting to be let in.

Malc, Nick and Fenn joined her, infected by her panic.

'Calm down, Lois, he's probably asleep,' Malc urged.

'I thought Luke was with you,' Fenn said. 'What happened?'

'Luke, open the door.' Lois ordered. 'Break the door down, please, someone, break the door down.'

'Calm down.' Fenn shouted.

'Beat the door down, please, please, someone, Nick, please.'

Nick thrust his shoulder at the door repeatedly, until the lock yielded and he staggered into the room. Luke, fully dressed, lay on the bed, his eyes closed, his breathing shallow. The bedside table held an almost empty bottle of Scotch and a bottle of Paracetamol tablets, both open. Lois screamed at Fenn to phone for an ambulance. He fled to do her bidding.

Lois found a towel, soaked it in cold water from the kettle, and instructed the others to wrap Luke in the duvet. She put the cold towel round Luke's neck began to slap his face, to force him to respond. Malc and Nick stood back, aghast at what had happened.

'How full was this bottle of Scotch?' she asked Malc.

'About three quarters full, I suppose.' Malc was just staring at her.

'And the Paracetamol?'

'I don't know. Sorry.'

Fenn returned and said, 'They're on their way. Here in five minutes, they said. I told them it was an overdose of Paracetamol.'

'Do you know many tablets he had?' she asked.

'He bought a bottle of fifty in Boots the other day. He had a headache. He took three, I know.'

'Count them,' she ordered.

Nick counted twenty-four.

'So he's taken about twenty. Oh, God, why does it take so long? Fenn, go down and look out for the ambulance. Wave them down. It will save time.'

* * *

The ambulance carried Luke down on a stretcher. Lois grabbed the bottles of pills and Scotch and hurried after them. 'Nick, bring Fenn to the hospital. Malc will come in the ambulance with me.' Lois, adrenaline building, explained the situation to ambulance men.

On arrival, Luke was rushed into the emergency ward. Malc and Lois waited outside, where Nick and Fenn joined them. Lois buried her head in Malc's chest and started to cry. He sat her down, waiting for the shock to subside. He, too, was stunned, unable believe what Luke had done.

A doctor came out to say they were about to pump Luke's stomach. He asked how long he'd been unconscious.

'He probably took the overdose between four and five o'clock this morning,' Lois said, recovering her self-control.

'Had he eaten in the preceding hours?'

'Yes quite a lot, but,' Malc added, 'he vomited most of it at two-thirty this morning.'

'Do you know how we can contact his next of kin?'

That really stunned them. 'I don't think he'd want them to know yet. Is he going to be alright?' Fenn was beside himself.

The doctor said grimly, 'Probably, but there might be liver damage. We are obliged to inform his next of kin and obtain his medical history.'

Fenn told the doctor all he needed to know.

A nurse brought them tea and asked whether Lois was ill. She said that they could ask for help, if the girl needed attention, but Lois insisted that she was fine. After a while, Fenn telephoned Luke's mother. Luckily, the doctor had already told her that there was no immediate danger, and no need for her to come to see her son immediately. She asked to be kept informed by one or other of them, and sent a message of love to Luke, saying she would come to see him soon.

Lois refused to move until she had seen Luke, so they sat in silence until three o'clock, when two of them were allowed to see him. Lois, seeing him lying in the bed, was shocked to see how much weight he had lost in the past months. 'Hello, Luke.' She bit back the tears.

He opened his eyes and murmured, 'I only wanted to sleep. I'm sorry.'

When they rejoined the others, the doctor came to speak with them. He explained that Luke was becoming anorexic, and it was up to them to help him get better. If they couldn't help, they must promise to make him see a doctor; he needed help, medical or psychological.

Nick drove back to the cottage, and the others took a taxi to Annedd Deg. After making a meal, which none had the appetite to enjoy, they persuaded Lois to stay the night. She slept soundly. The emotion of the day had exhausted her; Sly had hardly crossed her mind.

Malc and Fenn made breakfast, woke Lois and made sure she ate. She was impatient to find Sly, who wouldn't have a clue what had happened. Malc walked with her along the promenade to Alex. They met Gerry on her way out. She went up to the room with them. Sly had spent the night there, awake and alone, but was not there now. The beds were both tidy, and the ashtray was overflowing with cigarette ends. They told Gerry about Luke. Then,

Lois remembered that David was due to arrive for the party at any minute.

Gerry felt incredibly sorry for Lois, who had never meant to hurt Luke at all. She explained that Sly had decided to hitch back to Aber, while she waited for Nick to bring her home. There was more Gerry could have said about Sly, but now was not the time.

David arrived, listened grimly to the saga of Luke, and took Lois to lunch, for which she had no appetite. He took her to the hospital, afterwards, to see Luke, who looked a lot better. Malc and Fenn were there already. Luke could hardly look at Lois. The doctor had told him that her quick actions had made it much easier to treat him. Luke felt sick at what he'd done. Sooner, or later, he'd have to talk about it, but not now. He wanted the party to go ahead without him, he said, and asked them to save him some cake. It was probably for the best.

Next, they went to Sly's room. The door was locked. She saw through the window that the room was empty. Iolo came in and said that Sly had gone for a walk. David took her back to Alex and made her go to bed. He sat and read, and let Lois sleep. He hoped Sly would turn up soon. He woke her at seven, so they could get ready for the party. She seemed a lot calmer, convinced that Sly would be at the party, contrite and waiting for her.

When they arrived, The Union was already full. To enquirers, Malc and Fenn said that Luke was ill, but gave no details. Lois scanned the room but Sly wasn't there. Gerry arrived and made Lois dance, to distract her from thinking about Sly's absence.

It was ten-thirty, when Lois finally spotted Sly on the far side of the room, near the door, with Malc, who was gesticulating wildly, as though they were arguing. She went across, but Sly walked out, leaving Malc, who shrugged at her and shook his head. She raced after Sly and caught hold of his arm.

'Where are you going?'

He looked down at her hold on his arm; she released it, feeling uncomfortable. 'I'm going home, Lois. I only came to say Happy Official Birthday to Malc.'

'You could have said hello to me!' she said, knowing how pathetic it sounded.

'Hello, Lois. Goodbye.' He turned to leave.

'Sly,' she cried, 'for fuck's sake.'

'What's the matter?' He turned to face her.

'What's the matter?' she repeated.

'Oh, precious, what's the matter? You made your choice, Lois, and stuck to it?'

'What do you mean?' Her voice sounded far off. There was a roaring in her ears. The music from the party faded away. She could only hear his voice.

'You had a choice, Lois: me or Luke, your precious friend. You chose Luke.' He spat every word at her.

'I never chose, Sly. That's unfair. Luke was in trouble. He took an overdose; he's in hospital.'

The words took a moment to register, then Sly asked, 'Is he okay?'

'Yes. The doctors said it was a cry for help.'

'Or was it attention-seeking? Well, it worked.' Sly had gone too far to turn back. 'He got your attention, all right.'

'Sly, please, let's talk,' she begged.

'There's nothing to say, Lois; it's over, finished. Understand it.'

'You can't do this, Sly, please.' she implored him. 'I love you.'

Something snapped inside him. He pushed her back against the wall, his hand against her throat, unaware of the crowd watching now. David started forward to see what was happening. He stood dumbfounded.

Sly began to scream obscenities at her, concluding with, 'I have had enough; I don't need you; I don't want you; its over. I think I hate you' Catching sight of David edging forward, he said, 'Here's one of your disciples, Lois. You have her, David. You're fucking welcome to her.'

Sly's eyes were slots of bitterness and hatred. He pushed Lois viciously into the wall and turned away, taking the stairs two at a time and went racing out of the door. Lois slumped against the wall and stared blankly after him. David went over to her. The crowd dispersed, the show over.

'What's going on, Lois?'

She was pale. David caught her arm and led her to a chair. She stared blankly at him.

'Sly's finished with me,' she said bleakly.

'Why?' David was horrified.

'I don't know.'

David stopped a student, handed over a £5 note and asked him to fetch a brandy for the lady. The young man nodded and made for the bar.

In spite of all his efforts to dissuade her, Lois was determined to go and find Sly. To delay matters as long as possible, he gave her the brandy that had arrived, and told her to drink it.

'I need some air,' she said. 'I think I will go outside for a minute.'

David found Malc dancing with Gerry. 'Malc, Sly's finished with Lois.'

David briefly related what had happened.

When they went to find Lois, she had finished the brandy and was sitting with her head in her hands. Gerry went over.

'Lois.'

'Sly's finished with me, Gerry.'

Gerry hugged her, wishing she could take away the pain. Malc and David stood hopelessly by.

'He's out of his mind; he can't mean it,' Malc said with a sigh.

'He meant it, alright. I never saw anyone so angry,' David confirmed.

'Take me home, David,' Lois begged.

'Oh, Lois, stay,' Gerry said.

'Take me home, please, David.'

Desperately, David urged, 'Stay a while, please, Lois. It's Malc's party.'

'I just want to go home.'

Reluctantly, he led her to the car. He told Malc and Gerry not to worry, he'd get her home, and he'd see them the next day.

David saw her safely to bed and spent the night there, keeping vigil. He knew that, next time he saw Sly, he would want to kill the Welsh bastard.

9

After Sly: Empty Fun

LOIS AND DAVID LEFT for Chester early the next day but, after a couple of days there, he had to go to London and he took her with him. After a week away from Aber, Lois felt able to return and pick up the threads of her life at University; she knew that she had no choice, if she wanted that degree.

She felt physically sick, back in Aber, walking along Queens Road to Alex. When she reached the promenade, she put down her bag and looked out over the sea. The night was clear and the sea like a black mirror. Nothing had changed, Constitution Hill hadn't slipped into the sea because of Sly; it all felt much the same, and she felt very empty.

The first thing that struck her when she entered her room was that Sly had taken away all his belongings. His key lay on her desk. Lois unpacked, collected her sponge bag and towel, filled the bath with hot water, and enjoyed a long soak, while trying to decide what she must do to catch up on the work she had missed. Afterwards, she walked slowly back to her room, resolved to put on a brave face. As she turned the corner into Balmoral, she heard the sound of running feet. It was Gerry, delighted to see Lois back. She invited Gerry in for a cup of tea, and Gerry gave Lois the folder that she had been carrying. It contained carbon-copied notes from the lectures that Lois had missed. Gerry and Max had managed to cover them all. It would save Lois hours of work. She was so thrilled and touched at the trouble that Gerry had been to, it almost made her cry.

'We knew you would come back, you see. Not like Frankie, who finally gave up on everything.'

The two girls chatted. The whole College knew what had happened to Lois, at least, it seemed that way. Everyone had been asking Gerry about it. It was fortunate that Lois had gone away, and now it was last week's news. She told Lois that Luke's mother had been to see him and had stayed at the Belle Vue. Gerry said she was very sensible. Lois asked how Luke was.

'He spent a good deal of time talking with his mother, which probably helped.'

'What about the others?'

'Malc said he wants to see you tomorrow, at ten o'clock, in the Geography Concourse. He asked me to tell you. I was up in the Union with them when Malcolm came in, and I told them I didn't think you'd want to see Luke the moment you got back, although the others were keen to go to the hospital with you.'

Lois nodded gratefully. Gerry told her that she had obtained tickets for her, for the main events of Rag Week, and a ticket for the Rag Ball on Friday. Shakatak were playing. Lois didn't know whether David would be able to come. It was a long drive, to see Shakatak, but he might stomach it. She would ask him.

Lois gave a brief report on her week away, but added that, kind as David had been, there was no mileage in the relationship.

When Gerry had gone, Lois changed the bed linen, which had a lingering odour of Sly. She finally fell asleep at four in the morning.

It was strange to wake up and find herself alone. With time to kill before catching the bus, she looked through the folder of Gerry's notes and started making cross references to her textbooks. It was useful to have something to occupy her. Once again, she was grateful to Gerry. Lois donned one of her most outrageous outfits, a shimmering gold top with ruched sleeves, cut very low at front and back. With it, she wore a tiny leather skirt, gold tights, which she had just bought in London, and a pair of boots. She felt like kicking someone. She strolled down to the Bus Stop, and the Plyn boys hung out of their windows, shouting the Human League song at her, just as though she hadn't been away.

Lois's first lecture was Biochemistry. She concentrated hard and wrote furiously, wondering about the wisdom of university lecturers trying to teach degree-level Chemistry to people who had only an O-level in the subject. Max passed her a little note, welcoming her back. She smiled along the row. Once the lecture was over, she sidestepped Max and went over to the Geography Concourse, where she queued for a coffee and then joined Gerry and Malc. Malc stood up, kissed her and told her she looked great. Gerry tactfully said that she had to attend a lecture, and that left the two of them alone. Malc told Lois about the row he'd had with Sly after the party. Sly had turned up on Friday, to take Malc for a drink. He had refused to talk about Lois.

'Please don't think I'm being disloyal to you, but I'm worried about Sly. He's acting most oddly. If there's no one looking out for him… well, look at Luke!'

Lois understood; they'd all had a shock. She realised that she would have to be very guarded with Malc from now on, because she didn't want Sly to know how much she was suffering. They talked of other things until it was time for her to depart. When Malc promised that he would come and see her in Alex more often, she nearly told him not to bother.

She met her tutor, to go over the work she had missed. Luckily, it had been a fairly light week. The tutor asked nothing about the crisis that had taken Lois away. At two o'clock, they went down to the laboratory together. Everyone looked at her and she heard someone say softly, 'Oh, God, she's back, and what is she wearing?'

Back in Alex, she ate tea, worked until ten, and then called David. She asked him about coming up for Rag Week, but he said that it was impossible for him to come, due to work commitments.

It occurred to her that Sly could be going to the Ball, and with someone else. This thought kept sleep at bay for another night.

Amazingly, Sly hadn't been at either of the two midweek concerts. Blue Rhondo had been excellent, the audience small, the band marvellous. Everyone danced to the energetic, jazzy music, especially 'Me and Mr Sanchez' and 'Kalctoveesedstene'. Lois had a good time but thought how much better it would have been if Sly didn't hate her. Fenn was very attentive and stayed close to her all night long. She danced most with him. Malc commented on Sly's absence.

'I never thought he'd miss Blue Rhondo. He must be avoiding you,' he said, rather tactlessly.

'Well, if he's avoiding me, I won't have the trouble of avoiding him. If fact, we could let you have our social diaries and you could sort out all the clashes. You'd like that, wouldn't you?' She skipped off to catch up with Fenn, leaving Malc with Gerry. Gerry could hardly keep her face straight.

Huw, her hairdresser, took her to the Rag Ball. David made an overblown romantic gesture by sending her a dozen red roses from London.

'David won't have paid that much for them. He's probably screwing the local Inter Flora girl, and she made him a deal. He does things like that,' Lois said airily.

She had no lack of male admirers, and her social life was more than adequate, in spite of the yawning gulf left behind when Sly departed. Over the next few weeks, Lois worked hard and played hard. She continued to meet up with Malc, even though she still felt a bit miffed with him. He was proving to be quite useful in some ways. He told her where Sly was going to be, which parties, which Pier nights, and when he would be at the Union. It all helped her to avoid him totally. Gerry had become her constant companion and she put on a show of having a good time, but she was hurting inside, and she still cried in the night, reliving the forty-eight hours that it had taken to kill Sly's love for her. She had no idea what she could have done differently. She would never forget that terrible look on Luke's face, when he saw her with Sly, yet she seemed to find it difficult to conjure up Sly's face. The only memory she had was of his face contorted with anger. It was not conducive to restful sleep.

★   ★   ★

On Saturdays, they met Huw, ate at the Angel, dining on micro waved pies and oven chips, Huw's staple diet. Huw had a carefree personality and could make a joke out of anything. Lois often wondered what he was really like, but Gerry accepted him for what he appeared to be - fun. Huw did a great impersonation of Sly boy, as he and Gerry called him.

'Oh, chips! My favourite. Got any tomato sauce?'

Huw referred to Sly as spotty or zit-face. Lois sometimes forgot that Sly hated her and felt sorry for him, insulted on his behalf, but she laughed along anyway. It was for her benefit, after all.

Their usual routine was to go on a short pub-crawl and then on to the Union, which everyone else had practically abandoned. On the last Saturday of term, Fenn was there with Luke, who was now restored to reasonable health, and Malc was also there, which was unusual, because he was usually with Sly.

Lois was with Gerry and Huw, discussing her latest hairstyle, when they met Sly and Gina walking up to Pantycelyn. Gerry stopped to speak to Gina, whom she hadn't seen since she moved out of Alex. Lois took one look at Sly's face, detached herself from Gerry and moved a little way off. Huw noticed how Sly's gaze never left her until she had moved out of sight. Huw went after her, and Gerry, suddenly understanding the situation, quickly finished talking and went after them both. She apologised to Lois, who was reeling at the idea of Sly and Gina going to Panty at this time of night, alone. There was only one conclusion that she could reach. Gerry tried to get her to talk but Lois was still a closed book to her. She wanted her David. Now, there seemed to be no way of avoiding Sly.

* * *

The term, which had started with blizzards and snowdrifts, ended with a sudden burst of summer. Everyone shed winter clothes, and shorts and T-shirts reappeared. The visitors began to arrive, to sleep in their cars on the promenade.

On Wednesday, Fenn came round, selling tickets for a gig on Friday. It was very last minute. Lois asked for three tickets. Fenn said he would go round Alex, and then come back and go up to the Campus on the bus with her. Lois got dressed very quickly. Fenn, always fussing round, was beginning to annoy her!

Later that morning, she had time to go up to the Union, to get some stationery and stamps. She went to get a cup of tea, and as she carried her cup in, she noticed Sly sitting and reading something, drinking what looked like coffee. Hazel O'Connor, 'Stay Now', came to mind. She sat with her back to him and distracted herself by flicking through one of her books. Today, the scene from the large window looked bright and cheerful.

Nick came in and, seeing the two of them sitting miles apart, he almost walked straight out again, until he remembered Sly shouting at Malc's party, in this very room. He'd seen a lot of Sly recently, while he was helping out with preparations for Bent, and Sly had been in a foul mood on Sunday. Nick preferred Lois as a human being, although he admired Sly's many talents. He went over to her, sat down and they chatted.

'I've put the tickets you wanted in your departmental pigeon hole; I just haven't had time to get to Alex, and Gerry's are in hers.'

He asked her to come to the Bent first night party with him, but Sly and all his cronies would be there, she knew, and although Nick tried to persuade her to come, she was very reluctant. Nick promised to stick at her side, no matter what, and appealed to her motherly instincts by saying how nervous he was about appearing on stage. Finally, she agreed to go. Then Nick said he had not seen his fiancée since he started rehearsals, before he moved closer and asked her about Sly. Nick said that Sly had been in a bad mood after seeing her on Saturday, at the rehearsal. He'd seen her for thirty seconds on Saturday night, she said, and talk turned to safer topics until she had to leave.

Sly came over as soon as she left. He could smell her perfume, and the chair she had been sitting on was still warm. He remembered vividly the warmth and smell of her. It was the first time he had heard Lois's voice in a long time, and she had sounded carefree and happy.

'Sorry I didn't come over before. I didn't think Lois would like it.' Sly sat down, and Nick suddenly felt angry. Despite Lois's brave attempts to appear happy, she was clearly suffering.

'Sly, you said that you hated her, I think it's you with the bad vibes, not Lois.'

He apologised soon afterwards, knowing that, if he upset Sly over this, Gwyn would annihilate him; and they couldn't afford to lose his help. He didn't want Gwyn to have any more reasons to hate Lois.

By Friday evening, with the term's assignments handed in, Lois had only to attend some lectures, a Zoology debate and her tutorial. It would be lovely to enjoy the sunshine and see Aberystwyth at its best. She would soon be back in Chester with David, thank God.

To go to the concert, Lois put on a shocking pink suit with a short skirt and tightly fitted jacket. She had a silk vest-top underneath, for when it became too hot. Huw's perm was marvellous, and her reflection in the mirror showed a changed girl.

The Union was busy when they arrived, 'Play to Win' was playing, and the girls rushed in to dance. Gerry started her now perfected imitation of Sly dancing, and Lois laughed, until she saw Sly enter the hall with Malc. Sly could hardly fail to see Gerry's antics. She was dancing like a demented puppet crossed with a mime artist. Sly and Malc watched, grinning, and Luke joined them. When the record ended, Gerry saw her audience, came quickly over to Lois, and buried her head on her shoulder, cringing with embarrassment. Malc strode over to them.

'Why are you the same colour as Lois's jacket?' he asked Gerry.

'It's the reflection,' Gerry replied quickly.

Lois went to dance with Malc, to 'Life in Tokyo', Japan. She saw Sly approach Gerry and speak to her, and she laughed. Lois couldn't abandon Malc in the middle of a dance, but as soon as it was finished, she hurried over to Gerry, to find out what Sly had said to her.

'Well, he's bought us some drinks, and said that, as imitation is the sincerest form of flattery, these were a thank you. Then he asked how I was, and that's it.'

Lois was astonished. Sly was not good at taking a joke, especially about something as dear to him as his dancing style.

Gerry danced with Luke for most of the time. Lois danced with Max, Fenn, Malc, Huw. As Favourite Shirts came on, Fenn grabbed her just as she was about to have a quick drink. Sly came up unexpectedly, and asked her to dance. Fenn butted in front of him.

'She is dancing, so, sod off!'

Lois reeled from the shock of Sly speaking to her. Maybe, he was as sick of this whole charade as she was.

During that evening, drinks appeared as if from nowhere; Huw's new boyfriend, Evan, was the principle source; he was trying to impress Huw. Lois was too thirsty for alcohol and bought herself a pint of orange juice and lemonade. Everyone seemed intent on having a good time, Gerry was dancing non-stop. The band was brilliant.

Lois caught sight of Sly, who chose that moment to glance in her direction. Sly smiled at her, looking happy; Lois smiled back and turned her attention to the group on stage. The set ended far too quickly; the band did just one encore before Mitchell started the recorded music again. It was time to depart. Gerry was struggling to dance, and Lois had her reasons for wanting to go home. She asked Gerry if she wanted to stay with Luke, but Gerry, who had drunk far too much, wanted to go home with Lois. They crept away, saying goodbye to Huw only. Linking arms, they set off down the hill, singing at the tops of their voices. Lois asked Gerry about Luke. Gerry admitted that she liked him, but she wasn't sure if he liked her, because he was always friendly to everyone. She failed to mention her suspicion that he still longed for Lois.

In the final week, everyone had parties planned, and there was no escaping Sly, who attended all of them, even the more obscure ones. Gerry's friend, Mannon, probably gave the best one, during which, they danced all night to The Associates' 'Party Fears Two', and 'The Country Club.'

Although Sly was everywhere, it was easy enough to avoid him. Huw and Gerry made sure that Lois was never alone. Sly could only look at her, which was hardly a crime. The first night of 'Bent' was when she felt most vulnerable. She planned on going home with David on the coming Saturday morning, and Huw and Gerry wanted to see the play on the last night, which meant that Lois had only Malc and the aisle for protection. The play was powerful, poignant, and touched every member of the audience. Gwyn and Nick showed unexpected talent, and received a standing ovation, following which, Lois ran to find Nick in the dressing room, to congratulate him. Everyone was jubilant over the success of the production. Although Nick was on a high, he stuck to his promise not to leave her side. When he drove her back to Alex, she wondered why she couldn't fall for a nice boy like him. Why was she besotted still with Sly?

The next day, everyone was talking about Bent, and, in response to demand, two extra matinees were scheduled and tickets sold out within the hour. Even the Chemistry department seemed proud of their two dissenters. They had put up posters everywhere.

The worst party was in one of the tall Victorian houses squashed between the Belle Vue and the Welsh Halls. Lois didn't know the hostess but an invitation had been left in her pigeonhole in Alex. Gerry was screaming with boredom and persuaded Lois to go with her. The first two floors of the old house were packed with students, few of whom Lois recognised. Gerry knew more, of course. The Drama department was out in force. They could hear Bryan Ferry playing upstairs, and they went there and started dancing. There were half a dozen people in the room, and so they had plenty of space. They were messing around, doing Jerry Hall impressions to 'Let's Stick Together', when Sly came in and began to dance. With so few people here, it was impossible to ignore him. When 'Dance Away' came on, Lois could bear it no longer. Her heart was broken, and she wasn't going to dance away her misery in front of him.

Lois left Gerry to enjoy herself, went downstairs, got a drink, and fell into conversation with Josh Myerson, whom she only knew through Sly. They talked for ages about how the term had gone and what they were both doing. He, appropriately for an actor, lived in Thespian Street. He asked how she was coping with life after Sly, and she suddenly felt tears spring to her eyes. Josh took her to sit down in a quiet corner and gently allowed her to talk about it, saying all the right things. She told him that Sly was upstairs, and Josh asked if she would like to dance with him. It would keep Sly at bay, and they could have a very nice time. She agreed gratefully, and they went back upstairs and danced together. It didn't take long for Sly to slope off. Gerry came over and said, 'Thank Christ for that. What does he think he's playing at? Is he practising for the Wanker of the Year award?'

Later, Finlay came and joined them and they had a laugh, Gerry and Finlay, Lois and Josh. Josh walked the girls back to Alex, and Lois felt that she had made a new friend. It had been good to offload her troubles; she had been like a coiled spring recently. Sly had turned her into a mess.

* * *

By the last Thursday of term, it was really hot, people were letting their hair down, playing on surf boards, out windsurfing, and the promenade and beach were littered with students. Lois attended her last lecture of the term. David would arrive tomorrow.

In the Old College, a group of drama students were indoors, rehearsing for their production of 'The Caucasian Chalk Circle'. Dickie was making life very difficult, as usual. Finlay, Josh and Elin were painstakingly going over one particular scene, trying to follow his meticulous interpretation of every single word. They had been rehearsing for weeks, and it was difficult to unlearn what they learned. Dickie refused to let any of them go, even the technicians. The play was due on stage in less than a week, and it had to follow the success of 'Bent'. It would be a disaster, at this rate. Sly didn't even like the play, and wished he not become involved with it.

Dickie gave them a thirty-minute break and told them to be ready to begin again at four-thirty. When Sly went into the main hall to get a drink, someone came up behind him and slapped him hard on the back. Sly dropped his money and turned round angrily. 'Fuck off!'

It was Mickie, grinning as usual. 'Fuck off, yourself. How're you doing?' He helped Sly pick up the change. He also took a drink from the machine.

'I'm pissed off with this play. It's a pile of shit, and Bedford's full of shit, as well. Where've you been?'

Sly hadn't seen Mickie since the beginning of term. They went to sit on the windowsill, feeling the sunshine warming their backs. Everyone else was outside. They talked about what they had been doing since their last meeting, smoked cigarettes and drank their colas.

'Anyway, Sly, why are doing this play? I thought you'd settled on Art? And, how's the lovely Lois? Still gorgeous?'

Sly suddenly felt his shame very keenly. How could he tell Mickie what he'd done? He stared at his hands. Mickie thought that she must have finished with him. God, what a bummer.

'She's fine. She looks happy enough. I wouldn't know, not really.' He looked up at Mickie's concerned face and added, 'We've finished; it's all over.'

'Oh, for fucks sake! You have to be joking. Why? What made her finish with you? You must have done something really stupid? What was it?' Mickie was stunned.

'It's not like that. I finished with Lois; I don't think she wanted to; actually, I know she didn't want to.'

Mickie asked Sly again what had happened. Sly thought this interrogation was torture. He'd never be able to explain this to straight-talking Mickie. In a moment of mental acuity, he admitted to himself that he had no explanation for what he had done.

'I don't know; we had a row.' He was in despair,

Mickie persisted in twisting the knife, by asking for chapter and verse.

Sly began to tell Mickie about the break-up, but before he had clarified things for his friend, he sighed heavily, glanced at his watch, and said he was already late for the second half of the rehearsal.

'Look, I'll need hours to tell you. I'll come round when this is over. I'll talk to you about it then. Are you at John's? I'll be over about half nine, if it goes well.'

'Okay, Sly. I'll get some bevies in.'

Mickie wanted to find out what had happened, now, before he spoke with Sly again. He was more interested in what Lois would have to tell him than in Sly's version.

Mickie went along to her room, knocked on the door and opened it without waiting. It was empty, as he should have expected. He would wait until teatime. He came out of Alex, deep in thought, and spotted her. She was reading Barrington, a book he remembered from his own course. She sat with her back against the low wall that separates the promenade from the road. He hurried over. Seeing her dressed for summer was like seeing her for the first time. It almost took his breath away. He stepped over the wall and sat down next to her. Lois looked startled and, when she realised who it was, she threw her arms round his neck and kissed him on both cheeks, overcome with delight.

'Mickie, Mickie, where have you been? How are you?' Her face was beaming, it made him feel so good that he nearly forgot what he was here for.

They made conversation, while he studied her cautiously. Outward appearances indicated that she was not as hurt by whatever Sly had done as he had feared. After a while, he mentioned the photographs from January that had been in his portfolio when he went to sort out his M.A., the very mention of which caused a shadow to flit over her face. She recovered well but he had registered that look. He told her that he'd only just found out from Sly that they'd finished, and he asked her if she was upset still. Lois told him how she'd helped Luke. Sly, she added, had finished with her as a direct result. She spoke lightly.

'Hang on. What happened to Luke?'

'He took an overdose, I left Sly at a party, and went to try and find him. He had to go to hospital. It was awful. He's fine now.'

Mickie still couldn't figure this out.

'Why did Sly take exception to that?'

Lois shrugged, she didn't want to go over this again, it was still too painful to her. She couldn't explain it all to Mickie. Maybe Sly would, but she found it distasteful.

'So, he finished with you?' To Mickie none of this made sense.

'Yes, we were at Malc's birthday party. Sly almost throttled me, after totally ignoring me, and then he shouted all sorts of things about our sex life. That was that. Over.'

'Has he spoken to you since then?' Mickie was incredulous

'Oh, heavens above, that would be far too civilised. He wouldn't want to talk to me now. I'm totally beneath him. He just stares, likes to see me squirm, and likes to see how frightened I've become of him.'

'Lois, the Sly I have just spoken to isn't the one you are describing to me. He's really regretting what happened, he…' He didn't get any further.

'He can go fuck himself, for all I care. I'm not interested in him any longer. It's over and he finished it. I'm trying to get on with my life and I was doing okay until now.' Lois stared out to sea, a stony expression on her face. Mickie still felt that she was pretending, and decided to explore further.

'Lois, do you still love Sly, because if you do, you need to do something about it.'

Lois exploded. 'Do something! Me! What would you have me do, Mickie? I've just got used to not having him around any more. He said he hated me. What do you expect me to do about that, sit here and wait for him to change his mind? Or, perhaps you'd like me to get on my hands and knees and crawl back to him along the prom, grovel my way into his affection. He did it, Mickie, not me.' Lois stood up and walked over to the railings, trying to control her feelings.

'Listen, Lois, all I'm saying is that he's made a mistake; you just need to try to understand that.'

Again, she was furious; he had hardly given her a minute to get herself under control. She rounded on him. 'Understand? He said he hated me. What bit of that have I not understood? He might be your friend, Mickie, but I don't want anything more to do with him. This has nothing at all to do with you!' She began to cry and turned back to the sea, her hands clutching the rails, her knuckles white.

Mickie was speechless. Suddenly, she shook her head and sat down beside him again.

'Do you still love him?' Mickie asked gently, hoping that she understood that he was trying to help.

'Oh, Mickie, give me a break.' She paused, 'Of course I do. I can't just turn my emotions on and off whenever Sly clicks his fingers. It doesn't work like that for me. I was learning to live with it. I am nowhere near forgive-and-forget-land, believe me. Why are you interfering, when everyone else has just accepted it?'

After a pause, Mickie replied, 'It's because I left the two of you as love's young dream, totally besotted, Dancing Girl and Dancing Boy, together for ever. That's how you've stayed in my mind. I needed to get my head straight for my finals and have hardly seen anyone for weeks on end, so I didn't know about you. Sly's the first person I've seen. Everyone else has had time to adjust. I hadn't. I'm really sorry. I'm a dickhead.' He placed his hand on hers.

'Don't worry, Mickie, it's been good for me. I had been bottling everything up. I haven't talked to anyone about it because I've been waiting until I got home to David.'

'Who's David?'

'He's my friend back home. I trust him. Anyway, everyone else must think that I'm doing all right

'So, can you tell me the whole story?'

She told him some of it, and when she had finished, she asked, 'Please, Mickie, let Sly tell you about this. I really don't want to think about it.'

'Right you are, Lois. Shall I get us an ice cream? Make up for being such a total tosspot?'

'You're not a tosspot, Mickie; Sly is, but you've been sweet. It's not as painful now I've told you about it.' She smiled at him.

Mickie stayed with her until teatime. They didn't mention Sly again. Mickie decided to go and see Haircut 100 with them all, and said he would get a ticket and meet them the next afternoon. He could afford some time off now, as well.

10

After Sly: Haircut and David

THE EVENING WAS WARM; students packed the seafront pubs, or sat on the walls, enjoying the fresh air. Aberystwyth was preparing itself for summer. People said of the glorious sunset, that if you listened carefully enough, you could hear the sun sizzle as it sank beneath the horizon. They were all in the Sea Bank, and before Gerry left to do some more work, Lois told her that she had seen Mickie.

Fenn and Malc went off to the Union, and left Lois alone with Luke for the first time since that fateful party. Lois knew that he would want to say something about it. She tried vainly to stop him.

'Lois, I would like to thank you for what you did, for coming to find me, for making the others realise something was wrong. If you hadn't, God knows what might have happened. I never really said thanks. I'm sorry that Sly took it all so badly.'

Lois tried to make it easier for him by saying, 'It doesn't matter. I think he was just bored with me. He saw it as an excuse. He would have found something else if it hadn't happened that way. It's over. *C'est la vie.*'

To prevent Luke from saying more, Lois said she was going to help Gerry. She had had enough for one day. She found Gerry dancing to 'Ghost Town.' Lois knew she would do anything rather than work. Having looked through what Gerry had done and finding that most of it was rubbish, Lois found the relevant chapters in her textbooks, and made Gerry read them. Gerry, forced to concentrate, began to show a new interest in her course work.

*　*　*

Lois woke up after a long, deep sleep. She expected David to arrive at about eleven o'clock. Gerry had been up all night and looked exhausted, when she came to ask when and where she would find Lois, later in the day.

Lois said, 'We should be on the beach after lunch, somewhere towards the Pier.'

David arrived early, and it surprised Lois to realise how much she had been missing him. It was nice to know that he felt the same. Now she had her David, surely the worst was over. David looked wonderful, very tanned. He was wearing grey trousers, very well cut, and a paisley shirt with short sleeves. It suited him, although he seldom wore colours. He admired her hair, inspected it, touched it, felt how silky it was. He had bought her a new dress, which he wanted her to wear that night. It was a white, tube dress, very short, in a silky material.

David changed, and the two of them walked slowly along the promenade. David said he would be home for a week, then he had to go back to London, but he'd be back for her birthday. He asked about Sly boy and she told him everything. She felt much calmer after her outburst of yesterday, and thought it was just as well that it was Mickie, not David, who had caught the brunt of her despair; Mickie would talk to Sly; David would have hit him, for sure.

They had lunch and, afterwards, strolled down to the beach to sunbathe, where Mickie found them. He decided to tell Lois some other time about his meeting with Sly. Lois watched Mickie and David sizing up each other. David was hostile at first, but when

Lois explained that Mickie had been kind to her, he relaxed a bit. Mickie also seemed tense, but Lois thought he was probably tired after a long session with Sly.

While David bought some drinks from the Siop Y Prom, Mickie reported that he had seen Sly and said would write to her with details in the holidays. David came back with a Frisbee, and Gerry came along and joined them. It was an afternoon for relaxation, and the group of young friends played on the beach like children.

Lois and Gerry walked up the beach, to fetch ice creams for everyone, David and Mickie stood watching them, when Mickie noticed Sly sitting on one of the benches, from which he'd been spying on them. He waved to Sly, to let him know he'd been spotted. Sly waved back, but Lois saw him as well. She veered away suddenly, deciding to get ice creams from another shop, to avoid coming up the steps by where he was sitting.

'Do you know that wanker?' David asked, when he saw Mickie scowling at Sly.

'Yeah, he's a mate of mine,' Mickie said reasonably.

'After what that fucker did to Lois?' David said coldly.

'You fancy her?' Mickie said it very lightly.

'She's my best friend.'

'Well, she's also a friend of mine, and so is Sly. I reckon they will get back together. Sometimes, that's the way it is; you have to want what you know is right for your friends, even if you don't like it yourself. Friendships change.

David thought this over. 'You too?'

'Yeah, me as well.' Mickie couldn't fathom this arrogant bastard, but he obviously cared about Lois, and she would need a few people like that in her life.

'There's a queue, and I'm at the head of it. I've known her for years, and her mother thinks I'm a god,' David said loftily, as if the matter were henceforth settled.

Mickie merely raised his eyebrows and regarded David steadily.

He let the tension go because the girls were coming back with the ice creams.

A little way along the beach, the photographer from the local paper was taking photos of Haircut 100. Sly thought they'd sell more papers with Lois on the cover; she looked stunning in her bikini. He remembered Mickie mentioning that he'd seen Sly in the Old College library with Lois, and how he'd envied him. Well, the tables were turned now. He wanted to watch her, but Mickie had made sure that she saw him, and he felt awkward. She was hurt and he was making it worse. Mickie had made him realise that he would have to be patient.

Gina suddenly sat down besides him and said, 'Oh, God, look at that. Lois is out-posing Haircut 100. That little bitch gets everywhere, doesn't she? Who's that handsome blonde bloke with her?' Sly told her. 'Well, she doesn't hang round, does she, the little slut?'

'He's her friend, Gina, from Chester, they've been friends for years, and she's not a slut.'

'Jesus, Sly, you've changed your tune. Where's all this coming from? You've been slagging her off all term.'

'I think I probably over reacted. I don't hate her. I've just been really stupid.' Sly was pensive.

'Oh, for Christ's sake, don't expect us to rally round you again. You are being childish. Grow up and work out what you really want. I'll see you at the theatre.'

* * *

David left Alex first and went to the concert venue, while Lois struggled into her new, very tight dress. Gerry came in later, and studied her from all angles. Lois strutted up and down the room, to practise walking in the very high-heeled, new, silver shoes she was wearing. Gerry and Lois arrived at the Sea Bank that evening, later than every one else. Typically, David was holding forth about something, entertaining a small crowd, including some of the Plyn boys, who remembered him from his first visit. He stopped when she came in and said, 'Lois, your tits are everywhere!'

The girls greeted this with a laugh.

Once in the Great Hall, David went to the theatre bar, to buy some genuine champagne. He spoke to Fenn, whom he categorised as 'a sound chap,' which meant that he could talk to him about women and tell him filthy stories. Mark, from the band, had invited them to join the musicians for a drink in the Cellar Bar after the concert. Lois worried about that because, in her experience of back stage events, band members were always on the pull.

The concert venue was packed. Sly was there, talking to Malc. David went round with more champagne, and when he reached Sly, he looked over at Lois, who nodded, so he poured some into the glass that Sly was holding. David deliberately tapped the bottom of Sly's glass and its contents splashed into Sly's face. 'She might be civilised, but I don't fucking have to be. Keep away from her tonight, or I'll beat you to a pulp, you Mother Fucker.'

David calmly walked away. Mickie witnessed this without hearing what David had said. Sly was furious. Malc looked horrified, but Sly decided not to make a big deal of it; he would dry out eventually. He had received the warning, loud and clear.

The concert was very good and, afterwards, they all went to meet the band at their coach. Lois found the rest of the evening boring, overall, and was not sorry to leave. Together in her room, she and David finished a bottle of wine that he'd opened earlier that evening. They sat in the window and talked. David confessed what he'd done to Sly, omitting the little speech, and she laughed and said she wished she had seen it. She was tired and a little tipsy. David knew this wouldn't be the night to make a move. If she wanted him, he needed her to be stone cold sober.

11

After Sly: David

ON THE FIRST MONDAY after arriving in Chester, David took Lois to visit his mother in Shrewsbury; she seemed to be on good form, and David hoped she would keep fit and well. On Tuesday, Lois had to have two wisdom teeth extracted; David took her to the dentist and practically had to carry her to his car afterwards. They spent the rest of the week meeting old friends and visiting some of Lois's old haunts. By the end of the week, David concluded that Lois wasn't going to 'happen' this time. There would be other times and other places.

David hated it when she danced with Owen, an old acquaintance, but he wasn't in any position to object to that just yet. Instead, he thought of a gambit that might do the trick. He scanned the room, looking for the sort of girl he needed, and when he saw her, he walked over and sat beside her. 'Hi, you look like just the sort of girl I'm looking for. I thought I'd come over and say hello.'

The girl had already noticed David. Her friend had joked that she had seen him first. And, he found her attractive, wow! She didn't ask any awkward questions, like who was he, or anything, which was a very good sign, and he extracted information from her with ease. Having learnt all he needed to know about her, he asked if she would come outside with him, saying he was hot, it was smoky. He let her lead the way, walking behind her slightly, so that if Lois glanced up, she would think that he was going to the toilet. The girl was willing to have sex with David, and they found a quiet spot behind the club. Afterwards, to her chagrin, he left her and went back to his usual spot inside the nightclub, to watch Lois dancing. She had changed partners. At the end of the evening, Lois and David left the nightclub together.

David felt no remorse about letting a strange girl relieve his frustration. Until Lois wanted him, he saw no harm in behaving as he had always done. He slept later than usual the next morning. Lois was still asleep when David carried a tea tray upstairs to her bedroom. She lay on her back, the duvet hanging off the side of the bed. One breast was exposed. He'd seen this hundreds of times before; it had taught him self control. The cups rattled on the tray. He set it down on the floor, and Lois stirred slightly when he sat on the bed and covered her with the duvet. She opened her eyes.

'David.' She smiled sleepily, he looked at her and she looked at him, and then, to his amazement, she reached out her hand, pulled his face close to hers and they kissed. He couldn't quite work out how something for which he had so ardently wished for so long could suddenly be happening. After a time, a wonderful time, he bent to kiss her neck, her shoulders, and she was kissing him, opening his dressing gown, undoing the belt, looking into his eyes as she did so. She moved the duvet aside; they were already warm and it was only going to get hotter. Outside, the birds sang, the sun shone and the sky was still blue: inside, a miracle was occurring: David was making love to his Lois. Someone had once told him that man's biggest sex organ was his brain. This experience seemed to confirm it. He held back for as long as he could; wanting to give her pleasure.

Afterwards, Lois felt that she had used David because she had wanted sex, not with just anyone, but it hadn't all been for David. Sly had played a part as well. She hadn't thought of him, but she knew that this newly found sexual desire was directly related to her experiences with Sly. David watched her face, saw the range of emotions she was feeling. He had made love to her, but he would have to tread very carefully, to ensure that he obtained his ultimate goal. He kissed her on the lips, whispered thank you. He thought he would give her a moment to compose herself, and asked her if she would mind if he went to get his cigarettes. He kissed her again as he left the room, and thanked God that he'd had a shower that morning. Otherwise, he might have blown it all.

When he came back, she was lying on her side, waiting for him; he busied himself getting her orange juice and coffee, and she sat up in bed. He opened the window, lit his cigarette, and sat on her bed, watching her and thinking.

'Thank you again, that was awesome. I just want to say that I knew this might happen. I've been thinking about it a lot.'

Lois looked startled. 'You knew, how?'

'I know you don't want me to think about you the way I think about other girls. Let me say that it would be impossible. I feel love for you, respect; you have values, you are bright, you are funny, you can make me laugh, and I'm interested in what you have to say. We have shared experiences that only you and I know about. It is a world apart from a quick fuck. I even make love with you differently. I actually care that you have a nice time. With those other girls, all I care about is my pleasure.

'In fact, you've even got me thinking about the way I behave with these other girls. Nowadays, I try really hard not to lie, not to bullshit, to make it absolutely clear that I only want sex with them. Sometimes, it's all they want as well; if some of them want more, that isn't my problem. I'm trying to be straight. I've even considered celibacy, but I don't think that I'm really cut out for that, and anyway, it'd be a crying shame. Look at me.' He smiled and put on the 'David act' just for a moment, to make her laugh. She did, and then she smiled at him fondly.

'You made me think, made me see it was wrong to tell lies, to

123

have casual sex.'

To his horror, Lois started to cry. She was letting go of a lot of bottled-up pain. 'It's all right, David. It's just me. Sly must have lied to me. He couldn't have loved me, then hated me. I fell for the lies as well.'

David could have kicked himself for forgetting that she must still be hurting. He moved to sit next to her and put his arm around her.

'I feel so stupid; it's Sid all over again.' Lois wanted to tell him that she was no better than one of his floosies, that she had slept with Sly on the first night she had met him; that she had believed everything he'd said, but she couldn't speak for sobs.

'You can't be held responsible for what goes on his fucking mind. I bet you never thought it was going to be a one-night-stand, did you?' David said.

Lois shook her head. That much was true. She stopped crying, apologised and felt a little better.

'Anyway, you and I are not going out with anyone else. We haven't hurt anyone. You're not hurt by this, are you?'

She shook her head and he felt her relax.

'Hey, let's see what the rest of humanity is doing, shall we?' David fetched the newspapers, and they sat in bed, giggling, just as they usually did. David's heart was soaring with happiness.

★   ★   ★

In the afternoon, David had to leave for London, in order to avoid the heaviest traffic. Lois went out to the car with him, comforted by knowing that she'd see him again for her birthday. They hugged, their embrace longer and stronger than usual.

When he'd gone, she 'phoned Gerry, who was prepared for a long chat. The girls exchanged news and confidences, most of which came from Gerry, who confessed to having had sex with Luke. Lois tried to convince Gerry that she had a firm rock in

Luke; that he was very honest and open and would stick to his principles. Luke was a truly nice guy.

Lois put the phone down after they had been talking for almost an hour. She felt a little better, but began to ask herself if she was reading too much into the situation with David, who loved having a good time. She had enjoyed making love with him, and who better to enjoy good sex with than your best friend. However, she resolved to speak to him about it when next she saw him. She suspected that her mother was already planning the wedding.

She received Mickie's letter on the Monday; it was very long and very funny. The underlying message was that Sly regretted what he had done, realised that he had hurt her very badly and was willing to wait until she was ready to talk to him about it. The rest of the letter was chat about mutual friends.

On the day when David intended to take Lois and her mother to Paris, Lois thought they were off to Manchester, to buy birthday presents. She was none the wiser, until they turned into the airport.

It was Easter weekend and Paris was full of tourists, but they had the most wonderful time, visiting all the popular places. On their last night, Lois decided that the time had come to talk about herself and David. He needed to stay in Paris for a photo shoot and then fly to New York. He also planned a two-week holiday in Rhodes, after which, he'd be back in Chester, working part time in La Garda again.

'David, this has been lovely, this weekend, Paris everything.'

'I know. I've loved it as well, and I've loved being here with you. Making love has been so amazing. I adore you.'

He looked into her eyes and realised that instead of returning his ardent gaze, there was a guarded expression on her face.

'Darling, I'm worried about what this will do to our friendship, what will happen now that we are going to be parted for such a long time. I truly need you as a friend, and suppose we meet someone else, then what?'

'Lois, stop this. There isn't anyone else for me. I only want you, okay? Just don't try all this crap.'

Lois persisted, somewhat uncertainly, 'But, love, we have always been there for each other. If you get off with someone else, or I do, then what will happen? You are going to be away; I have to go back to Aber. How can we commit to each other? Are we friends, or lovers? What exactly is going on here?'

David considered his reply carefully, trying to find the response she needed to hear from him, true, or untrue.

'We are friends, we've had a nice time, and we won't spoil it. Our friendship means the world to me. I don't want anything more from you. I love your body, I love you, but I would rather settle for friendship than try to pretend that we can go on like this. I don't want to hurt you, I don't want you to hurt me. We are friends, first and last, just friends.'

Lois felt relief flood over her because he felt the same way she did. She wished he would look at her, the tone of his voice was unsettling but he had said what she wanted to hear.

'Thank you, David. I don't feel ready for a new relationship just yet and, while I love you dearly...'

David asked, 'Still thinking about Sly? Has he ruined this for me?'

'Yes, I think he did. I don't feel able to trust anyone at the moment.'

'Not even me?' David was getting really riled. 'Lois, I've never let you down, never; so don't equate that bastard with me.' He spoke louder than he had intended to.

'No, you've never let me down, but you haven't got the best reputation in the world, have you?'

'Please don't insult me. You are not one of my floosies, and you know that. You are my Lois; this is not the same; I adore you.' He stubbed out his cigarette and walked over to the bed. He sat down next to her and tried to control his feelings.

★   ★   ★

They parted on good terms next day. Preoccupied with the thought of driving her mother home from Manchester airport in a borrowed car, Lois had not concentrated when she said farewell to David, and failed to note his look of extreme sadness.

Lois had a suitcase bursting with summer outfits to wear, ready for when she arrived back in Aber for the start of the new term.

Malc called in to see her, to say he'd been visiting Julia, Gerry's old mate. They had seen quite a bit of each other over the holiday, as they both came from Blackburn. Lois wondered if romance was in the air. Malc had also visited Sly in Monmouth. When he mentioned it, she changed the subject. She went out for a drink at the Sea Bank with Gerry and Luke, where Huw joined them. He said he had parted from his boyfriend, but wouldn't elaborate.

There was less social life now, as the pressure of exams increased. The Union disco had almost petered out, and the friends only went out on weekend evenings, usually to the Pier.

Nick reappeared and came round quite often to see Lois, cadging notes and offering advice on Biochemistry. He'd worked hard over Easter, he'd had nothing else to do, as his girlfriend had become engaged to an old school friend. Nick seemed okay. Like everyone else, he was more preoccupied with work than before. Lois hadn't seen Sly and was glad about that.

12

After Sly:
Mickie's Reward

LOIS AND MALC arranged to meet for lunch in the Arts Centre. She was late and there was a long queue at the food counter, but Malc had already got their meals, much to her relief. He said how tired he was, now that he was working harder, with the exams in prospect. On the wall was a poster advertising the theatre production of 'Taming of the Shrew.' He asked her if she would like to go, but Malc had just been labouring the point about how much work he had.

'Are you inviting me?'

'Not exactly; a friend of mine asked me to ask you, that's all.' Malc explained casually.

'Oh, yes. Who, exactly?' she asked.

'Sly.'

'You're joking!'

Malc tried to put Sly's point of view, but Lois was unyielding. 'What will we talk about: the play, the characters, the themes?' Lois was being sarcastic.

'Look, you said that you'd like to see the play, he's got tickets. It's only Sly, for goodness' sake.'

'Yeah, but which Sly, the one I went out with, or the weirdo one that blew up at me last term?'

After Malc tried again, Lois thought it over. It was only the Theatre, they would talk about the play and she could always make an excuse and leave, if things turned out badly. She would go, she decided.

'Good girl. Now, he might give me a bit of peace and quiet to get my work done. He'll meet you at seven o'clock, here in the bar; I'll take you to lunch on Wednesday, and you can fill me in on all the gory details. He left the tickets with me, sure that you'd go with him. You'd better have them.'

There was no sign of Sly, when she walked in at five minutes past seven. She bought herself a drink and sat at one of the little tables. At seven-twenty, there was still no Sly. She was furious. She was about to leave, when she saw Mickie approaching. 'It's great to see you. You look lovely. Is it a hot date?' He sat down beside her and smiled.

'Are you going to the play, Mickie?' Lois hoped Sly would turn up now, find her with Mickie, and be gutted.

'I haven't got a ticket. I came to check on some details for the exhibition.'

A boy suddenly appeared at their table, red-faced and panting. 'Excuse me, are you Lois Bartlett? I have a message for you. Sly's had to go to an audition, he won't be able to make it this evening, he's very sorry. I should have been here earlier but I missed the bus, had to walk up the hill, nearly killed me.'

'Date with Sly? Mickie raised an eyebrow.

Lois explained and Mickie laughed aloud. 'Oh, Christ! I can't believe my luck. Sly stood you up and bought two tickets to see 'Taming of the Shrew', and I can come with you. Right! Let's go and take our seats. I'm going to love this.' His laughter was infectious.

They found their seats moments before the house lights went down. Rather than go to the bar in the interval, they sat in their seats and talked about the play. Afterwards, Mickie suggested going for a drink in the Union. They held hands as they walked across the concourse. The evening was beautiful, the sun had just set and the sky was full of pink and orange clouds. There were students everywhere. Lois saw Fenn and Luke, and she waved at them. Being with Mickie, she felt safe and special.

Later, they walked back through the campus and she remembered the first night she had walked down to Panty with Sly. The scent of flowers reminded her; everything was in full leaf again, just as on that night. Mickie threw his arm around her shoulder, she slipped her arm around his waist, and they walked very slowly, enjoying the evening air. They ended up standing by the railings in front of Alex, watching the waves lap the pebbles. Mickie kissed her, and it seemed to make perfect sense. When they broke apart, she took his hand and led him through the front door and up to her room.

Lois made tea and Mickie looked at the magnificent view outside the window, which was slightly open, admitting the smell of the sea and the coolness of the night air. He looked down and saw Sly standing exactly where he and Lois had been, only minutes before; he was looking out to sea, his hands gripping the rails. Mickie knew that he should warn Lois that Sly could make his way up here, to apologise for letting her down. Sly turned, looked up and saw Mickie, who closed the curtains.

Lois brought the tea over to him. She kicked off her shoes and regarded him thoughtfully, her head on one side. Mickie sat down on the bed and told her to come and sit with him. She sat on his lap, legs straddling his. Tea forgotten, they kissed and made ecstatic love, driven on by raw desire.

'Oh, God, Lois, I'm so sorry; this is dreadful,' he said, having just experienced the most amazing physical and emotional sensation of his life. He laughed.

'Why are you laughing?' Lois was seriously worried; no one had ever laughed at her in the moments after making love to her. What had she done wrong? It had felt wonderful to her.

'Oh, God! I'm not laughing at you.' Mickie took a few deep

breaths, still smiling inanely. He took her hand and tried to explain the strange sensations he had felt. 'You're a great lover, Lois.'

'I used to think that men were the lovers, women were loved,' Lois murmured, her eyes closed.

'Well, considering this is our first encounter, shall we say we have gone at it like rabbits? We've just made the best love ever; why shouldn't we be honest.'

They spent the night together, but Mickie had to be up early, with work to do before his finals, and he woke her before he left. 'I wish I could stay, and I wish this had happened some other time. I really enjoyed last night. Perhaps, tomorrow. I've got a gap until Friday afternoon. If I get through all that post-modern stuff, I'll try to come round then.'

Lois, realising that they were talking finals, said, 'No, don't worry, just come to me when you want to.'

'If I did that, I'd be here all the time. I'd better go, let you get some more sleep. I'll see you soon.'

Later, Gerry woke her, by throwing a set of notes at her. 'Get up, you lazy cow. Natasha says you had a man in here last night, and I want all the sordid details.'

'Not until you get me tea and tell me all about the lecture.'

'I don't know what the lecture was about. I hope you can decipher the notes.'

Mystified, Lois picked up the notes and asked, 'What does this mean?'

'I have no idea. I arrived late and probably missed something. It's bound to be in the book. Anyway, here's your tea. What's the news?'

'I had a wonderful time at the theatre, and rather a late night.' Lois teased her.

'So, it's all back on with the Sly-spotty-one, then?'

'It's not Sly. He stood me up. It's someone else.'

Lois told Gerry what had happened and how Mickie had

escorted her, in the absence of Sly. While they joked about this, Malc knocked on the door and walked in.

'What's all this about you and Mickie Marshall? Sly's just been to see me, and he's pissed off.'

'Good morning, Malc, nice to see you, too. I suppose that Sly forgot to tell you that he never turned up last night.'

'He had to do an audition for the summer production. When he went to Alex, to explain and apologise, he found you and Mickie boy snogging away in the moonlight.'

'Good,' said Gerry.

'What are you playing at, Lois? Do you realise that Mickie is still living with Pauline?'

'He and Pauline have been finished since Christmas,' Lois said.

'Yes, and we all know why, don't we?' Malc snapped.

'No, we don't, actually, so do tell,' Gerry said sarcastically.

'Sly is really upset, Lois, and I promised to come round and find out the score here.

'I'm going to the toilet. I really have no wish to talk to you while you're in this mood.' Lois got out of bed and made for the door, leaving Gerry to continue the conversation.

When Lois returned, Malc apologised

'I thought you liked Mickie.'

'I do, but it's a shock to think of you and him like that. Sly really was upset at letting you down, and he was devastated at seeing Mickie here, staring down at him.'

'I'm starving. Does anyone fancy lunch at the Cabin?' Gerry asked, in order to create a diversion.

★　★　★

Lois began to revise for her exams; however, she found it harder to concentrate than she had hoped. She kept thinking about her night with Mickie. She felt good inside, despite Malc and Gerry insisting that it had been just a one-night stand. It was nice to feel this way again; she wondered whether she had felt like this with Sly.

The next day brought the usual round of lectures and tutorials, and she found Mickie filling her thoughts. He was not someone she saw every day, and now it occurred to her to wonder what he did with himself. At half past ten at night, Mickie appeared at her door.

'I've worked as hard as I could tonight, and I wondered if you'd like to go for a drink, last orders or something. I can't believe I'm saying this, asking the most attractive girl I've ever met in my life to come out for a quick drink. I hope you understand, this is a really bad time for me, but I do want to see you.'

'Yes,' Lois said, throwing her arms about his neck, 'I understand. I'm just so glad you came anyway. I've got a bottle of Chianti somewhere; we'll drink that here, and you can tell me about your exam.'

It was five o'clock in the morning when Mickie woke her, to say it was time for him to go.

'Will I see you tonight?' she asked.

'I can't. It's bit difficult. Actually, it's Pauline's birthday and we're having a dinner party. It's been arranged for ages.' Lois was awake now.

'What do you mean?'

'Well I've known her for a long time, we're still very close; she'd be heartbroken if I wasn't there, especially if she knew the reason.'

'You mean she doesn't?'

Mickie sat down on the bed and took Lois's hand. 'Look, this is a case of bad timing, from just about every angle. I will tell Pauline that I'm seeing you, but I can't do it in the middle of her finals; it wouldn't be fair. She's been on a knife-edge all year, mostly due to me, and I'd feel a right shit if I pushed her over the edge.'

'Well, how do you think she'll feel when she finds out later?'

'I'll lie, it's easier.'

Lois and Mickie argued about the situation, but Lois knew she had the upper hand over Pauline, and the pair of them stopped the confrontation.

'Anyway, go back to sleep, dream of me. I'll come round tomorrow evening and take you out to Gannett's. We'll have a proper date, okay?'

Lois smiled in agreement, Mickie kissed her quickly and left.

★　★　★

On Saturday, after shopping, Lois and Gerry took coffee in The Cabin, with Luke and Malc. When Lois left them, she walked slowly up to her third floor room and found Mickie sitting on the floor outside her door, reading a book. He wanted to go for a walk, in spite of a fine drizzle falling. Mickie and Lois wandered hand-in-hand along the promenade. Lois wondered what would happen if they met Pauline and whether he would drop her hand when they reached the terrace where he and Pauline lived.

During that day and into the evening, Lois learnt about Mickie: who he was, where he came from and how he came to be studying art at Aberystwyth. Having started on a quite different path, he changed to art, which was why he arrived in Aberystwyth, three years older than everyone else and not knowing what to expect. He met Pauline and life had been straightforward, until the final year.

Mickie took Lois to Gannett's and showed her the frescos around the room, which he had painted last summer. He told her that he sometimes had free meals, in part payment. She drank a lot of wine but Mickie hardly touched a drop. When she mentioned going to the Union, he greeted the idea with unexpected enthusiasm.

'I hope Sly will be there. I can't wait to see his face when we walk in together. What a picture!' Mickie laughed. Lois shook her head.

* * *

On the morning of Mickie's last final examination, he left Alex at five o'clock. Lois hardly stirred, knowing that she would see him later. He ran joyfully along the promenade towards South Marine Terrace. The sea was like glass and made almost no sound as it caressed the pebbles on the beach. The last two weeks before the most important exams of his life had been almost unbearable, and then, there was Lois.

At six-thirty, he was sitting at the kitchen table, notes and books strewn around him, while he did last minute revision. He would have lunch with Pauline and John and cook a meal for Lois in the evening, at Alex. He was vaguely aware that it was about time to wake Pauline. When John walked in to the kitchen, Mickie was surprised.

'All right, what are you doing here?'

Mickie hadn't heard John come in, which meant, possibly, that he had slept here. John had met up with Pauline last night and, he said angrily, she was upset. Sly had told her about Mickie and Lois, and she felt unable to face going home to an empty house. John was angry that Mickie hadn't told him anything about Lois, and he wanted to know what the hell was going on. Mickie was close to losing his temper, because an evening in Pauline's company seemed to have turned John against him, and he loved this guy like a brother.

'For Christ's sake, John! You ask what I am doing to Pauline. We've been over for months and you know it. I have tried to be as fair to her as I can be, but I can't live my life for her any more. She's trying my patience. I can't be held responsible for her any longer, I just can't. Meeting Lois was like a gift from God, and I took it.'

'You've only just met Lois. What are you talking about?'

'John, I have felt this way about Lois ever since I first saw her. You know that.'

'Are you saying you finished with Pauline, because of Lois.'

'Yes, partly. When I saw Lois, I knew she was the only girl for me. Why don't you know this; how can you know me but not know this?'

'I don't know, Mickie. You joke a lot. Tell me all about it, okay?' John said.

Mickie tried to explain his feelings to John, who was scornful in his response. 'You're letting your knob do your thinking for you, mate.'

'No, you're wrong. If it was just that, it'd be fine, but I love everything about her: the way she talks, the way she is so intense over work, the way she's so vulnerable, so open to everything.

Oh, come on. You used to think this way about Pauline.'

'I did not.' Mickie was emphatic. 'I never said I loved Pauline. That's one of the things that bugged her, but I can't tell Lois any of this, in case I ruin it all, She's just not ready. I can only make it as good as it gets, then sit back and wait. I've even thought about asking her to come to Birmingham with me, or of me doing my Masters here, even of asking her to marry me, but I know she'd run a mile, she's just not ready, she's only nineteen.'

'Girls mature faster than boys, you know.'

'Oh yeah? Remember when you were nineteen? Even if she were to fall for me, I'd still be terrified of this hold that Sly has on her. Suppose she lived to regret it? I'd be too frightened.'

'How do you know how she feels? What if she's waiting for you to say something?'

'I know she likes me, wants my body, but Sly has power over her and I don't know why. There's no love, but she thinks there is.'

'You're very certain of all this.'

'Oh yeah. Too right. I think about nothing else. I'm well practised at it.'

'You, Mickie, are always the first person to help other people, always Mister Nice Guy. Everyone thinks you're the golden boy. The only person I've ever seen you be nasty to is Pauline,' John said.

'I was trying to be cruel to be kind.'

Mickie squirmed as John continued to probe. 'Yeah, well you're not very good at it. It might have been nicer to be cruel to be cruel. How do you think she felt, on the day after her birthday, when Sly tells her, "Hey, guess what, Mickie's shagging Lois, Happy Birthday,"?'

'There was never going to be an easy way out of the Pauline situation,' Mickie said. 'Yet, but for Sly, I would probably never have met Lois. I suppose I have to be grateful for that.'

'So, what will you while Lois grows up enough to see through Sly and learn to appreciate you?'

'God knows. I'll just have to stick it out. Anyway, I've got the small matter of an exam in a bit over an hour.'

'I'd better get back to Hazel, she'll be wondering where the hell I've got to.' John rose to go.

At that moment, Pauline came into the room, and from the look on her face, they knew she had been eavesdropping.

'I don't want a row. I'm going up to the department,' she hissed. 'I'll see you in the exam. I think we need to talk, don't you?'

Mickie made a move towards her, but she turned aside, with a show of dignity. 'There's nothing to say now. We'll argue. I'll get mad.' Mickie caught hold of her arm but she shrugged him off.

'I'll see you after the exam. I know how important it is to both of us.' Turning to John, she added, 'Thanks for staying last night. I hope Hazel understands.'

★ ★ ★

If God had been good to Mickie until now, He had just reconsidered. Mickie finished checking his final, final essay, which had occupied him for three hours, planning and sorting, and writing until his fingers ached. He watched the clock tick away the final seconds of his last exam at Aberystwyth. It was midday, when the examiner asked the students to put down their pens. Mickie had forgotten about Pauline until now.

Sally, his tutor, asked him to follow her out of the room. The other students were still sitting in their places. As soon as they got outside, Sally told him as gently as she could that his father had suffered a massive heart attack that morning. He was in hospital, unlikely to recover. His family wanted Mickie to join them at the hospital as soon as he had finished his exam. Sally said she would drive him to Liverpool immediately, and asked if he wanted Pauline to come with him.

While he was trying to make sense of this awful news, Pauline arrived from somewhere. Sally quickly explained what had happened and Pauline, shocked, stared at Mickie.

'You'll have to tell Lois for me, Pauline. I'll write her a note and you can take it to her, please. There's no need for you to say anything to her.'

'Oh Mickie, even now, it's still her.'

Pauline had been about to offer to come with him, knowing the new burden of responsibilities that would be his from now on. Silently and sadly, she handed him a pen and A4 pad, with which he wrote his note to Lois. As he handed it to her, Pauline shook her head. 'I can't believe this.'

'I'm sorry, but I can't just go without telling her where I am and what has happened. Please make sure she gets it.'

Pauline thought she hated him, but recognised in the same instant how much she loved him. Even this service she would render.

Once he and Sally were on their way to Liverpool, Pauline was tempted, briefly, not to deliver the note. She happened to board the same bus as Gerry, and asked her to give the note to Lois. It was all over for Pauline: her finals, Mickie, her university life, even her childhood.

13
After Sly:
End of the First Year

WHEN GERRY APPROACHED HER with Mickie's note, Lois was chatting to Nick. Having read the note, she stared out of the window on a world so sunny and bright, where students liberated from exams exulted in their new freedom. It seemed hard to believe that, somewhere in Liverpool, Mickie was coping with his father's grave illness. She handed Gerry the note to read, and Gerry proposed that they buy some wine and stay indoors in the evening. She guessed that Lois would not be in a party mood. Gerry and Luke were drifting apart already, which grieved Gerry, but Gerry kept her own concerns to herself and allowed Lois to talk of Mickie.

They spent Sunday browsing round Clarach open-air market, and, in the evening, took the boys out for a drink in the bar at the hall on Penglais Hill. The doors were open and students spilled out to sit on the grass outside. The sunset over Cardigan Bay was spectacular. From one of the nearby student blocks came the strains of David Bowie's 'Hunky Dory'. Suddenly, everything seemed very precious; it seemed incredible that their first year was nearly over.

Lois telephoned Mickie and learnt that his father had stabilised and was expected to recover in time. Mickie thought he would not be back in Aber until after the end of term, and added that Pauline would be joining him in Liverpool, once the exam results were out.

'Don't let anyone make a big deal out of this. Pauline's a friend of the family, and I couldn't stop her, even if I wanted to. At present, we need all the help we can get.'

The next day was the worst, having to pack up and leave the place that for many had grown to feel like home. The third years were the saddest and most anxious, as they waited for their results. A Botany and Zoology Social Evening was to take place, and the exam results would be out. This usually coincided with the Going Down Ball but, this year, there was to be a disco in the staff room instead. Thunder was rolling among the distant hills, but Aber was bright and sparkling under a blue sky. Lois and Gerry laughed as they crossed the Pantycelyn car park, on their way to the disco. Waiting for them was Sly.

'Lois, I wondered if I could speak to you, alone.'

He ignored Gerry, who hoped that Lois would tell him to get lost, but she told Gerry to go on ahead, she wouldn't be long.

They walked to the back of the hall. 'Malc told me that you would be here. I needed to see you; I haven't seen you all term.'

He asked about Mickie's father and her exams, and she answered him cautiously, waiting to hear what he had to say. The smell of the polish in the hall evoked disturbing memories. When they got to his room, like hers, it was almost empty because he, too, was packing. Sly went to fetch two cans of lager from the fridge, while she stood alone and wondered who would have this room next year.

'The Art Department results are out tomorrow. The rumour is that someone has been given a first, probably Mickie.'

Feeling impatient, she asked, 'Sly, why did you want to see me?'

She didn't want his small talk. He sat down on his bed and gestured for her to sit down on the chair.

'Lois, I just wanted to say that I have never in my life regretted anything as much as I regret losing my temper with you in February, frightening you and finishing with you. I was so stupid, stubborn, and I wouldn't listen to what you said, or what Malc has said many times since then.' Her face was impassive. He continued, 'I still love you and I need you back in my life. I just wanted you to know that, before you go away from here.'

Lois believed he was sincere but there were too many other things on her mind, and she couldn't throw down the barriers she had erected. She was seeing Mickie, and he didn't deserve her to fall for Sly and his little tricks again, especially now.

'Well, Sly, you've made me wait a long time to hear that; maybe too long.'

Sly's face showed surprise that things were not going as he had predicted. She should be in his arms by now. He recovered himself. 'I'm so sorry. I know that you are seeing Mickie, so I am not expecting anything to happen right now. I would just like to know if there is any chance for us. All the time, I think only of you.'

Lois looked away from him, not trusting herself to look into his eyes. Sly leant forward and touched her hand, willing her to speak.

'I think so. I still love you, Sly. I haven't stopped, not for a moment.'

'Please mean that, Lois. I would give the whole world if you meant that.'

'I do meant it, but I don't trust you, and I need to feel able to trust you if we are going to be together again. I trust Mickie, I am with Mickie, and I like that,' she said slowly. 'Please try to understand. I need to see you as a friend, a person in my life that I can rely on, and then we might just stand a chance.'

'Take as much time as you need. I will prove that I have learned from what happened. Take my word for it.'

Lois knew that she would regret it if she stayed longer, for he was already weakening her resolve to resist him. 'What would you have done if you hadn't seen me tonight, Sly?' Lois picked up her bag and walked to the door.

'I would have written to you.' He hadn't even considered the possibility.

'Well, write to me, anyway. I'd like to see what you would have said.'

* * *

Lois arrived when the annual review had five more minutes to run. Gerry and Max had saved her a seat and she tried to slip into it inconspicuously. At the end, there was a mass exodus of students, all headed for the notice boards on the ground floor. Lois, Gerry and Max crept forward. Lois quickly found her name and saw that she had As in Zoology and Botany. Gerry also had passes. Glancing back at her own name, Lois noticed an asterisk, indicating that she had won the Zoology prize; quite an achievement for a first-year. Gerry and Max congratulated her heartily.

At the party, everyone was in good humour. Once the music started, the results were quickly forgotten.

* * *

The coach journey to the site of the end of term field course seemed to take forever. Gerry fell asleep, exhausted by the term's events, exams, and Luke robbing her of much needed sleep. Lois watched the Welsh countryside speed past the window and let her mind wander. A year ago, almost to the day, she had finished her A-levels, and enjoyed the most carefree summer of her life, often with David for company. She thought about Easter and wondered why she had needed him so badly. She hadn't felt a physical desire for anyone a year ago, so why had she picked on her best friend?

What about Mickie? Why did she feel such lust for him? She smiled at the memory of their first night together, and his confusion and embarrassment. Then, she thought of Sly, the jolt she had received on meeting him, the good times, the bad. Why was she making him wait? Was it lack of trust, or was she punishing him? She was playing a dangerous game that could leave her without any of them. Whom would she miss the most, who was the most important. Her heart said Sly; her brain said David; so where was Mickie?

'Lois, you are talking to yourself,' Gerry said, suppressing a yawn,

'They say that's the first sign of madness, don't they? I was just thinking aloud.' Gerry asked what Sly had needed to say, and Lois told her. 'What a nerve that bloke's got. Hasn't he got any brains at all?'

Lois laughed at the way Gerry always saw everything in black and white.

They carried on their discussion, and their only conclusion was that things were bound to be awkward with David.

The field course was great fun and lasted until Saturday, when they returned to an almost student-free Aberystwyth, where everyone who was still about the place headed off to collect their belongings and bid each other farewell. Gerry's brother was waiting for her at Alex. Lois brought her stuff downstairs. The hall was empty and her sandals tapping on the tiled floors sounded eerie. She was on her third trip up to her room when she found David waiting for her, standing in the bay window, looking like Lord of all he surveyed, cigarette in hand. Her heart leapt at the sight of him.

'There you are. Come and give me a kiss.'

14

After Sly: France

SUNNY LA ROCHELLE, Lois thought grimly. She was lying on the beach, surrounded by people seemingly having the time of their lives, and she had never felt so miserable. They were in the middle of a drought and a heat wave, everyone looked tanned, and David was the colour of a walnut, his blonde hair almost white. Last year, she had been waiting for her exam results. Now, Lois wished he would give her some space and time to get things into perspective. However, he stuck to her side, and paid her the utmost attention, although he had problems of his own. His parent's relationship seemed to be rekindling and, now that his father was virtually retired from the business, he regretted the time spent away from his family.

Lois looked over to where David was playing football with some German and French boys. Although they were still able to talk, laugh and enjoy each other's company, there was too much about which she was unable to talk to him. Sly and Mickie were certainly taboo subjects. She knew David's views on girls who slept around. Her fear was that of losing him as a friend. She had come to rely on him always being there for her, and she hoped she was there for him. How had it all become so complicated?

She walked to the water, cooled her feet in the surf, and came back to find David drinking bottled water.

'Are you all right, Lois? Were you thinking about Sly?'

'About Sly?' Lois laughed. 'No, actually, nothing much, just about all the times we've been here.'

'I've been coming here since I was a child. It was a good move my old man made, when he persuaded Uncle Frank to spend their inheritance on something the whole family can enjoy. I love it here. This is the best weather we've ever had,' he said. 'Have you 'phoned Mickie?'

'No, he asked me not to. We write to each other. His father is on the mend and the doctors say he will be home soon.'

'Good. Do you know how he got on in the finals?'

Lois was surprised at his sudden interest. 'No, but he must know now. Why are you thinking about that?'

'I don't know. I suppose I was thinking that someone is always waiting for something momentous, whenever we come here. Not this year, though, eh?'

Lois thought he had more to say, but he couldn't say it, whatever it was. 'No, nobody is waiting for anything this year.'

'I told Rich we'd go out tonight, as it's his last night.' Lois pulled a face, but David said crossly, 'Come on, Lois, he's been here a fucking week, and I haven't been down to the club with him yet. He's getting pissed off, and I don't blame him.'

'Well, you go. I don't fancy it tonight.'

'I don't like to leave you on your own.'

'I don't feel very sociable.'

'So I've noticed.' He reached for his cigarettes, lit one and then stared out to sea.

'I'm sorry. I've got a good book to read, and I ought to write to some people back home.'

David continued to stare icily out to sea. He was angry.

'Look, I've got my period; I just don't feel like dancing.'

'You always feel like fucking dancing.'

The argument flared, and they both said things they didn't mean. Aware that they sounded petulant and childish, Lois suddenly grinned, her anger dispelled. 'Look, I don't know what's wrong with me. Take Rich out tonight; I'll be fine, honestly.'

'Okay, come on. I'll buy some doughnuts.'

She recognised a peace offering when it was offered.

The rest of the day went pretty much according to the normal plan. David played volleyball and swam with the usual group. Rich came down to the beach in the afternoon, looking very pleased with himself, which meant he had scored last night.

Lois went shopping, glad to be alone at last. Her best friend, David, was sulking and she could do nothing about it. Her behaviour had soured the new relationship they had enjoyed, and jeopardised the long friendship that used to exist between them. The boy she was supposed to love was back in Aberystwyth, acting the role of a sea slug in a stupid drama, and the man she was supposedly seeing was somewhere in Liverpool with his ex-girlfriend. None of it made any sense at all. Gerry would be able to laugh about it!

When she returned to the villa, David and his brother, Rich, were getting ready to go out. They tried once more to persuade her to join them but she was resolute. Rich had even brought her a bottle of wine, and a stuffed chicken breast to cook for supper. She was surprised, but the gesture was not enough to dispel her feeling of dislike for Rich.

'Don't get back too late,' she warned, knowing that they probably wouldn't be back until morning. Once they had gone, she felt lonely, and couldn't be bothered with the chicken. Twice, she almost decided to join the two brothers but, after three glasses of wine, she couldn't be bothered. She had tried to think about Sly and Mickie, but the person uppermost in her mind was David. What would happen if they were still in this awful state of tension when they got back to Chester? She was losing her best friend, they were drifting apart and there seemed to be nothing that she could do about it.

Lois heard someone return to the villa at around two o'clock.

She decided it was probably David, and was vaguely surprised that he should return before kicking-out time at the club. She was almost asleep, when she thought there was a knock on her door. She must have fallen back to sleep while waiting to see if the door would open, or if there would be a further knock. There was neither.

David woke her the next morning, so that she could say goodbye to Rich. It was already eleven o'clock but Lois felt as though she hadn't slept a wink. She was very thirsty and, even before she opened her eyes, she knew she had a bad hangover.

'I've brought you some Paracetemol and some sparkling water. Rich will be leaving soon.'

She took the pills, drank the water, and immediately felt nauseous, but she managed to get out of bed and help to pack the last few of Rich's belongings. As they waved goodbye to him, she hoped that his departure might take some of the tension out of the situation. David wanted to hit the beach; she wanted to go back to bed. He eventually went alone, but not before irritating her by acting as though he had never drunk too much in his entire life. She was in a bad temper by the time she returned to sleep, and it wasn't helped when she was woken by the maid, who came in at 2 o'clock, to tidy the room.

Lois felt better, and went down to the beach, where she hoped that David and she might have a late lunch. She found David sitting at a table with three girls, and turned on her heel, but David saw her and caught up with her.

'Hey, hang on. What's the matter? Where are you going?' David fell into step with her.

'To the beach. Don't let me drag you away from your dollies.'

'You're not. I was just chatting. Why don't you come and have a hair of the dog?'

'No, thanks.'

'Why not? What's the matter with you?'

'Nothing,' she said. 'I'll see you at the beach.'

David watched her walk away, wishing that he could resolve this dreadful stalemate, and yet, he had no idea what he was doing wrong. He had brought her here, had paid full attention to her, he had not been out until last night and, even then, he had been back before the club closed. He could have had his pick of the girls, but he had walked away. He was trying so hard to make this easy, to be friends. It was eating him up, seeing her half-naked on the beach, watching her around the villa, being so close, yet so far. He was beginning to lose patience.

Lois started to read but fell asleep, and David, returning to the beach later, covered her with his T-shirt, to protect her from the sun. When she awoke, the headache had gone and, when she felt the T-shirt covering her, she felt quite touched by David's thoughtfulness. He and a handful of friends came over and joined her when David saw that she was sitting up. Martyn and Renate, a Swedish couple with whom David was friendly, asked if Lois would like to go to the club that evening. By the time she and David left the beach, they had arranged to meet half a dozen of the others at 8.30, to eat and go on to the club. David reeled off the music that she would dance to: New Order, King Creole, The Clash, even Duran Duran at a push. She was beginning to look forward to it.

When they got back to the apartment, the maid had left her room spotless and tidy. It was all a long call from Aberystwyth student life. Maria had returned her laundry, spotlessly clean and freshly ironed. She expected to find her white jeans amongst the clean clothes, but they were missing, so she went to ask if David had them by mistake. She found him trying to sew on a shirt button. He knew better than to ask her to do it.

'Have you got my jeans in your laundry?'

She found them, but when she tried them on, she could scarcely do them up; they would be agony to wear.

'They've shrunk.'

'Let's have a look.'

Lois was facing the mirror, bending this way and that, trying to stretch the waistband, to make them more comfortable.

'They look fine,' he said, looking at her reflection in the mirror, thinking how wonderful she looked. He stood close behind her; it was unbearable, he couldn't say anymore.

'I won't be able to move in them, I'll have to wear something else.' Her voice trailed off as she saw his expression in the mirror. She stood quite still, meeting his gaze.

David found his voice. 'You look gorgeous.'

She watched as his head bent slowly towards her neck. He kissed her shoulder, looked in the mirror, watching to see what her reaction would be. He expected to be slapped round the face at any moment, but it was worth it. Anyway, he couldn't help himself, he couldn't be this close and do nothing. She stood still, watching intently. He risked some more. His hands came round her waist; one reached upwards towards her breast, the other moved down over her hip, then slowly over her stomach towards her pubic bone. Again, he glanced at her expression. She was watching his hands, as if she were transfixed. He bent to her neck again, kissed the soft hair, smelt her freshly showered skin. His breath was hot. Suddenly, she turned. He flinched, expecting a slap in the face. She seemed to pounce on him, and caught him unawares. She grasped his face between her hands and kissed him ferociously, bruising his lips, exploring his mouth with her tongue. Lois had taken control and David was in for a tempestuous ride.

They hadn't uttered a single intelligible word throughout the entire proceedings. He wanted to say, 'I love you.' It came out as, 'I'm knackered.' She smiled and released her legs from his back. He withdrew from her, and she pulled herself back onto the bed. He collapsed beside her, she turned over into the foetal position, and they fell asleep.

David slept only for a few minutes, momentarily drained. He

had lain for some time watching Lois, hoping she would wake up and smile, and turn to him, but she was fast asleep. He thought his friends would not mind too much about being stood up, but hunger prompted him to think about food. He left Lois a note and went in search of something special. He returned to the villa with a freshly prepared salad, wine and cigarettes, and all he could think of was how shocked he'd been by her response. He'd never seen her like this, so different from the girl she had been at Easter.

Lois was still sleeping when he returned, so he arranged the salad and went to sit on the balcony. Eventually, as the sun began to set, he went to the room and she stirred. He sat down on the bed and kissed her gently.

'Come on, sleepy head, get dressed. I've made dinner for you.'

She came onto the balcony a few minutes later, wearing a loose silk dress, her hair combed straight back from her face. He handed her a glass of red wine and she looked at the table, impressed. Then she thought better of it.

'You didn't make that.'

'No, I ordered it from the restaurant. I thought you'd like it. Come on, let's eat, I'm starving.'

'Me, too, thank you.'

They busied themselves with their meal, sharing the bread and eating hungrily. Once they had emptied their plates, he took them away and returned with the grapes.

'I think we'd better talk, don't you?' He felt able to talk to her now; no longer frightened by what she might have to say.

'I think we better had. You can start, though; I'm not sure what to say.'

'I meant what I said at Easter. If you're not happy with this, not comfortable in anyway, then we'll be friends. I'd rather have that than nothing at all. I would settle for that, although I don't want to. Now, after what's just happened, I'm confused. How do you feel? Are you happy?'

'At this moment, yes, I'm happy. I feel relaxed and warm and good.' She shrugged her shoulders. 'But we're here on our own, there's no-one else who knows us, or anything about us. What just happened was very definitely between just us. There's no brother Rich, evaluating my every move, looking down his nose at me, thinking that I'll ruin your life. There's no mum, rubbing her hands and planning wedding hats. No Gerry, saying, "I told you so," no Sly, no Mickie, just us.'

David's eyes narrowed and he looked confused.

'Why did you include Mickie?'

Lois had been caught off guard but she didn't want to lie, there had to be honesty now. She told him, in brief, what had happened between her and Mickie Marshall, and David looked hurt, unable to meet her eyes.

'I couldn't tell you, David. I knew you'd be hurt. Fuck knows why; you see a different girl every week, probably, but I'm not supposed to mind about that.'

'You see how this changes things between us,' David interrupted. 'I've told you...'

'Yes, I know, but you'll still do it, until I say I don't like it any more. What sort of friend am I, to say you're not to see other girls? I don't own you, any more than you own me.'

'I knew there was something you hadn't told me. I thought you'd got back with Sly.'

Lois resolved instantly not to tell him about Sly. 'This isn't about Mickie, it's about us. Yes, I'm happy now, but I don't think it can last. Once we get back home, it will change, it will be too difficult. Christ, I don't know how my life became so complicated. It used to be so easy; even when Sid finished with me, it felt like a clean hurt, but it didn't hurt like breaking up with Sly did. Things were once so straightforward; you were my friend; you are my friend, my best friend. Friends don't screw each other, they just don't.' She became agitated, and walked to the edge of the balcony.

'One of us will get hurt. We can't just have sex and expect to be friends between screws; it's neither one thing nor the other. What happens if I get back with Sly, or Mickie? Or, if you get off with someone else? I've seen you cast off so many girls like that. What becomes of us then? I'm frightened.' She turned back to face him, defiant.

'That's not the only answer, is it? We could make a go of it, properly. I mean, we have no one else.'

'Oh be realistic, David. I'll be back in Aber in a few weeks. You've got that modelling agency now, and won't be able to come down like you used to. We'll be pissed off with each other. You'll get bored, I'll get restless, and there'll be Mickie. It's just not feasible, it wouldn't happen.'

David was losing the plot. Lois was trying to push him away, convince him that there was no future for them.

'How does Mickie fit into all of this?'

'I don't know, somehow, I guess.'

David raised his eyebrows and shook his head. None of this would sink in. He was fighting a losing battle for her.

'I wish I could tell you why he's the one. I can't explain but my head says one thing and my heart says another.'

It wasn't much of an explanation, but it was the only one she had.

'It's just a matter of time,' she finished weakly. 'I'm sorry.'

No matter how hard David tried to pin Lois down and elicit some graspable facts about Mickie and himself, she was like an eel, too slippery to hold. Sly was the real danger.

David thought about Sly and Lois getting back together again and, remembering how he'd treated Lois, he felt his anger rise. 'If Sly hurts you again, I'll fucking kill him.'

Lois had heard this fighting talk before. David's aggression was so much a part of him, she barely thought about it any longer. It was odd how he always came back to Sly. He seemed to find

Mickie less of a threat.

David no longer felt euphoric, just bitterly disappointed, beginning to wish he hadn't asked her to talk. She had been honest, he should have wanted that, but now he knew that he would have been happier with deception. He took two cigarettes, lit both and handed one to her. Lois watched him, unaware that he was suffering so badly. There was another moment or two of silence, until David spoke again. 'I'm frightened, too. You know how I feel about you. Everyone, Rich, my mother, they all say it's only because you were Sid's girl that you're not available. The impossible attracts me. They both reckon that if I had you, I wouldn't want you any more. It seems so unfair, to judge me like that, to look at the things I do and try to deduce how I feel about you. Rich says I'm not cut out for long term, monogamous relationships, and that idea frightens me. I think I love you. It feels so real, but what if they are right? Suppose I fucked up, got laid by some girl, hurt you. Then what would I have? I'd have nothing, not even belief in my own emotions. I'd have no self-respect. I have so much to lose, if I lose you. The prospect of being without you is, well... I just can't face it.'

It had taken some courage to reveal his deep-rooted fear. This was a test of himself and a chance to get a relationship right.

Lois began to see that there was no real answer. He loved her far more than she loved him, or, a least, in a different way. She had given in to sheer lust that evening, and it had irretrievably changed their relationship. She had to find a way out without hurting him.

'What are we going to do?' Lois tried to sound calm.

David ground out his cigarette stub and sat down again. 'I'm glad you ask, "What are we going to do?" rather than, "What am I going to do?"'

'What do you mean?' Lois looked surprised.

'Well, at Easter, all you seemed to be thinking about was what you had done and what you wanted.'

Lois was horrified. He didn't usually criticise like this. 'I was confused,' she admitted, thinking back, trying to determine whether he was right or not.

'You never sounded confused, just fucking selfish. I was pretty pissed off with you.'

Lois wondered why he was telling her this now but, on balance, it was probably right, she had talked more about herself than him, last time they had tried to discuss this. 'Why didn't you tell me?'

'It would have sounded like sour grapes. I'd just been denied what I wanted. Anyway, I forgave you, just like always.'

'I'm sorry, truly I am. Tell me, next time I act like that. The point is: what can we do? Here we are, talking like friends, and a few hours ago, we were shagging like there was no tomorrow. I'm telling you things about Mickie and Sly, although I shouldn't discuss them with you, but you're my friend, you're like Gerry. I expect you to be able to cope.'

'Hardly' David said grimly.

'I'm terrified that I might lose you. For five years, you have been part of my life, always there. Tell me how to cope with this mess we've made, and how to survive it.'

'It would be easier if we both wanted the same thing but, at the moment, we don't seem to.' It sounded so brutal and so hopeless.

Suddenly David asked, 'Have you ever had a holiday romance?'

'No, you know I haven't.' Lois was irritated by this irrelevance.

'Neither have I.'

'So?'

'Well, why don't we have one? We are alone here; we could have a fantastic week, really enjoy ourselves and enjoy each other, and then go home and get on with our lives, live on the memories, no ties. It would be something tremendous that happened, and can't be recaptured in Chester.'

'Do you really think that could work?' she asked warily.

'It has to be worth a try. Okay, so when we get home, we'll

have to adjust, but like you say, we will both be busy soon, and there won't be much time, anyway.'

He tried to sound casual, desperate to retrieve something, even if it was only a few days. Lois thought about how far away Chester and Aberystwyth seemed at that moment. She was sure she could pull it off, but she was less sure of David, although he seemed keen. 'Who would you tell?'

'I don't know, how about you?'

'Not my mother, for a start. Maybe, Gerry.'

'Your mother will know anyway, it's a mother's intuition. I'll probably tell Rich. What about Sly?'

'I don't think so. I suppose I might, just to piss him off!'

'Mickie?'

'Definitely not, and you're not to tell the lads.'

'Definitely not the lads.'

'Lois?' David had been thinking. 'When we make love, is it special to you?'

'Of course it is. You're my best friend and I love you.'

'It means the world to me. I've had sex with loads of girls, probably hundreds, but with you it's so different.'

'That's because you feel something for me, it's not just a physical act, or I hope it isn't.'

'No, it's a lot more than a physical act. It has feeling, emotion. It feels so good.'

They both fell silent, thinking.

'Lois, did you sleep with Mickie?'

Lois paused before she answered, she couldn't decide whether he could take all this honesty, but if she lied, she didn't think he would believe her anyway. She told him yes.

'How was it?'

'David!'

'No, okay, sorry, don't tell me. I'm sorry.'

'You can't do this, it's not fair.'

'I know. I'm sorry. It was just a bit of a shock.'

Lois thought of Mickie and wondered what he would feel, if he knew where she was.

Desire for David drove Mickie from her thoughts. Her experience with David was a joyous one. Perhaps all she had needed was a holiday romance to clarify her feelings for all three of the men in her life.

15

After Sly: Slugs

ON THEIR RETURN TO CHESTER, David went home for a few days, to make the transition from paradise to normal life. He and his father bickered every night, until finally, David cut his losses, stuffed some clothes into a carrier bag, and drove himself back to his true home, at 102 Houle Road.

Lois's mother made him very welcome and set out to spoil him with his favourite food. With Lois, he was wary. He had said that the holiday romance idea would work, and now he must make it work. On Friday, when Lois was to return to Aberystwyth with Gerry, he could get back to normal and find himself a floosie for the weekend. He wasn't sure that he could be bothered.

Lois and Gerry were going to Aber to see Mickie's exhibition. When Lois telephoned his home in Liverpool, Pauline answered and sounded unfriendly. Mickie came to the telephone and said that his father was home, apparently getting along well. Mickie also had his exam results; he couldn't wait to tell her, 'I hate to brag, but you are now speaking to Mickie Marshall B.A., First Class with Honours. Just bow a little!'

His exhibition opened in the Arts Centre on the following Monday, and he was thrilled that she would be there. It was also the end of the summer production, so there would be a party to attend. Mickie said he would not be in Aber when she arrived, as he had an appointment with his tutor, and he couldn't back out of it.

She and Gerry were going to stay at Huw-the-hairdresser's, so it didn't matter if Mickie wasn't there. He thought he might be able to come to Chester and see her, later in the summer, and that was a bonus.

Lois met Gerry, on Friday morning, at ten thirty, in Shrewsbury, intending to hitch lifts to Aberystwyth, as both girls were short of cash. Neither David nor her mother knew about this. Lucky with lifts, they took three and a half hours to complete their journey, and arrived at Huw's salon when he was on a coffee break. He told them that he was going back to London before much longer. The girls were horrified but he was adamant. With plenty of students around, life had been stimulating, but when they had all gone down at the end of the summer term, it had grown too quiet. They could come and see him, he promised, and it would all be fine. He had bought them tickets for 'The Little Mermaid', anticipating that they would want to see Sly being a mollusc.

Malc arrived at the salon, with Julia in tow. Huw was working until five-thirty, so they left their bags with him and went to buy an ice cream to eat on the beach. Gerry told Lois that Luke had finished with her. Lois tried to cheer her up and said she hoped that the split would be amicable, that they would still be friends, because they were sharing a house next year, and it could be difficult.

'I fucking hate him,' Gerry yelled.

Lois had never seen her friend so malicious; she was usually laid back about her love life, never getting too involved with anyone. Lois realised that she had underestimated the strength of Gerry's feelings.

Back at the salon, Huw thought that the girls might have had an argument, judging from the expression on Gerry's face. Lois told him about Luke, and Huw rushed to Gerry's defence. 'How come that bastard finished with you? What happened?'

Gerry hated being centre of attention, and all this sympathy made her feel worse. She decided to joke about it. 'I trod on one of his Joy Division records and he said he never wanted to see me again.' They all laughed.

Keith, Huw's current friend, turned out to be far too nice for Huw, who would walk all over him. Keith had studied History and Theology, and had stayed on to do his M.A. He cooked them a lovely meal, and afterwards, they went to the Theatre, which was crowded, mostly with parents and young children, eager to see the show. She had met Sly here, nine months earlier, but she wouldn't have recognised it, it seemed totally transformed.

The production was brilliant, very lively. Lois thought that Josh Myerson was excellent as The Shark, Finlay acted the Prince superbly, even if he was typecast, and Elin Jones, as The Sea Witch, probably stole the show. Soon, she was completely enthralled, and when Sly finally appeared in a gang of sea creatures, it came as a shock. He spotted her immediately, and his face lit up with a smile. Then, it was over, and when the cast came back on stage to take their bows, Sly waved to her and she waved back. It was a good start.

They had just left the Theatre to go and join Keith at the Belle Vue, when Sly caught up with them. He called her name and ran down the theatre steps, still wiping off his stage make-up, and waving his denim jacket.

'Hey, wait for the minstrel by 'ere.'

'Sly, that was wonderful. I really enjoyed your interpretation of your part. Very French, very Hunchback of Notre Dame,' Gerry exclaimed.

Sly was smiling. 'That was for your benefit, I thought it might brighten up the proceedings, but I've just been bollocked by Bedford for arsing around. Pretentious twat!'

He asked them if it was okay if he tagged along with them to the Belle Vue. Huw and Gerry fell into step, leaving Lois walking with Sly. This was the first time they had walked together since they had split, and Lois couldn't decide what to do with her hands, having no pockets in which to put them. They chatted about this and that, and he casually asked where Mickie was.

'He's had to go to Birmingham, something to do with his M.A. He'll be back on Monday, for his exhibition.'

Malc and Julia, Keith and Huw and the usual crowd were at the Belle Vue, all delighted to see Lois back amongst them again. Some of the other drama students came in and spoke to Lois, but Sly made no attempt to join them; he told Lois he was getting rather bored with the 'darling' routine by now. Everyone was chatting together, and as she was sitting next to Sly, they fell into conversation. It all felt very natural. Malc was just telling everyone that Sly's new health regime was driving him mad, and he was getting to be a bore, when Evan came over, looked at Sly and said,

'I never knew that you were a friend of Huw's. Next time you come in, I'll give you plenty.'

Sly went red with embarrassment, until Evan explained, 'I work at the Dolphin, the fish and chip shop; he's one of our best customers.'

'I have pass it on my way to the Theatre and it's hard to resist the smell.'

When the barman called time, Malc said he didn't fancy going to the Pier; they wouldn't play Japan, no matter how many times he asked. Huw was going back with Keith, who gave Gerry a door-key, so they could get in when they got back. Sly, Lois and Gerry were in the mood for some bopping. Gerry was already rather drunk. Sly put his arm around both the girls.

'The night is young, I have two lovely ladies for company and I need to dance. I've been watching too much 'Fame'!' Lois couldn't imagine Sly watching that. He wanted to update them on the new features at the newly refurbished Pier, and Lois asked how he knew so much about it.

'I came here with Mickie. We had a laugh. It's a proper eternal triangle we are having.' He chuckled, and Lois wondered why.

They left when the smoochy records began, even though Lord John started with a favourite of Lois's. Sly bought them beefburgers and chips, which they sat on a bench on the promenade to eat. They linked arms and walked back home, although Gerry was very much the worse for wear. They made tea in Huw's kitchen, and Gerry said she felt awful and wanted to go up to bed. Lois believed her, knowing Gerry wouldn't leave her alone with Sly otherwise. Lois wanted Gerry to talk about Luke because the problem with him was more far-reaching than Lois had suspected.

Sly drank his tea. He and Lois had drunk sparingly during the evening, each needing a clear head. They sat in the kitchen, speaking softly, until Sly felt it was time to make a move because he had two performances on Saturday. He stood to leave and she followed him. He bent to kiss her and she offered him her cheek.

'Playing hard to get, are we? Anyway, thank you for this evening. I've had a really good time.' He smiled.

'So have I. It's been lovely.'

When they parted, she was pleased that he hadn't demanded or expected anything more.

★　★　★

Sly slept very well indeed and was up with the crack of sparrows. By the time Malc surfaced, he was showered, dressed and had done the shopping. They eventually headed for the beach, to have some fun on this their last Saturday in Aber for some time to come. Sly spotted Lois and Gerry walking along the promenade, looking for him. He ran towards them, waving like mad. Gerry felt terribly hungover and went to buy a fizzy drink from the prom shop, to settle her stomach. Sly was thrilled to see Lois walking towards him, remembering how dreadful he had felt in March, when she was fooling around with Mickie and David on the beach.

She laid out her beach towel, and stripped down to her minute bikini, which displayed her tan to perfection. Sly could hardly bear to look at her. She joined in a game of football with him, Malc, and Finlay, seemingly unaware of the affect she was having on him and Finlay. Malc was oblivious to her charms. They bought ice creams, once they were weary of football. Then she and Sly ran down to the sea, intending to swim to the offshore buoys. Gerry returned and soon drifted off to sleep. Gina and Ali arrived and put their towels close to Gerry. Gina spotted Sly and Lois in the waves, splashing each other, behaving like children.

Gerry woke up and Gina asked her what was going on with Sly and Lois. Gerry was non-committal, said she thought Lois and Sly were just friends, and Gina said that Sly used to hate Lois, but Gerry wouldn't be drawn any further. After a while, Lois and Sly came running up from the sea, sat down and began to dry themselves. Sly asked Gerry if she wanted to help him fly his kite. Gerry failed to understand him and looked puzzled. He repeated himself, deliberately affecting a strong Welsh accent. Gerry fell about laughing, and Gina shook her head. Sly was usually the quiet one of the group; today, he seemed to be full of energy, trying to impress Lois.

They ate lunch together before Sly went off to prepare for the two o'clock matinee. The evening performance would start at seven-thirty. Sly held Lois's arms as he said goodbye. 'Thanks for this morning. Sorry I can't stay any longer. I'll see you tonight? I can't wait.'

He kissed her cheek and, just to normalise the situation, he kissed Gerry as well. The girls went back to the beach to wait for Mickie who was due anytime now.

16

After Sly: After Slugs

SLY LEFT THE THEATRE immediately after the evening performance, ignoring Dickie's invitation to come and have a drink with
the cast. Gina stayed just long enough to make her presence felt
and then went to look for him. He wasn't in the Belle Vue, and
she assumed that he had gone straight back to his room. Many of
the drama students were here, waiting for the party to start, and to
escape from Dickie.

Gina knew that she was about to break his heart. He was
dressing ready for the party, when she found him.

'You look nice,' she said, studying him carefully.

'Do you want a drink?'

'We've made enough punch to last the whole evening; Finlay
was pouring more vodka in it when I came in.'

'It'll be fine, don't worry. Have a glass of wine.' He opened a
bottle and poured out two generous portions into mugs. He smiled
at her and said, '*Iechyd da*, here's to a fabulous evening.'

'Sly.' She hesitated, bit her lip, then dived in. 'I've just seen
Lois in the Belle Vue.'

'Oh, yeah.' Sly was puzzled. 'What's up?'

'She was with Mickie Marshall.'

'Shit!' He was stunned.

'Didn't you know he was coming back today?'

'No.' He should have guessed that Mickie would come down
for the party. He'd done most of the set design. Sly sighed heavily.

'I should have realized. Did you know?' he asked, feeling incredibly stupid.

'Yes, Gerry told me today.'

'You should have told me.'

'When? You've been so busy looking after Lois, and performing.' She was defensive.

'Yeah, I know. It's my own fault. I just thought that tonight would be the night. I'd sort of banked on it.'

'Oh, Sly, why do you have to play such a complicated game? Why can't you fall for someone else?' Gina was becoming annoyed.

'Well, you never know, perhaps she'll be overwhelmed by my expensive after-shave.'

Gina looked sympathetically at him, not knowing what to say. Speculation had been rife all day, particularly after last night, and Sly, with Lois around, seemed like a new person. Soon, a number of people knew that Mickie was back, yet Gina was the only one with the balls to tell Sly.

The sound of loud music and laughter drifted upstairs. The party was starting.

'You'd better go down and check that punch. I'll be down in a minute.' Sly poured more wine into his mug.

'Oh, no, you don't. I'm not having you festering in your pit all night, drowning your sorrows. This is our last night party; there are people downstairs who won't be here next year, and you'll come down with me and have a good time.'

Sly obediently followed her downstairs. 'Well, one of those who won't be here next year is Mickie,' he said.

Gina didn't dare tell him of the rumour that he'd passed up his place at Birmingham for another year in Aber.

They found the party well under way, some people dancing, some sitting around, and some heading straight for the kitchen. There was already a crowd there, and more to come; it had all the makings of a very good party. The first person Sly saw was Mickie, who was talking to Finlay, but he had his arm around Lois's shoulder. He looked so relaxed and easy. Sly envied his effortless way with people, his ability to make friends easily. Mickie was one of the most likable people Sly had ever met, and he had Lois.

Sly had already detected one or two raised eyebrows in his direction, and he chose to go over straight away and say 'Hi', before he lost his nerve. He tried to sound relaxed and happy and it sounded convincing, even to his own ears.

'All right, mate, how'd it go?' Mickie asked.

'Fine. I can't believe it's over and that I go home tomorrow.'

'Would you like to try this punch Finlay made?'

Lois looked wonderful. Sly ached with longing to touch her again.

'Yeah, but go easy on it. I hear it's wicked,' Sly said, surprising himself.

Lois moved away and left the two of them alone. Sly couldn't help a smile.

'What are you doing here, Mickie?'

'You invited me, remember?'

'Yeah, but I thought you'd be away until Monday,' Sly muttered.

'What, and leave Lois for you? You scally.' Mickie laughed.

'That is what I thought you'd done.' Sly was sulky now.

'You must be joking. I'm not stupid, you know. Pauline says there's been talk about you and Lois getting back together.'

'Oh yeah?' Sly said, even though it was an empty victory now. 'Yeah.'

'What does Pauline think of that, then?' Sly was interested.

'I'd reckon she'd be pretty pleased, don't you?'

'Probably. What about you?'

'I think it'll happen if you play your cards right, but not tonight, not with me here. I'm not conceding defeat; it's still my time.'

'Thanks for nothing.'

'Listen, mate,' Mickie said seriously, 'this is probably my last night with Lois until you screw up next time, and I'm making the most of it.' Mickie was almost admitting how scared he was of Sly's hold over Lois.

Sly shook his head. 'I won't screw up again.'

'That remains to be seen. Even if I will be in Birmingham, this isn't over yet.'

They both looked over to where Lois was worming her way through the dancers, balancing three drinks in her hands.

'You lucky bastard,' Sly murmured.

Mickie took his drink, put his arm back around her shoulder and smiled at Sly. Sly left the two of them alone. He needed someone else to talk to, and something else to drink. Getting drunk was one solution to the problem of how to survive this evening without making a complete fool of himself. It was a struggle to find any one else who was unattached. Even Malc was chatting up one of the town girls, who looked about fifteen years old. Sly spoke to Finlay and Lynne, and tried to calm Gina, who was diluting the punch, which did appear to consist almost entirely of neat vodka. Lois and Mickie were sitting down, talking and laughing.

He almost tripped over Pauline, who was sitting by the wall, legs curled up underneath her. She looked completely serene, her face calm and untroubled, but her eyes were riveted on Mickie.

'Hi, Sly, how are you? Long time no see,' Pauline said, and added, 'I remember watching Lois at the pier, when this record was playing. She was sitting on a table, swinging her legs, looking at all the people dancing and singing along to this record. It was just after you finished with her. She looked so unhappy. Why did you do that?'

Sly shook his head. They both watched now, Sly couldn't quite capture any of his thoughts, and Pauline seemed enveloped in her own.

'Until then, I thought it would be all right. I know he'd been besotted, but I still thought he'd get over it, until you threw them together that night,' Pauline said sadly.

Sly couldn't bear to watch Lois and Mickie any longer, and he wondered why Pauline was torturing herself in this way. She was very drunk and yet she was very beautiful, even more so than Lois, in some ways.

'He won't look at me now. When he talks to me, he pretends he's very busy; he looks everywhere but at me. Why is that, Sly?'

'I'm sorry, Pauline. I never meant all this to happen, believe me. It was just a crazy mistake. I hurt too.'

'Perhaps we should close the circle completely, Sly?'

He failed to follow her line of thought. She touched his arm and looked deep into his eyes. She had beautiful, blue eyes.

'What do you mean?'

'I mean us. How would they feel if we completed the swap, went to bed together?'

Sly was shocked, in spite of being very drunk himself. Mickie and Lois had left their seats and were walking towards the door.

'I don't think they'd notice if we made out, right here on the floor,' he said, while wondering where they were going.

'Want to try?'

'I think I'll wait until Mickie's in Birmingham and have another try with Lois.'

Pauline sighed, 'Yes, you're probably right. I'll have to wait, too. Good, old, faithful Pauline is just waiting for Mickie, same as usual.'

Sly found Pauline too maudlin; he needed cheering up, not dragging down. He got the feeling everyone was full of sympathy for him. He wished Mickie would give Lois back. They all knew she belonged to him, so why was she making him pay so dearly for one piddling mistake. He went out into the hallway, where Gerry was sitting alone on the stairs. She looked very pissed off.

'Sorry about Luke, Gerry.'

Gerry blinked hard, as if trying to place him. She smiled. 'Sorry about Lois, Sly.'

'Great party.'

'Fantastic.' They sounded as though they might be at a funeral.

'Where's Lois?' he asked, after a long pause.

'She went outside with Mickie, to discuss Birmingham.'

'What does Lois know about Birmingham?'

'What does Lois know about anything?' Gerry sounded very bitter and it surprised Sly. They were always together; he couldn't believe Gerry was angry.

'Are you pissed?'

'Yes, and I intend to get pissed some more. Are you pissed, too?' She slurred her words.

'Yeah, I guess I am.'

'Best thing. If in doubt, get pissed. Why don't you beat him up, or something?'

'I don't want to. I like Mickie, he's my mentor.'

'Well, you should just punch him, or Lois. They've ruined everything.' Gerry produced a bottle of vodka from her handbag. 'It doesn't taste; have some in your punch.' She filled up his tumbler and they clinked glasses.

'What did you mean about Mickie and Lois ruining everything?'

'Oh, it doesn't matter. Well, yes, in a way it does. Luke finished with me because Lois started to see Mickie. He knew it wasn't going to work.'

Sly wondered why Gerry was talking in riddles.

'What wouldn't work?'

Gerry sighed and then explained very slowly and carefully, as though she were talking to a child. 'Luke only went out with me to make Lois jealous. When she started to see Mickie, he realized he had failed. I know, because he told me when he finished with me.'

'Nice guy,' Sly said.

'Sure is.' Gerry drained her glass. 'So now, there's you and Lois, all spoilt, over Luke; Pauline and Mickie, all spoilt over Lois and Mickie; and me and Luke, all spoilt over…whoever. All spoilt.' She shook her head sadly. 'Poor Sly.' She patted his hand. 'Poor old Sly.'

'Poor Gerry. I never knew. I thought Luke had got over Lois.'

'People don't get over Lois. She screwed David, you know. Poor David, all he'd ever wanted given and taken away again.'

'David?' Sly's brain wouldn't work.

'Yes, you know David, blonde Adonis, David. Mr totally fucking gorgeous?'

'Yeah, I know but…'

'Didn't you know? Sorry if you didn't. I shouldn't have told you. It's a secret.' Gerry pulled a face and giggled.

'I bet.' Sly wondered if Mickie knew about this extra complication. Maybe Gerry was just drunk.

'Don't worry, you'll get her back, you eat away at her, she's crazy about you. Can't help it. You have a hold over her.'

Now, this was more like it; he could listen to this all night. 'Really?' He was eager to hear more.

'Sure, Sly. She says you make her go weak; even last night, she was pleased about seeing you. She's obsessed with you.'

Gerry leaned closer towards him and he bent forward to hear the next revelation.

'She says you're brilliant in bed, too.' Gerry giggled again.

'She told you that? When?' He loved this; it was exactly what he needed to hear.

'Oh, sometime when we were talking. She doesn't usually tell me things like that, but I know she's crazy about you, you'll get her back and it will be just like before. Poor me. No Lois, no Luke.' She looked crestfallen

'We can share her,' Sly decided. 'You can have her during the day; I'll have her at night.'

'It's a deal.'

★ ★ ★

Malc had avoided girls recently; tonight, he was in the mood to tap off with someone, young Mandy was evidently receptive, and he was just about to get her outside via the back door, when Finlay found him and said he really ought to find out how bad Sly was. Malc gave Mandy strict instructions not to move. In the hallway, they saw Sly slumped against Lynne's shoulder, while she tried to hold him up. He was muttering to himself and his eyes were glazed. One or two concerned people gathered round, and Malc suddenly felt very impatient.

'Oh, fucking hell, Finlay, how'd he get in this state?'

'I saw Gerry giving him neat vodka earlier on,' Lynne said, pushing Sly upright again and struggling to hold him. Sly was practically unconscious.

'Where is Gerry?' Finlay asked.

'I think she's in here,' someone standing outside the downstairs bathroom called. Malc banged on the bathroom door. Gerry was inside, vomiting noisily. Her legs seemed to have abandoned her. She leant her head on the rim of the toilet and closed her eyes, hoping to stop the room spinning. It made it worse. She was sick once more. She splashed some cold water on her face. Malc banged again on the door, and it took some time before she could summon up the courage, or the energy, to open it.

While Malc sorted out the casualties of the night, someone went to try to find Lois and Mickie.

Mickie had been anxious to get Lois on her own, ever since he had arrived in Aberystwyth that afternoon. Of course, Mickie hadn't wanted to be away from Aber, just as Lois arrived. He anticipated that Sly would jump on any opportunity, in his absence, but he hadn't reckoned on the immense speculation that would greet his own return to the fray. Mickie went to see Lois, after his initial encounter with Pauline. Pauline told him all the gory details, when he had called in to pick up a change of clothes for the evening. He'd rather hoped that she would be going out somewhere else, but it seemed as though she had stayed in on purpose to report.

Pauline turned up at the party, no doubt invited by Lynne, and Mickie saw her watching him and Lois like a hawk. When Pauline started to talk to Sly, Mickie took Lois outside, to get some fresh air. It was becoming noisier, hotter and smokier indoors, and many people were the worse for drink. There were many raw emotions brought on by the potential parting of the ways that would come tomorrow. Thank God, Sly would be gone then. As they stepped outside, the quietness contrasted suddenly with the scene they had just left.

It was well after midnight, the pier had already discharged its revellers because of the strict Sunday drinking laws. The lights along the promenade were dim, the water was calm and inky black. They sat in one of the shelters and looked out over the darkness. Whatever happened in the next few months, Mickie banked on this evening to set the scene for their future together. He knew he had to find something monumental to say, he had even toyed with the idea of coming right out and telling her how ardently he loved her, but she wasn't ready, and he was a coward when it came to that. He wondered why he'd been so brave earlier.

Pauline had told him that Lois and Sly were back together, but he hadn't believed it. He had gone to see Huw, found out from him where she was, and had walked in, knowing that she would be pleased to see him, and he had been right. He couldn't have asked for a better greeting, and it had buoyed him up. He had felt brilliant all night, until this moment. They had said nothing since they stepped outside. Lois nestled against him, her head on his shoulder. It felt marvellous just having her there with him. How would he cope without her?

He began to tell her about what had happened when he was in Birmingham, what his prospects would be if he went there instead of staying on in Aberystwyth.

'Lois, I can't stay here. I could do my MA here, but it's not viable.'

She was only just within reach of him, trying to read his expression.

Mickie continued, 'I can't stay, for two main reasons. Firstly, I'm scared that if I stay, I'll end up like John, tied to the place for no particular reason, unable to make the move. I should go to London, but I can't quite face it. Liverpool's my city and I don't like the idea that London is the place to be, although I'll have to accept it, one day. Birmingham is a compromise. It will give me all the opportunities I need. It's exactly right, my tutor's ace, I'd be doing the right course, and now there's the job. It's all working out really well. Secondly, I'm afraid to change things because I think you and Sly have some stuff to work out yet.'

Lois stood up suddenly and faced him. 'Don't say that. Everyone thinks that we will get back together again, but I'm with you, and I don't want you to go.'

Lois knew she wouldn't stop him going, even if she could. He had to move on.

'I think you know it, too, Lois, if you're completely honest. There's still something unresolved between you and Sly, and I'm not part of that.

'Please don't say that. Don't make it real.' She was standing just in front of him, he wanted to reach out to her, but he had to make her understand this.

'Words don't make things real. This is real, whether I say it or not; it's still there, whether we speak about it, or just pretend this is an ordinary situation. We both know it isn't ordinary, that it could all come to pieces, for a million different reasons. What I say means nothing. It's what we feel and think that matters. Words are just deceivers.'

Lois tried to make sense of his words.

'Listen. I'm here now. We have each other for now. You think in the short term, you think about next year, I've got my mind on something else.'

This was the moment, even though there was a physical space between them; he could feel the moment on his fingertips, it was real, a presence. She moved her head, her face pressed against his fingers. He felt the electricity of the touch, which had captured the very essence that words could not convey. She might never understand the moment, but she wouldn't forget it, and that was the crucial point. This was his monumental moment; he had created it, and they had both felt it. It would have to be enough.

'Come on, give us a kiss.'

She asked, 'Is that how you Scousers treat your women? "Come on, then, give us a kiss".'

'Actions speak louder than words.' His instinct told him that the business with Sly would burn itself out, but it was a hell of a risk to take. He took her in his arms and kissed her.

Malc and Mandy were similarly engaged, also in a shelter on the promenade, close to Lois and Mickie. Malc heard Mickie's voice and came over to them.

'Hey, you two, I've been looking for you everywhere. Gerry's in an awful state, pissed out of her head, up in Julia's room. Gina's with her. I think you should go and look after her.'

Lois smiled back at him grimly. 'Thanks a lot, Malc.'

Malc, his duty done, turned his attention back to the lovely Mandy.

Mickie took Lois back to Gina's room. They met her coming downstairs, and Lois thanked her for taking care of Gerry.

'No problem. Did Malc tell you that Sly's in an equally bad state? He's in room 21, and he's asking for you, too. If you're interested, Pauline's mouthing off about you to anyone who'll listen. Sorry.'

Mickie and Lois exchanged looks of despair.

'Come on, let's deal with the easy one first.'

They found Gerry, good-humoured, lying fully clothed on top of the bed. Lois helped her to undress, found her a glass of water, and Mickie managed to open the window to let in some fresh air. Finlay looked in. He was suffering from a massive guilt trip, after doctoring the punch. He had been getting an ear bashing about it all night, from Lynne and Gina. Finlay and Lynne had been with Sly for about an hour and the Good Samaritan act was wearing thin. Lynne had sent Finlay down to find Lois.

'Sly's upstairs, very drunk.'

'We know,' said Mickie impatiently.

'He wants to talk to you, Lois. He's in a hell of a state and threatening to come downstairs if you don't go up.'

Lois followed Finlay upstairs to find Sly. He showed her where Sly's room was. When Lynne saw Lois, she said she was going back to the party, to make sure she was missing nothing of the fun. The room was very dark. Sly was lying in bed, covered by a sheet. He clutched to his chest a tape and a letter. He appeared to be asleep.

'Lois, is that you?'

'Yes, it's me.'

'Would you put this tape on for me?'

She took the tape and put it into his tape deck. Sly closed his eyes and they listened to the music in silence. Then, Sly said, 'I'm drunk. I've made a real fool of myself, haven't I?'

'Not really.' She sounded very cool, but sitting this close reminded her of so many times that had gone before, and she was glad he had his eyes closed.

'I couldn't bear to see you with Mickie. I couldn't cope, so I got drunk.'

'You could have just enjoyed yourself,' she said.

'I can't enjoy myself without you. I need you.'

'Oh, Sly!'

Words like this cut her to the core. Stirred to pity, she reached out towards him and grasped his hand. He held it to his chest, and the letter, addressed to her, fell onto the duvet. 'What's this?' she asked, holding it out to him.

'It's the letter I wrote, the one you asked for. I wanted to give it to you tonight. It explains some things better than I have yet been able to. Don't read it until you get home. On the first morning, read it sitting up in bed. That's how I've imagined you reading it, when I was writing it.'

She put the letter in the pocket of her dress.

'Where's Mickie?' Sly asked.

'Downstairs, looking after Gerry.'

'What will happen to you two?'

'I don't know. Nothing, probably. He'll be in Birmingham next year.'

'Come back to me, then?'

'Maybe, I will.'

'I love you,' he said simply.

'Perhaps, but I've never felt that you liked me much.' She spoke very calmly.

'I don't suppose this has helped.'

'It hasn't hindered it either; it's just one of those things. Listen, Sly, I must get back to Mickie, and see how Gerry is.'

'I can sleep, now you've got the letter. You will read it, like I said.'

'Yes.'

'I love you, Lois.'

His words sounded empty, possibly because he was drunk. Quietly, she left the room and padded downstairs. Gerry was snoring and Mickie was gone.

★ ★ ★

It was nearly two in the morning, the punch had taken its toll, and the majority of revellers had departed. Julia was crying in the corner; she looked a mess, Gina was comforting her. Neither Mickie nor Pauline was to be seen. Lois poured a small amount of punch into a cup and topped it up with orange juice. Finlay came in, put some slices of bread in the toaster, and asked if she wanted some toast.

'Do you know where Mickie is?'

'I'm not sure, Lois. I think he took Pauline home. She was drunk. She thought you were upstairs with Sly.'

'I was.'

'Yes, I know. Don't worry, I'm sure he'll come back.'

Lois tried to remember how Mickie had reacted when she left him to go and see Sly. He'd been pretty cool about it, but she had no idea what he was thinking. Finlay changed the subject. He couldn't tell her anything more about the row between Pauline and Mickie, but he distracted her for a while with theatre gossip. It was late and Lois was exhausted. She needed to ask Gina where she was to sleep that night, but Gina was still caring for Julia.

Just at the right moment, Mickie returned and came straight over, smiling. Lynne followed him. Mickie sat down next to Lois and Lynne took Finlay away.

'How's Pauline?'

'Same as ever. How's Sly?'

'Asleep, and so is Gerry, so that's all the problems sorted out.'

'Not quite,' said Gina. 'I hate to ask you, but could you help me get Julia upstairs? I can't do alone.'

Mickie got wearily to his feet and grumbled, 'Jesus, I'm going to start charging for this. Who made that punch?'

Between them, they got Julia upstairs, put her in the bed next to Gerry's, and went back downstairs. They finished off the punch, well diluted with soft drinks.

'Do you mind if I join you for a while?' Gina asked, flopping down beside them. 'You two will have to sleep down here, if you're going to stay. God, what a party! Malc disappeared with that schoolgirl, and poor Julia's got such a thing for him.'

'I thought this party would be good fun; everyone got on so well during the production, like one big happy family, then, pow! It's been a real disaster. Sly, Gerry, Malc, Julia, Pauline, Mickie.'

'I'm not responsible for Malc and Julia.' Lois defended herself quickly.

'I didn't mean it like that. Gerry was lethal. She gave Sly neat vodka, and was bad-mouthing everyone. Have she and Luke split up?'

Lois nodded.

'I wonder why,' Gina said reflectively.

Lois didn't know, but she would find out at the earliest opportunity. When Lois finally curled up in Mickie's arms, she was shattered. They slept soundly, until Mickie woke up, early next morning. There were people moving around upstairs, and soon they would come in and want to make tea and breakfast.

'Come on, we're going for a walk.'

Lois peered at him, her eyes heavy, and a headache starting. She longed for more sleep, and closed her eyes again.

'Come on, you can sleep this afternoon, before Huw's do. It's a beautiful morning; let's go and look at it.'

She dressed and downed a glass of orange juice, before they set out to walk along Tanybwlch. It was very quiet, nobody was about yet, but chip papers and litter stirred in the breeze. The sea and beach looked sparklingly clean in comparison. The tide was ebbing and they were able to reach a secluded cove, where they made love on the sand.

By the time Mickie and Lois had completely indulged themselves and returned to Aber Glasney, it was mid morning, and the place was bustling with people, some feverishly packing, others eating toast and swallowing pain-killers, to cure their hangovers. Gerry seemed none the worse, having slept well, been heartily sick and drunk plenty of cold water. Malc turned up, having been kicked out of the house by his youthful companion's furious father. Mandy was asleep in bed, he added, while he slept on the sofa, just in case anyone was in any doubt.

Sly slunk downstairs, looking very much the worse for wear. He could hardly bring himself to look at Lois, who made him endless cups of tea and acted as though nothing extraordinary had occurred.

Sly and Malc had to finish packing, and Mickie and the girls went up to say their farewells. Lois hugged Malc and then Sly, who kissed her on the cheek, watched by Mickie. There were too many people around to say anything significant, so Sly just looked at her. Mickie took her hand as she left the room, and Sly wanted to die. He tortured himself a little more, by watching them walk slowly down the promenade until they were out of sight.

Mickie was up with the lark again, to check that all was ready for the exhibition of his work. Lois was getting worried about leaving him for a long time. She felt cocooned in his love, and secure. She didn't want to go back to being on her own in Chester, and she hoped that Mickie would come and see her. She drifted back to sleep, thinking of him.

Lois and Gerry arrived at the Arts Centre shortly after eleven o'clock, to view the exhibition. The place was packed, Mickie was busy, and everyone wanted to talk to him, or take his photograph. He was not enjoying all this attention. Lois and Gerry wandered round and studied his work. Usually, in an Art Gallery, Lois would move through quickly, looking for something to attract her attention, then observe it carefully and try to work out what was special. All of Mickie's work interested her. He had a preoccupation with boats, there were many that she recognized to be from Greece, and she liked those. Her favourite exhibit here was a collage, very intricately assembled to form the face of a woman. He joined her as she was scrutinizing the piece.

'It's my mam. I wanted to show how complex human life is, all the tiny pieces of information you need to have in order to get any sense of a person. I just started producing these tiny things that make up me mam. I did it over a long period, and then, I put them together and worked them into her face. I've only just finished it.'

They stood looking at it. He draped his arm around her shoulder, pleased with her choice.

'Has she seen it?' Lois asked, thinking of how beautiful it was, and how his mother's heart would burst with pride, love, and admiration for her eldest son.

'No. I never told her about it, in case it didn't work. I'll give it to her when I go home.'

Gerry preferred a huge nude, done with acrylic paint, in oranges and pinks, very garish. Mickie laughed, when she told him.

'Oh, God, that's horrible. I'm embarrassed with it. I only did it for a laugh. I was having an argument with John and he dared me to submit it. It only took about an hour to complete, but the tutors like it, they think it's modern art, and it's a joke!'

The three of them laughed helplessly. Lois would have avoided the photographs of herself and Sly; which bought back too many painful memories, but Mickie made her come and look. She had forgotten how good they were. Eventually, Mickie had enough of being centre of attention, and they left. Most people there were busy congratulating themselves for helping the genius.

They met Huw and Keith for lunch and the girls talked about hitchhiking home. Mickie walked with them to Llanbadarn Road, where they hoped to obtain their first lift. After a lengthy wait, a lady stopped, said she was going to Welshpool and wanted some company, which was ideal. Mickie stood waving at the car until it disappeared; he felt totally devastated.

In Welshpool, they had a pub lunch of scampi and chips, during which, Lois took the opportunity to ask Gerry about Luke. Gerry was reluctant to bare her soul at first, but Lois was insistent.

'Luke said,' she growled, 'he had the fucking cheek to say, that he'd only ever gone out with me to try and make you jealous.'

Lois was horrified, but before she could say a word, Gerry went on, 'I think he quite enjoyed making me suffer, too.'

Lois put her arm round Gerry's shoulder. 'I thought he was a nice guy, Gerry. I'm so sorry.'

'He said that, once you'd started to see Mickie, when he knew it wasn't going to work out for him, and he didn't want to carry on using me. I was only ever nice to him.'

Lois hugged her again. 'Well, I think he's a complete shit, and he can't dance,' she said firmly.

Gerry laughed and said, 'There you go. We can't have Boogey going out with someone who can't dance, can we?'

Gerry seemed to have cheered up. She wondered why she hadn't told Lois earlier, because it had helped her to talk about it. Lois was learning about girlfriends at last.

17

After Sly: the Owen Thing

BACK IN CHESTER AGAIN, Lois's routine quickly re-established itself. She had a temporary job, working four hours a day at La Garda, either morning or afternoons, and she and David swiftly adjusted to their Chester way of life, after La Rochelle. Perhaps the holiday romance scenario had really worked for them, or maybe, because they had enjoyed a Platonic relationship so often in Chester, it was easy. The tensions that had been present in France were gone. They continued to visit the Grot on Thursdays, and Chico's on Saturdays, David behaved outrageously, and all seemed to be back to normal.

Then, something happened which tested their friendship to its limit, and it began one Saturday night, when David was virtually ordered to attend his father's sixtieth birthday dinner at The Butcher's Arms. Lois was disappointed not to be able to go to Chico's, but her sister, Ronnie, said she would like a night away from domestic bliss with Bryan, and they arranged to meet in the Bacchus wine bar and have a girlie night out.

Lois arrived at seven o'clock and ordered a white wine spritzer. Theo, the bar man, talked to her between serving customers, and, by seven-thirty, when Ronnie had still not turned up, she became agitated. The plan had been to have something to eat and then go to Crispin's, a gay club that David totally refused to visit, even though they played brilliant music.

'I have enough trouble fending off all the women who want to shag the living daylights out of me, without starting a queue of fucking benders as well,' he had said.

When the bar telephone rang, it was Ronnie calling, weeping and almost incomprehensible. She and Bryan had had a row, she said, Bryan had left the house in a fury, and she had to go and find him. Lois said that, in that case, she might as well go home, watch television, and drink some wine. Theo wanted her to stay, and gave her a free drink. He finished work at eleven, he said, and he would like nothing better than to take her to Crispin's, because he had overheard her conversation, and he had the capacity to dream, just like we all have. Theo was busy, and the place was filling up by eight o'clock. She was on her third white wine spritzer, when the lads arrived, out to party. They were amazed to find her on her own.

'Where's David? How come you are here all on your own?'

They bought their drinks and formed a laddish circle, so that they could all join in the banter and have a good chat. They were very excited tonight, and Lois decided that she would rather go home, instead of waiting for Theo. She had just picked up her bag, when one of the lads, Owen, left the others and came to join her at the bar.

'You're not leaving, are you? Where is David ? He'd never let you come out on your own, if he knew we were around. Let me get you another drink. I'll look after you.'

She asked for lemonade and lime. The only thing she knew about these lads, whom she had met through David, was who liked to dance to which records. Owen loved new romantic: Alex, Kid Creole and the Coconuts, and anything funky; Will the Clash and rock in general. She had never had a proper conversation with any of them. Owen seemed determined to give her a nice time, and Theo watched from a distance.

'I'm starving,' Owen said. 'Would you like to go and have

something to eat?'

It was nearly nine o'clock, and she was hungry, so they left the wine bar and walked down to Narni's restaurant, where she chose seafood tagliatelli, and Owen had a pizza. While they ate, she told him about Crispin's and said how much David hated going there. Owen seemed desperate to take her. 'I love Crispin's. They play everything I like there. I don't have to sit out a single thing. Please, let's go, it will be fabulous.'

Lois needed little persuasion. Owen was an enthusiast and could think of nothing better than a night on the town with David's Lois. They went and had a fabulous time. Owen was a good dancer and they hardly sat down all night.

Owen had gone to fetch them each a drink and was coming back, when she noticed David's brother, Rich, approaching, which meant that David was here as well. David came over, and arrived while Owen had both hands occupied with the drinks. David punched him full in the face. Owen fell against the mirrored wall, and glass shattered and flew everywhere. David picked him up and hit him again. Lois watched in horror as David hit Owen for a third time. Galvanised to action, she tried to get between David's clenched fist and Owens's face, which was already streaming with blood. David slapped her hard, sending her crashing across the table.

He laid in to Owen again, and then the bouncers were there, restraining David, and Rich turned up. Lois was beside herself with fury. Her David had hit her! She struggled with the bouncer who was pulling her towards the door. There is something humiliating about being ejected from a nightclub for being involved in a fight. Two bouncers were struggling with David, and Rich was supporting Owen, who continued to bleed freely. The bouncers wanted them outside, but one was concerned enough to go back inside and telephone for an ambulance for Owen.

The moment the bouncers released him, David head-butted

Owen, sending him down once again. Lois wondered whether he would ever get up. Rich also seemed to be concerned. He bent over him and slapped his face, trying to bring him round. Lois had no idea what was going on.

David turned on her. 'You fucking bitch. What the fuck do you think you are doing? You slag.'

Seemingly satisfied that he had knocked Owen unconscious, David lit a cigarette and straightened his shirt. This seemed to calm him a little. 'Right, you are fucking going home, you, bitch. Get in the fucking car now,' he shouted.

'She touched her face where he had hit her. 'I'm not going anywhere with you. You hit me. You're mad,' she screamed.

The David she saw now was a complete stranger, a violent, abusive, implacable maniac. He continued to shout abuse at her, until Rich intervened.

'Do as he says; it'll be easier for you in the end. I'll stay with Owen. He'll be fine, honestly.'

Owen was still unconscious and bleeding heavily, but she suddenly felt defeated, and there seemed to be no alternative but to obey David. The Triumph Stag was parked near the club. David forced her into the passenger seat, climbed behind the wheel and drove away at top speed. He jumped two red lights and was doing sixty miles per hour through Chester town centre.

'Slow down, or you'll kill both of us,' she urged.

'Like I give a fuck, and you have just lost the right to tell me what to do about anything.'

He swerved to miss an on coming car. Lois was beginning to think her life was seriously in danger. When he pulled up outside her mother's house, she was shaking all over. He killed the engine, removed the ignition key and sprang round to the passenger door, opened it, pulled her out and frogmarched her up the path.

'Get in there, you fucking bitch.'

Once in the kitchen, he seemed to calm down a little. He took a bottle of brandy from her mother's cupboard, poured himself a healthy glassful, and lit a cigarette. Lois, trembling from shock, stared at him.

'So, are you going to tell me what the fuck you were doing at Crispin's with that complete bastard? You said you were going out with Ronnie, or was that just a fucking cover story.'

Lois explained about Ronnie and that all she and Owen had been doing was dancing.

'Who saw you?' David asked quickly.

'Everyone saw us.'

'I want one fucking person who can confirm that this just fucking happened, and you're not lying to me. If you are lying, you are dead, and so is Owen Fucking Burke. Both of you, dead fuckers.'

'Ask Ronnie. Ask Theo. He was working at the bar.' Lois was indignant but she was beginning to realise what jealousy was capable of doing to David. 'David, nothing happened, nothing at all. We danced; that was it.' She forced her voice to sound calm.

'Yeah, right, well, I guess you were about ten minutes away from a fucking snog. Do you really think he would have been happy to spend an evening with you with nothing more than fucking dancing? Of course he fucking wouldn't, not when he had the chance to humiliate me at his fingertips. For years I have been inflicting pain on that fucker, tonight was his chance for come-uppance, and he fucking took it. You are so fucking stupid. You, with your big brain, stupid as fuck.'

'What do you mean, you've inflicted total humiliation on him for years?' Lois moved over to stand nearer the table.

'The bloke is a monogamist. He's really doesn't like all this fucking around. It doesn't sit very nicely with his middle-class upbringing, does it? Ever since he first had a girlfriend, I've given him two weeks with her and then I've fucked her. Then, he's forced to move on, meets someone else, and off we go again.'

David flicked his ash onto the table and took another swig of brandy.

'But why, David, why would you want to do that to someone? I just don't understand.' Lois sat down opposite to him at the kitchen table. She felt cold in the face of so much hatred.

'It's because of my old man, the infernal bastard. Owen's father is his business partner; they've known each other for years, they play golf together. They have been comparing us forever, and, in their eyes, that wanker has always come out of it better than I have. He's got all the O-levels and A-levels and the fucking degree. He's an accountant, for fuck's sake. My father simply does not appreciate that I am the epitome of cool. Shit-face Owen Burke knows that I am fucking super cool and God's gift to everyone. That's why he took the chance to take you to Crispin's, you fucking idiot. Jesus, if I hadn't have got there, you would have made me, David Stachini, look the biggest fool in the whole world. How often have I told you what the lads get up to? Haven't you always said that you never wanted to get involved with them? Haven't you always despised the girls who allow themselves to be used and fucking abused? You're no better than the rest of them. You just think you are, you fucking conceited bitch.'

David lit another cigarette and poured some more brandy. He was thinking hard about something, and so was Lois. She had let David down big time, and behaved like a fool. Her naiveté surprised her yet again.

'Right, I'm off to fucking bed. I've got an early start tomorrow.'

'Why?' She was puzzled.

'Because, first thing tomorrow morning, I'm off to see Ronnie, and you'd better hope that her story is the same as yours, or I'll fucking kill you.'

Once he had gone, Lois poured herself a large brandy and thought about the events of the night. Ronnie would put him right, and Theo would tell it like it was. He would know that she had just been very stupid, but not malicious. Everything would work itself out in the morning. David had left his cigarettes and she smoked two in rapid succession.

* * *

Next morning, Lois expected to get sympathy from her mother, who had just made a pot of coffee and was sitting staring out of the kitchen window, deep in thought, when Lois came downstairs.

'I wonder that you can show your face to me.'

'Why?' Lois was astonished that her mother was angry with her.

'After that stunt you pulled on that boy last night! God, my own daughter! I have never been more ashamed of you. Never.'

She went to the sink and rinsed her coffee cup.

'You know that David hit me last night?'

'You deserved it. I feel like slapping you myself, you stupid little cow!'

'Mum, I am your daughter, for Christ's sake, and you are siding with David?'

Her mother was relentless in her condemnation of Lois and her support for David. Lois began to see things were more serious than she had imagined.

'Where is he now? Has he gone to see Ronnie?'

'He's been to see Ronnie and Theo, and he came back here to see me. We had another talk and now he's gone home.' Her mother was very angry still.

'Home?' This really was serious.

'Yes, home, to all those people he doesn't like very much: his father, his mother and his brother. He's taken his belongings with him. Does that give your tiny brain some idea of how much damage you have inflicted?'

'Oh, my God, Mum. What will we do? What will you do?

You'll really miss him.' Lois was at a loss.

'I most certainly will not. He'll telephone me three or four times a day, as he always does when he's not here, and when you go back to that wretched place and start playing silly idiots with that Welsh boy all over again, David will come back to me. Next time you think you can come back here, we'll have to think again, won't we?' She sounded very determined.

'Mum, you wouldn't kick me out. Where would I go?' Lois was horrified.

'Ronnie says she'll have you. You drive me to distraction, running around in your fantasy world, too blind to see what is right under your nose. I'll have a real man around, thank you very much.'

Lois was mortified that her mother had turned on her so viciously. She knew that she was fond of David, but she had no idea that it was running so deep with her. Her mother continued to berate Lois, and showed a surprising knowledge of things in Lois's life that she thought were secret. David must have been her informant, and when Lois asked her mother if that was the case, her mother admitted as much.

'The question you need to ask yourself is how I know that Owen is David's most hated rival. I mean, he has others, but Owen is the ultimate. I know it, and yet you, who claim that you are his best friend, are in the dark? I'll spell it out for you because, quite honestly, I think you need that. The trick is that I listen. I am David's best friend; not you. You are just someone to whom he is incredibly attracted; you look so wonderful together, and he would like you to be his 'one and only'. To be honest, I don't think you are up to it. If he decides to throw you out of his life forever, you are getting your just desserts. You will spend the rest of your life looking for someone to replace him, and you will die unhappy.' She turned away.

'Mum! How can you say that to me? I'm your daughter!'

'I say it because it is true. I say it because I love you, not because I don't. You need to hear this and, if it can change the way you think, it might just help you.'

'This is absolute nonsense. If I phone him now, I can sort this out.' Lois was convinced of it. Nothing had happened, and she couldn't lose David over this.

'Go ahead and try, you arrogant little chit. He said he doesn't want to talk to you, or have anything to do with you, until he's had time to think whether he wants to put himself through this absolute misery because of you, or not. He wants to be certain before he decides, and that's why he has gone home. Whatever happens now, I will always be a part of his life but will you, Lois? In some ways, let me tell you, I'd like him to decide not to continue with you, even though it was my dream to see my perfect couple walking down the aisle, married. I'm not sure I would choose you for my David now.'

With those parting words, she went out into her beloved garden, leaving Lois feeling very angry and confused. She dialled David's father's number and Rich answered. She asked to talk to David.

'He's not here.'

'Rich, I can hear him. Ask him to come to the 'phone. Please.'

'He doesn't want to talk to you, he said so expressly. I was just trying to save your feelings. So, fuck right off, you are history.'

She dialled the number again but they had left the receiver off the hook.

* * *

Several times during that day, she tried calling David's number, without success. Her mother was miserable and walked round her garden in tears. In the afternoon, she went out.

When the telephone rang, Lois answered it immediately, assuming the caller to be David. It was Owen.

'Lois, please don't hang up on me. I need to speak to you, please.'

'I have nothing to say to you,' she said, forgetting what Owen had suffered by taking her out.

'Lois, whatever David said, I didn't go out with you last night because of him. I've always liked you. I love you. Please believe that. I love you.'

'Listen to me, Owen, I'm glad that you are still able to walk and talk but I don't ever want to speak to you again. You can't love me; you don't even know me. Don't ring here again.' The conversation had been distasteful to her.

Her mother came home and went to bed with her book. Lois convinced herself that things would get back to normal before long, but Monday was, if anything, even worse. Her mother talked to David on the telephone, but whenever Lois tried, she heard the engaged tone. Lois didn't want to talk to anyone; even Gerry couldn't understand what she was going through. On Tuesday morning, she woke early, determined to drive over to David, sure that they could sort it all out. Doubts assailed her on the way. If David had been out last night, he could have got off with someone else. Seduction was, after all, his life's mission.

When she drew up outside the beautiful Georgian mansion that was David's family home, she took comfort from seeing his Triumph Stag on the driveway. She parked her mother's car next to it. The fact that she had not asked to borrow the car and that her mother might be in need of it only now occurred to her. Full of trepidation, she rang the doorbell. The housekeeper, Mrs. Munday, answered the door and took Lois to the kitchen, where David was slouched on the sofa, tea in hand. He was surprised to see her.

'Oh, what do you want? You are the last person in the world I want to see.'

Lois turned to Mrs Munday, who had started to stack the

dishwasher, and said, 'Mrs Munday, I know that you will think that I'm being horribly rude, but could you leave us? I have to speak to David about something, and I would rather be alone with him. Could you find something else to do for the moment, please?'

'If you want to talk to me, we can do it in the conservatory. That one listens at doors.' David marched ahead of her and she followed meekly.

'What do you want? Have you driven here? I thought that you hated driving?'

'I needed to see you, David, that's why I am here. I have to speak to you because I love you, you are my friend, and I now realise that what I did was stupid, unthinking and cruel, and that I have hurt you beyond measure, and the very worst thing is, that I never meant to. I just didn't think, and I am truly sorry. I am here to find out how to put this right.'

'Oh, fuck off. There's nothing you can do. You've destroyed yourself and me, you fucking bitch. Don't you know that we were special; when we were together people looked at us and died of jealousy because they would never be us, the perfect couple? We had it all, and you just threw it away.' He was still incensed.

'I do know, but that is just an image. It's not real. We have more than that, we understand each other.'

No matter how hard she tried, Lois was getting nowhere fast. 'David, there must be something I can do to prove to you that I am sorry, there just has to be.'

'Well I suppose one of those blow jobs you produced for me in France would go someway to doing it.' He lit another cigarette and regarded her coolly.

'I can't do that; the answer to this is not sex. We are talking friendship here, not sex.'

'The answer is always sex, and you're a Biologist. You people make me sick. With all your stupid qualifications, you think you can intellectualise anything. You are all so stupid. It's not about pieces of paper; it's about living your life, being true, being what you really are.' He drew on his cigarette. 'If you haven't come here to fuck me, fuck off, right out of my life.'

'So, this is it, is it? All those times we've spent together, wasted; all that shared angst about Sid, your father, my mother, all the talking and talking; it's all come to nothing, is that it?'

'Too right, it is. My life is far too short to include you in it, Lois. I'm going to be a long time dead. Unrequited love is for fools, and I am not one. I know that, and if I can find the strength of mind to throw you out of my life forever, it will be the very best thing I have ever done. I torture myself over you; I am eaten up with it.'

Words failed her. She realised now that this was the end, she would have to learn to live without him. Tears blinded her, she felt as though her heart was breaking yet again. When she reached the door, she pulled it open but something forced it closed again, before she was outside the house. It was David. He held out his arms to her and she fell into them. He held her close. She was shaking all over. David stared over her shoulder at the familiar hall and wondered why he was so desperately weak. He could see all the sense in parting from her, but could not put it into action.

'It's okay, it's fine, and you don't have to go.'

'I don't have to go?' she asked, giving him a look that nearly broke his heart all over again.

'No, you don't have to go. Let's go and have some tea.'

He could see from the terrified look on her face that she was unsure whether to believe him. David apologised for everything, doing his best to reassure her.

'You frightened the life out me; do you know that?' she said, almost collapsing onto the sofa.

'I know, and that's when I realised that I couldn't throw you out.' David sighed heavily. 'I need you in my life, not out of it. What I'd like now is to be in bed with you, having a nice cuddle, not sex.

David was spooning sugar into their mugs but he soon stopped when she said, 'You don't want to have sex with me?' She was open-mouthed with amazement.

'Not if it makes you feel bad about Zitface. A cuddle will do.'

'But I don't feel bad about Zitface.'

'You don't? In France you said you did.' It was David's turn to be bewildered.

'That's a long time ago and, since then, Aber feels almost unreal, I can't even be sure it exists, that he exists. He's not a reality for me at the moment.'

'He's not a reality? Then, what is?' David asked.

'You are?' She was emphatic.

'Well, why haven't we been having gorgeous sex with each other? What's that been all about?' David's hand still hovered between the sugar jar and her mug.

'When we were in France, we agreed to have a holiday romance, and stop having sex when we got back to Chester. It's what we said would happen.'

Both of them were horror struck at the idea that their poor communication had let them down.

'I want to have sex with you; you want to have sex with me. What are we doing, standing here? Let's get going.'

* * *

David's father requested David's presence at a meeting with Owen and his father, Charles Burke. The two fathers had decided to try to reconcile their sons' differences, although Charles would have preferred to give David a thrashing, or haul him before the court for assault. David had broken Owen's nose, but business is business, and young men are always fighting over girls. David was the last to arrive. In spite of reluctance to take part in what he saw as a waste of time, he had a plan to keep everyone happy. Charles Burke and David's father were talking together, glasses of scotch in hand; Rich sat on one of the drawing room sofas, and Owen was standing and looking out of the window.

'Oh you're here. We can start.'

David lit a cigarette and went to stand as far from Owen as the size of the room permitted.

David's father began a rambling peroration about a boyish misunderstanding, Owen paced the floor and stared down at the carpet, and David studied his battered face, his black eyes, and a nose swollen to twice its usual size. David interrupted his father.

'Yes, Dad, there was a misunderstanding, but it wasn't between Owen and me; it was between me and Lois. It's all sorted out now, and we understand each other completely. I was angry. I was probably drunk; I went too far. I'm sorry.'

He was, in fact, only sorry he hadn't killed Owen, for whom his hate had never been stronger, and he'd hoped that he would never have to see his face again. He waited until Owen was back at the window, walked over to him and held out his hand. Owen looked resentfully at it, then at David's face. David was surprised to see that Owen harboured envy, not hate. However, he shook hands briefly and David drew Owen close, as if to hug him. Very quietly, he whispered in Owens's ear, Touch her again and you are fucking dead.'

The two fathers were delighted to see what they took for reconciliation. Rich was staring at the floor, trying not to laugh and give the game away. Luckily, Charles and Owen Burke had to leave very soon after that, but David's father wanted to talk to him.

'There now, that went well, didn't it?' his father said, satisfied.

'I am only here because that 'chit of a girl', as you called her, implored me to come. As for Owen Burke, I fucking hate him. It was a waste of time. Owen means nothing to me and Lois means everything. She is my whole world. If you don't understand that, you don't even know me. You're only interested in saving your face at the golf club.'

David left without waiting for any reaction. He had reached the end of his relationship with his father, whose money he would continue to take, nevertheless, and fritter away.

18

Before and During Sly

FOR THE REST OF THE SUMMER, Lois devoted herself to David, while corresponding with her friends from Aber by letter. She told Gerry exactly what had happened with regard to David, after Gerry had sworn to keep it strictly to herself. Lois cancelled Malc's planned visit to Chester and refused to go to Luke's birthday party in the lake District, or the Futurama, even though it was just outside Chester. She concentrated on helping David plan and organise his birthday party, at his parents home. Everyone, except Owen and any of Lois's friends from Aberystwyth, was invited. The party was a great success, and Lois took this opportunity to demonstrate her undying devotion to him, for which David was grateful to her.

After the party, Lois's began to think about Aber again, and Sly. He sent her a limited edition copy of 'A Promise' by the Bunnymen, which she played when David wasn't around.

David offered to take Lois down to Aberystwyth for the start of term. The weather was perfect, sunny and warm, and they drove with the top down and the music blaring. They stopped in Welshpool for lunch. The car pulled into a lay-by just outside the town, and Lois asked why they were stopping. David said he had some things to say to her, and her heart dropped. All day his mood had been good, now, suddenly, he was serious.

'I've been doing a lot of thinking about you and us over the last few weeks, since that Owen thing. I meant what I said that day, when I nearly let you go out of my life. I really do suffer over you. I have never experienced hurt or torment like this before. Some of the things my family said, Rich in particular, made me realise that I must try to protect myself better than I have before, so, I won't be coming to see you this year. It isn't going to be a re-run of your first year. You will be busy and so will I, and I suspect that you will get back with Mr Fuck Face, and I really don't want to deal with that. Do you think that you and he will get back together?'

'I honestly don't know what to think, I'm very confused about everything. I don't want to go back at all. I would much rather run away to London with you, but Mum would be dreadfully disappointed, and so would I, in the long run. I've tried hard to make up for my stupidity over Owen, and to thank you for giving me another chance. I can hardly think about Sly.'

'I know that you've tried, and I much appreciate the fact that no one has mentioned Owen again. Owen was not Sly. Sly-boy would be a bridge too far for me. I know I want to smash his face in, and that would be unpleasant. Let me just say that, if you do decide on him and he fucks up again, I will be around to help you pick up the pieces. Whatever happens, you are the love of my life, the last person I will think about when I die.'

David continued in this vein for a few minutes, during which, Lois began to cry. She felt as if her heart were breaking all over again. Why couldn't she just love David in the way he loved her? Why was she holding back on him? David had been thinking hard about this when he was away from her, and all she had done was listen to Sly's stupid record.

'I will miss you,' she whispered.

'I know, and I will miss you, but I can't see a way around it. If, at any time, you tell me that it is all over with Mr Zit Face, I will be here instantly. Can you tell me that now?' Lois shook her head and cried even harder.

'There you go, then.'

David threw his cigarette out of the window and started the engine. He drove with a look of grim determination on his face. Waves of sadness washed over Lois, who felt totally at a loss, very immature, very out of her depth.

* * *

Once they got to South Marine Terrace, David was all politeness and charm, and carried Lois's luggage to her new room. He stayed only long enough to drink a cup of tea, although Lois tried to persuade him to stay and have something to eat, but he told her he was doing himself a favour by not prolonging the agony. He said he would see her at Christmas, as long as she didn't have 'that wanker' in tow. Lois was sobbing as he drove away without so much as a backward glance. She wasn't to know that the pain he was feeling was so acute that he could hardly drive.

Gerry came to find her; Lois gave her an up-date, and Gerry sided firmly with David, and said couldn't understand why Lois chose Sly. She told Lois that all this confusion was due to so many things going on in her life, and she needed some stability. Gerry warned her against taking up with Sly-boy too quickly, and advised her to take time to allow her feelings to settle, and then, made her laugh by telling her that she had found a copy of 'Disco Duck' and sent it to Luke as a birthday present. She left Lois unpacking, went down to make tea, and refused to tell Luke, Fenn and Malc what Lois had confided, knowing that, if she did, it would go straight to Sly. Malc told Sly that the girls had closed ranks, and he had no idea what had occurred between David and Lois.

Huw's leaving party took place that evening. Lois put on a brave face, and she and Gerry enjoyed themselves in the Angel pub, dancing and larking around with Huw for one last Aberystwyth time. Sly took the opportunity to ingratiate himself with Gerry, and invited both girls to come and see his new room in Caerlon that he was to share with Dafydd, who had yet to appear.

The term began and the girls were busy with their field course, leaving little time for adjustment. Luke and Malc cooked their tea and generally did the household chores for them. Malc hoped they could eat together once a week and remain good friends. Luke was very kind to both the girls, and it was difficult to stay mad at him, even if he did dance like a duck. Once lectures began, it was just as though they had never been away. To Lois's delight, David wrote and enclosed a large enough cheque to see her through the term.

Then things began to happen, some ordinary and not surprising at all, some weird and very different from last year. Lois and Gerry received invitations to some parties; Finlay and Josh visited, and Lois had spent most of the night talking to them, while Gerry got off with some bloke from her course. The girls re-established their Saturday morning grocery shopping routine, and Malc started hanging around with Gina, Ali and one of Gina's friends, Emily.

Lois and Gerry obtained part-time work in the cellar bar at the Marine Hotel, their duties coinciding on Friday, or Saturday nights. They also worked a couple of evenings in the week, not long enough to affect their academic work. They routinely lunched with Malc at the Arts Centre on a Friday, but on the third Friday of term, he told them he was to go on an Industrial Society Trip and Sly would meet them instead. Lois had not seen much of Sly, as their paths had hardly crossed; Gerry thought that Lois was avoiding him, and hoped it was because of what she had said.

Sly came round to South Marine Terrace on most evenings, and Malc would sit downstairs and chat with him. Gerry joined in, when she wanted an excuse to stop work. Lois had many essays to complete, and corresponded regularly with David and Mickie, who seemed to have little to do except write to her, so that she had little free time.

When they met Sly at the Arts Centre, he exuded charm. After exchanging small talk, he mentioned Gina's planned Fetish and Perversion party, scheduled for a week on Saturday, to which they were invited. He then invited them to come to the Pier that evening with him.

'I have changed quite a lot since last year. I'm trying not to take life so seriously.' He looked significantly at Lois, who quickly looked away, not wanting to embarrass Gerry. Finally, they agreed to meet in the White Horse at eight.

Sly made a huge effort to impress Gerry, having understood that she exercised considerable influence over Lois. Finlay joined them on the Pier, and the four of them had a fun time. Gerry seemed partial to Finlay; they had a lot in common, including a shared sense of humour. Sly and Finlay walked the girls home afterwards, and came in for tea. Lois was tired and went to bed early. Sly seemed rather put out at this and followed her upstairs. When he knocked at her door, she opened it, and he asked if she was okay. Tired and rather irritable, Lois told him she wanted to sleep. He wished her goodnight, in Welsh, and she found it difficult to drop off after that.

★ ★ ★

Gerry masterminded the Fetish and Perversion party outfits. The event was a huge success and well attended. Afterwards, Sly offered Lois his arm as they walked through the town, and back to Caerlon. The inevitable happened, the old magnetism was as strong as ever, and Sly was euphoric when she let him take her to bed; he had her back, all to himself, at last. It gave them a chance to catch up on one another, re-kindle the old flame, and forget the past.

★ ★ ★

Everyone had pitched in to buy a rib of beef joint, and Malc was to be in charge of cooking it. Luke accepted vegetable-preparation duty, and Gerry made profiteroles, under Lois's supervision. Lois was also in charge of roast potatoes and Yorkshire puddings, and responsible for averting culinary disasters. Malc put the joint in the oven without seeing to the timer, which was on 'delay'. Lois sent him upstairs to his work on the Stoke-on-Trent silk industry, while she set the oven, rescued Luke's lumpy cheese sauce, and supervised the chocolate sauce that Gerry was making. The rest of the day was unremarkable, except for the food, which was delicious.

All in all, Sly and Lois formed a normal relationship, akin to the one they had so much enjoyed before, but a couple of things happened to jar their happiness and send Sly into a sulk which lasted most of the term. It began when Lois discovered just how secretive he was being about them being a couple again. Lois was giving Sly a lesson in fellatio, when the door burst open and Emily walked in, took one look, apologised profusely and left. Sly went after her. Lois was highly embarrassed and remembered the last time someone had witnessed a scene such as this one. Sly brought Emily back to the room and left her with Lois, while he went to brew some tea.

'I am so sorry. I had no idea that you and Sly were back together. He hadn't said anything at all. I've just got so used to coming round here. It's really sad, because it's always been me who was sorted out, and my friends whose love lives were crap; now it's the other way round, and I feel such a saddo. I know he's intensely private, but I thought he'd tell me, if only to prevent something like this happening. Oh, you must hate me. Please forgive me.'

Now that Lois stopped to think about it, he used to be so careful about locking doors. He didn't want people to know that he was back with her, and it made her feel uncomfortable. Once Emily had gone, Sly quickly got back to where he was when she first entered the room, but Lois let her mind wander from the task in hand and mouth. Did Gina know, for example?

The next unsettling happening was far more wide reaching

than the business with Emily. Sly had lunch with Malc and Malc let slip that, when the friends went to see Japan in Birmingham, in two weeks' time, they would be staying with Mickie. Sly was waiting in Lois's room to tackle her about this, when she came down from College.

'What's wrong with that? You like Mickie. He's your friend.

'I don't want you staying with him, I won't let you go.'

Lois argued back and forth, reminding him that Malc and Gerry were going and that Mickie lived in a one bedroom flat.

'What are you expecting us to do; have sex on the floor with those two as an audience? Why don't you trust me?'

Sly, in a jealous rage, refused to see reason and became irritable and stubborn. Gerry came to investigate all the shouting, and when Lois explained, Gerry offered to tell Malc and see if he could help. Lois went back to her studies, having offered Sly food, which he refused. He found fault with everything, accused her of being uncaring, whined with self-pity, and behaved like a naughty child.

Gerry was appalled by Sly's demands, and Lois was almost relieved that the relationship was going to be over before she became tangled up with him again. One thing he did was demand that she hand him the letter he was certain she had written to Mickie. She told him she hadn't written a letter, and that she had not given up her intention of going to see Japan and, therefore, Mickie. In a mood worse than the night before, Sly roared at Lois, who tried to stay calm herself and not antagonise him. She just tried to remain passive. Sly stormed out in a fury and walked back to Caerlon, where Emily joined him a little while later. He poured out his complaint to her, and she told him he that he was right to react like this, which was music to Sly's ears. After Emily left, he tried to think of a way to show Lois how strongly he felt about Mickie.

Thus, Sly's bizarre form of punishment for Lois's disobedience began. No meetings, no lunch dates, no evening dates of any kind were arranged. They might dance with each other if they met by chance, but they hung around in separate groups. Lois was usually with Gerry and people from her course, Sly with Malc, Gina and Emily. Many evenings out ended with Sly detaching himself from his group and re-attaching himself to Lois when it was time to depart. He never spent a single night away from South Marine Terrace. Gerry was incensed by his behaviour and couldn't bring herself to speak to him. Lois tried to hold her head high, and think of the times when he was so generous with his lovemaking.

They were getting the nights right; it was the days that were screwy. Every morning started with lovemaking, followed by Sly adopting his sulk mode. On the morning when the friends were to catch the train to Birmingham, he pretended to be asleep, so she kissed him goodbye and set off defiantly.

Lois felt a huge sense of relief on leaving Aberystwyth; it was easy to forget just how intense the place could be, how remote from the real world. Gerry used the journey to have another go at Malc for not doing more to get Sly to be reasonable towards Lois. Lois tried hard to detach herself as Gerry ranted on.

'Actually, Gerry, I have tried, but there is nothing anyone can do when Sly goes into a sulk. It's exactly like last time. At least, he hasn't stormed off, and Lois is big girl, she can take care of herself. She could kick him out if she wanted to, she's not stupid, you know,' Malc said.

Lois was almost grateful to him. 'Sly will come round eventually, Gerry, he's just in a mess at the moment, he's not thinking straight. I am choosing to put up with it all.'

'Yeah, well, I wish you could just flick a switch in your brain and stop loving him. I never want to fall in love if it stops me doing things logically. I'd rather hold onto my brainpower. If love makes you want to put up with his nonsense and let him treat you like some cheap tart, we can't stop you.'

Lois wished that Gerry and Malc would mind their own business and leave her to sort out her own problems.

★ ★ ★

The concert in Birmingham was brilliant. Mick Karn was really on form and David Sylvian's crooning was first class. Lois felt her heart lurch on seeing Mickie, who held her tight and kissed her. Malc wasn't there to witness that. He said she looked tired and asked if she was okay. She murmured that she would tell him later. Malc came from talking with the performers, and Mickie, oozing charm, steered them to the nearest pub, so they could listen to his hilarious stories of people on his course.

Mickie had found a desirable flat with one bedroom, and a studio for his work, and some of his pictures were on the walls. One took Lois's fancy and Mickie told her she could have it once it was finished, which might take a while, as it was something he worked on in his spare time. He was the perfect host, entertaining them with food, wine and amusing anecdotes. Malc and Gerry asked if they might retire to bed, before Lois and Mickie were ready to sleep, which left them with an opportunity to talk together. Eventually, with a twinkle in his eye and a smile on his lips, he asked about Sly.

'It's pretty dreadful, really. He's absolutely furious that I'm here. He wanted me not to come.'

'Oh, that's brilliant! What a wanker! He has you all day and all night, back in Aber, while I'm stuck here in Birmingham, and he's making a fuss. Tosser! So, what's been going on? Mickie couldn't hide his pleasure that Sly was messing up, big style.

Lois studied her nails, humiliated and hurt by everything that had happened. Her eyes filled with tears. Mickie was round the table, the moment he realised that it was no longer funny. He held her close while she told him exactly what Sly had achieved in the last few weeks. Mickie was horrified.

'Have you told anyone else about this?'

'Gerry knows, and she's absolutely livid. Every time it comes up, she has a real go at me. She thinks I should just tell him to piss off, but I can't. It's humiliating enough, being treated like a subhuman. Gerry sees everything as black and white, but to me it's all grey. David's abandoned me. He seemed to know something like this would happen and he said he didn't want to have to witness it.'

'What about your mum, or your sister?'

'Ronnie thinks the same as Gerry. I can practically hear her telling me to tell him to go and fuck himself. I can't talk to my mum about this; she's too biased towards David.'

'Well, you need someone to talk to. You're bottling it all up and that won't get you anywhere. You can 'phone me, I'll listen, and I won't try to tell you what to do. Is that all right?' Even as he said it, he wondered why he was taking a sucker punch. David had the right idea: stand back and let it happened, then step in as a knight in shining armour.

'Shall I write to the Dick Head?'

'God, no! He'll go ape-shit. If he knew that I'd told you, he'd go mental.

'He must be warped if he thinks that you'd come here and not tell me what he was up to!'

They continued to talk and Mickie was put even more firmly in the picture, but there seemed to be nothing Lois would allow him to do to help. She looked exhausted, and he suggested that they should get to bed.

'I can't sleep with you, Mickie,' she said sharply.

'I know you can't, but I can hold you, stroke you help you relax, so you can sleep. You need some kindness.'

Lois was worried about Malc, but Mickie told her that he would sleep on the floor, once she was asleep, and Malc would be none the wiser. He insisted that he just wanted to do something to help her.

After a late breakfast, they went to the city centre and started to do some serious shopping, made more enjoyable after weeks of deprivation in Aberystwyth. Malc had a list of obscure records as long as his arm, to purchase for himself, Luke and Sly. Lois wanted to go shopping for clothes, and Mickie took her into the indoor market, where she found many items to tempt her. She hadn't yet cashed David's cheque, and the only reason why she might have done so would be to buy her mother a decent Christmas present. Mickie begged her to let him buy her some clothes. He had just been sent some money from his mother, who was clearing the house out, ready to move nearer to her family.

'Me Mam has been selling some of me paintings. She's doing really well, trudging around Liverpool and getting some ridiculous prices. She's threatening to go down to London and see what she can do there. It's scary. It's becoming a reality, trying to make a living out of me work. Suppose people don't like it.'

'Of course they'll like it, they'll love it, it's brilliant!' Lois was utterly convinced.

'Anyway, let me buy some things for you; I never get the chance to do something like that.'

She had to admit that the idea of Mickie buying her some clothes and her not telling Sly was already making her feel better. In the end, he bought her two pairs of boots, black and red, and a long, black, net dress that clung to every curve. It was see-through, but Mickie persuaded her that, with a black bra and panties underneath it, Sly boy would be terrified of her.

Mickie waited for an opportunity to have a quiet word with Gerry about her handling of Lois. It came as Malc and Lois went off to the toilet on the railway station, before they caught the train back to Wales.

'Gerry, go easy on Lois. She's really hurting over all this Sly stuff. You're a nice girl, and you clearly care, so don't be telling her what to do all the time; just let her talk.'

'I'm only trying to get her to see that he's using her,' Gerry replied defensively.

'Yeah, but you've got to let her find her own way through it. She's got a pure heart, and she wants this to work out with Sly. She thinks she's in love with him.'

Gerry cottoned onto this very quickly. 'You don't think she really is in love with him, then?'

Mickie smiled, sorry to have said too much. 'No. She's in lust with him, if anything. Listen, if he finishes with her, she'll implode. Make sure I know about it. She might not be keen, but just call me. She'll need every friend she's got, and I'm a friend, believe me.'

Gerry did believe him, he was very plausible, honesty itself. She was pleased she'd found the answer to Lois's problem with Sly. It was Mickie.

★ ★ ★

Saying goodbye to Mickie was hard. Gerry fell asleep at Shrewsbury and Lois stared out of the window, trying to imagine what Sly would have in store for her, now she had disobeyed him. She imagined that this would be the end of their re-born relationship. In fact, Sly failed to show up at all, and Emily came to mind. Gerry was overjoyed that he had not showed up, and wanted to know if this would now be the end of his bizarre behaviour.

'I really don't know, but I'm skiving off Plant Ecology, so you'd better take some carbon paper with you. I know he's free then, and I'm going to find out what exactly is going on!'

19

During Sly: Honesty

STANDING OUTSIDE SLY'S ROOM, Lois heard voices talking softly, intimately, and she was afraid that she might be about to discover something unpleasant. She knocked and Sly called out, 'Come in.'

He sat in the bay window, opposite Emily and without acknowledging Lois's presence, he carried on speaking earnestly to her, almost as if he were compelling her not to look towards Lois. Lois regarded them in silence and leant against the wall, her mind a blank. Sly continued to ignore her, which filled her with indignation, and she went up to him and spoke his name. 'Sly, have I suddenly become invisible? I am here to see you.'

'Sorry, Lois, I'm talking to Emily at the moment.' He resumed his conversation, leaning past her, to face Emily. Lois swore at him and left the room, and Sly made no move to follow her. Gradually, her outrage turned to pain, and she sought out Gerry, who greeted the news with something approaching glee; all the signs indicated that this was indeed the end.

Lois tried to concentrate on her work, but she was always conscious of a feeling of emptiness. Gerry tried in vain to persuade her to go out to a Carp party at the Pier, but Lois needed time alone, to think. She was working on her essay, wiping away tears, when there came a knock at the door and Sly walked in. He regarded her thoughtfully and asked her why she was crying.

'You are the absolute limit, Sly, asking me why I'm upset, when it should be clear as daylight. What do you want? You aren't expecting me to sleep with you, are you?'

'Of course I am. It's been two nights, and I need you.' He seemed puzzled.

'Where were you last night?' Lois was angry again.

Sly slumped onto the bed, and said, 'I drank a bottle of vodka and passed out, if you must know. I would have been here, if I hadn't got drunk.'

Lois stared at him, and said loudly, 'You have come round here to have sex with me now, when you wouldn't even acknowledge that I was in your bloody room this morning! You can't be serious.'

'Oh, but I am.' Sly's tone was very even.

'Sly, this isn't fantasy land; you can't treat me like this,' she said angrily.

'I do have an explanation, but I don't think you'd understand it?'

'Why don't you try me? What exactly was going through your tiny mind?'

Sly began to explain something of his jealousy and sense of betrayal, knowing that Lois slept with other men, David and Mickie, and possibly others of whom Sly knew nothing. He had carefully thought through the tangle of his emotions but doubt-ed whether Lois could be made to understand them, and, if she did, whether it would alter her feelings in any way. Sly, in his darkest moments, had contemplated and rejected the idea of murdering his rivals, and all he had left was exposure of his wounded soul, for her to pity, love or scorn, as she chose. Unable to jump to the nub of the matter, he wrapped his feelings in a cocoon of verbosity that confused Lois, who tried to understand him. She asked why he had found it necessary to inflict physical pain and humiliation on her.

'You made me jealous, and when I'm jealous, I just see red. You made me see red because you wanted me to be reasonable, and I'm not a reasonable person. I chose not to speak to you today because I wanted to hurt you like you keep hurting me.'

'I have never hurt you,' she insisted, completely confused.

'You slept with Mickie and David. I hate both of them. I could kill anyone who has ever had sex with you. Or, perhaps I should kill you, and then you'll never be able to break my heart.' No one had ever spoken to Lois like this, not even David. The coolness with which he spoke was chilling.

'Stop it, Sly, you're scaring me.'

'Good. I want you to be scared; I want you to suffer, but you've nothing to fear from me. I can threaten it, but I know I could never hurt you. I've thought about it endlessly, and I know that I'm not capable of physical violence against you. Anyway I'm a pacifist.'

Lois laughed out loud. 'Ha, a pacifist who threatens to kill? You're mad!'

'Lois, I talk about killing people, I choose not to; that's pacifism. I knew you'd never understand.'

Sly gave vent to all his pent up frustrations, asked her intimate questions about her behaviour with his rivals, challenged her to justify herself, mocked her and tormented her, until she was losing hope of explaining to him that Mickie and David only came into the equation after Sly had raped her, following that fateful goodnight kiss. He left her with the knowledge that his love was all consuming, as destructive as a furnace, yet capable of refining gold. This conversation engineered a new level of understanding between them. Lois was beginning to see how Sly's mind worked, and this settled many of her doubts about their relationship.

When Gerry asked about it, Lois said that Sly had apologised and they had made up. Lois kept telling herself that she had an extraordinary boyfriend, and the feeling pleased her. Sly had been ridiculously honest with Lois, and she seemed to love him even more as a result. He had felt the change almost straight away. He had thought hard about what they had said to one another, and he began to see that he probably didn't need to be so selfish towards her. There might be some room for him to show affection outside of Lois's bedroom. He made excuses for this lack, putting more blame on her than himself, for he still had much to learn about her and about himself.

He was seriously considering marriage to Lois, but a marriage couldn't depend entirely on sex. They had some things in common; why didn't he make more of them, why didn't he show any interest in her work, when it patently meant so much to her? Was there a missing piece, or pieces, in the jigsaw of their complex relationship that had not yet occurred to him? If there were anything lacking, he could not see what it might be. Sly, like all men, thought that a little papering over the cracks would keep his sex kitten sweet.

He went round to South Marine Terrace and waited for Lois to return from her practical session. He sat on her bed, trying not to harbour thoughts of Mickie, or David, or Luke. He heard Malc come in. In a burst of total selfishness, Sly had decided that he would lie through his teeth, if he had to, in order to secure her services. When Lois returned, Finlay was with her, and this sent another shock through Sly's system. He had never seen them together before. Finlay explained that he only wanted to borrow a book from her, and she had brought him up to her room to get it. This event triggered a stream of questions in Sly's brain, which he would ask at a more auspicious time. Had he imagined it, or was Finlay pissed off to find him in Lois's room? Sly was not sure, but diverted himself with the prospect of sexual gratification to come.

'Not now, Sly,' she protested, because he had waited until Finlay's departure and then grabbed her. Before she had a chance to continue, Sly trotted out the prepared text, explaining that his love for her had changed, that he was afraid of losing her, that he would always love her, and all the rest of it, while gazing at her with wide-eyed innocence and apparent sincerity.

'You're not going to lose me. I feel closer to you now. I feel that I understand you in a way I never did before. I've seen your worst side, and I still love you. It hasn't made any difference, except to explain why you've been acting weird.'

'Yes, but something Gerry said about us, that we only ever dance and have sex together, made something beautiful sound so sordid that I realised that I do care what other people think, if it means that they don't know what a truly wonderful person you are. If they think any less of you because of the way I treat you, then I'm doing you a real disservice.' Sly grasped her hand and began to stroke it.

'It doesn't matter what other people think, only us,' Lois insisted.

Sly hadn't realised just how convincing he had been the other night. 'Yes, but I don't have to behave that way. I have other choices, but because I've been so enraged, I hadn't stopped to consider any of them. There have been so many things going on in my brain; perhaps I should have shared them with you, rather than just thinking about making love with you. I want to marry you, and this is not the way to treat a partner for life. So, I'm sorry.'

Lois could hardly believe that she was getting the apology that, until a few days ago, she had felt she fully deserved, and now she didn't need. She shook her head in disbelief. 'What things have been going on in your head?' she asked. She didn't feel ready to get married, even to Sly; she had a degree to get and a research scientist to become, so she avoided that side turning.

'Well, you and Mickie and David. I know something happened there, because Gerry told me when she was drunk. There's Emily, and my da, and worries about work, and not knowing what I want to do, when so many other people have their lives mapped out, and why I find it hard to think straight sometimes, and not being able to control my emotions, and shit like that.'

'Emily, why Emily?' Lois seized upon this one name before

she even had time to ponder.

'Well, she's significant to me. We don't talk about me and you; that's why she was shocked when she walked in when we were on the job. We've never discussed it since then. She's a bit of a prude really; she talks about God a lot. I wondered what you thought of me making a new girlfriend; sorry, I mean making a new friend who is a girl, just as we get back together.'

'Look, I understand about friends, I've got David in my life, or at least I did have.'

It just slipped out, Sly pounced on it immediately and they began to bicker again, about Mickie and David, about Emily, and about Sly's temper and jealousy, until it suddenly dawned on him that the Christmas holidays were approaching and that Lois would once again fall into David's clutches. He sought desperately for a way of stopping this happening. It came to him like a flash of lightning.

'Could you come to Monmouth for the Christmas holidays?'

'No, Sly, my mother would never forgive me,

'I thought not, so that means we will have to be apart from each other for a while, and I will find that very difficult.' "Me, too," interjected the limbic system of his brain. 'Because I love you.' "Nice touch," added the limbic system.

Sly bent to kiss Lois, who was feeling a weird range of emotions: relief at being able to see David at Christmas, surprise at the sudden about turn with Sly, and turned on by the kissing.

'My da's sent me some money, and I want to buy you something really nice, and take you out to Julia's restaurant, to say sorry for neglecting you and not being easy to deal with. I'll book a table. How about the last weekend of term?'

20

During Sly: Dishonesty

FOR THE REMAINDER of the term, Sly was as good as his word, starting with the first Dance Society party, when he called round to the house to pick her up. Lois had made an extra effort with her appearance that evening, and when Sly saw her, he felt a thrill of excitement. They danced to all of their favourite songs; the meal at Julia's was sublime, as was the sex afterwards. With one week until the end of term and the rooms in South Marine terrace to themselves, they enjoyed themselves. Sly was feeling more balanced and his mood was better than it had been for months; but this was only the start of winter, and there were more long nights to come.

Parting at the end of term was painful, and they both wept as her train to Chester drew away. They spoke on the telephone often, and wrote to each other at least twice a day. Lois felt perfectly calm about their love; nothing had ever felt so sure.

When David came home for Christmas, she was thrilled to see him. They went to the Malt and Hops, which was the traditional place to go on Christmas Eve. This year, they had to buy tickets beforehand, to guarantee your place. David and Lois used their time to catch up with news and find out what mutual friends had been doing. Lois spotted Owen across the room and stuck very close to David, who didn't seem remotely interested in the general exchange of Christmas kisses going on around them, until he also spotted Owen.

'Come on, then, give me a kiss, Lois,' he said.

'I can't, David,' she said, thinking of Sly.

'Oh, for fuck's sake, remember Owen.'

'You can't blackmail me about that forever.'

'Just fucking watch me. Remember Owen and give me a fucking kiss.'

David's face was set. She felt that she had to comply, and they kissed, tamely to begin with, and Lois felt oddly distant from the embrace. However, as David caught Owen watching them from the bar, he decided to hot up the embrace, especially for his benefit. He ran his left hand down Lois's back and over her bottom, while he cupped her left breast in his right hand. She responded immediately, and he jerked her bottom towards his groin. 'Let me take you home,' he whispered croakily, while continuing to caress her neck.

'Take me home,' she replied.

'Good girl.'

Much to Lois's consternation, they got no further than his Triumph Stag. She allowed David to fuck her in the car park, but the moment it was over, she was overcome with remorse. As he lit a cigarette and started the engine, Lois tidied her clothes, hoping that no one had seen.

'Oh, my God, what am I doing? I'm not the type of girl who has sex with David Stachini in the Malt and Hops car park,' she groaned.

This greatly amused David, who replied, 'I am sorry, my dear, but I hate to differ; you are exactly the sort of girl who has sex with David Stachini on the Malt and Hops car park, and I have a dirty big love bite on my neck to prove it.'

'But, David, this is madness. You won't have any respect for me, and what about Sly?'

'Listen, I hold you in the very highest respect, and I assure you that no amount of shagging you will ever change that. As for Sly boy, I won't tell him, if you don't.'

'Yes, but what about my self respect? I know what I've done. I love Sly. I don't want to behave like this.'

'Oh stop fucking beating yourself up over this, for Christ's sake. You are nineteen years old and you look fucking gorgeous, you ooze sexuality, and your body is enough to turn every bloke in the pub on fire. I am twenty-four years old, and I fancy the fucking pants off you. You're not married to the prat yet; you've got years ahead of you before you have to worry about fidelity. You're young, free and single, and you are very sexy. Your libido drives you to want sex, and I have no problem with providing it, whenever you please.'

'But what would my mother say?' Lois was in despair.

'She'd probably be very pleased to begin the wedding hat routine. I might even mention it to her.'

'David, you wouldn't!'

'Why not? I've told her about everything else.'

'I don't believe you.'

'Well, you might like to think that your mother is too old to have had sex herself, or doubt that she could hold a perfectly decent conversation about it, but I know differently. I've always talked to her about everything I get up to and, just because you are her daughter, it doesn't make you any less interesting to her.'

'David, I forbid you to talk to my mother about us having sex.'

'Tough fucking titties! When you introduced me to your mother and I adopted her as my own, you lost any right to dictate to me concerning what I talk about with the woman who is more like a mother to me than any other woman in the world.'

* * *

Back at home, Lois reverted to the subject that was uppermost in her thoughts. 'David, it's wrong for us to have sex like this; we are supposed to be friends.'

'I don't see what you think you will achieve by pretending that you aren't keen on it. I've already fucked you, so I know what you are capable of. You are a hot bitch,' he said, with a leer.

'For years, I have seen how you treat girls, and I don't want that to happen to us.'

'I know all that, Lois. You've told me hundreds of times, but what you fail to see is that there is a difference between them and you. I fucking love you and I love fucking you, as well. I'll give you something to think about. You haven't had a drop of alcohol tonight; you were stone cold sober when we fucked in the car park, even though the rest of them in the pub were off their faces. They say that drinking alcohol can't make you do things that you don't want to do, but I've fucked hundreds of girls when they were pissed, and I've had them do all sorts of things I am sure they wouldn't dream of doing when they were sober. Some of them couldn't look at me in the morning, and I certainly didn't want to look at them. You are not like that, and the sex we have seems like good, clean fun in comparison. So, are you going to let me fuck you again, or what?'

David ground out his cigarette and poured more wine for both of them. Lois shook her head. She couldn't understand how this could have happened again. What was she playing at? David shook his hair back and licked some wine from the corner of his mouth.

'Don't do that,' Lois snapped at him.

'Do what?' David was surprised.

'That, that thing with your tongue,' Lois replied helplessly.

'Why not?' Suddenly, he understood, and smiled. 'Oh, I see.

You are going to let me fuck you again, aren't you, you little minx?' And he did, right there, on her mother's kitchen table.

* * *

David slept in Lois's bed with her. She seemed to have thrown caution to the wind that night but was mortified when she awoke at eight o'clock on Christmas morning and found that David was up already, and by the side of her bed were an empty cup and a glass of her mother's customary wake-up call to David, whenever he stayed with them. Her own mother had come into her room, to bring David's refreshment, after a night of sheer debauchery. She was incredulous, and, embarrassed beyond belief, she went downstairs. David was coming up.

'Oh, there you are. I was just going to come up and see if you wanted a little Christmas fuck. Now you're up, we can do presents and you'll keep for later, won't you?' He licked his lips suggestively.

Like families throughout the land, they unwrapped their presents, thanked the givers, and spent Christmas day normally. However, for the rest of their time together, whenever she was on the telephone to Sly, David would lick his lips, give a V-sign towards the telephone, and mouth "wanker" at her. While David found it hysterically funny, Lois had difficulty concentrating, and Sly began to detect this. She felt bitterly ashamed of herself, and resolved not to tell Gerry how low she had sunk, so there would be no chance of Sly finding out. David found endless reasons for the two of them to slip away, so they could enjoy as much sex as possible. David calculated that Lois's inflamed libido was a direct result of Sly's groundwork, and he loved the fact that he, David, was reaping the benefits.

* * *

Before Lois caught the train to Aberystwyth, she showered and scrubbed every inch of her body, and did her best to ensure that David had left no mark on her. He seemed to know that there were limits to her tolerance. He had pretended to give her a love-bite, on numerous occasions, but only to wind her up, and she was unmarked. She tried to convince herself that Sly couldn't possibly know what had happened, but his letters had had become less regular and his telephone manner was different. Carrying her burden of guilt, she wasn't looking forward to seeing Sly.

He was waiting for her at the station. He kissed her and took her luggage from her; so far, so good. He whispered to her that he couldn't wait to be inside her, and they walked hand-in-hand to South Marine terrace. Once inside her room, Sly wasted no time at all in removing all her clothes. Rather strangely, he didn't remove any of his, so that he was still dressed in his customary Bunnymen mac, and all of his clothes, including his baseball boots. Lois, on the other hand, was completely naked and writhing on the bed while he kissed her all over. She thought the clothes thing was odd, but was concentrating too much on pleasure to be concerned about it. After a while, he stopped and stood away from her bed, gazing at her intently. 'Lois, I can smell David on you.'

Silently cursing herself, she spoke calmly, reassuring him. 'No, you can't, it simply isn't true, Sly.'

His enquiring gaze made her very uncomfortable. 'Lois, you've had sex with David over the holiday. I can tell.'

'No, Sly, I haven't.'

'I think I smell something different about you and it feels like David. I'm going for a walk. I need to think about what to do. I don't trust you, Lois. I think you've betrayed me. I didn't have you down as a slut, but now I think I may have been wrong. Emily thinks you are a slut, the very worst kind of slut.'

There was something about the way Sly said the word slut in his soft Welsh accent that seemed to make it one of the worst words in the English language. Still staring at her intently, he spat the words at her.

'Emily! What has she got to do with it?' Lois was at a loss.

'Emily came to stay with me over the holiday. You couldn't come, but she wanted to. She says you are a slut, and we shouldn't be having sex. She doesn't approve of sex before marriage.'

'You have had Emily to stay, and you never even told me!' Lois was incensed.

'Why should I tell you anything about my life? You've been screwing David; I am sure of it.'

'Sly, believe me, I haven't.' Lois continued to be defiant.

'I don't believe you. I wanted to marry you. I was going to ask you, but you don't want to marry me, do you?' He was still maintaining eye contact.

'Sly, I do love you, but we are too young to be thinking about marriage.'

'What's age got to do with it? If you love me now, what is going to change? We will still be together, but what we do together won't be immoral. I don't like the idea of immorality.'

'Has Emily put this into your head? Is that it?'

Sly shook his head. 'If you examine your memory, Lois, you will find that I first mentioned marriage to you after knowing you for six hours. This has nothing to do with Emily. The fact is, you don't want to marry me, do you, Lois?'

Desperate to improve the situation, Lois said, 'I will marry you, if that's what you want.'

'You are lying again; you don't want to marry me. I'm going for a walk. Stay here. I will decide what I'm going to do.' He left very quickly, slamming the door behind him.

Lois put on her dressing gown and paced the room, her hand over her face, saying, 'Fuck, fuck, fuckity fuck, this is all my stupid fault. I am so stupid. Shit, shit, shit, shit.' She stared hard at herself in the mirror, wondering how she had fucked up so comprehensively, and why she had ever thought she could keep it from Sly. Eventually, she stopped, and tried to think of ways to convince him. She could tell him to ask Gerry, or even David, but he probably wouldn't do it, and she couldn't be sure that David would lie for her. He would like nothing better than their relationship to be over. In desperation, she walked down to the shop and bought ten Silk Cut cigarettes. Sly returned about two hours later. He sat on his haunches, folded his arms across his knees and spoke very softly.

'I think, I have decided what to do. I remember something you told me about mallard ducks, and I think that will fit my plan. If he's fucked you, then I will have to fuck you more. I don't understand why you have done this, Lois. I am at a loss. You told me you understood me better than ever, after I told you about my jealousy, and what have you done? You have given me reason to doubt you yet again, and I am in a rage and seeing red all over.'

'Sly, I haven't done anything wrong. You can ask Gerry, ask David, if you like.'

'Oh yeah, and they wouldn't lie for you? It's like a fucking conspiracy around here; everyone is ready to lie for you, and the only person who should tell me the truth is you, and you won't because you're too afraid of the truth. It's like always being trapped in the same situation. I'll never get to the truth of this. You seem determined to torture me for the rest of my life, and you claim to love me. You don't know what love is, Lois. Emily is right. You are a slut. Every time you deny it, the more it convinces me you are lying. Why are you smoking? You don't normally smoke, or have you been enjoying post coital cigarettes with David? Got hooked, have you?'

Shit, Lois said to herself quietly. She should have seen that one coming. 'Anyway, if I'm going to fuck you, I'd better get on with it, so take off your dressing gown and lie on the bed for me.'

'Sly, this is hardly putting me in the mood for love making,' Lois argued.

'Listen to me. You are a slut, you do not deserve my love, and you are not worthy. The only thing you can do to make me feel any better about the fact that you have been fucking David in Chester, while I have been thinking of you until my fucking head nearly exploded, is to spread your legs for me now. Or do I have to make you?'

Sly's voice was menacing, and Lois couldn't see any way out of the situation. He removed her dressing gown and pushed her roughly onto her bed. He kissed her all over, except on her lips and, without removing a single item of his own clothing, he took her. When it was over, and Lois was glad that it was over quickly, he did up his trousers and told her that he was going to buy some vodka and would be back when he was ready. 'And you had better fucking well be here, ready for me.'

★ ★ ★

During the next few days, Sly spent his time in her room, staring into space, eating nothing. Lois made do with an occasional piece of toast, and smoked cigarettes. Sly forbade her to drink any wine, while he drank vodka by the tumbler. He spoke to her only to ask suddenly, 'Did you have sex with David, Lois?'

Gerry was due back on Wednesday. Lois looked forward to it because it would mean she could get away from Sly and work with Gerry on their Ecology field study. On the other hand, Gerry would notice Sly's odd behaviour and make her opinions forcibly clear. Lois had already decided not to tell her about David. She could be as stubborn as Sly, and it became a matter of will, not to allow him to win over this particular issue. Occasionally, she tried to reason with him. He seemed to be less angry, calmer, and positive that he knew what was best.

'Sly, how long is this going to go on for? Gerry is coming back tomorrow, and she already thinks you are barking mad,' Lois argued.

Sly ploughed over the same old ground, insisting that she had slept with David, no matter how often she denied it. In the end, she almost told him she had slept with David, tons of times, but instead she asked again, 'Sly, what makes you think that I will put up with this dreadful behaviour?'

'Well, it's your punishment for betraying me by fucking David, so you have no choice; you have to put up with it for as long as I say.'

'I do have a choice. I could just kick you out, and lock my door.'

'You won't do that. A locked door has to be unlocked sometime. There is always a way.'

Lois shook her head and lit a cigarette, stared out of the window some more, and then decided to have one last stab on Emily. 'Did you sleep with Emily over Christmas?'

'No. I don't think I'll ever be able to sleep with anyone else but you, unless I think about you while I do it.' Sly replied in a matter of fact way.

Lois regarded him contemptuously. 'Oh, God, that is really sick.'

'Hardly. I imagine that a lot of people think about someone else while they make love. That's not sick. Having sex with someone else, when you claim to be deeply in love with me, that's what I would call sick.'

'Can't you at least be civil to me? Gerry is going to have a field day when she gets back here. You said you didn't like anyone to think that our relationship was sordid, didn't you?' she pleaded.

'Yeah, but that was when it felt beautiful, and now it doesn't, it feels sordid because you've fucked it up, so I don't care what Gerry thinks, and if she thinks that I'm a nutter and you are a slut...' He paused. 'Well, she'll be right, won't she?'

'I am not a slut.' Lois shouted.

'Yes, you are, you are a slut and a whore.'

'Sly, a whore takes money for sex, for Christ's sake.'

'I'm quite sure that David gave you some money, bought you some nice clothes to wear. So, what would you call it?'

Lois had had enough, and she made to leave the room. Sly

took her arm and held her firmly.

'You're not going anywhere, Lois, without my say-so. You have humiliated me, and demeaned my love, and me; you will stay here and pay me back for everything. When you are totally humiliated and demeaned, and you can admit it to me, then we will move on. Until then, you stay. If you want to admit the truth, things will move faster. If you want to finish this at any time, you only have to say. If you desire me, and you want this relationship to continue, you are in for a very difficult time. Is that clear?' Lois nodded. 'Good, then let's get one of these pay back fucks out of the way.'

★ ★ ★

Lois heard Gerry come in during the afternoon. Sly was sprawled across the bed, still fully clothed, sunk in an alcoholic stupor. Relieved to get some time off from his dark brooding and penetrating stare, she could actually feel herself soften towards him a little. Earlier she had asked him, 'What colour is your love for me now, Sly?' Despite his inebriated state, he had replied without a moment's hesitation, 'Grey, like the sea and the sky. Endlessly grey.' And she had felt so sad that she had wept silent tears as he drifted off.

Lois went downstairs to greet Gerry, taking her cigarettes with her.

'Hello, darling, how are you?' Gerry greeted her cheerfully. One glance at Lois's appearance told her instantly that something was terribly wrong. Gerry was certain that Sly was involved, and she asked, 'Where is he, the perverted one? What has he done this time?'

'Upstairs, drunk.' Lois sat down heavily on one of the kitchen chairs.

'That's a new one. I'll make a cup of tea and you can tell me all about it.' Lois felt guilty about inflicting her woes onto Gerry, who had just come in after a long journey and had not even had time to take off her shoes.

'Sly thinks I slept with David over the holiday.' Lois started, realising that she must tell Gerry everything, because there was no point in lying to her.

'Oh, come on, Lois, the bloke is an Adonis. How could any woman resist. Every woman in the British Isles would do the same.'

'I know, and it all seemed so funny at the time, but Sly is absolutely heartbroken, and I feel so shitty about it.'

'Have you told him, then?'

'No, he just knew.'

'Fuck! How weird is he?' Gerry burst out laughing.

Lois told Gerry just how weird Sly was, and, predictably, Gerry found it all hilarious. 'Right, what are you going to do about it?'

'Nothing, just wait and hope that he will come round eventually, I suppose.'

'Lois, these are supposed to be the best years of your life, and you are spending them with a complete tosspot. Kick him out and find some one not so weird. What about Mickie, David, even Finlay? You can't have missed him sniffing around you.'

'I can't do that, Gerry, don't ask me why.'

'Okay, so, we'll do lots of Ecology and get ahead of the term, and go out, have a few laughs to counteract the weird one, and get you through it. The Bunnymen have a new album out soon, and they are going to tour, so how about getting him tickets to see them when they are in Liverpool? That should cheer him up.'

Practical solutions to weird problems did offer Lois some respite from her agony. She showered, dressed and began to organise her Ecology notes. Lois and Gerry were making some Welsh rarebit for tea, when Sly suddenly appeared.

'How are you feeling?' Gerry asked cheerfully, setting a glass of lemonade and two Paracetemol down in front of him.

'I feel terrible, truly awful,' he said, and he looked it.

'That'll be the vodka,' Gerry said gleefully.

'It's got nothing to do with vodka. It's mental anguish and emotional torment.'

Gerry quickly turned away, to hide the smile that she couldn't repress.

★ ★ ★

Sly, who had now ceased to care about personal hygiene, along with his other oddities, told Lois, 'I don't want you to discuss any of this with Gerry, or anyone else. This is private. I will let you go to the Biological Sciences Library to do your Ecology, but you are not to go anywhere else. I don't want you to go for a drink with Gerry, or do any dancing, or drinking wine.'

'That's going to be fun, then, isn't it? Just how exactly are you going to stop me?'

He regarded her thoughtfully and said pompously, 'I never said that I would try to stop you, I am merely telling you what I would like, so that you can use it as a guideline by which to measure your behaviour. I am trying to help you, Lois. You obviously need a lot of guidance and monitoring in conducting your life. Despite your best efforts, and I do really believe you think you have tried, I am generous enough to give you that, you have fallen well short of my exacting standards, and have managed to hurt me yet again. So what you do is up to you, but you also know what I expect of you by now.'

Gerry was very angry about this. She could not understand why Lois allowed herself to be bullied by Sly, a drunken, cruel, weirdo.

'It is bad enough that you allow that tosser to ruin your life, without allowing him to ruin mine as well. It's no good for me, going out with other people. It's not the same without you, and no one else can dance with me.' But Lois was adamant. 'Just tell him the truth, then. You'll probably have to do it in the end, and maybe he will sort himself out faster.'

'I just can't,' Lois replied helplessly. Gerry pressed her. 'I think that he might kill me.' She had owned up to her darkest fear, that the truth would, indeed, push Sly over the edge, and he would lose it all together.

'Lois, is that the real reason why you won't tell him the truth, because you are frightened of him? I just don't under-stand. You are sleeping with a maniac, who might want to kill you! Can you hear what I am saying? For fuck's, sake get real.' Once Gerry had calmed down, she tried to encourage Lois to at least try to stop Sly drinking. The number of vodka bottles that he was getting through was stupendous, and even Malc was concerned that Sly's depression showed no sign of improving. 'And, you can stop smoking. He's done enough damage to you, without ruining your health as well,' Gerry concluded.

Lois did try pointing out to Sly that alcohol was a depressive drug and was unlikely to make him feel any better about anything. He was unreceptive, began to swear at her, and told her that vodka was now his only friend. Lois couldn't discover if he was doing any work at all. He seemed to be a fixture in her room at South Marine Terrace, there when she left for the Campus in the mornings, and there when she came back at six o'clock at night, but he refused to say what he did with the rest of his day. One hopeful sign was that, on weekdays, he began to restrict his drinking to the night, when Lois was asleep, and he started looking after his personal hygiene again, which was a relief for Lois. The weekends were the worst, from six o'clock on Friday night until early on Monday morning, when he was continually drunk. His conversation, such as it was, concerned death and how depressing everything was, the weather, the sea, Aber, Lois, music, everything.

* * *

When Echo and the Bunnymen's third album was released, on 28th January 1983, Lois had her hopes pinned on it. Sly was already dressed and ready for the day when she awoke, saying that he wanted to go and buy the tape and vinyl copies of it for both of them. Lois protested that she wanted to buy his, and he refused, knowing that David's money would be paying for it.

'My da's not short of a bob or two either; we are just not flashy with it.'

He told her to return at lunchtime and they could listen to it together. They didn't speak at all until the tape was finished and Sly had returned it to its box.

'Well, what did you think? Did you like it?' Lois asked keenly. She could imagine dancing to some new Bunnymen tracks.

'I don't like it; they've put trumpets on; they've sold out. Mac thinks he's a pop star now, and they'll be on Top of the Pops next.'

Lois was severely disappointed. Sly found fault with the soloist, the band, the lot. It seemed that their differences now extended to the one thing she thought could never change: their beloved Bunnymen.

* * *

On the day of the next Dance Society party, Sly told her that he would not speak to her, or dance with her, at the event, and that she was not to drink or dance. She lost her temper again.

'Fuck off. Who are you, to tell me what to do with my life? I've helped to organise this and I'm damned if you are going to fuck it up for me.'

'I've told you, Lois, I am trying to help you. I am the boy you claim to love while you happily shag other boys, and that's why I have a right.'

As Sly left the room, Lois picked up the nearest thing to hand and threw it at the door after him. She had broken David's Christmas teapot, to add to her troubles.

She prepared for the party with a heavy heart, angry with Sly and adamant that she would show him just how much of a good time she could have, despite his stupid attempts to get her down. She dressed carefully in the clothes bought for her by Mickie. She did Gerry's make up for her, and they shared a bottle of wine before they got anywhere near the Talbot Hotel, by which time, she was drunk enough to face the evening. Dancing, laughing and drinking, they had a great time, until Lois grew too drunk to co-ordinate her dancing. Gerry took her into the bar area, to try to sober her up a little. When they found Finlay there, Lois launched herself at him and flirted outrageously with him for the rest of the evening. Gerry and Finlay had become quite friendly, while Lois was not around. He was a real scream and their sense of humour was very similar. Finlay plied them both with more drinks and flirted right back, having a whale of a time. When Lois tottered off to the toilet, he asked Gerry about Sly's status in Lois's life. Not very helpfully, Gerry replied simply, 'Don't fucking ask.'

Sly seemed to be spending his time with Malc, Gina and Emily. It was difficult to tell whether he was enjoying himself; his expression was as sulky as usual. Once, he came into the bar and glowered at Lois and Finlay, who were far too pissed to care. Gerry thought it was hilarious and shouted, 'Oh, don't come in here, you might get contaminated!'

At the end of the evening, Gerry had to ask Finlay to help her get Lois home, as she could barely walk by this time. Laughing at nothing in particular, they dragged Lois along to her room. Gerry was a little concerned that Finlay might try to take advantage of Lois's condition, so she made it very clear that they would get Lois safely installed in her bed and then have a cup of tea downstairs. They were surprised to find Sly boy already waiting for them, a face like thunder.

'I'll take her from here, thank you.'

Finlay was shocked, never having seen Sly like this, and he tried a friendly, Woops, sorry mate, I seem to have got your girl friend drunk!'

'She doesn't need any help; she is perfectly capable of getting drunk herself, thank you.'

Gerry took Finlay away, Sly undressed Lois and put her to bed.

* * *

At four o'clock in the morning, Lois woke up with a raging thirst and a thumping head. She had never before been drunk and incapable, and although she was not nauseous yet, that would come later. She was absolutely at rock bottom. She had become one of David's floosies, the person she had always said she would never be. She had flirted with someone she hardly knew, and she probably would have slept with him, and done all sorts of unimaginable things that she would never have wanted to do. She had behaved appallingly, and she was brimming over with remorse. It was over. Sly had won. She had no fight left in her. At this moment of truth, she suddenly realised that Sly was crouched in his corner, watching her, lucid, and waiting

'Did you fuck David over the holiday, Lois?' he asked, the moment he was sure that she had seen him in the gloom.

'Yes. Yes, I did,' she replied in a hollow voice, no longer caring what he did to her.

'And do you now feel totally humiliated and completely demeaned?'

'Totally, completely and utterly,' she answered mechanically.

He seemed pleased. 'Utterly, yes that's a good word, you chose well.' He stood up and moved over to her bedside. 'Now, that wasn't so hard, was it, a little honesty?' He helped her to the toilet like an invalid and made her drink some sparkling water and take some Paracetemol. As he lifted her back into bed, she felt him get in beside her, naked, and spoon his body into hers. Whatever she had been expecting, it certainly wasn't this.

Gerry came down in the morning, to see how Lois was, and to say that there was no way on earth that she could go to any lectures. Sly wouldn't let her into Lois's room, but he stepped out onto the landing and said in a chilling voice, 'Listen to me. This morning, Lois told me the truth about David. I know you two share all your secrets, so you probably knew already. Know this, then: her will has finally been broken; she has learned a hard lesson. I will take care of her today, so please don't disturb me.'

Gerry stared at him with hatred, every hair on her body bristling with rage. 'You really are some sick fucker, mate, really sick. You should be taking lithium.'

Sly regarded her coolly and went back inside to hold his Lois while she slept.

Lois woke again at ten o'clock, when the nausea really hit home. Sly was ready with a bowl. He gently rinsed out her mouth with some mouthwash, and wiped her face.

'You should try to get something down you, something sugary. Would you like a cup of tea?'

Lois nodded and fell back onto her pillows. Tending her and producing more sweet tea whenever she vomited the previous cupful, he explained that sugar helps to counteract the drink in her system.

'How do you know all this stuff?'

Sly smiled for the first time all term, and confessed, 'I know all there is to know about getting drunk, I've been doing it since I was eleven.'

'I feel like Brenda Last,' she whispered.

'You are like Brenda Last,' he said gently, with another smile.

The syrup seemed to do the trick and this time she fell into a much deeper sleep. When she had slept again and woken, feeling better, he helped her to bathe.

'Why are you being so nice to me?'

'Because you have told me the truth. It's all I wanted.'

'What happens now?' Lois had begun to realise that there was a method to his madness; he was following some sort of plan.

'Well, I will have to continue to punish you; you understand that? Don't look so frightened, the worst is over now. You've been really brave, and there is nothing to fear. You have proved yourself equal to me. It will go back to how it was last term, before you went to Birmingham. That's not so bad, is it? You can cope with that, can't you?'

Lois nodded. Nothing could be worse than the last few weeks.

★ ★ ★

Gerry was thrilled that Lois was allowed out again, and she was impatient to get to the Union on Saturday. In fact, everyone seemed thrilled to see her. Fenn played 'The Cutter' within moments of her walking in through the door, and Lois enjoyed dancing to it. Then, Luke played 'I Could Be Happy' so that Fenn could dance with her, and Joy Division, 'Love Will Tear Us Apart' so the he could dance with her. At the end of the song, Luke kissed her on the cheek and told her that she was fantastic. Malc and Sly came along later and danced to everything. Sly seemed happy, he smiled a lot and, in the middle of 'Jeepster', he said, 'You give me great joy, Lois. There cannot be too much joy.' She felt happier than she had done in ages.

At the end of the Union, Malc offered to walk Gerry home, so that Sly could walk down the hill with Lois. On the steps near Biological Sciences department, Sly stopped her and said, 'Smell that. Twenty-seven different varieties of *Cotoneaster*.' She looked surprised and he added, 'I never forget anything you say to me.'

This harmony continued for the next few weeks, while Lois was busy catching up on the work she had missed and continuing her studies. Sly hung out with Malc, Gina and Emily, as usual. There was much more security in his relationship with Lois. She began to try to acquire tickets for The Bunnymen concert in Liverpool. Gerry thought that Finlay had contacts, and said she would talk to him about it. Everything seemed to be going well, at last.

21

During Sly: the Finlay Thing

LOIS WAS NOW ATTENDING every one of the thirty-eight sessions available in the University week, still working at the Marine Hotel and keeping Sly happy at night, and she became exhausted. She bumped into Gina on her way back from Finlay's house. Gerry had given her the message that Lois should see Finlay about the Bunnymen tickets, and give him the information he needed for his contact.

'He won't get you the tickets unless you go round in person. Perhaps he hopes that once you see his 'Lurve Nest', you will see the error of your ways with the Sly spotty one,' Gerry teased.

On the Friday night, Lois and Gerry went to the Pier for a Pernod promotion, at which Lois drank nothing, and there was no sign of Sly and gang. Finlay told Lois that the tickets would be with her next week. When they got home at around twenty past two in the morning, Sly was not there, and she found it hard to get to sleep, not knowing where he was. He was not back by morning, and Gerry was still in bed, so Lois walked along to Caerlon. The door was open, as usual, and his room tidy but empty. It gave the impression that he had gone way for the weekend. She thought it unlikely that he had gone home without saying anything to her. Malc could shed no light on Sly's whereabouts, but he reminded them that he had invited Sly to his birthday meal, on Sunday.

'I told him that he had to come, after he fucked up last year's.

So, he'll be there, don't worry.'

Having made a half-hearted effort to write an essay, the following evening, Lois went to bed early, straining her ears for a sound of Sly coming in. A gale raged outside, shingle battered her windows and waves beat against the promenade.

The friends helped to prepare the food for Malc's party, to which Sly turned up, sloped into the room and studiously avoided Lois. In fact, he spoke only to answer questions from Malc. Gerry was incensed and complained loudly about his behaviour. She seemed hell bent on getting drunk, and Lois was almost tempted to follow her example. The meal was lovely, but it was difficult to enjoy anything, when one person refused to speak and get in the mood. Lois began to feel sick with fear and could hardly eat a thing. Gerry was drunk when she finally cracked and turned on Sly.

'Oi, you, fuck face, what exactly is the purpose of you being here?

'I am here as Malc's guest,' he replied coldly.

'Well, try to lighten up a bit. It's his fucking birthday, remember?'

'I haven't forgotten, Gerry.' There was an awkward silence around the table, and Sly got up from his place and put his napkin down on the table.

'Just for once, Gerry is right, I'm not in the mood for parties, I will leave. Malc, can I have a word with you, in private?'

He left the room, Malc also left, without comment, and Lois followed him.

'Oh, let him go,' Gerry shouted. She shook her head and poured herself more wine, saying, 'Well, I'm going to have a good time, even if the rest of them are determined to bathe in misery.'

Lois was shaking all over because she couldn't fathom what was going on, but she knew that it was pretty disastrous. When Sly came downstairs, he made to pass her, but she grabbed him by the arm. She implored him to say what was wrong, but he looked at her with contempt, and growled, 'I don't want to talk to you. I have nothing to say.'

'Sly, please, you owe me an explanation.'

'I don't owe you anything, except, maybe, one last fuck.' He pulled her roughly into her bedroom. She had never seen him so angry. He was very rough with her and she derived no pleasure from this experience. 'I hate you, Lois. I hate everything about you. You make me sick to my stomach. I have bile in my throat.' He withdrew from her and pushed her roughly onto the bedcovers. She pulled the sheet round her. Again, she asked what had happened to make him so angry, but he abused her verbally and told her never to come near him again. He just picked up his bag and walked out. Lois followed him, pleading for an explanation, begging him not to leave her. He ran downstairs and out of the house, slamming the door behind him. Lois sat back on the bed, shivering. Luke came running upstairs to her.

'What's happened? Oh, my God, what has he done to you?'

She asked for Gerry, and Luke had to explain that Gerry was horribly drunk.

Luke asked her to tell him what was wrong, but Lois could never talk to Luke about this; he was too innocent, and this was just too awful.

'Leave me alone for a moment, please, Luke. I need to wash and get my clothes on.'

Luke was disturbed by all of this, and particularly at Lois's reluctance to speak to him about it. He gave her a chance to sort herself out while he fetched a glass of brandy for her. Next, Finlay turned up. He had entered the house, found Gerry out cold, and come upstairs. He had just knocked on Lois's door, when he heard voices. At a glance, he took in the situation.

'What has he done to you? It's Sly, isn't it? Gerry told me he's a shit.' Luke stood by as Finlay took command. Finlay insisted that she must tell him what Sly had done. The brandy was kicking in, and he was very persuasive.

'I can't tell you with Luke here.'

'Fucking great! Thanks, Lois. You've known me for over a year and this pillock for two minutes, but you still won't let me help you, when you must know how much it means to me to help,' Luke said bitterly. 'Fine. I'll finish the washing up and get Gerry to bed. I do have some uses.'

Lois woke early; Finlay was slumped on the armchair in her room. She went to the bathroom, and when she returned to the room, she asked, 'What are you doing here?'

'I thought some one should stay, in case you woke up. I'll go, if you like. Gerry came down at four o'clock. I told her what had happened. She was very upset that she hadn't been able to be here with you. Is there anything you want, a cup of tea?'

Lois shook her head. Then she asked, 'Has Malc gone up to the campus yet?' Finlay didn't think so. When Lois found him, she asked him to try to find out what was wrong with Sly. Malc held out little hope of success, but said he would do his best, anyway. She decided to go to her lectures, where Max tried to engage her in conversation, but she remained silent and Sly-like.

In the evening, she told Gerry about everything that had happened. Gerry called what Sly had done rape, and tried to persuade Lois that it would all be for the best in the end, if she finally broke with the weirdo. Lois considered her options; there could be no more running home to David; she would have to cope on her own. Newly found resolve meant she could go and see Malc, immediately he came in. She wasn't running away, and she wasn't expecting anyone else to do her dirty work for her. Maybe, she was coping, finally. Malc confirmed that Sly simply was not speaking, which was what she expected.

On Wednesday that week, something serious happened, for which Lois blamed Gerry. She had been working, when Gerry and Finlay came in and Gerry said that Finlay had something to tell her. He sat down on the bed and looked rather pleased with himself. Gerry left, which Lois found strange.

'Where's she gone?' Lois asked puzzled.

'There's something I wanted to tell you. I've finished with Lynne today.'

Lois wasn't quite sure what to say in reply. So she said, 'Is that good?'

'Yes, I should have done it ages ago. I don't love her any more, and now I've met you, I just knew I had to do something.'

'What ever do you mean, now you've met me?' Lois asked, feeling sick to her stomach.

'Well, you and Sly are over, and you can't doubt that I love you. I can't think about anything else.'

He looked at her, his face full of optimism. Lois was burning with anger and indignation. She gave Finlay no cause to doubt the reception she gave his declaration of calf-love. Any other man would have fled before her fury. Finlay was very calm in reply.

'I know that you haven't really considered me, Lois, but it doesn't matter, you are still in trauma, I know that. I just wanted you to know that you've given me the courage to finish with Lynne and I feel totally liberated. It's good and, even if you don't want me, it doesn't matter because I'm still free of her, at long last. I am not expecting anything from you. I just want to be your friend and to help you get through this. I won't demand anything. Honestly.'

Lois refused to go for a drink with them that evening. She sat and stared out at the sea, trying to work out why everyone around her was completely barking mad. Gerry came in to see her later, ready to apologise to her. Lois cut her short and sent her away. Things would never be the same again.

On Friday night, Finlay came round and said, 'Lynne is coming to Aber this weekend; she say's she would like to meet you.'

'Meet me? She's already met me, and I got the impression she disliked me. Why would she want to meet me?'

'Well, she has been my girlfriend for a long time, and I have told her all about how I feel for you.'

Lois choked with anger. Finlay had not heard a word of what she had told him, and now he offered her this impertinence.

Once again, a storm raged, and its noise made it difficult for her to sleep. She snatched a couple of hours and woke very early. She sat in the window and watched the waves building and breaking, expending their pent up violence on the rocks. It suited her mood. She wondered whether to let David know what had happened, remembering what he had said to her when he brought her back to Aber. It seemed like a lifetime away. She decided to wait until she was back in Chester for Easter. Aberystwyth could make everything seem worse than any other place she had known. Was it the remoteness, or the greyness, of the seaside town? At last, she pulled herself away from the window and made breakfast for Josh and Rachel, two friends who were visiting and staying in the same house.

Lois worked hard all day and prayed that she wouldn't bump into Zit face in the evening. Tonight, because she was supposed to be meeting Lynne, she dressed and made-up with care. Finlay arrived, without Malc, at seven o'clock. Lois hoped that Malc was with Sly. Lynne was sitting at the bar, when they arrived. She made a show of greeting everyone, and for the rest of the evening, so it seemed to Lois, Lynne talked non-stop about the catering business. Lois wished that she could just leave, but she didn't want to draw any attention to herself. Josh took pity on her and engaged her in conversation. Rachel soon took part in this, leaving Lynne and Finlay chatting happily together, and Lois wondered why he had finished with someone with whom he clearly got on so well. She glanced up just as Sly, Gina and Emily came into the pub. They got drinks, and, yes, shit, they were coming over.

Lois stood up and said, 'I have to go now. Please excuse me.'

Lynne regarded her coolly, but Finlay had also understood that Lois and Sly could not remain together.

'What's up? I thought we were going out to dinner.' Lynne asked indignantly. 'She just said that nobody has eaten yet. Why don't we all go out together and eat somewhere?' Lois erupted into fury. 'You stay, Lynne. I will go home. This is all causing far too much trouble. You can go fuck yourselves, the whole lot of you; except for Josh and Rachel, you are all tossers.'

After they had eaten, they went to the Belle Vue for a brandy and found a seat in the window. Outside, the storm continued unabated. Lois suddenly missed Mickie and wished he were there, eyes twinkling, with something funny to say to her. Gina, who always seemed to arrive with bad news, came in and sought out Finlay.

He picked up his coat and said, 'I won't be long. Gina says Lynne is threatening to kill herself. Like, I actually care, Lois thought.

★　★　★

The wind showed no signs of abating, and it was getting late, when Finlay showed up again. He appealed to Lois for help to end his relationship with Lynne, the corollary being, of course, that Lois step into her shoes. Lois was too tired to think straight, and she tried to get Finlay to leave. However, Finlay could be very persuasive, and begged her to come right away. When Lois reluctantly agreed to come to Caerlon and do what she could to help him, he promised that she wouldn't have to come upstairs. She could wait just inside the hall, and no one but he would even know she was there. He only needed to know that she was waiting for him, and that was enough. She and Finlay battled the raging elements once more, and arrived at Caerlon wet and bedraggled

Finlay left her downstairs, and the sounds of shouting filtered down to her. She couldn't make out what was said, and her eyes were itching from tiredness. Finlay took a long time to pluck up the courage to leave Lynne. After she had been shivering in the hall for fifty minutes, Lois heard footsteps above. Finlay had started his move, and Gina was following him. Lois heard her booming, actressy voice. 'Finlay, you are leaving a human being for an empty vessel.'

Lynne's voice was audible now; begging him not to leave. She heard Sly say, 'Come by here, and wait a bit, until she's calmed down.' He seemed to have sided with Finlay amidst all this female hysteria. However, Lois had had enough, and she wanted to go home. She marched upstairs and surveyed the scene from the kitchen doorway. Lynne was slumped at the kitchen table; Gina sat beside her, one arm round her shoulder. Emily was on the other side of her. Finlay was closest to the door, and Sly was skulking by the sink.

'Finlay,' she announced, 'I am going home. I've had enough of this nonsense.' Sly looked shocked, and Finlay made to move towards her, but Lynne was the fastest to react. She plucked a knife from the table and lunged at Lois, yelling, 'You fucking bitch, I'm going to kill you.'

Finlay and Sly leapt at her and one of them snatched the blade from her hand. Lois spun on her heel and left. The wind was already dying.

★　★　★

The next morning, she told Gerry all about it. 'Fucking pretentious wankers,' was her typical reply. Lois started work on a physiology essay, and she was halfway through it and about to make a cup of tea, when Finlay reappeared. Lois made him a cup of tea, as well, and asked Gerry to join them, so that he wouldn't have to repeat his sorry tale.

'So, how's Sly? Did Lynne cut his willie off?' Gerry asked. 'That would have been poetic justice.'

'No, he cut his hand and had to have stitches. Did you hear what Gina said about you?'

'Of course, I did. She was yelling her head off.'

'They all really hate you.'

'I know they do,' said Lois.

'But why? Why are they so keen to poison my mind against you? The things they said were awful, and I'm sure they aren't true. Have you ever had a boyfriend called David here? They seem to think that he's an outrageous type.' Lois and Gerry exchanged significant looks but said nothing.

*　*　*

It took the Drama crew the rest of the week to persuade Finlay to stay with Lynne, and he came to the house to say that Lynne had forbidden him to acknowledge Lois if they met in the street.'

'Gerry will be sad, She's the one you've let down, and I think you need to talk to her, not me,' Lois said.

Gerry came down to see Lois after Finlay had left, she apologised for setting Lois up with him, and agreed that it had made matters worse, not better.

For Lois, the worst was not over. As she and Gerry worked in the Marine Cellar Bar on Friday evening, Sly walked in with Gina and Emily, and a few more people that Lois didn't know by name. It was almost ten o'clock, and they had clearly been enjoying a night on the town. They waited in a group by the door until Gerry was busy, when Sly went up to Lois, who was washing up glasses, and ordered a round of drinks, which she gave him. Gareth was on duty this night and, as it was quiet, he was seated at the bar, enjoying a pint. Sly and friends gathered near the jukebox, and

Lois continued to wash up. Presently, Sly came back to the bar.

'Excuse me, but you seem to have given me an empty glass. Do you see this glass? It's empty, like you, Lois,' he said, loudly enough to attract attention. His friends brayed with laughter.

'That glass wasn't empty when I gave it to you. It had lager in it.'

'What's the matter, Lois?' Gareth called over.

Sly turned to him, quite deliberately making his voice more Welsh than ever. 'It's this English girl, by 'ere; she tried to serve me an empty glass.'

'Give the man a drink, Lois, and try to concentrate,' Gareth told her. Lois took the glass and filled it once again with lager.

Gerry looked incensed. 'Don't serve him again. Let me do it. I'll fucking kill him.'

'It's not worth your job, dear. Don't let the turkeys get you down, remember.' Sly knew what he was doing. The moment Gerry was unavailable, he came back.

'Excuse me, but this glass seems to be dirty, See, by 'ere, it's a dirty glass, like you, dirty.'

Gareth had gone to change a barrel so he wasn't there for this one.

As Lois refilled a new, clean glass, Gerry suddenly said, 'See this glass, you shit-for-brains, it's cracked, just like you, mate.' Unfortunately, Gareth returned in time to hear this, so she got a telling off. Again, Sly waited his turn and was once more back at the bar. The group was now rolling around, so funny did they find it.

'Excuse me; you seem to have given me the wrong drink. I asked for a gin and tonic and this is vodka. You clearly don't listen, or you're not very bright, or maybe both.'

A smile came over his face. Gareth was getting agitated so Lois poured vodka into the glass.

'Well, sir,' she said, returning his smile, 'you've still got the tonic and, because we have a promotion on at the moment, gin is more expensive than vodka, so you owe me twenty pence. Service with a smile.'

This baiting continued all evening, until Gareth lost patience and so did Lois. 'You can stuff your job,' she said. 'I'm going home.'

* * *

The next night, when Gerry and Lois walked into the Union, Sly and his cronies were already there. Gina came over and told them to leave, so that Sly might enjoy himself, which was impossible with Lois, the bitch, in the same room as him. Gerry was ready to fight her corner over this, but Lois wouldn't stay.

'It's no use, Gerry, I just haven't got the energy to fight.'

Gerry grew more and more worried about Lois, who complained continually of sickness and lack of appetite, as well as insomnia. When she took off her jumper, to don her lab coat, Gerry was horrified to see that she had lost an awful lot of weight. She had a dreadful cough, as well, probably due to the cigarettes she had smoked, earlier in the term, but this was exacerbating her sickness. Gerry resolved to take action. She found Mickie's home telephone number, but someone else answered and gave her his work's number. Mickie was certain to be there, she was told, because they had a show opening next week.

22

After Sly:
Mickie to the Rescue

MICKIE WAS IN A FOUL MOOD, suffering from last minute nerves, impatient with the young people who were trying to arrange the exhibits, when someone called him to the telephone. Instantly he thought of home and his family, hoping that it wouldn't be another crisis in the wake of his father's death. The call galvanised him into action, and he left his assistant, Rosemary to cope as well as she could.

He drove down to Aberystwyth under a blue sky. The storm had petered out and left a glimpse of spring in the air. He found Lois in her room, she gazed at him in wonder.

'Oh, Mickie, I thought I'd heard your voice. I couldn't believe it. I thought I'd gone completely mad.'

'I've come for the weekend, if that's alright.'

His eyes twinkled; Lois didn't think she has ever seen anything so beautiful. He explained that he had abandoned his exhibition, to come and visit her, and now that he had seen her, he was concerned that she had lost weight and was so pale. His sympathy melted her heart and she told him what she had been through since the last time they had been together.

'Oh, the bastard, bastard, bastard! He can do that to you! He is sick. How do you feel? Do you need counselling, or something? I mean, that's rape, no matter how you look at it.'

'Mickie, I know it sounds crazy, but I'm suffering from

something much more than rape. It's not how he chose to finish it that is getting to me; it's the whole thing. I feel as if, ever since he went nuts in the first year, he has been trying to make me suffer. It seems to have been his lifetime's work. I'm not focusing on that one time, when I think about it. Total humiliation has been his aim, even when he said he loved me. I don't need counselling, I just need a new brain, one that doesn't contain any mental traces of Sly Davies.'

'But there are rules to prevent these sorts of things happening. Can't you tell your tutor or someone?'

'We are supposed to be grown up, Mickie. This sort of thing happens in schools, not here.'

Mickie asked what he could do for her, and she reminded him how he had sent her to sleep in the old days, by stroking her skin. Lois found that he still had the knack, and she slept well for the first time in months. Mickie spent the night thinking about Sly, until he drifted to sleep at seven o'clock in the morning, certain that he had the answer.

They breakfasted at the café in the cattle market and, afterwards, they went shopping in the town. Later, he made a lunch of scrambled eggs and Parmesan cheese, with smoked salmon. She was cleaning the pots when he said, 'Lois, it's time for me to go out.'

'You're not going to see Sly, are you?'

'No, of course I'm not. It's my old pal John. He's having a hard time at the moment. I can't come all this way and not go to see him. Hazel's making his life a misery, and I just need to go and see if he's all right. You don't mind, do you? You said you had some work to do.'

'I have,' she agreed, but he saw she was disappointed.

'He's my friend; you know that.'

'It's just that you always seem to be rushing off somewhere. Your feet don't touch the ground.'

'I'll only be gone for about an hour, and when I get back, I'll be all yours, I promise. I'll wash your hair for you. How about that?'

'You'll do what?'

'Wash your hair. I've got sisters. I know how to wash hair. You'll love it.'

* * *

Mickie felt bad about lying to Lois. Although John had none of the problems Mickie had described, he still needed to see him. He found him watching the International Rugby match, a can of lager in his hand.

'You going to watch the game with me, then?' John was settling back into his armchair.

'I hate rugby even more than football.'

'So, what's going on?'

'I'm here for Lois, John. I need to find Lynne.'

'Oh, not that again. I thought we'd done all that.'

'Tell me where I can fuckin' find her?'

'She is working at the Cabin.'

'Magic. You're a star, terrific. Thanks, mate. I hope Wales get stuffed.'

'Fuck off.'

* * *

Lynn was there, waiting on tables, when Mickie walked in.

'What are you doing here?' she asked, smiling.

'Well I've come to see you, my old friend. Is there a chance you can take a break? See if you can get a cigarette as well.' He sat at one of the tables, where she joined him.

'Charlie says I can have thirty minutes, and he says hello. You're lucky we're not busy. So, what are you doing here? Why aren't you in Birmingham?'

'There's no sense beating about the bush. It's Lois.'

'I though you'd got that sorted out,' Lynne snapped impatiently.

'No, I haven't. I'm here to sort it out, and I need you to tell me what has been going on? Why is someone as seemingly sorted as you waging a hate campaign against her? Her life is a misery and she's ill with it. Have you seen her?'

Lynne looked annoyed. She lit a cigarette.

'Get real, Mickie. Your little poppet is in crisis and you come all the way from Birmingham to sort her out. What a nice guy! You must be mad.'

'Please tell me what has been going on, Lynne,' he said simply.

'Your little poppet tried to steal my Finlay.'

'No, she didn't. You're just deluded. She isn't interested in Finlay. It was just a stupid idea of Gerry's, Lynne, to try to shove them at one another. Finlay was bored and lonely, and he fancied her, but that doesn't make her what you called her, a worthless, empty vessel.'

'She flirted with him at the Dance Society disco.'

'She was drunk. It's no wonder, either, after she had been subjected to Sly's psychological tricks.'

'Oh, I don't believe this,' Lynne spat at him. 'You are wasting my time. I really should know better. Pauline told me all about you and that girl, last year, how you fell for her, became obsessed, fell in love. Couldn't get enough of her, could you? You're the worst!' She pointed her finger in his face. 'You're worse than all the rest, you've got it bad, you're deluded.'

They argued back and forth, getting nowhere. Mickie defended Lois against all the poisonous accusations levelled against her by Lynne, and Lynne lost all patience with him.

'Why don't you just take her back to Birmingham? She causes too much trouble here.'

'I would love to do that, but it isn't the answer. She'd come with me now, but only to escape from you lot and Sly, and that's not a good enough reason for me. So, get the Department off her case, give her some respite.'

'It's not the whole Department.'

'Yes, possibly, but what's happening is juvenile, and you're meant to be an adult, so act like one.'

With that, he left her, hoping it would be enough. Lynne had taken him seriously. Mickie returned to Lois, convinced that his conversation with Lynne would make a difference. He was less certain what to do with the knowledge that Sly believed Lois had cheated on him with Finlay. In the end, he decided that it was best to let Sly to find out in his own time just how warped he was.

Lois was clearly pleased to see him when he got back. As he had promised he would, he gently washed her hair. Once he had finished, she thanked him.

'Any time. That was one of the most intense moments of my life.'

Lois began to cry again and he took her back to her room and held her gently in his arms as she wept.

'It's all right, don't break your heart. I know what you are thinking, believe me.'

'No, you think I am crying over Sly, but I'm not.'

'I never thought you were. You are crying for me, because you would like to feel for me the way I feel about you, and you don't. It's all right. It's not my time yet, but it will be one day, don't worry about it.'

'Mickie, I think I love you. Why do I feel that way?'

'Look, you don't love me. I'm being kind to you, when everyone else is giving you a hard time, and you're feeling gratitude. It's not love, not yet, but it's lovely that you want to love me. It's enough, honestly.'

Lois looked at him very hard and asked, 'How do you know me so well, Mickie?'

'I just do. I love you and I always will, until Aber falls into the sea, eh?'

He took her to Gannett's for a good dinner. Lois rejoiced to witness the absolute joy that everyone who had ever known Mickie displayed on seeing him again. They did make love that night. Mickie wanted her to be sure that she was ready, and she was. On Sunday, he had to get back to Birmingham. It took every ounce of determination, to prevent him from visiting his old tutor and begging for an M.A. place here. He longed to take Lois back to Birmingham with him, and he had come to hate Sly passionately.

Once Mickie had gone, Lois felt lonelier than ever before. Even Gerry could hardly reach her. She sat through lectures and practical sessions on automatic pilot and, at night, she spent hours looking out to sea. Her physical condition had never been worse. She neglected her make-up and no longer cared what she wore. She longed to be in Chester.

At the end of term, Gerry travelled with her as far as Shrewsbury. She gazed at the passing countryside, her mind blank. She wanted to fall into David's arms and have him take over where she had failed, and tell her what to do, what to say, what to eat, how to get better. For a second, as she stepped off the train, David's face lit up, but when he saw that state she was in, he came close and asked, 'What the fuck has he done to you this time?'

23

After Sly: a New Lois

ON SATURDAY 16TH APRIL,1983, Ian Stephen McCulloch – Lois's Mac, if you didn't know – and Lorraine Fox married at a traditional church wedding in Warrington. It was in all the papers, including Lois's, and Mac was quoted as saying, "I know it's a tradition, but so's going down the pub, and I like doing that as well." It was the day that Lois's life changed forever.

* * *

On her return to Aberystwyth, Lois was different. She settled back to work, starting with a Marine Biology field trip, which she enjoyed immensely; it coincided with her twentieth birthday, and she was showered with gifts, some from people she hardly knew. David was back in her life as well. Apart from the field trip outing, she worked, cooked food, and hid in her room. Sometimes, Gerry would knock on her door, when she knew she was there, but Lois wouldn't answer. David had paid to have locks fitted on both Gerry's and Lois's doors on the very first day of the term. He wanted her to feel as safe as she could. Lois stubbornly refused to go out socialising. At weekends, she went home to Chester, or David came to see her, arriving in his Triumph Stag late on Friday evening and leaving early on Monday morning, to get back to London and his modelling.

They had dinner in the Belle Vue, or in South Marine terrace, and had many trips out to stately homes and gardens in the county.

Lois couldn't get away from Aberystwyth often enough. David was still able to turn on the charm whenever he wanted to, and could swiftly attract an admiring audience for his tall tales.

The Aberystwyth weather continued to reflect Lois's mood; thunderstorms came in off the sea, swept over the town, lost themselves in the mountains, and came back to the sea again. Gerry continued to try to re-establish contact with Lois. She began to accept that there was no chance of dancing, but she wished that Lois would talk to her. Sly seemed to have evaporated into thin air.

Towards the end of term, Fenn and Luke tried to persuade Lois to come to the Union once more before they left. They failed. Gerry thought of a way to guarantee that Sly and his posse wouldn't be there, and she was determined to talk to Lois about it. It was a beautiful day, sunny and warm, and the visitors had started to arrive. Lois was reading and she felt happier than she had for a long time. The absence of Sly from her life was doing her a power of good.

Gerry found her and announced, 'I've thought of a way you can come to the Union. We'll get Malc to take Shit-face out somewhere else. I'll even pay him. Fenn and Luke and I will be able to be with you. We miss you so much.' She started to weep. Lois had never ever seen Gerry cry. She took her hand, and Gerry continued, 'We miss you, Lois, we miss you so much'.

'I'm here, darling,' Lois replied. 'I've never been away. I'll always be right here for you. Listen, I've been meaning to say, we're all going to France with David this year, me, mum, Ronnie and Bryan. We want you to come, too.'

Gerry couldn't believe her luck. 'All Summer? Ace; we'll have a ball.'

'There's something else, but you must promise me that you won't tell anyone. I don't want Sly to know'.

'Of course. There's no way I'd tell that wanker anything about you. Believe me, I'd rather die'.

'Okay, I'm not coming back in the autumn'.

Gerry was aghast. 'Lois! What do you mean, you're not coming back in the autumn, for fuck's sake? You're on for a first'.

'I won't get a first now', Lois replied. 'He made sure of that. I'll be happy with a two-one. I will finish my degree. I'm just not coming back this autumn. I'm taking a year out. I want to make absolutely sure that Sly boy can't fuck me up again. I want it guaranteed.'

'What will you do?' Gerry asked, puzzled.

'I've got a place as a research technician at Aston University, doing interesting Bio-technology work. I've always wanted to do that, anyway.'

'But what will I do without you? Shit, Lois.' Gerry started to cry again.

'You could do it, too. You just go to the careers office and ask for a placement. It's easy; it's called an industrial year'

'And you wouldn't mind?'

'Course I wouldn't. Don't be stupid. I'd love to have my final year with you, zit-free, imagine.'

'Oh, but that's great. Loads of people are having a year out, Mannon, all the linguists, even Brown R. She's having a year off because her dad's ill.' Gerry was warming to the idea rapidly.

'We'll be fine, just as long as Sly doesn't find out. He'd take a year out just to make sure he could give me a hard time. He's perverse that way'

'Lois, there's one more thing. Can you tell me why you are sick all the time?'

'It's just that I keep getting these waves of emotion, and then I feel sick. There's nothing I can do about it. I can't stop coughing, and when I cough, I feel sick. Please don't worry about it; my doctor says there is nothing anyone can do. It will just take its course. I saw him at Easter. David made me go. He checked me out. I'm fine, honestly. Please don't worry.'

'But you're getting so thin, you look dreadful.'

'Thank you, Gerry, but I can't help it. I keep being sick, that's why I'm losing so much weight, it'll be all right in the end, just give me time.'

'Everyone thinks that you are bulimic.'

'Believe me, I hate throwing up. It is not serious. It'll pass, in time.'

Gerry was uncertain how much to believe, but passed on the information to their friends, who were equally sceptical, but grateful that Gerry had at least tackled Lois.

★   ★   ★

After Lois's last examination, she left for Chester and safety. David had driven up that morning and cleared her room of all her clutter. Gerry had hoped that Lois would stay for a celebration lunch but had to be content with the forthcoming summer holiday in France. Gerry was pleased not to be doing her third year next year. She had planned her industrial year to coincide with Lois's and was going to work for an Agrochemical company. She stretched out on her bed and fell into a light sleep, from which she was woken shortly afterwards by a knocking at her door. She was horrified to open the door and see Sly.

'What do you want?' Gerry asked. Sly looked worried about something.

'I want to know where Lois is. Her room is empty. I need to talk to her. Where is she, Gerry?'

'She went straight home after her exam. Now, leave me alone. Piss off.'

'Has she gone to Chester?'

'Just fuck off and leave her alone. She's going straight to France, anyway, sailing tonight with David. You'll never find her again, you fucking wanker.'

'But I have something to tell her, something she will really want to know. I want to tell her what happened.' Sly was speaking very slowly, as though he simply couldn't take in what had happened. 'Malc told me that she finished her exams today. He made me wait until she had done the last one. She should be here. He didn't say she was going home straight away.'

'Well, he probably didn't know. We've not discussed anything about Lois with Malc, because we know it would get straight back to you. Now, fuck off and leave me alone.'

'I can't,' Sly spoke very firmly. 'If I leave this room, I will fall off the edge of the world. It's as though there is nothing out there for me anymore.'

Gerry was starting to get angry. Sly was staring at his hands, unmoved by anything she said. Gerry suddenly had a burning desire to hurt him in someway. She visualised herself kicking him about the body. No sooner had the thought developed than she was in action. She launched herself towards him, screaming. 'Fuck off, fuck off, fuck off, fuck off.' She hit and kicked viciously; landing blows on head and body. Sly tried to defend himself, but Gerry was enjoying herself so much, after all those months of pent up frustration. She stopped when she realised that Malc was standing in her doorway, staring open-mouthed at the two of them.

'Eeh, you two, cut it out. I'm trying to revise for my finals here, and you're having a fight. What the fuck is going on?'

Malc reached down and helped Sly to his feet. Sly gave Gerry a look of pure hatred. Malc dragged them into his room and asked what had happened.

'This bastard is trying to get me to tell him where Lois is; says he needs to speak to her. He is off his rocker. If you value this lump of shit as a friend, Malc, then get him seen to before too long. I can't imagine what you see in him. Lois is worth a hundred million of this sad bastard. Haven't you got any loyalty at all?' Gerry asked, and left them alone.

Malc asked Sly what was so urgent that Lois had to be told about it. Sly said he had to tell Lois first.

'Well, I don't want to be rude but I'm supposed to be revising.'

Sly stood up. 'It's all right,' he said. 'I want to be on my own, anyway. I'll be in her room, if you want me. When do you have to leave?'

'By Saturday. Why?'

'I'll be in her room until then.'

Malc went back to his revision, found it hard to concentrate, and went to make some tea. He looked in on Sly and found him in the corner of the room, a bottle of vodka in his hand. Malc got no response from him, and decided that he must make Sly see a doctor before he went home. Lois's room looked very empty. Malc could smell her perfume.

The Aberystwyth doctor who examined Sly was not long out of medical school. She knew what was wrong with him, gave it a name and said that she could treat him.

He tried to telephone Lois, doubtful whether Gerry had told the truth about her sailing immediately. Malc had said that Gerry was going to France with them, and that she was not leaving until Saturday, but he delayed mentioning that Lois would not be coming back in the autumn. Lois's mother answered Sly's call and put down the telephone when she realised who was on the line. He tried the next day, and discovered that the number was unobtainable because the family was now ex-directory.

He asked Malc to do one final thing for him regarding Lois. He was to write her address on an envelope, so that she would recognise a friendly hand and open it. He wasn't to know that David had taken charge of all correspondence to Lois and that the letter went into the bin. She never knew that Sly had tried to contact her. In desperation, he went to her house in Chester. It was empty, the curtains drawn. He tried asking her neighbours, but nobody could, or would, tell him anything.

24

After Sly: Su Su

MALC WISHED for the hundredth time that he could see into Sly's head. There was a rainstorm coming in across the bay and the sky was black. Sly sat immobile, as if he had forgotten Malc's existence. Malc knew better than to ask what he was thinking of; the answer was always Lois. Malc asked himself why he kept coming here, only to go through the whole scenario yet again. Sly had been smiling on the previous day, which had given Malc hope that he would soon get over Lois and start to live again. This morning, Sly was back in the window seat, staring out to sea, evidently in one of his black moods. Malc had tried to discover what had brought about the change, and Sly said it was a dream of Lois. Since then, Malc had been reading, but now he was bored. The only bright spot on the horizon was the fact that Gina and Ali were going to come out with them tonight. Gina brought out the best of Sly.

Malc was afraid that he would have a go at Sly soon, then, feel guilty because Sly couldn't really help himself. Sly was seeing his doctor regularly, Malc knew, so if it really were depression, she would surely have given him something to help lift his mood. Sly was reluctant to talk about his health.

'Why don't we go shopping, Sly?'

'We don't need anything, I've got it all.' Sly was about to turn away to look at the sea again.

'I'm bored. I can't take much more of this. You're doing my head in. Let's go and look round Galloways, or Andy's records, anything.'

Sly didn't move, but Malc found his jacket and made him put it on. They would go shopping, if it was the last thing they did. It was raining hard and a stream of water ran down the gutter. When Malc went into Andy's records, Sly stood outside in the rain, sulking. They went on to Galloways bookshop. Sly once again stayed outside, staring mournfully across the road, while Malc took his time amongst the bookshelves. Sly, impatient, wet and cold, looked through the window, trying to find Malc, who was in conversation with a girl who looked vaguely familiar. Malc was talking to her urgently, holding her arm, emphasising something, and Sly was intrigued. Malc moved towards the counter as the girl came out of the store. She walked past Sly, glanced up and turned her face away and hurried down the street. Sly had a strong desire to follow her. Something intriguing had happened.

Malc, carrying a brown paper bag, left the shop and walked rapidly away. Sly ran after him and caught his arm. He asked what was happening, who was the girl in the bookshop, but Malc hurried on. He wished Sly would go away now, and leave him alone.

'That was Su Su, an American friend, here for the day. Listen, Sly, sorry, but I have to go home.'

Sly still tagged along, asking questions that Malc had no intention of answering.

'Look, Sly, I wouldn't be doing this if it weren't important, would I? You could do me a favour, though, and meet my friend Penny off the train.'

'But I don't even know her.'

'She'll know you,' Malc assured him, before he ran off, leaving Sly standing in the street.

★　★　★

That same afternoon, in Birmingham, Gerry was unloading groceries from her car. She had bunked off work and stocked up on goodies for the weekend. David and Ben were coming up from Chester, and she was looking forward to having some fun. Lois would be home soon, ready to have a sherry with her. As Gerry went in, the telephone was ringing; when she reached out for it, it stopped. She waited a minute, and it rang again. The voice that said, 'Lois?' was one she recognised.

'It's Sly.'

She told him to fuck off, and slammed the receiver down. To be on the safe side, she left the telephone off the hook, and began to ask herself whether to mention the call to Lois and David. How did Sly have their Birmingham number? Surely, he hadn't obtained it from Malc.

When Sly rang again, the line was engaged, but he had recognised Gerry's voice. Sly had looked in Malc's address book and found only one Birmingham number, unidentified by a name, but now confirmed as Lois's.

Lois was late home, and Gerry ceased pacing up and down, trying to think what to do. If she told Lois, she would worry. If she told David, he would go mad at her. His life's work was keeping Sly away from Lois. Gerry had a premonition of trouble ahead and, because she was unusually quiet, Lois knew something was wrong. Before Gerry had time to offer an explanation, David and Ben arrived, followed shortly by a taxi bearing Malc.

* * *

Sly told Gina and Ali that he had a migraine, an excuse that had come in handy over the last twelve months, particularly during stressful times. He bought some vodka, without which he would never sleep. He asked Gina and Ali to meet Malc's friend Penny off the train from Blackburn and look after her until Malc returned.

Malc woke Sly in mid-afternoon, opened the curtains, and picked up the almost empty vodka bottle. He told Sly, unsympathetically, that he would kill himself if he carried on drinking so much. He asked about Penny and Sly said that she was with Gina and Ali. Malc sighed, made a pot of tea and poured two mugs full, and heaped sugar liberally into Sly's.

'I went to Birmingham, to see Lois,' Malc said, watching Sly's face.

'I knew you had, but I don't understand why? What was so urgent that you just took off? Why couldn't you phone her? You had her number in your address book.'

'You'll find that it's been changed, by now. David will make sure of that.'

'Didn't you think that I would be terrified at you going away like that? Is Lois all right, Malc.'

'She's fine.' Malc said impatiently.

'What has that American girl got to do with this? Please don't bullshit me, I need to know.'

'Su Su has hardly seen anyone since she moved back to the States. When I met her yesterday, she was hungry for information. She knew Lois vaguely; she liked her, used to talk to her on the party circuit, that sort of thing. She heard that Lois wasn't coming back next year, because, she thought, you were doing your M.A. here. I'd already told Lois that you weren't. I just wanted to check with Lois whether it was true or not. I didn't want her to think that I was plotting with you to stitch her up again. That's why I went.' Even Malc thought this sounded pretty feeble.

Sly wasn't convinced either, and he protested, 'All that way, so suddenly; it could have waited, at least until Sunday.'

'Sure, it could have waited, but I don't want Lois to suffer anymore. I know what happened. You've never admitted it to me, but the others have told me, and it sickened me. It was after I let you send that letter, Sly. I had a real battle with myself at that time; I couldn't work out why I would want to be friends with someone capable of raping of one of my closest friends.'

Sly looked thunderous. They had never discussed this before, but it explained why Malc had been so impatient with him over the last year. He must hate him.

'I don't understand why you are still here, either. I've never admitted to anyone that what you say is true. I admitted nothing to you, not because I didn't want you to know, because I was afraid I'd lose your friendship. I deserve to lose it. I deserve everything I get, including this silence from Lois. David is doing a good job of protecting her from me. He deserves her; I know that now, but I still want to explain something to her. I can't allow anyone else to do it. I will find a way, if I have to wait forever.'

Malc was losing it now. 'What the bloody hell is this thing you have to tell Lois? Tell me. I'll let her know, for Christ's sake, and then maybe you'll be able to move on with your life. You having been talking about this for a year and it's boring, Sly.'

'I don't deserve to move on.' Sly sipped his tea, thinking. 'Are Lois and David together?'

'How would I know? Malc was angrily pacing the room now. A pointless shouting match developed, until Malc walked off in search of Penny and the girls.

25

After Sly: Aber Again

IN THE LAST WEEK of September, Gerry, Brown R and Lois returned to Aberystwyth for their final year. Autumn came early that year; the leaves were already turning golden. Lois felt trapped from the moment she stepped out of the car. So much depended on this year and she prayed that she would get her degree. Brown R and Lois had come down in Brown R.'s battered Ford Escort. Gerry let her brother drive her back. Brown R had been having her year out, had lost the love of her life, and was about to face her final year at University.

Gerry and Lois now had rooms in Cwrt Mawr, a newish hall, at the very top of Penglais Hill. The University seemed to have run out of money when it was built, and the interior walls were bare breezeblock. They would soon get used to life there, they thought, and, by self-catering, they would spend less money. Brown R had a room in the Clarendon Hotel, on the sea front. Mannon, another old friend, was living in Cambrian Road.

'Well, don't expect me to visit you up there. I thought you had more sense than to live in that horrible place,' Mannon said, when they met in the Belle Vue lounge bar. It was actually better than Mannon thought. There were eight people sharing a communal kitchen, and everyone got along quite well. One of the most popular was Maggie, a post-graduate Biochemistry student, who liked a drink and was hopeless with men. There were two Welsh boys, and Kosh, a Pakistani boy reading maths. Kosh made wonderful meals for them and introduced them to char. Lois would live to regret never learning how to make it for herself. The others were just odd, but they got on all right.

Lois went home every other weekend, returning just in time for Animal Ecology, on Monday mornings. She still enjoyed dancing and dressing outrageously, but her spark had gone. Gerry, Luke forgotten, fell deeply in love for the first time in her life, and after this, she rarely talked about anything except her beloved Charlie, a fellow Zoologist. Lois worked hard, and Gerry was more motivated now, although she still socialised, got drunk, and went to the Pier, now with Charlie in tow. Lois spent more time with Brown R and Mannon, talking about what they all wanted from life. Mickie came to see Lois whenever he could, and took her out to the cinema, or for an evening meal. She was grateful for his love and his patience; he demanded nothing from her, just turned up, took whatever she had to give him and went away, leaving her feeling better about herself, and knowing that she was loved. David saw her mostly in Chester; he was always there when she was.

Mannon had changed little in her year out; she was still outrageous and still wanted to hold the ultimate party, which she soon did, and it was successful. Mannon never got involved with any other nonsense afterwards. The party was her last fling before she grew up.

A little after this party, Gerry managed to persuade Lois to come to a tropical evening at the Union. The mid winter weather of Aberystwyth was a far cry from tropical, but they went to dance. Mannon tried to engineer a date for Lois with a fellow she introduced as Bu.

'Sorry about this. I was at the bar and she just grabbed me. It's a bit awkward, see. I've got a girlfriend already.' Bu blushed and fidgeted.

'It's all right, Bu. Mannon likes to play matchmaker. I don't want a boyfriend. Let's have a chat and, maybe, a dance, and then she'll leave you alone. What are you reading?'

'Zoology.' They quickly established safe, common ground upon which to discourse, and the evening passed pleasantly for them both. Bu's friends came to collect him from her at the end of the event. Bu introduced them as Simon-Bu and Claire-Bu, and Lois asked whence they obtained their names. It transpired that Bu, formally registered as Huw, had named himself Bu when he was too small to articulate correctly, and the name stuck. His siblings, to differentiate themselves from other children, assumed Bu as an informal family surname.

At Christmas, Gerry and Charlie went to stay with Brown R and her friend, big Sue, in the aptly named Loveden Road. Lois, no longer amused by the antics and conversation of the other girls, went to Chester, to see David and her family.

In January, Lois started to help Bu with his studies, as she had promised on that first evening. He was making good progress, with her assistance. Lois wanted to complete her dissertation early because there was to be a two-week course on Psychology at Swansea University at the end of term, and her tutor arranged for her to go on it. Sly was still in Italy. By the time he returned, it would be the third term, and Lois would be heavily into her revision and on her way to her finals.

26

After Sly: Swansea

ON THE WEEKEND when Lois was due to travel to London from Swansea, David arranged a dinner party for the Saturday, after which, they would return to Chester together. Bored with modelling and the travelling it entailed, David thought about becoming a salesman in his father's business, where he would be based in Chester. He dreamt that Lois would begin to recognise that she couldn't live without him. Once she finished with University and started her job in the research laboratory in Warrington, life would assume a pattern, and this seemed to be what he wanted.

In Swansea, Lois was also thinking about the weekend and worrying about staying in London, but her mother had persuaded her that it would be fine.

'You need some time off. You've been working too hard, and there are your finals coming up. One night isn't going to make any difference, is it?' She was probably right.

Lois was just going through the motions of checking through her assignments, which she had to hand in the next day, but her mind was wandering. She decided to take a break and watch the news. She had used her time to good effect; not only had she completed the course, she had spent the entire term, beginning in Aber, preparing for her finals; all her background reading was finished, all of her revision notes made. She could now afford to spend Easter doing whatever she pleased. In the forefront of her mind was the expected reappearance of Sly, and she was beginning to feel that she would cope with it. In spite of her confidence, she dreaded bumping into Sly, still fearing the unexpected telephone call, and thinking warily of him when she picked up her post.

She turned on the television and started to fill her kettle for a cup of tea. A fellow student, by the name of Chris, knocked on her door, intending to invite Lois to come out for a drink with him, fairly certain that she would decline.

'Great. I was bored out of my mind. Chris tried to hide his amazement, but Lois reassured him, 'No one can work all the time.'

'We can take a taxi. A friend of mine is an assistant warden in one of the halls, and it's her birthday party; there will be plenty of food and more booze than usual.'

'It doesn't matter; it will be nice to be out of this room. It's driving me mad. I ought to get a bottle of wine or something, and get changed.'

'We've no time, and, anyway, you look great, so why bother? We can get a bottle from the hall bar as we leave.'

'Well, for heaven's sake, give me a moment to tidy myself up a bit.'

Together they walked to the hall bar and bought a bottle of wine to take with them. Lois asked who would be there, and if she would know anyone. Chris didn't think so, but he promised to look after her. He mentioned his hectic social life, and Lois was surprised at him, but of herself she said almost nothing.

'I don't know anything about you, Lois, except that you are at Aberystwyth University, where ever that is. Why all the secrecy? Is it a man you're hiding?' He had asked the question he had meant to avoid.

'No, not really. There is someone, but it's not a completely normal situation.'

'Is it a married man?'

'No, he's not married! He's more of a friend. We haven't managed to work things out yet, and, maybe, we never will, but he takes up all my energies. I had my heart broken and he was there to pick up the pieces. Now I'm getting better, we need to readjust. It's complicated.'

The mood between them had altered, which was exactly what Chris had been trying to avoid. He wanted her to know that he was a good bloke, and he had hoped to have a fun time with her. Lois asked about him, and he told her he had a working class background, had finished his education by his own efforts and landed a university place. There were similarities to her own story that she recognised at once. Chris introduced Lois to some of the party people, and she quickly discovered that she was enjoying herself. They moved out of the main room and stood in the relative darkness of the doorway, Chris pointing out more people, whose names Lois immediately forgot.

One person attracted her attention, however. Sly was there; it seemed too incredible. She stared at the figure, uncertain at first, but convinced when she realised that he had seen her, as well. Someone distracted him by asking if he wanted a drink. Lois turned urgently towards Chris and said, 'Chris, talk to me.'

'What? Why?' Chris looked baffled. 'Lois, what's the matter? You've gone quite pale?'

She babbled nonsense at Chris, who was a little too drunk to recognise it for the panic it was.

'Lois?' Sly's voice sent a chill up her spine; she turned and met his gaze.

'Sly, what are you doing here?' She feigned surprise.

'I should ask you the same question. I'm staying with Robert, my cousin. Gemma, our party hostess, is his girlfriend. How about you? I knew you were in Swansea, but I never thought I'd see you here.' He found it so easy to lie to her.

'Oh, I'm here with Chris. Chris, this is Sly; we were at

Aberystwyth together for a while.' Her words trivialised their relationship, but it was more civilised than saying, "This bastard has ruined my fucking life, and he raped me twice."

Chris shook Sly's hand.

'Do you mind if I sit down a minute.' Sly asked. 'So, how's the course going? Psychology, isn't it?' She told him that it had been hard work but very fulfilling. 'So, are you off home, then?'

'No, I'm off to London. David's holding a mega swish party to mark my end of term. We'll go back to Chester on Sunday.'

Careful, slow down a bit, her brain instructed, and don't drink any more punch, for God's sake. Lois placed her cup on the floor, out of harm's way. Sly continued asking questions, apparently innocuous ones. Lois remained polite, asked him how his MA was shaping.

'Slowly. I've just come back from Italia, '*Es una campagna bellissimo. Molto bellisimo,*' he replied, with a wide smile.

Their conversation eventually turned to Mickie and his planned onslaught on London. Sly, to divert her, told her he'd seen David in *The Face* magazine.

'How is he? He's getting around a lot; I seem to see him everywhere. To be in *The Face*, that's really cool. Has he still got his Stag?'

Sly was probing, reinforcing information that Malc had given him. Malc had not mentioned any new boyfriend on the scene, but his vagueness concerning Lois and David had infuriated Sly. However, Lois herself had just confirmed that, close as they might well be, that was still all there was to know about David.

Sly asked about Cwrt Mawr, which meant that he had her new address. She told him that it wasn't as nice as living in town, but they had managed a few laughs along the way. During this conversation about mutual friends, Chris felt decidedly left out. He fetched them some drinks and then asked, 'How about going to see if they have any Bunnymen tapes?'

'Good idea, Chris. See if you can find something better than this seventies stuff; Bowie or Ferry, if you can't.'

Chris went away and stayed away.

For Lois, the evening was extremely strange. She was enjoying being with Sly. He had changed; he was more confident, more relaxed, and more able to laugh. Sly had come here expecting to be bored, talking to some friend of Gemma's that she and Robert had lined up for him. Now, here he was, having a ball, catching up on news. Okay, so it wasn't exactly a deep talk, but it was a start. It might lead to him to being able to tell her what he needed her to know.

By three-thirty in the morning, most people had gone home. Chris helped to tidy up and decided that he had had enough. He knew that Sly was Robert's cousin, and he would be staying overnight, so he imagined that Lois would be, as well. He went over to say goodbye.

'Are you off so early?' Lois consulted her watch. 'Jeez! I had no idea of the time. I'm just coming.' Turning to Sly, she said, 'Well, it was nice to catch up with you, Sly. I'd better go; I have to go to a final day seminar tomorrow, today, whatever.'

Sly wanted to walk her home but she said that she and Chris would share a taxi.

'Listen, Lois,' Sly said, pulling her close and speaking quietly, so Chris couldn't overhear. 'Now we've spoken, won't you let me explain things? Please, this is killing me, really.'

Lois froze. This was far too close a call, she must not give in, and she must not open herself up to all his evil again. This was Sly-boy, the nutter. She looked at him; his eyes were kind and beseeching; she was on the brink of submission when she remembered her looming finals.

'I'm sorry, Sly, this has been really nice but I have to concentrate all my efforts on my exams. That's what this has all been about. Maybe, in the summer, you can write to me, but please wait until then. Please.'

'All right. I can wait. I've waited long enough already. I'll let you finish first, then we'll talk. I will write to you.'

Chris hurried and Lois almost had to run to keep up.

'Hey, Chris, slow down, what's the matter?' she asked stupidly. Chris told her. 'Listen, Chris, I'm really sorry that you are mad. I never thought that he and I would get on so well. At first, I just wanted him to go away, but in some ways, it's good we talked; it makes me hope that I might really be over him. He's the one that broke my heart; he's the sad fucker who threw me away.'

'Why would you go out with someone like him? He isn't much to look at?'

'It's not all about looks; we share an interest in dancing and music, and there's just something about him, I mean, there used to be.'

'Judging by tonight's performance, he still does it for you.'

Lois tried to explain about Sly; how he had finished with her, twice in fact, which Chris found difficult to believe. They shared a taxi back and Chris walked her to her block.

'Lois, can I ask you something?' He didn't wait for a reply. 'Will you give me your address, so we can keep in touch? I'd be really interested to know what happens.'

She fell asleep, musing over the mysterious workings of Sly Davies's mind.

27

After Sly: the Degree

ON THE DAY that the results were posted, Lois packed, dismantled her room, took down her postcards and pictures, and Gerry spent the day in bed with Charlie, intending it to be for the last time. Too many university romances failed later, and she wanted nothing left to deal with from a distance; that takes too much staying power.

Gerry and Charlie were both upset at the mutually agreed parting of the ways, and Lois tried to console Gerry as they went to inspect the examination results. Lois spotted Gerry's name before she saw her own. Gerry had a two-two and Lois knew she'd be thrilled.

'You've got a two-one!' Gerry screamed. Lois couldn't believe it. She was not disappointed not to have a double first, although the Zoology department hadn't given anyone a first for many a long year, and it would be another twelve months before they would do so. Most people had obtained what they called "the drinking man's degree", but Lois was in the top echelon of those who had gone one better. It was a glorious day, sunny and hot, the sea sparkled in the sunlight, and Aber felt like the happiest place in the world.

Sly went up to the Zoology department, to see how she had done. He looked at the list and found her name. He felt sad and guilty, when he saw that she had missed a first.

Lois called her mother, and then David, who shouted his delight and promised to come down right away to help her celebrate. She told him where to look for her.

Most students were hell bent on getting drunk but Lois persuaded her small group to do the sensible thing and have something to eat in the Sea Bank. Presently, David arrived. Having squeezed Lois until she could hardly breathe, he ordered champagne for Lois's friends. They ended up on the Pier, all rowdy, all drunk, except Lois and David, who danced a little and then sat talking, watching the antics, and trying to keep an eye on Gerry.

David took Lois to bed. He wanted her so much, and she had no energy to resist him. Now, Malc could tell Sly, she thought, as they lay together in post-coital harmony. Lois left Aberystwyth on the following day. What could not be stowed in David's car went into storage for collection later.

David drove her back to Aber for Graduation Day, but because Ronnie and Lois's mother came down, too, he borrowed his father's more capacious car. Lois's mother wept when Lois went up to receive her certificate, and there were more tears outside. Lois liked to think that she would see again all those who had helped her at a difficult time of her life, most of them without even knowing it. Then, it was time to go off to La Rochelle again.

As they drove way from Aberystwyth, Lois wondered if she would ever feel like going back. So much had changed since David had first driven her there on that first Sunday. She remembered crying when she watched his taillights disappear as he drove away from her along the promenade in the year BS: Before Sly.

28

After Sly: Ben

MALC WAITED FOR LOIS to get to France. She had agreed to telephone from there, and give him the go ahead to talk with Sly. In fact, Malc and Lois had a carefully laid plan concerning Sly, and Lois was keeping her side of the bargain. As the time drew nearer, Malc considered that she might try to back out of the deal. He was even more worried that David might stand in her way, whatever she decided, but she telephoned and told Malc that it would be fine.

The chance meeting with Sly in Swansea had gone a long way to helping the situation. Lois had already provided Malc with all that he needed to show to Sly. Malc called Sly at home, and asked him to come to see him in Leeds. He said that he couldn't do what he wanted in Monmouth or Aberystwyth. He had deliberately called Sly from work, first thing in the morning, so that Sly could set out immediately. Malc knew that he would do this, when Malc said it was to do with Lois, and he'd tell him all when they met. Sly rang back to say that his train was due in at five forty-five.

Sly packed an overnight bag and asked his da to drive him to the station. He said he would be back the next day. The journey was subject to delays, and Sly was bursting with impatience. As the train got closer to Leeds, Sly began to exhibit all the symptoms of a 'flight or fight' situation, with sweating and shortness of breath. Malc could have no idea of the physical and mental anguish that he was suffering.

Malc was standing by the barrier, smartly dressed, the very image of an archetypal successful businessman. Malc told Sly that there was a pub nearby, where they could talk. The pub was quite busy for six o'clock on a Tuesday evening. While Malc went to get some drinks, Sly found a corner seat and sat down. Malc was taking an age, and Sly stared at his back, willing him to hurry, yet dreading what was to happen next. When Malc sat down, Sly could wait no longer.

'Malc, what is it, for fuck's sake? I am going out of my mind here, please tell me.'

Malc took an envelope from his briefcase, placed it on the table and slowly extracted a photograph of a small boy. He handed it to Sly, who looked at it uncomprehendingly. The child looked strangely familiar to him but he was sure that he didn't know him; he didn't know any young children.

'This is Ben. This is Lois's and your son, Ben.'

The enormity of what Malc had just said echoed between them. Sly looked at the photograph again. His son! How had Lois managed to produce a son without ever telling him anything of it? That's why he looked familiar; he looked like Sly had looked when he was a child. Ben had curly hair, big eyes. He was a bit sulky.

'Look, there are more here. These Lois had copied for you.'

Malc open the envelope and dozens of photographs fell onto the table, some of a baby, others of a toddler. As Sly, hands trembling, looked through them, Malc tried to give him some facts.

'He was born on October 18[th,] 1983, he's twenty-one months old. That top photograph is the most recent one of him. He likes Thomas the Tank Engine, tractors and football. He's a very good boy, and Lois is a wonderful mother.'

Sly looked again at the photographs. There was one of a very new baby in someone's arms. Was it David holding him?

'My son! How long have you known about this?' Sly couldn't

believe that he had a son, or that Malc knew of it before he did.

'Do you remember Su Su, the girl in the bookshop? She knew about Ben. Lois told her, when they met by chance in London.'

'When did Gerry know? Was it when we had that fight?' Sly's brain was slowly coming back from the brink.

'No, David wouldn't trust her with the news until she had left Aber. They told her when she went to France with them.'

'How come you didn't tell me last year? Why now?'

'David insisted that Lois should have left Aber with her degree before you were told. I persuaded Lois that, one day, Ben would need to know who his father really was. It would be wrong for him to think it was David, which would be a strong probability. She wants to be honest with Ben, and I persuaded her to allow me to tell you, once they completed the third year. I know all about not having a father, and she does, too. David opposed the idea; but Lois, for once, did what she wanted, and is agreeable to you meeting with Ben.'

Sly felt as though his brain had received a huge jolt, everything was up in the air, none of his thoughts were accessible to him, he couldn't think, he grabbed at any thing that came into view, he was demented.

'When was he conceived, Malc, do you know?'

'I don't know; the baby came early, that's all I know. You'll have to ask Lois.

'When will I see her and Ben?'

'They are in France now, and I don't have an address or telephone number. I've no way of contacting her. She always rings me or writes to me. David wants to keep her safe, which means out of contact with her friends. Lois's mother will sort out your first contact with Ben, if you want to see him. Do you want to?'

Sly was aghast that Malc could think for a second that he wouldn't want to meet with Ben, be with him, be part of his life, be his father.

'Right, Sly, Mrs Bartlett will oversee your first visits, and then, maybe, Lois will see you. That's as much as I know. You need to write to Lois's mother. She's always been on your side about the baby.'

Sly sat and thought about this; amazed that Mrs. Bartlett had shown him any sympathy. Malc told him when the family would be back home, and urged Sly to have his letter to Mrs. Bartlett sorted out by then. Sly gave way to his emotions; he felt as though the last two years had been leading up to this, and now his tears flowed.

They spent the evening in conversation, while enjoying a Chinese meal. Sly was impatient to see Ben; the reality of having a son would require time to absorb. He talked of Lois and Ben, and of what they meant to him. Malc listened to Sly and felt glad to be relieved of the burden of keeping this secret. Both of them had passed a significant milestone in their lives.

29

After Sly: It's DAVID!

THE FRIDAY BEFORE LOIS was due to see Sly in Aber, David was preparing to fly out to Rio de Janeiro, departing on the Saturday. Lois wanted to have David far away, in Brazil, by the time she boarded her Aber-bound train. She had had a busy day. Ben had constantly demanded attention, and she was tired and devoid of patience. For this visit, Lois was going alone to see Sly, and Ben was to stay with Ronnie. The boy was fretful and wanted to come with her to the seaside. Just when she thought she would never finish packing, Ben fell asleep.

With the packing done, Lois settled down to some serious thinking. While she was on the Gower, decisions had come so easily. Now that seeing Sly again was a reality, she was less sure of herself. Ben was so demanding of her time during the day, and she had many adjustments to make to her life. On the one hand, she was excited at the prospect of sharing Ben with the only person in the world as biologically interested as herself: Ben's real father. David was besotted with the child, but how would Sly be? Sly's handling of his first visit to Ben had impressed Lois's mother. Lois smiled at her memories, and they weren't all bad. Perhaps everything would be all right. She heard the back door shake; it was on the security chain. Then, someone rang the bell. She knew it had to be David; she could make out his outline through the frosted glass.

'I thought you were waiting for your flight to Rio,' she said, as she opened the door and David strode angrily through it.

'Yeah, I bet you did. Why are you going to Aber to see that wanker? Why not see him here, where there is someone to protect you? Why not see him with me, so that I could make sure he couldn't hurt you again? We have all this secrecy and protection and, then, you calmly waltz down to Aberystwyth to see him, the moment you think my back is turned. You owe me some answers.'

'Did my mother tell you?' she asked. David was still pacing, he wasn't interested in the question, he ignored her. She repeated herself.

'What does it matter? I know, and, yeah, your mother told me.'

She felt as though he had caught her red-handed, but she was resolved to stay calm and be patient. 'I was trying to protect you,' she said.

'I don't need protecting. You're the one he forced himself onto. I'm stronger than he is, you're not, it could all happen again. How many people would go back to face their rapist on their own, defenceless? Only you, you stupid fucking idiot.'

'David, please listen, I have already seen him once and it was all fine. When I was down in Swansea, I met him at a party, we talked, and when we parted, he asked if he could write to me. I asked him to wait until the summer, because I knew that Malc would tell him about the baby, once I'd left Aberystwyth. When Sly found out, he wrote to ask to see Ben, and he said there was something he had to tell me. I have to face him, otherwise I will never feel safe again, and he wants access rights to Ben.'

'That's what I got you a solicitor for, to sort out access. You don't have to see him. You are putting yourself in danger, and I can't understand why!"

'If he is going to be a part of Ben's life, David, I want us to be civil to each other. Children are very sensitive to these sorts of things, and I don't want to screw up Ben because I'm too scared to look his father in his face. This is for life, David, not just for now,

Ben needs to know who is father is. There are other things that have to be decided on. Meeting Sly's father is one, money is another.'

'You don't need a penny of his money. Don't I do enough for you? Mention that you need something and I get it for you. You want for nothing,' he shouted.

Lois went upstairs and closed Ben's door, and then came down and poured David a small glass of wine.

'Do you know what I was going to do in Rio? I was going to buy you an engagement ring. I was going to ask you to fucking marry me, once I got back. If you'd said no, I was going to take off round the world with Rich, and drive you out of my system. If you'd said yes, then I was going to move back up here and settle down with you, for ever.'

Lois stared at him, incredulous. 'I don't think it would work, David. I thought we had some sort of deal going, something about being best friends. I don't know. I need time to think about it.

'Oh, Lois, please think and please come and live your life with me. I'd die happy. We'd have more great kids, they would be gorgeous, and I'd never let you down, never.'Lois sighed heavily. She was not against the idea of life with him. Perhaps, she had just been too young and stubborn before.

'Tell me that you won't have sex with that bastard this weekend,' David suddenly said.

'I have absolutely no intention of it,' Lois replied hotly.

'That's not the same as saying you won't, and you know it. Come on, we are practically engaged to be married; you've got to promise me.' David was smiling, happy enough to joke now, because he knew that she would have said no, if she hadn't changed her mind.

'We are not practically engaged to be married at all. I said I would think about it, that's all.' Lois smiled back.

'You didn't say no. That's enough for me.'

30

After Sly: Sly Again

SLY HAD TAKEN A FLAT in the top two floors of a house in Bath Street, almost opposite the cinema, which he shared with two Welsh students, Iwan and Dylan. Sly was downstairs, in a little bedroom on the same landing as the bathrooms. He loved his room, although he missed the sea. The three of them cooked together in the spacious kitchen, and there was a pay phone in the hall. The flat also had central heating, a rarity in student accommodation in those days. Sly liked Dylan and could confide in him about Lois without Dylan getting judgemental or bored. Iwan, on the other hand, was a gossip; he loved scandal and tittle-tattle, and Sly did not share secrets with him.

Iwan tried to interest Sly in girls, some of whom he brought home to the flat, all of them pretty. Sly might have been tempted, but he resisted their charms to such an extent that Iwan thought he might be gay. His every waking moment was filled with Lois and, when he slept, she was in his dreams. Iwan knocked on his door in the middle of the morning, to ask about domestic arrangements for the weekend. Dylan and his sister had gone off to walk up Snowdon. They would eat out.

They sorted out the trivia of the day, and Sly said nothing at all about Lois.

The moment he was sure he was alone, he made some tea and sat down to write a shopping list. He knew exactly what he needed but he didn't want to leave anything to chance. At a little after twelve o'clock, he set off happily and by the time he returned to the flat, he was getting nervous. He had walked round the shops, rehearsing what he would say. After lunch, he cleaned the oven and prepared their evening meal. He cleaned the kitchen and the bathrooms. It kept him from sweating over the meeting with Lois. Next, he sorted out a few tapes and finished sticking the photographs of Ben into an album. He had taken them with his Pentax camera when he met his son at Mrs. Bartlett's house in Chester.

Lois spent the journey time revisiting in her mind the chain of events that had led her to be sitting on the train, on her way to meet with the guy who had robbed her of every last shred of dignity and crushed her with his strange mix of love and hatred. I must be mad, she thought to herself.

The train to Crewe was crowded with Saturday shoppers and tourists. Lois stared at the floor, but she couldn't think about Sly, for that she needed quietness.

At Crewe, she bought some cigarettes. As she lit the first one, she wondered if Sly still smoked. She and David had tried to give up when she was pregnant. David found it easy. Nowadays, they sometimes smoked when they were out together. She imagined that, whenever it became uncool, he would stop; he was like that. The cigarette calmed her a little. The train to Shrewsbury was less crowded, and she propped her head against the window, leant on her jacket and fell asleep, until someone shook her awake as they drew into Shrewsbury station.

She bought herself a cup of tea and revived a little. She had forgotten how much she hated these train journeys, and had begun to wish that she had driven. Her beaten up Mini Metro would just about have made the distance, but it would have meant that she could leave at any time, if she needed to, and not have to wait for a train out of the Godforsaken place. Suppose Sly pulled a trick, like last time, then what would she do? David had said he feared for her safety so the same thought must have occurred to him. She knew what Sly was capable of, when he was in the mood. What was he so desperate to tell her?

She very nearly didn't board the train to Aberystwyth. Frozen in panic, she stood on the platform, trying to work out what to do for the best. For a moment, she couldn't move, although the train was almost ready to go. She should go home now. A woman's voice brought her to her senses.

'Sorry to bother you, but could you give me a hand with this lot, please? I can't find a guard anywhere.'

A heavily pregnant woman stood before her, a small boy, a little older than Ben, held one of her hands; with the other, she was struggling to fold a buggy and carry a suitcase. They found some free seats in a non-smoking carriage, stowed away the cases and buggy, and fell into a conversation about babies. The woman was on her way to Borth, the stop before Aberystwyth. When the train started again after the woman and her child had disembarked, Lois was twenty minutes from seeing Sly; she had been unable to sort out her thoughts.

In the kitchen in Bath Street, the cawl was simmering nicely, filling the house with tantalising aromas. Sly laid the table, his spirits soaring. He had made it. The day had dawned, and he had prepared as much as he could. He told himself that nothing could go wrong now.

At that moment, Iwan walked in. Sly turned on him.

'Get out, Iwan. I want some privacy tonight. You told me you wouldn't be in this evening, so what are you playing at, and leave the food alone.

'I'm not going anywhere until you tell me who the lucky person is.'

'No one you know, just an old friend, someone I used to be friends with before I was lucky enough to meet up with you, shit head. Now, if you don't go, I might just let slip to Anwen that you didn't come back here on Thursday, and whoever you were with, it wasn't Olwen.'

This seemed to do the trick. Before he actually departed, Iwan asked for a loan of ten pounds.

'Where are you meeting this mystery friend, then?'

'At the station, not that's any business of yours.'

'Where is she coming from?'

'Shrewsbury, dickhead.'

'Well, boyo, I have bad news for you. The Shrewsbury train came in ages ago.' Sly ignored him. 'No, really, that's why I'm here. Ivor went to meet his girlfriend off it. It says on the timetable that it gets in at eight, but it always makes up time. It's early; it's been in the station for ages. Honest, Sly, I'm not arsing around. I've just come from there. It's in.'

'If you're joking, Iwan, I will kill you later. Don't touch anything. No, on second thoughts, here's ten pounds. Now fuck off down to the pub and stay there. I'll see you later.'

Sly eventually pulled up outside the station and parked on double yellow lines. If Iwan were right, Lois would have been waiting for ages. She could have gone to find him, walked to Bath Street. It was hardly the best way to start their time together. He realised that Iwan had been telling the truth because the station was deserted. They had already pulled the iron gates across the exit. He ran onto the forecourt. It was empty. He had missed her. Panic rising, he asked the ticket collector.

'She's over there, mate, by the ticket office.'

There she was, his lovely, lovely Lois.

* * *

Lois had made up her mind during the train ride that things would take their course and she would handle it. Sly had no hold over her; she had the upper hand, she told herself. Even so, when the train stopped, she let the carriage empty before she stepped onto the platform, intending to make him wait. She held her head high, determined that he would not see her fear.

A stream of travellers was dispersing, Sly wasn't amongst them. She went to the barrier, to hand in her ticket, and was surprised when the ticket collector mumbled, 'Welcome back.' He must have seen thousands of students arriving in his time, yet he recognised her. She went into the station forecourt, and Sly wasn't there either. Lois couldn't believe it. Of all the eventualities, the idea that he wouldn't be there had never occurred to her. She swore softly to herself, angrily threw down her bag on a bench and lit a cigarette. She watched the other people filter away from the station until she was the only one left. The ticket collector closed up his office and walked past her.

'Been stood up, have you, love? She wanted to reply, 'Don't call me love, but she flashed him a smile instead. 'Don't worry. This train always gets in early; the driver is in the Rheidol darts team and likes to get some practice before the game.'

Lois was grateful that he was trying to make her laugh, but when they drew the first iron gate over the exit, she wondered what to do if Sly failed to show at all. She was damned if she would go to Bath Street. There might not be any more trains for a couple of hours, but there might just be a bus to somewhere in the real world. She could go to Swansea, where Chris would put her up.

The timetable showed that there was a bus to Swansea at half eight. She was furious with indignation. Early train, or not, Sly should have been here by now. She turned to leave, and there he was.

31

Sly and the Mysterious Something

SLY WAS UNPREPARED for the sight of her. There was something self-assured about her now, she was no longer the immature student; this was a splendid woman. Sly spoke humbly, apologised for his lateness. In the same way that Sly was getting a reality shock, Lois was experiencing any number of emotions, one of them was fear. He helped her with her luggage and exchanged pleasantries as they walked to the car. He asked about Ben, and she told him that he was fine and staying with Ronnie and Bryan for the weekend.

They arrived in Bath Street and she felt odd because everything was so familiar, yet it was strange to think that nothing had changed since she left.

'Do you mind if I smoke?'

'No, not at all. I didn't know you smoked.'

He found her Iwan's ashtray. He wanted to warn her of the dangers of smoking, demand that she desist in front of Ben, and start to control her again.

'I don't smoke with Ben around, but it's nice to have a break from all that responsibility for a while.'

Unable to express his innermost feelings, his own guilt, his pride in Lois, his possessive love for his child, Sly went to see to the supper.

They enjoyed their meal. Sly looked healthier than she remembered him, and he ate with relish. When they had finished, he proposed that they visit the Crystal Palace, meet Dylan and his sister, Lowri, then go up to the Union. Lois felt excited by the prospect of dancing. Something about her enthusiasm reminded Sly of the girl whom he had first met almost five years previously.

Dylan and Lowri were waiting in the pub, intrigued to meet Lois. When Iwan saw the two of them waiting at the bar, he was over like a shot, demanding to know who she was. Sly turned apologetically to Lois, and introduced his flat-mates and Lowri. At half ten, they went to the Union, which seemed to be unchanged, except that Lois could recognise none of the faces. They all looked too young to be at University. While she and Sly were dancing, someone ran up to them. It was Bu. Lois couldn't have been more surprised when it transpired that Bu knew Sly. She was pleased to see him. He told her that was doing really well, said he felt that he was on target for a First. Lois was delighted for him.

'Yes, and it's all down to you. After all that help you gave me, I did really well in my First Year exams, and I took your advice about which subjects to take in my Second Year, and I did what you told me about research, and it's all going brilliantly.'

Lois felt envious of Bu, and thought of how she had missed out because of Sly. Bu asked where she was living, and she wrote down her address for him. He asked the DJ to put on some Wham, and they danced together. When a new band came on, the dance floor became very crowded with Freshers, and Lois wondered what would happen to them while they were here. When Sly suggested that they go home, she was ready; she was getting to old for all of this.

Back home, they talked of Malc and Gerry, Fenn, and Luke, who had settled in London. After they had dealt with all other subjects, Sly said, 'Don't you think it's time we talked about Ben?'

'Okay. What did you want to say?'

Sly had thought about this moment many times. He had every version stored in his head, had mulled it over repeatedly. There were endless possibilities to the conversation they were about to have. Much would depend on her reaction to his first words. He knew that he had to start at the beginning, which was so painful that he wished he could avoid it, but it was a vital part of the future, too.

'Lois, when I forced you to have sex with me, that time, in Marine Terrace, I was ill.'

'Ill?' This was unexpected. Mad, possibly. She'd thought about that one many times. She felt he had outmanoeuvred her once more; she didn't want to start playing games all over again.

'This isn't a game.'

'I know it isn't. I'm just trying to make you understand. My doctor diagnosed me as having Seasonal Adjustment Disorder. Have you heard about it?'

'Yes, we studied it here, in fact. It's connected to the pineal gland; birds' navigation, that sort of thing.'

'Well, I'd never heard of it. It came as a complete shock to me. I knew that every winter, in January, February, I would begin to harbour dark, black thoughts, find it hard to see anything positive. I thought that it was connected to the anniversary of my mother's death.' Lois nodded, but allowed him to speak. 'The treatment is easy. I sit under a light-box, in the winter evenings. I take better care of myself now that I've learnt to value my health. No more junk food, no more vodka, it's just white wine for me now. I've started jogging and I do Karate. For the last two winters I have kept well, and now I think I'll be all right.'

Lois was shaking. This was a rational explanation, finally! She lit another cigarette.

'My illness doesn't explain everything. There's Emily as well. Emily was playing mind games on me. She managed to persuade me that you were having a fling with Finlay.' He waited until the impact of his words sank in. Lois was horrified.

'How? Why?'

'Well, she wanted me to replace the boyfriend she had lost. Gina started it, by telling us that she had seen you come out of Finlay's house in the middle of the day. Emily used it to make a mountain out of a molehill.'

Lois couldn't remember why she had gone to Finlay's. It was something trivial, in view of subsequent events.

Then she remembered: 'Bunnymen tickets! Finlay had a friend who could get us Bunnymen tickets. I wanted to get them for you, to go to their concert in Liverpool. Finlay's friend sent them. I ripped them up in the end.' She started to cry. The futility of it all epitomised the whole saga of Lois and Sly.

'You didn't go?'

'Of course I didn't go. I was pregnant, I was ill, I was heartbroken, and I was in pieces. The Bunnymen might be a great band, but even they couldn't help me to get up from rock bottom.' She fumbled for some tissues in her bag. Her pain was palpable and his guilt burnt like a red-hot poker. 'Go on with your revelations, Sly,' she said, closing her eyes and shuddering.

'Emily's gossip came on top of that business with you and David. You were lying to me about that. Why should I find Emily's tales incredible? You do see, don't you, Lois? I saw Finlay at your place, and I know he stayed the night. What else could I do? How could I know what was truth and what were lies?'

Lois was horrified at the involvement of so many meddlers, who had almost destroyed her. Sly poured them both some wine and waited for her to respond.

'But that's incredible. I mean, I can understand your illness, but as for the rest, I just can't imagine.'

'All the pieces of the jigsaw fitted together, all making a perfect lie. Finlay told me the truth in the end.' Sly could see that she was mystified. He explained. 'Lynne told Finlay that I thought you'd been having sex with him. He told her immediately that it wasn't true, and she knows him well enough to understand that it really hadn't happened; they'd all just thought it had, me included. Mickie realised right away that the key to all of this was Emily.'

'Mickie. What has he got to do with all of this?' Surely, Mickie wasn't involved.

'Mickie came down from Birmingham to see you. He went to see Lynne while he was here, to discover what had been going on. He convinced her to tackle Finlay about their relationship. Lynne couldn't imagine anyone finishing with her over a girl he hadn't even taken to bed. Mickie knew you better. He convinced her to ask Finlay. Finlay decided that I had to know the truth. Finlay's just a big kid and he can't keep secrets, can he?' Lois smiled; it was all perfectly true.

'There's just one more thing. Don't worry, this is a nice thing. Gerry had a go at Gina and made her see sense. She told her how ill you were, so Gina nagged the rest of them to give you a break. It came too late, but she tried. I thought that you'd want to know.'

'Gerry's been so good to me, she's stuck by me through thick and thin, all those awful times. Bless her.' Tears flowed from Lois's eyes.

'It must be very difficult to hear all this so quickly. It's no wonder you're upset. I tried to tell you all these things, but it was impossible to get through the barriers David had set up around you. I guess that Gerry told you about the fight. He came back here, after he taken you home. He waited in my room on the Saturday and, when I came in, he beat me up. He's much stronger than me. I never stood a chance. He beat the shit out of me, broke my nose and took a piece out of my ear. I had broken ribs, and, for a while, the doctors thought my kidneys were damaged, as well. My da was furious, wanted to bring in the police, but I didn't want that.'

Why?' Lois was intrigued.

'Because I had raped you, and I understood how he must have felt about me. I'd defiled you, his precious Lois, his most dear

290

person. If I had been David, I would have wanted me dead. I never believed I was capable of such an act. I behaved like an animal. Rape! It's an evil act, and I raped you.'

'I try not to think of it as that.'

'You should. That's what it was. Have you talked about it with anyone?' Sly asked, needing to know.

'Mostly with Gerry. She was great, listened and was sympathetic. I called it rape to begin with, but in the end, I decided that I had to take some responsibility as well. I'd had sex with someone I hardly knew, when we got together in the first year. I had tolerated so much crap from you when I should have kicked you out. I failed to protect myself. There were many times in the second year when I consented to have sex with you, when I didn't really want to, when you were being weird. I got my reward for it, didn't I? It was mutual sexual pleasure, not that time, however. Gerry made sense all those times when she told me you were a nutter. I had also stopped taking the pill, which only happened once, when I forgot to stock up, and it all came at the wrong time for us both.'

'Please, can I say sorry to you for that? I have thought about it everyday, and everyday I have been sorrier about that than anything else I have ever done.'

A huge wave of emotion almost overwhelmed Lois at these words. She gasped for breath and wracking sobs shook her body. Sly had little more to say about the past. He had placed every card on the table and Lois had examined each one.

'Shall we talk about something more cheerful? Would you like to see the photographs I took of Ben?'

Sly was beginning to see her world and learn what had happened to her in the past two years. She knew that her decision to see Sly, and try to work out how to include him in Ben's life, was the right one.

They continued to talk; neither of them could ever exhaust

this particular subject, their son. Sly had one question to ask, but he postponed asking it until it came from his lips of its own volition.

'Do you know when Ben was conceived?'

She knew exactly what he meant. She had often wondered if Ben had been a product of his hatred towards her, especially in the early months of her pregnancy before she felt him kick; then, she'd stopped caring.

'I don't know exactly. There's no knowing. He arrived earlier than we expected.'

'I feel so relieved about that. At least, there's a chance that he was conceived in pure love.'

★ ★ ★

Having reached the pinnacle without disaster, Sly offered to play her some music, which wiped the slate clean, at least for the time being. They talked some more about the Bunnymen, about what the future held, whether they would stay together, about music in general. Sly noticed that Lois looked drained; the whole evening had been an emotional roller coaster, and they were talking banalities. It was bedtime for her.

★ ★ ★

Lois felt very calm and relaxed when she woke. After breakfast, they decided to take a walk along the seafront.

'Did you know that there is a local custom that says it's lucky to kick the end of the prom?' Sly asked. 'My da told me. I never knew, either. Amazing how we can underestimate parents, isn't it? I've talked a lot to my da recently, well, since David gave me a beating. He made me tell him everything, and he's helped me to work out a strategy to cope with the loss of you. I haven't been able to tell him about Ben yet because I needed to know what you wanted to do. I didn't want to tell him that he had a grandson and then tell him he couldn't see him. I thought I'd wait until we'd sorted out things better. We need to talk about this. Do you have any thoughts? I don't know anything about access, maintenance, stuff like that, do you?'

'No, but David found me a solicitor, he wants me to do everything through him. David went ballistic when he found out I was coming here. He hadn't realised that I needed to face my fear alone; he is still very protective of me.'

'I want to be part of Ben's life, Lois. I know that you have many friends who are already part of it, and that's what I'm after, to start with, so he knows me as a person. I would like to spend time with you and him. That's very important to me. Perhaps I could come to Chester, rent a flat near you, so I could help out, and be babysitter, that sort of thing.'

She smiled. 'There's a queue, you'll be behind my mother and my sister, and they squabble about it endlessly.' Sly looked mortified, until she explained that she was joking.

'What does David say about my involvement? Is he still jealous?'

'David finds this whole thing hell on earth. He wanted to marry me, adopt Ben as his own, the whole caboodle. He adores Ben and I have to work very hard to prevent him from spoiling him to death.'

The air was fresh and cold, the sea creamed with white on the wave tips. Sly put his jacket round her shoulders.

'How can I thank you for coming here without David? It was everything I had hoped for.'

'Mickie has been very supportive, Sly. He didn't react well to the baby, but now Ben is becoming a little boy, it is easier. Mickie is competitive; he didn't like to see David so at ease with the baby, not that David would change nappies unless he absolutely had to.'

'So, what did Mickie do?' Sly was interested. For his own peace of mind, he had to know; so that he could face up to what he had destroyed.

'He's a very special person, is Mickie. He gave me some very valuable advice, which I took. David knows nothing about it, in fact, I'm not sure that I should be telling you.'

'Do you think Mickie's the one for you, then, the special bond?'

'I think it will be David, but I still have some serious thinking to do. I'd rather not talk about him. It is too private.'

As they walked home, Sly offered Lois his arm, and was amazed at how much it pleased him just to do this simple thing. He asked her why she had named the boy Ben.

'I decided on Benjamin because I don't know anyone called Ben, and it seems like such a nice name, so open and clean. His middle name is David.'

'What would you have called her, had she been a girl?

'Oh, that was easy; I'm a Biologist, so, Zoë, life!' She was smiling.

* * *

By the time Lois caught her train home, they had agreed that he would come to Chester at the weekend, stay at a hotel, and use the time to look at flats. He could write his M.A. anywhere; it didn't have to be in Aber. David would still be away, so that Lois would have time to talk all of this through with him before any permanent decisions were made. Sly would also get a solicitor in Chester, ready for anything legal that might arise. They could spend some time with Ben, and see how that felt. They were beginning again; this time, it was in a more controlled, adult way. Lois mused over all that had happened. Maybe, things would work out, after all.

32

After Sly: David

SLY BOOKED A HOTEL ROOM and let her know that he would arrive on Friday evening. She worked during the week, and Ben attended a private Infants' School, paid for by David, who wanted the boy to have the best of everything. Lois usually collected him on her way home in the evening, or Ronnie took him home with her.

Lois was impatient for Sly to arrive on Friday. She was also looking forward to telling David that she had finally resolved to marry him. She had just arrived back from work, having picked up Ben from the Montessori school, when Sly turned up. He assisted her with Ben's supper, bath and bed routine, read a little story and kissed Ben goodnight.

Next morning, Sly was there in time to give Ben his breakfast. Sly wanted to look at flats before taking Ben and Lois to the zoo. Lois, with her knowledge of zoology, felt sympathy for the caged beasts, pacing up and down, hating life, longing for freedom. That evening, Sly helped to put Ben to bed, and was sitting with him and waiting for him to fall asleep, while Lois took a shower. She had just wrapped a towel round herself, when she heard a crash downstairs. She pulled on her dressing gown and flew down, to find out what was going on.

The sight that met her eyes was appalling. David was standing in the middle of the kitchen, his fists up, a look of intense hatred on his face. Sly was slumped on the floor, his back against a kitchen unit, half-dead, his face covered in blood.

David took one look at her and shouted, 'There you are, you bitch. Very cosy!' He struck her across the face with the back of his hand; it caught her off balance and she crashed into the wall. She tried to speak but the breath had been knocked out of her. This seemed to stir Sly, who got to his feet and made towards David. David looked round, looked at Lois and swore again.

A knife was lying on the table, next to the chopping board.

Lois screamed, 'David, no! Please, just listen to me!'

David snatched up the knife. He had come back from Rio, to be with Lois, and had walked in to a scene of domestic bliss. That fucker was chopping onions in Lois's mother kitchen, like he owned the fucking place. David's early return was meant to be a wonderful surprise. He lunged at Sly with all his strength. Sly blocked him, using a Karate defensive technique. David tried again, aiming for Sly's face. Sly Karate-kicked him, and caught the knife, which crashed to the floor. David changed position suddenly, looking to grab the knife back, and Sly's kick accidentally caught him on the side of his head. David's knees buckled and he fell to the floor. Sly was still in position, arms out, ready for the next onslaught, but David lay motionless.

Lois looked at David, wondering when he would get up. She wanted to go to Ben, to make sure that he was all right.

'Are you all right?' Sly asked anxiously.

Lois nodded, still staring at David. 'I want to go to Ben.'

Sly took David's wrist, and bent his head towards David's face, listening for something. Then he said, 'Lois, stay calm. I need you to ring for an ambulance; David isn't breathing.'

Lois did as he said, while he began to give David mouth-to-mouth resuscitation.

'What's the matter with him?'

'I kicked him in the head. I didn't mean to; he moved after I took aim.' Sly looked at her white face, hoping she could hear his words. Sly continued to work, but he was fighting a losing battle and he knew it. He couldn't give up while Lois continued to sit and watch. After what seemed like an eternity, ambulance men dashed in and took over. Lois was now standing by the wall, watching in absolute horror.

'Listen, Lois, you'll want to go to the hospital with him. I'll stay here.' Sly knew that the police would be arriving at any moment. 'Who can I get to come to be with Ben?'

'My sister will come; her number's on the board, next to the phone, or Mrs Whittingham from next door.'

Sly called Ronnie and briefly explained the situation. Ronnie said she was on her way. Lois, in a daze, followed the ambulance men. As they were putting David in the back of the ambulance, the police arrived, expecting to find just another case of domestic violence.

Afterwards, Lois could hardly remember the drive to the hospital. One of the ambulance men placed a blanket round her shoulders. She couldn't take her eyes off David. They thumped his chest, fitted an oxygen mask over his face and gave him an injection. She wanted them to leave him alone. At the hospital, they rushed David away. When she tried to follow, a nurse stopped her and said that she had to give particulars about the patient. She told them as much as she knew. They left her in the Accident and Emergency waiting area, still shaking. Eventually, David's father arrived, and when he recognised her, he came over and hugged her. He was crying. Why was he crying?

The doctor came out from behind the double doors and took David's father away. Rich arrived and went in the same direction. People were scurrying about, but they ignored her, passing and re-passing as if she didn't exist. She closed her eyes, trying to obliterate the vision of David, white, immobile, close to death.

Someone came and held her hand, took her pulse, shone a light in her eyes. They gave her tea with a lot of sugar in it. Why wouldn't they let her see David? She asked that question endlessly. Nobody replied. A nurse came and took her into an office, where David's father was waiting for her. He told her that David was dead. The kick had done damage to his brain. He had stopped breathing; his brain, starved of oxygen, had given up. Her David was gone. She felt as though she was falling off a cliff.

She went with David's father, to see David's body. He looked peaceful, rather pale, and a little blue around his lips. She cried and flung herself across his body. David's father was crying as well, and he asked her to leave him alone with his son. Lois went outside, where she found Rich, who was crying, too. She went to sit in reception, where Ronnie found her.

'Where's Ben? What have you done with him?'

Ronnie was supposed to be with Ben. Ronnie said she had left him with Bryan.

'Where's Sly?' Lois couldn't understand why he wouldn't be there, at home with their son.

'He's been arrested, taken into custody.' Ronnie tried to tell Lois about this. Lois said it was an accident and that Sly hadn't meant to do any harm. Why couldn't the police see that and leave him alone? Ronnie said that the police were on their way to the hospital, to speak to her because she was the only witness and they needed to take her statement.

The police officer arrived and sat down beside her. He asked her to tell him exactly what had happened. He asked if she'd been wearing only her dressing-gown, and she said she had been in the shower. The police officer gave her the impression that he suspected that she and Sly had been up to no good, and that's why Sly had killed David. She just wanted them to go away. Before he pocketed his notebook and left, he told her that she wouldn't be able to have any contact with Sly until his case went to court, because she was the sole witness. She became hysterical and a doctor gave her a sedative. Ronnie took her home, where, unable to enter the kitchen, she went up to Ben's room and sat on his bed, looking at his little face, until Ronnie took her to bed and the sedative sent her to sleep.

When she woke the next morning, her mother was sitting on her bed, crying. Lois sat up and held her mother, knowing how much this must mean to her, knowing that she loved David beyond measure. After a while, her mother asked Lois what had happened.

'I don't really know. I was upstairs, having a shower. David must have just arrived and found Sly cooking. He wouldn't have known that he'd be here.' Lois's mother could understand exactly what would have happened. 'When I came down, it made things worse; David took a knife and was going to kill Sly. Sly was badly hurt. He didn't mean to kill David, he was just trying to stop him. He tried to keep him alive, he did mouth-to-mouth; he really tried to save him.'

Lois told her mother that she had decided to marry David, and that Sly knew about this decision and approved, on the understanding that access to Ben would be permitted. At this, Lois's mother wept again.

'What about Sly's parents?'

'He only has his father. The police should have fetched him, shouldn't they?'

'I'll see what I can do for him, Lois. I'll ask my solicitor.'

That day seemed endless. Lois's mother telephoned some people and told them what had happened. Lois called Gerry, who said she was already on her way. Unable to contact Mickie by telephone, Lois wrote a letter and sent it to his most recent address in London. Malc and Luke would come as soon as she asked.

Rich called round and spoke to her mother. Lois stood at the kitchen door and watched, unable to make out what he was saying. Her head throbbed with pain. Eventually, Rich turned away, and her mother called out after him, 'Just you try it. Wild horses couldn't keep me away.' She slammed the door shut behind him. Lois led her mother into the kitchen, sat her down at the table, and asked her what it had been about.

'He tried to tell me that we weren't going to be allowed at the funeral. They didn't want you there. Don't worry, they can't stop us. We will go. David would have wanted us there.' This brought fresh misery.

Lois went upstairs to David's room, which was very tidy. Her mother must have prepared it for his return from Rio. It felt odd, with no mess, no unmade bed, and no clothes on the floor. She wanted to find something that still bore David's smell, but everything had been laundered, and smelt of detergent. Lying at the bottom of the wardrobe was the cricket jumper her mother had knitted for him. He must have just dropped it there. She was so thankful, that she sat on the bed and wept again, holding the jumper away from her tears, terrified they might wash away the smell.

Gerry arrived not long afterwards. Sly had killed David. It was too horrible for words. How would Lois ever recover? She went to get Lois some cigarettes from the garage over the way. When she got back, Lois's doctor was there, giving her the once over. With her mother, he left some sleeping pills for Lois. Lois thought that her mother was more likely to top herself than she was and she made her mother give the pills to Gerry.

In the evening, David's father turned up, looking haggard and grey, and asked if he might speak with them. Lois's mother showed him into the front room, where Lois and Gerry joined him.

'Mrs Bartlett, I understand that my eldest son came round here today and told you that you would not be welcome at David's funeral. I apologise. He shouldn't have done it. The family recognises that you and Lois are, were, two of the most important people in David's life, and I wouldn't undervalue that.'

Mrs. Bartlett began to weep and Gerry and Lois moved to sit beside her on the long sofa.

'Rich isn't coping very well with David's death. None of us is, but it seems to have hit him particularly hard. He was just lashing out.'

Lois wondered how David's father could bear to be here, with his son dead, and it was all her fault.

'David once told me that, if I didn't understand about you, Lois, I didn't understand anything about him. I didn't believe him at the time, but since Ben was born and he spent even more time with you, I knew that it was true. Because of you, we became closer. I understand that he was seriously thinking of moving back to Chester, and that you'd said that you would marry him. He called Rich from the airport on his way to Rio, and told him.'

Gerry looked gob-smacked, Lois cried harder. Her mother spoke for her. 'Lois told David that she wasn't saying no, not this time. He has asked her hundreds of times. He knew that she would agree in the end.'

'So, last night was just a tragic accident. He found Sly here and went ballistic. That's very much David's style. He always had a very quick temper.'

Mr Stachini opened the bag and took out one of the books. 'Did you know that David kept a diary?' Lois looked up sharply at him. David would never have kept a diary, it was just the sort of thing he hated. Mr Stachini seemed to know that she didn't believe him. He went on, 'Not a proper diary, obviously not used every day. There are infrequent entries, but they record his feelings. He writes all about you two and your importance in his life. There's very little else in them. I thought that you'd want them, to keep until you are ready to read them. Perhaps we, David's family, could come and read them as well.'

Lois felt deeply sorry for him; he looked so lonely. She stood up and put her arms around him. He clung on to her and the book, and broke his heart all over again.

'I don't suppose that David will have told you this either,' he said. 'I had to ask him to make a will when he turned twenty-one, to do with his partnership in the business. He named you, Lois, as his sole beneficiary.' Lois looked at him in total astonishment. He tried to smile at her. 'You are going to be a very wealthy young woman.'

Lois shook her head, turning away from him. 'I don't want his money. I just want my David back.'

Mr Stachini stayed a little longer, had a sherry with them and promised to let them know when the funeral would take place, and when David's body would be in the Chapel of Rest.

Gerry managed to wangle a couple of days off work and stayed to help look after Lois and her mother. The police came and interviewed Lois again; her solicitor was present. They told her nothing about Sly. The only person allowed to see him was his father. Sly sent her a message via his father, who told her that Sly wanted her to know that he was fine. It was all because of his Karate: he had a deadly weapon and had used it. The police had charged him with manslaughter, and he had been granted bail on condition that he stay at his father's house until the trial.

* * *

There was a crowd in the church for David's funeral. Many of the old gang, including Luke and Malc, were there, even Mannon, Brown R. and Maggie, all people who had hardly known David but had known Lois and Sly. The one person who was missing was Mickie. Lois and her mother had been included as family and, therefore, arrived last. Mr Stachini bravely spoke about his son.

The chapel service was followed by the cremation, which was for family only and was the very worst bit, especially when the coffin disappeared through the curtain. At the funeral tea, back at the Stachini house, Rich was nice to Lois, which made her feel even worse. Ronnie and Bryan left early, to pick up Ben from nursery school, so that his routine would be normal. Lois had a strong desire to go home and weep on her own. It was hard to be brave, when you've lost your touchstone. She thought that things could never get any worse than that.

33

After David: Sly

A WEEK OR SO after David's funeral, Lois contemplated returning to work. On Saturday morning, she woke at half past ten and everywhere was very quiet; there was no sound of Ben. She found her mother sitting at the kitchen table, her eyes red from weeping. Lois wondered whether they should move to another house, to save her mother from having to cook in the room where Sly had killed David. Her mother said that Ronnie had taken Ben to see Bryan's parents and that she didn't want to go out, and seemed as if she did not to want Lois to go out either. It was as if she were waiting for something.

In mid morning, a smartly dressed stranger rang the doorbell, and when Lois opened the door, he said, 'You must be Lois. I am Sly's father, Selwyn Davies.'

He held out his hand and she shook it, remembering that the police had told her that they weren't allowed to talk. She started to protest but he interrupted her by saying, 'It's all right. There won't be a trial now.'

Lois, puzzled, invited him in and her mother came to see who was there. Mr. Davies explained the reason for his visit.

'Sly was allowed home on bail, on Thursday. I am sorry to bring you this news, but on Friday morning, he was gone when I awoke, and I found him in the garage, in my car. He had killed himself.'

'Sly's dead? He can't be. Why? Why? It can't be true, not Sly as well as David!'

Lois was hysterical. Her mother made her sit down, took her in her arms and rocked her, while Mr Davies gazed blindly out of the window, tears pouring unchecked down his face. When Lois was calmer, her mother went to make tea, and Mr Davies waited until she came back before he continued his sad tale.

He asked if he might see Ben, and her mother explained that the boy was with his aunt for the day, and promised that they would arrange the meeting. Lois suspected that her mother had arranged for Sly's father to call that day, and she confirmed it as she poured the tea.

Mr. Davies felt in his pocket for a letter, which he gave to Lois. He said, 'Sly, had thought everything through. He wrote me a long letter and gave meticulous instructions for his funeral. This letter is for you.'

Lois was surprised to observe that the envelope was open. Sly had written:

'My lovely, lovely Lois,

You might remember that I once said that I wouldn't want to live in a world without you in it. I meant every word. I don't want to. I also don't want to live in a world where you blame me for the death of your very dearest person, your David. You might argue that you don't blame me, it was just an accident, that you would learn to live with it, for Ben's sake, but I know that you would, deep, deep, deep down. You would always try to hide it from me but I would know. I would be able to see the pain in your eyes when you looked at me, or fear, or emptiness, or indifference, and I would die a little each time. I would rather die right now than die a little every day. I don't want you to live your life lying to yourself and to me. You would want to do the right thing by me, you are obsessed with doing the right thing, you are trying too hard to be perfect, and you need to learn to be yourself.

You have given me great joy in my life. For the last two years, we were estranged, and at the end of it, I found out that you had carried my child, despite the fact that I hurt you beyond measure, in the basest way possible. You found the strength to have our baby. You came to see me in Aberystwyth, very brave, on your own, despite all the objection that people must have put to you, David, I know, didn't want you to come. Have you any idea how happy you made me by those acts? Please remember that pure joy; like no one else has ever given me, you did that for me, Lois. And you wanted me to be a part of our son's life, so noble and true. He gave me great joy as well. I know that I leave him in your very capable hands; he will come to know about me because you will talk to him, like a proper mother, as mine was. Dancing, Echo and the Bunnymen, just talking with you, holding you, seeing your beautiful face, being with my son, all these things are my favourite moments. Not one of my favourite moments has been shared with anyone else. How about that for true love?

Please don't be sad for me. I need to do this, to take my own life, now, before you have any more pain inflicted upon you. You have been my life, every moment of it.

I love you,

Sly.'

Lois read the letter and then held her face in her hands.

'Why me?' she cried. 'Why me? Two people are dead because of me. What did I do wrong? It's all so pointless. How am I supposed to live, knowing that they died because of me?'

Her mother held her close, knowing that she would have to cope because of Ben. Mr Davies asked if he could read Sly's letter. She handed it to him wordlessly, thinking he must already have read it, since the envelope was open.

He read it, and said, 'I only really came to know my son because of you. He used to bottle things up after his mother died. Then, when he needed help with you, he had no choice and we talked endlessly. He hadn't told me about Ben, though, not until I first went to see him in prison. He loved him very much, and you as well. He had hoped to find a way back to you. I guess he just couldn't cope with the idea of losing you all over again; he'd put up with too much. I only have Ben now. My wife's dead, my son is dead, Ben is my only link to them. I hope that you will allow me to see him, get to know him, be his *taid*, his grandfather.'

Lois nodded, unable to speak. Then Sly's father became more business like; he wanted to tell her about Sly's wishes for his funeral.

'He just wants family and a very few friends; you, your mother, Ronnie and Bryan, Gerry. He wanted Gina, Luke, Ali and Malc, and his Welsh friends from Aberystwyth, and that's about it. He specifically said, and I have no idea why, that he didn't want Mickie to come.

Lois knew exactly how Sly felt about Mickie. It was funny that he'd come to admire David but had been unable to forgive Mickie.

'He has chosen the hymns, all Welsh, and he wanted the service to be in the Methodist Chapel in Monmouth. He believed in God; did you know that? He told me that he had made his peace with God, before he took his own life.'

Lois tried to imagine why they had never spoken about something as fundamental as religious belief in all their times together. She wasn't sure that she believed in a God who could let these terrible things happen. Finally, Sly's father told her that Sly wanted to be cremated and have his ashes scattered on the sea at Aberystwyth, where he had been happiest.

Lois was numb, only half absorbing what Mr. Davies was saying to her. The thought uppermost in her mind was that the man's beloved son was dead because he had known her too well.

'There will have to be an inquest, of course, but it should be fairly straightforward. He left two copies of the letters he wrote to us; yours is open because they had to compare it with the copies, to ensure that nothing was omitted from what the coroner will see. I will let you know when the funeral arrangements are finalised, then, you can tell the people that you know.'

Ronnie returned earlier than expected, while Mr. Davies was still in the house. He played with Ben for a short time and Lois sat and watched, wondering how she would be able to tell Ben about his father who committed suicide. Lois's mother was worried about Mr Davies going home to an empty house, but he said that had plenty of support.

★ ★ ★

Gerry drove Lois to Monmouth for Sly's funeral, and they listened to the Bunnymen on tape. Lois thought of all the times she had heard them with Sly. The chapel was half-full when they arrived. Many of the mourners were Sly's relatives. Gina stood with Luke, crying even before the service started. She broke away from Luke and came to Lois's arms. She sat next to her and Gerry.

Sly's bearers were his first cousins, healthy young men, as Sly once was. The singing was beautiful and helped to resolve Lois's problem with regard to God. She could go to church, sing lovely hymns and try to find consolation. She could no longer ignore religion. Sly's father was brave and dignified, and she wondered at his incredible strength that enabled him to sit so calmly through his son's funeral service.

34

After both: the End

DAVID, HAD HE LIVED, would have celebrated his twenty-eighth birthday on 24th August 1986, and Lois wanted to mark the occasion in some way. She thought of the people who had visited her often throughout that painful winter when she lost David and Sly. Gerry had been there most often, with her faithful Charlie, from whom, in the end, she had found it impossible to part. Gerry had let Lois talk and cry, shout and scream, and had given her things to structure her thinking, had offered solace in Lois's darkest hours.

Lois's mother had adjusted slowly to not having David around. David's parents and Rich were frequent visitors, and Rich gave the impression that he wanted to take the place of his dead brother in Mrs. Bartlett's affections. The Stachinis were working it through by now.

Sly's father had moved to Wrexham and he was able to take the boy to church and Sunday school. Lois went as well, sometimes. Mr. Davies was being a wonderful *taid*, and the growing boy loved him dearly. Long before Lois knew that Sly and his father wanted Ben to bear the name of Davies, she had registered him as a Bartlett. Once she knew Sly's wishes, she left the legal business in the hands of the solicitor, who said that it was no problem to sort out the change.

* * *

Luke and Gina came to the memorial barbecue party. With Gerry, they were Ben's godparents. Lois, while still undecided about God, had had Ben christened shortly after Sly's funeral, and promised to bring him up in the Christian faith, so that he had a choice in later life, whether to believe, or reject it.

Lois invited all of her stalwarts, as a way of saying thank you. Her mother took Ben with her to stay with David's family, who often invited the pair to their spacious house and spoilt little Ben with gifts of every kind. Gerry wanted Lois to invite Mannon, just for a few laughs and because the last party before they left Aberystwyth had been Mannon's final fling.

The invitations asked people to arrive on Saturday morning and stay overnight. Luke agreed to take charge of the barbecue, with help from Gina. They were living together now, and seemed to be happy and settled.

Gina had baked a cake, very chocolaty, beautifully decorated, and Luke looked so proud of his girl. Mannon, who was now a typical London girl and thinner than ever, drove up in a slinky, black BMW car. The other guests came armed with bottles and edible goodies. Malc was the only one still missing by twelve o'clock. Everyone else was in the garden and Lois was in the kitchen, sorting out what to cook first. Presently, she heard Malc's voice; he had arrived with Mickie. When Lois peeped out into the garden, she saw Mickie talking with Luke and Gina. He had a bottle of beer in his hand.

'All right, Lois, how are you?' Mickie called, waving the bottle at her.

Lois was so angry; she couldn't trust herself to reply. She went back inside, and Malc hurried after her. He didn't want to be the one responsible for upsetting her today of all days.

'What have you brought him here for, Malc?'

'I thought you'd be pleased. He called me, I told him about the party, asked him along. What's the matter with that?'

She forced a smile and told Malc to go back outside, assuring him that she would be fine, she just needed to get herself under control. What a cheek! There had been absolutely no word from Mickie for almost a year, despite David and Sly both dying and her desperately needing him. Now, he shows up without a by your leave. She'd show him. She wouldn't even speak to him; that would serve him right. She put on a brave face, but she was still scowling when she went to take the chicken drumsticks out to Luke.

Lois was in a foul mood, while everyone else was having a good time, eating her food, drinking her wine, laughing their heads off. She wouldn't let anyone help her. She rushed to and from the house, fetching and carrying, expending her annoyance by physical exertion. Mickie talked with everyone else but her, and the longer it went on, the angrier she became.

Gerry came inside, to try to get her to give the washing up a rest and come outside. She had never seen Lois in such a rage.

'I'm fine here. I'll have to see that fucker out there, if I come out, and I don't want to.'

Finding her entreaties ignored, Gerry sighed and went out again. Malc raised his eyebrows at her but she shook her head. Mickie, who had been observing the signals keenly, felt that now would be the best time to speak with Lois, while everyone else was busy eating, drinking and gossiping. He came to the doorway of the kitchen and saw Lois noisily loading the dishwasher, wrestling with a glass jug that was too large to fit in the basket. It broke, sending shards of glass into the machine. Lois jumped back in surprise, and started to cry. Mickie was over in an instant, pulling her towards him, not saying a word. She began to push him away.

'Come on, now, calm down. You're upset. I'm you're friend, you need me.'

'Need you!' She thrust him away. 'Need you, ha! I don't need you. Look at me, Mickie. What makes you think that I need you?'

'I know you do.'

He looked at her steadily, and she glowered back, openly hostile. He was right. She did need him; she had needed him for a whole, long year. Mickie put his arms around her and held her close. She wanted to kiss him; she wanted him. The desire was intense and unexpected; all the feelings that had lain dormant for so long were awake. All she saw on his face was benign concern.

'It's all right.' Mickie murmured.

'What is?' she asked.

'Everything, everything you think and feel is all right.'

'How do you know?' She had an irrational anger that he had not come here to seduce her, and that her physical need of him was making her vulnerable again.

'I'm here now.'

Something of her passion, like an electric current, passed to Mickie, who put his lips to hers and kissed her. She felt herself yield to his embrace, forgetful of her guests, the spitting barbecue, the burning sun on her back. She felt as if she had returned home after a long period in the wilderness.

'Excuse me.' Gerry was standing in the doorway, a great big grin on her face.

'Could I get to the fridge, please? We're running out of beer. Don't let me interrupt you. Carry on.' Gerry went over to the fridge. 'I'll take these beers round, then, I'll give you some help, if you've finished with Mickie, that is.' Gerry went out, laughing and carrying two four-packs of lager.

'I'm so sorry, Mickie.' Lois felt embarrassed.

'What are you sorry for? That's one of the nicest things that ever happened to me! I'm just sorry that Gerry wanted a beer.'

Lois sighed. 'I don't know what happened to me, I just felt so… I lost control. I really wanted you.'

'Wanted?'

'Want. I want you very much indeed.'

'I want you, too; that's not in doubt, is it? The point is this: I

312

love you. I always have. It's always been you, right from the start, and you know it. I decided to play this clever game, to get you. I thought I could do it, too. I thought I was so clever.'

'What do you mean?' Lois was puzzled. 'What game?'

'Listen, we'll talk later. I have so much to say. I'm here now and, this time, I'm going to put it right with you.

'I just feel confused. I kept wondering why you hadn't come to find me, why you deserted me when I needed you so much.'

'I went round the world, to try to forget you; I did a David, abandoned you. It wasn't the right time. This time, it's going to be all right.'

Inevitably, Mickie and Lois, under the influence of that greatest magnet of all time, found themselves in her bed, happily rediscovering what they had long since forgotten.

Gerry's voice floating up from the garden, making ribald remarks about the pair, motivated them to get dressed and rejoin the others. When the cool of the evening descended and gnats performed their merry dance, some of the guests smoked cannabis, or drank more beer, Mickie pulled her away from the others, led her upstairs and reaffirmed his love.

He began to speak about the past, trying to explain why he had held off, left her to go her own road.

'I needed to get you to trust me. I just knew that trust was the most important thing. That was my game. I'd hang around, being Mr Good Guy, let you make all your mistakes and help put you back together. Once you trusted me and you'd grown up a bit more, you'd want me, Mr Dependable. You never trusted Sly, did you?'

'I was always nervous of him; I never knew what he would do next. It's hard to trust someone who is totally irrational at times. I think I finally came to know him, and then he killed himself.'

'Do you think about Sly and David a lot?'

'Yes, all the time. They never really go away. People say it's hard for me because Ben looks so much like his father.' Mickie nodded agreement.

'That doesn't bother me. Ben's a little person in his own right. He's not his father, he's not me. I really miss David, though. All the time, there's a huge void that nothing can fill; nothing ever will. He was such a good friend. I never fully appreciated him when he was alive, and now it's too late. I was entirely selfish when it came to David. I can't believe he stuck around so long.'

Lois shook her head. 'I miss him all the time; I talk to him in my mind, telling him things that have happened, explaining why Sly was there, trying to relive that night, make it happen differently, so that we could all be alive. I feel so responsible. I loved them both and they are dead.'

'I feel responsible, too, you know?' Mickie said. Lois couldn't see how. 'I feel responsible because I wanted you to come to me voluntarily. I could have made a more serious play for you at anytime at all. For instance, that first summer, I could have come to Chester; I could have done my M.A. in Aber. I thought about it, but you hadn't got Sly out of your system, so there was no point. Lynne told me to take you away from Aber, that time when I came to see you. She said you were so low, you probably would have come, but only because you were desperate for anything to cling on to. You were already pregnant, too. I made a real balls-up of that one, didn't I? David was a special guy. He was like a father to Ben. I never knew how he could put up with that. I didn't think that I could.' Mickie waited for a reaction.

'David was at the birth with me. It helped a lot. If I hadn't been so obstinate, it might have worked out for us. People make a go of less than we had.'

'Did you think of me?' Mickie tried to keep his voice light, but wondered why he was bothering, because the importance of his question must scream from his voice and his expression, no matter how nonchalant he tried to look.

'Yes, I tried to let you know about David's funeral. That's when I found out that you'd left the flat in London. When I tried your mum's address, there was no reply from there, either.'

'She's moved to the Wirral.' Mickie explained.

'Oh. I tried everyone I could think of, even Finlay, who couldn't help. After that, I just assumed that you'd wanted to lose contact with me.'

'I did. That's why I went round the world. When you let me know you were going up to Aberystwyth to see Sly, I just caved in. I spent two days trying to resist the urge to come up to Chester to try to persuade you not to go. I thought that you would go back to him. I just couldn't do it again. It was so frustrating. You were writing about Ben, and Sly being the father, and all that crap, yet your desire to see him again was so obvious. I gave up, went home to see my mam, and poured out my heart to her. It was she who suggested that I go round the world, and forget Sly. That's what David did, in your second year, abandoned you to save himself, didn't he? It seemed like a good idea and I decided to try it.

'I had the money my mam had saved after selling my canvases. Not writing to you was the most difficult thing. I hoped I could leave it all behind and come back a different person. Actually, I think I became closer to you on that trip. I thought about you constantly.

'My mam came out at Christmas and we explored Australia together. If she knew you had tried to get in touch, she never mentioned it.'

'She must hate me,' Lois said regretfully.

'No, she was just trying to protect me. I'll take you to see her tomorrow, if you like.

'How did you find out what had happened?' Lois was hungry to find out why he had decided to come back into her life now.

'I went to see Pauline, just for a drink. I didn't stay the night. I'm not proud of this, but a year was a long time. We met in a pub in Covent Garden, and she told me all about what had happened to everyone. I couldn't believe it at first. I called Malc, who filled me in on some details. I didn't know whether I would be welcome or not, and that is why I let the time slip past, but Malc let me know about this party and I decided to come and own up to everything, and to stay, if you'll have me.'

'Stay? How long?' Lois was surprised at how important his answer was to her.

'Well, I mean to stay forever.'

Lois rested her head on his chest. He stroked her hair gently.

'Until Aber falls into the sea, remember? That's what I mean about staying for ever. I'm not leaving, this time, unless you throw me out. I've made such a mess of things, I can hardly believe it. Lois, dear girl, I know that it's not the easiest thing in the world for you to do, to agree to take me as I am and let me stay with you for good. You'll be thinking about Ben.'

Lois nodded, tears streaming down her cheeks.

'He's already lost two fathers. I can't allow him to become attached to anyone else and then be deserted again. He's too little to understand now, but he will want the full story one day.'

'Listen, Lois, you can trust me; you always have, just trust me again. I don't profess to be great with small babies, but I'm good with kids. I never understood how David coped when Ben was tiny. I hope that I won't always think of Sly whenever I see Ben, but I love you enough to make this work. I want you and I know that Ben is part of the package. I just hope that you've forgiven me for what I said when you told me you were going to have him.'

'You mean about the abortion?'

'Yeah. You've got to understand what a shock it was to me. That piece of news wrecked everything, just when I thought I could take you for the asking. When I came to Aber and you cried, it was the first time you acknowledged that you wanted to love me. You didn't, but you wanted to. I always felt I could compete with the other two in most respects. David was a golden boy; anyone could see that. Yet, for all his charm, good looks and money, he had never really succeeded with you. That was a good sign. As for Sly, he was a good dancer, and you obviously fancied him like mad, but I knew it would only be a matter of time before the whole thing fizzled out.'

'Yes, Sly seemed to know that, too. He almost finished it twice, before it had run its natural course and burnt itself out. I know that now. We were so good together physically, but he always loved me more than I loved him. I couldn't accept that. It seemed as if the reverse were true. Once David was dead and Sly in prison, I recognised it for what it was. Sly wrote me a letter at the end, to let me know that he killed himself because he knew I would never forgive him for killing David, and he was right. I couldn't forgive him, but I didn't wish him dead because of it.'

'I suppose that all that stuff about David and Sly put me off coming back to see you earlier,' Mickie said pensively. 'Once I knew you were pregnant with Sly's baby that was it. He was always going to be the most significant one in your life. I couldn't understand why you wanted to keep his child. I knew that, no matter what happened, we would never be free from him because he was the baby's father. Even if we had children of our own in the future, you would never be pregnant for the first time by me. It sounds so childish, doesn't it? You will never know the strength of feeling I had about little Ben. I could put it down to one of those biological things about genes and offspring, but, at the time, I was almost senseless with rage. The way I went on about the abortion makes me ashamed, yet I knew you weren't even listening to me.'

Mickie explained how he had seen David accept the baby and enjoy him, make provision for his future, prove how caring he was, and how it had altered his own outlook on everything.

'I'm sorry. I was just so jealous, not of Ben, of Sly. You'd been through all of those things for his child, not for mine. I was a total wreck. So when you said you were going back to see him in Aberystwyth that day, I just took off.' He kissed her hair again. 'I'm so sorry.'

'Don't be. I don't know now what made me so determined to have this baby. I would have given the same advice if Gerry had been pregnant. I would have gone to the clinic with her, held her hand, but I would have believed that an abortion would have solved the problem. I don't remember your reaction being so strong, anyhow. I thought we discussed an abortion but concluded that it wasn't to be. You see, you weren't the first to suggest it by any means. David was with me when I first discovered I was pregnant. He'd practically booked the clinic and the abortion, before I said I didn't want to have one. It took him months to come round to the idea of the baby, Sly's baby. My mother, Gerry, everyone advised that an abortion was the only way forward. I think part of me really wanted to have Ben, a tangible reminder to everyone that Sly and I had really existed. Of course, I hadn't bargained for the reality of Ben, and how much I would love him in spite of everything. But, initially, maybe, I did have him out of spite.'

Mickie noticed her photographs on the bedside table, pictures of Ben and David, not Sly, he noted. There was a Welsh love spoon, and he asked her about it. 'Sly carved it for me. Look, it's got a Bunnyman on it.'

'It's beautiful. He was really talented. What a waste.'

There was also Mickie's own framed and mounted cartoon drawing of Lois pregnant with Ben.

'You still have this?' Mickie picked it up and studied it.

'It's about the only thing I have of yours, except the letters. Do you know, I haven't got a single photo of you? Oh, Mickie, I was so convinced that you would come back. I expected you daily after Sly... after he died. When the report went in the *Liverpool Echo*, I was convinced you'd read it, and come and get me. As time went on, I began to harden towards you. I felt bitter because you were able to get on with your life when mine was falling to pieces.' Lois took the cartoon from his hand.

'This frame has been in the bin more times than I care to remember. Mum says I've always been a dependent person. I remember all the men I have leant on. First, there was Sid; then, David; then, Sly, and there was you. In this past year, I've come to rely on myself. I think I've grown up at long last. We're equals now, and I still want you. I wasn't sure before today, but I do love you, really love you, not just wish I could love you. Stay with me, Mickie. Don't go. Be here when I wake up.'

'Reaching out to touch you in the morning will be just the first step. I'm not going anywhere. When we wake up, we'll make love, and then go and get Ben.'

Lois smiled and said, 'Mum will bring him round; he's too much for her in the morning.'

They slept curled against each other, totally at peace with their love. When Lois woke, she looked first at her bedside clock, then at Mickie, still sleeping beside her. It was nine forty-five, and they were just about to start living the rest of their lives.

Other titles from the popular **dinas** imprint

A journey of humour and tragedy…

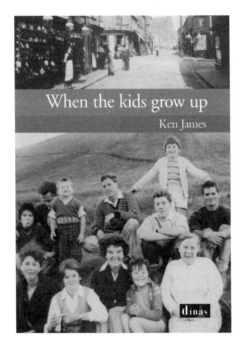

WHEN THE KIDS GROW UP
Ken James
A gripping drama based on a true story, spanning three decades,
set in Dowlais.
0 86243 716 4
£6.95

… and a magical, scary mystery!

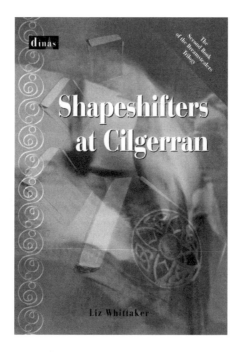

SHAPESHIFTERS AT CILGERRAN
Liz Whittaker
Join in Leo and Ginny's thrilling adventures. Book 2 of the
Dreamstealers Trilogy.
0 86243 719 9
£5.95

Titles already published

For more information about this innovative imprint,
contact Lefi Gruffudd at lefi@ylolfa.com
or go to www.ylolfa.com/dinas.
A Dinas catalogue is also available.